After ten years as a television camerawoman, **Ella Hayes** started her own photography business so that she could work around the demands of her young family. As an award-winning wedding photographer she's documented hundreds of love stories in beautiful locations, both at home and abroad. She lives in central Scotland with her husband and two grown-up sons. She loves reading, travelling with her camera, running and great coffee.

Jo McNally lives in coastal North Carolina with one hundred pounds of dog and 200 pounds of husband—her slice of the bed is very small. When she's not writing or reading romance novels (or clinging to the edge of the bed), she can often be found on the back porch sipping wine with friends while listening to great music. If the weather is absolutely perfect, Jo might join her husband on the golf course, where she tends to feel far more competitive than her actual skill level would suggest.

You can follow Jo pretty much anywhere on social media (and she'd love it if you did!), but you can start at her website, jomcnallyromance.com

ITALIAN SUMMER WITH THE SINGLE DAD

ELLA HAYES

HER HOMECOMING WISH

JO McNALLY

MILLS & BOON

First Published in Great Britain 2020
by Mills & Boon, an imprint of HarperCollinsPublishers,
1 London Bridge Street, London, SE1 9GF

Italian Summer With The Single Dad © 2020 Ella Hayes
Her Homecoming Wish © 2020 Jo McNally

ISBN: 978-0-263-27869-9

0220

MIX
Paper from
responsible sources
FSC www.fsc.org **FSC™ C007454**

This book is produced from independently certified FSC™ paper to ensure responsible forest management.

For more information visit: www.harpercollins.co.uk/green

Printed and bound in Spain
by CPI, Barcelona

ITALIAN SUMMER WITH THE SINGLE DAD

ELLA HAYES

For Mum

CHAPTER ONE

'TILT IT UP! No! More…more! There…no, there! Now, don't move.'

Olivia Gardner gripped the silver reflector and gritted her teeth. She couldn't understand why Ralph Holdsworth became so obnoxious the minute they arrived at a wedding. He was tolerable the rest of the time, albeit a little highly strung. He might be the go-to wedding photographer for those wealthy enough to afford him—his talent was undeniable—but assisting him was not the dream job she'd imagined. Most of the time she felt as if she was walking on eggshells. If she hadn't been learning so much about wedding photography she'd have walked out months ago.

He stepped back, lowered his camera and motioned to the bride. 'Okay, darling, let's move over to the window. Liv! The dress…?'

Olivia parked the reflector and dropped to her haunches, fanning out the dress the way Ralph liked it. She hated the way he called all the brides 'darling'. How hard would it be to remember their names? She made a point of memorising the names of the entire bridal party ahead of any wedding.

Today's bride, Sophie, was a sweet-faced girl with porcelain skin, blonde hair and a slender figure. Her wedding dress was ivory silk embellished with tiny pearls and it felt soft and papery between Olivia's fingers as she pulled it out and smoothed it down. She tried to ignore Ralph's impatient glance as she moved onto the veil. It was a full veil, fine antique lace, a family heirloom probably. The bride's 'something old'.

Carefully, she draped the ornate edge over Sophie's shoulder and the girl smiled at her, mouthed a thank you. She could sense Sophie's nerves, gave her arm a little squeeze before she turned to pick up the reflector, but Ralph was waving an impatient hand in her direction.

'I don't need that now! Go pap some guests.'

She swallowed her irritation. She knew he didn't mean to be offhand, but it was annoying when he spoke to her like that in front of clients. Without a word, she picked up her camera and slipped out of the room.

Slowly she made her way along the wide hallway towards the staircase. She wished she had the courage to strike out on her own, but she was wary. She'd been down that road before. Armed with her photography degree, she'd started freelancing for an independent arts magazine but the circulation was low, the pay dismal. She'd stuck it out for a year to build a portfolio then tried to break into other magazines, but it was impossible. Magazines had their pet photographers.

She'd been working as a part-time barista when she met Ralph Holdsworth. He'd offered her a job and she'd jumped at it. He was a top wedding photographer, well-connected! At first he hadn't let her touch a camera. On wedding days she scurried around with reflectors, fluffed dresses and made sure that the right people were arranged into the right groups for the family photos. At

the studio he set her to work editing an endless stream
of wedding images which, he told her, would be an education in itself, and she handled all his paperwork too
because he hated anything that wasn't creative. Twelve
months and over forty weddings later, he'd given her a
camera. She was to be his second shooter, responsible
for the candid shots and the little details he didn't want to
do, but he still expected her to help with the bridal por-
traits and to assemble the guests for the formal pictures.

Today's wedding was taking place in the garden of
Kensall Manor, the bride's family home. The house was
Tudor, all oak beams and half-panelled walls with mellow plaster above. On the galleried landing she paused
to watch the comings and goings in the grand hall below:
catering staff bustling about with trays, guests looking
for somewhere to leave wedding gifts. And then the hall
suddenly emptied. She was about to make a move when
a tall, dark-haired man in a morning suit strode in carrying a shallow open box containing the men's button-
holes. There was something powerful in the set of his
shoulders, something about him that made Olivia press
herself closer to the balustrade to get a better view. He
was looking around, for the groomsmen she supposed,
then quite unexpectedly he looked up and caught her
eye. She barely had time to catch her breath, to register
the tiny, indefinable reaction in his eyes before he broke
into a smile.

'Hello, up there! I don't suppose you've seen the bride-
groom…?'

Blue eyes, something shining through them. She could
feel her heart thumping in her chest, an unwelcome flush
of heat rising through her as she called up a mental list
of the wedding party. This had to be Zach Merrill, the

groom's older brother and best man. As she cleared her throat to speak, she prayed that he wouldn't notice her blushing. 'No, I'm sorry, but if I see him I'll tell him the best man's looking for him.'

He looked bemused. 'How do you know I'm the—?'

'You're wearing the weight of responsibility on your shoulders...'

He lifted an eyebrow then broke into a smile which stole the breath from her lungs. 'Is it that obvious?'

She nodded.

'Zach!'

A man's voice rang out from somewhere off the hall and he turned to look, made a gesture of acknowledgement then lifted his eyes to hers once more.

'You can call off the search! I've found him.'

Blue eyes staring into hers. Somehow, she found her voice. 'That's lucky! Can't have a wedding without a groom.'

He laughed, started to walk away then stopped and looked up again. 'Goodbye then...'

She smiled softly. 'Bye.'

She watched him disappear then shook herself. Fraternising with the best man wasn't going to get her anywhere; she was supposed to be working. As she trotted down the stairs she pushed him to the back of her mind and tried to concentrate on the little tingle of excitement she always felt at the start of a wedding day.

She loved photographing weddings. Everything from the smallest details to the grandest gestures, but most of all she loved the ceremony. The way the bride and groom looked at each other...little nervous smiles, eyes glistening with happy tears. She found something compelling about the ritual of commitment, about the idea of two people starting out together, taking their first steps into uncharted waters. No loose ends. The thought of it always made her feel happy.

As she stepped out into the warm spring sunshine she hung the camera around her neck then followed the broad path that led to the southern aspect of the property. She could see guests mingling on the long terrace next to the house. She could hear the buzz of conversation and glasses tinkling and she knew she ought to go straight over, but instead she cut across the immaculate lawn to where rows of chevalier chairs were set out for a ceremony in front of the ornamental lake. It was perfect! She gazed at the scene, lifted her camera and put her eye to the viewfinder. For a moment she pictured herself in the frame, standing with the man she loved, her fingers laced in his, their eyes locked, lips pledging love and fidelity, and then…the kiss.

She lowered the camera and watched a lone coot swimming across the glassy surface of the lake. She wished she could switch off her old teenage fantasy but it was always there in her head, playing on a loop. She didn't understand where her silly romantic notions came from. Her own parents had never married—they were far too modern for that!

She came back to herself and glanced over her shoulder. If Ralph caught her staring down the aisle when there were guests to photograph she'd soon be out of a job. It didn't take much to set him off when he was in the thick of a wedding shoot. She supposed he was a victim of his own success—under pressure to produce astonishing images all the time. The last thing she wanted to do was provoke him. Besides, she thought as she made her way towards the terrace, 'papping' guests was a step up from carrying his camera bag, even if she knew that she was capable of so much more.

From the periphery she scanned the crowd then lifted the camera with its long paparazzi lens. She snapped close-ups of smiling faces, bright hats, animated groups. She moved around, working the different angles, picking out details—champagne flutes sparkling on a tray, an elegant woman with immaculate red lipstick and long red nails. She spied a little girl with dark serious eyes peering through a sea of legs. She was a pretty little thing, so Olivia crouched down to play peek-a-boo from behind the camera. The girl buried her small fingers into the fabric of a woman's skirt, eyes brightening. Olivia pulled a funny face and the girl returned a shy smile. She fired a burst of frames then winked at the child and stood up. She liked photographing children—no hangups, no vanity.

With a couple of hundred shots done, she left the terrace and walked across the lawn to take some wider views. The old house must have been extended over the years. She could see the different materials in the two wings that flanked the original Tudor construction but the meld was pleasing, the exterior softened with an ancient wisteria and a rampant, scrambling clematis. All Ralph's clients owned properties like this. Sometimes she couldn't believe that this was her life now: every weekend spent in some elegant home or some fancy hotel. It was a far cry from the small Sussex cottage where she'd grown up.

She checked her watch. The great hall would be set for the wedding breakfast by now, which meant she'd be able to photograph the room in its pristine state. Lifting the camera from around her neck, she set off towards the front of the house but as she stepped onto the sweeping driveway she stopped, toes pressed to the tarmac. Up ahead, the groom was chatting and laughing with his two groomsmen—and Zach! She felt her heart flip over and land in her stomach. The way Zach was standing, the way his shoulders shifted under his morning coat as he moved... It would be so easy just to stand and watch...

Get a grip.

She took a deep breath and forced her feet to move. There was no avoiding an encounter if she wanted to get back into the house, so she'd just have to play it cool. As she drew nearer, she tried to concentrate on the ushers' names. Charlie and Will—or was it Bill? Cousins anyway. They were a little shorter than the Merrill brothers and infinitely less nervous from the look of things.

Far too soon she found herself standing in front of the little group.

'Good morning!' She could feel Zach looking at her, but she fixed her eyes on the groom. 'Lucas, we haven't met before. I'm Olivia Gardner, Ralph Holdsworth's assistant.'

Lucas extended a hand and shook hers warmly. 'Hi, Olivia. Pleased to meet you.' She noticed a tiny fleck of toothpaste at the corner of his mouth, the lopsided rose on his lapel. He motioned to Zach. 'This is my brother, Zach, and these good-for-nothing hangers-on are Charlie and Will.'

Charlie threw a playful punch at Lucas's arm. 'Good-for-nothing hangers-on? You're going to pay for that!'

As a friendly skirmish broke out, Zach stepped into the space between herself and the jostling men. It was a gallant protective gesture but it meant that he was now rather close. She took a little step back, lifted her eyes hesitantly.

He rolled his eyes then smiled. 'See what I have to put up with?' He held out his hand. 'It's nice to meet you properly, Olivia. Are you here all day?'

His palm was warm and dry. It felt nice. 'Yes. Until after the first dance…'

'It's a long day for you.' His gaze shifted to the camera in her hand. 'That looks heavy.'

His dark hair was on the long side, combed back from a lightly tanned face. She noticed fine lines etched into the skin around his eyes and, now that she was close, she could see kindness in his gaze, something else too that she couldn't quite pin down. She suddenly realised it was her turn to speak.

'It is… Heavy, I mean…but you get used to it.'

Lucas was straightening his jacket. 'Will you take a picture of us, Olivia?'

'Of course.' She hung the camera around her neck and stepped forward. 'Can I sort your buttonhole first?'

He glanced at the crooked rose on his lapel and pulled a face. 'Charlie, you idiot! You've roughed me up.'

She smiled. 'It wasn't Charlie's fault.' She flipped over Lucas's lapel, pulled out the long pin then fixed it back into place. 'Roses are heavy—they can easily slip to the side if they're not pinned properly.'

'Is mine okay?'

Zach was looking at her. She tried to ignore the little rush of heat rising through her as she stepped towards him and turned back the lapel of his jacket. This close, she could smell his cologne—citrus top note, woody base.

He lifted his chin while she worked at the pin. 'You have an eye for detail.'

'It's an occupational necessity.' She lowered her voice as she re-pinned the flower. 'Lucas has toothpaste at the corner of his mouth. Perhaps you could mention it to him before I take the photo…?' She stepped back and lifted her eyes to his. 'Okay?'

There was amusement on his face as he adjusted his collar. 'No problem.'

She turned away and drew a steadying breath. Zach Merrill was giving her vertigo. As she put some distance between herself and the group, she felt her heart drumming against her chest and when she turned around to line up the photograph and adjust the camera settings she was all fingers and thumbs. She took another deep breath. 'Okay, gentlemen—' Four pairs of eyes looked her way. 'Lucas and Zach, can you stand shoulder to shoulder, please, then Charlie and Will, can you take the wings?'

'Wingmen!' Will laughed. 'I like that!'

They shuffled into position and Olivia framed the shot. It was hard to concentrate on Lucas when Zach's face kept drawing her eye, but she simply had to—it was *Lucas's* day—she had to make sure that *he* looked perfect. She took some shots, adjusted the zoom, took a few more and then suddenly she went cold. Ralph always photographed the groom and his attendants. She wasn't supposed to be doing this.

'Can we do a fun one?' Lucas was looking at her expectantly.

She smiled. 'What did you have in mind?' Her stomach was churning. She couldn't refuse. Lucas *was* the client after all, but Ralph was going to arrive at any moment and he wouldn't like it.

Zach was smiling at her and there was something in

his eyes that chased her fears away. 'He wants to do a leaning shot. Look! We'll show you.'

She glanced at the big entrance door. No sign of Ralph—hopefully, he was still busy with Sophie and the bridesmaids. She tried to push him out of her thoughts as she watched Lucas and the men arranging themselves into a line. On a count of three, they canted their bodies at a forty-five-degree angle and burst out laughing. She couldn't help laughing too and fired off a succession of frames. This was what she loved about photographing weddings, being part of spontaneous moments like this.

'Olivia!'

The camera skewed in her hands. She took a breath and looked over to the vast doorway where Ralph was standing, rigid as a statue. A small shiver of guilt forked through her limbs and then slowly, deliberately, she tucked it away. She'd done nothing wrong. He was just being cranky as usual. She looked over at the men, who were still laughing and jostling each other. They didn't seem to have noticed anything and she was relieved. She pinned on a bright smile and stepped towards them.

'Ralph's here to take your formal pictures now.' She could feel Zach's eyes on her but forced herself to look at Lucas. 'Have fun! I'll see you later.'

As she walked towards the house she wondered if Zach was still watching her, but then she pushed the thought away because Ralph was waiting for her in the doorway, his eyes flinty, his mouth a grim straight line.

Zach Merrill couldn't help noticing the way Olivia had reacted to Holdsworth's voice. She'd sort of curled into herself, then quickly conjured up some fake brightness before walking away. He'd watched the pair of them talking in the doorway. He couldn't read their lips but he could read their body language. For some reason Holdsworth had been remonstrating with her, and from the tilt of her chin he could tell she'd been fighting her corner, whatever that might be.

He couldn't imagine what Holdsworth was upset about. Olivia Gardner struck him as polite and professional. How subtly she'd handled the issue with the lopsided rose on his brother's lapel, the rogue spot of toothpaste. She had an eye for detail, an easy, engaging manner, a lovely smile... She was clearly an asset and he hoped that Holdsworth could see it. Zach certainly knew which one of them he preferred. He came back to the moment, focused on what Holdsworth was saying.

'Okay, guys, walk forward now, swing your arms, talk to each other...laughing's good, keep it natural.'

The photographer was lying on his stomach, a plastic sheet spread out beneath him. He was pointing a camera in their direction. They only had to walk towards him but he was making them do it again and again; it was getting hard to keep up the fake chatter and laughter. As they set off for the umpteenth time Lucas leaned in and whispered to him that Holdsworth was costing Sophie's parents a small fortune so maybe doing every shot a hundred times was how he justified his fee. They both laughed out loud at that one, then laughed all over again when Holdsworth called out, 'That's the money shot!'

He was doing his best to be sociable, but now that the ceremony was over Zach was feeling restless. He'd caught up with his family, mingled with the guests, but he'd only been half listening to conversations, smiling in all the right places. It was his brother's wedding: a special occasion. He knew he ought to be enjoying himself, but it felt too much like work. He'd rather have been talking to the band. He'd seen them rocking up in their van, jaunty strides as they unloaded their amps and speakers, the big black cases for drums and keyboards. Guitars!

He lifted a fresh glass from a passing tray and retreated to a quiet corner of the terrace. He watched Holdsworth directing Lucas and Sophie into romantic poses at the lakeside, waving his hands about, cameras swinging from his shoulders, full of nervous energy. An image flashed into his head—Olivia and Holdsworth in the doorway—an altercation. He scanned the edges of the crowd, looking for the girl's nimble figure, her chestnut ponytail, the red camera strap around her neck, but she was nowhere to be seen.

She'd been there during the formal family photos, organising them all. Addressing them by name, adjusting ties and corsages, gentle hands on shoulders—turn this way a little please—flashing her warm, bright smile. He hadn't been able to take his eyes off her. She was lovely... and so good with people, so polished. She'd caught his eye a couple of times and then she'd smiled and blushed a little bit and he'd found himself smiling too because she was flirting with him and for some reason he liked it. In no time at all the family photo session was done. It had gone so smoothly that if he hadn't seen them fighting he would have assumed that Olivia and Holdsworth were the best of friends.

He shifted his gaze back to the lake. Lucas was facing Sophie now, forehead to forehead. Sophie was giggling and Holdsworth was calling out instructions from behind the camera. 'Keep it! Hold it!'

He felt a smile growing on his lips. Sophie and Lucas

were besotted with each other, perfect for one another. He could see a happy future for them because they were soulmates. That was what he'd written in his speech anyway, but as a deep ache filled his heart he wondered if he'd be able to say those words at all. The climbing voices around him suddenly felt too loud. He parked his glass and slipped away into the garden.

The grounds of Kensall Manor were extensive. As he walked, the voices on the terrace dwindled to a burble then gave way to birdsong. He passed through a wrought iron gate into an orchard and wandered through gnarled apple trees laden with blossom, alive with the buzzing and humming of bees. He let his mind drift to memories of his own wedding day. He could still see Izzy walking towards him through the lemon trees, patches of sunlight dappling on her skin, splashing the silk chiffon of her dress. She'd had that look in her eye, that secret smile she kept for him alone. His heart had buckled in his chest as she'd turned towards him and threaded her fingers into his. She had been his one perfect love, his life, his everything, and now she was gone, snatched from him in a tragic instant. He swallowed hard, plucked a blossom from a low branch. Marrying your soulmate was not a passport to a happy future. The future was as delicate and destructible as the flower he held in his hand.

He drew a steadying breath and checked his watch. He wondered if Alessia had woken from her nap yet. So many new faces, and this big strange house in the English countryside—it was bound to be tiring for a three-year-old. He hadn't been sure about bringing her at all, but of course his mother was always keen to see her granddaughter, and Lucas had insisted that his little niece should come to the wedding.

He crushed the flower between his fingers and let it fall to the ground. In half an hour the guests were going to be seated for the wedding breakfast and the more he thought about his speech, the more anxious he felt. He checked his inside pocket, touched the paper folded up inside. He wasn't nervous about speaking in public—as a hotelier, talking to people was an integral part of his life—but the speech he'd written about soulmates and everlasting love would unravel him, he just knew it. Perhaps if he altered some lines here and there, skimmed over the emotional stuff, he'd manage to hold it together. He just needed a pen and a quiet place to do it.

'Oh, I'm sorry—' He stopped mid-stride, the breath catching in his throat. Olivia Gardner was sitting in front of a laptop surrounded by camera equipment. 'I was told this room was empty.'

'It's almost empty.' She smiled hesitantly. 'There's only me here.'

He noticed a faint colour in her cheeks as she held his gaze. He noticed his own pulse. 'Can I come in?'

'Of course.'

He stepped into the room and closed the door. 'I need to look at my speech.'

She plugged a device into the side of her laptop. 'Don't mind me—if you want to practise, I mean.'

'It's not speaking I'm worried about.' He reached into his pocket for the thin wad of paper. 'I need to revise what I'm saying.'

'Ah.' She pressed a key and looked up. 'I get it! You're having second thoughts about giving your brother a roasting…?'

'Something like that.' He couldn't tell her that he was

trying to avoid embarrassing himself. 'I don't suppose you've got a pen?'

'I have.' She rooted through the pockets of the jacket hanging over the back of her chair. 'Somewhere…'

He stepped closer, noticed thumbnail images filling the computer screen.

'Here!' She was holding out a silver pen, warm brown eyes fixed on his.

'Thanks.' He took the pen, motioned to the laptop. 'Editing already?'

'No. Just downloading and backing up. We bank images as we go along, just in case.'

'Can I see some?'

She glanced at the door and it wasn't hard to read her thoughts.

'You don't have to worry—Holdsworth's at the lake with Lucas and Sophie.' He smiled. 'It can be our little secret.'

She hesitated then met his gaze squarely. 'It's not—Ralph's a very talented photographer—'

'Who's difficult to work with, I imagine…?'

Her lips were quirking into a half-smile. 'He can be challenging…'

'Extremely challenging, from what I've seen.'

She was pressing her lips together hard, trying to suppress a smile but her eyes were giving her away. 'Ralph's…okay.'

She might have issues with her boss but she was keeping them to herself. Zach admired her loyalty though he wondered if Holdsworth deserved it.

'I'd really like to see your pictures. What about the photo you took of us leaning? Will you show me that one at least?'

She scrunched her face up. 'Well, I do have to flag some photos for a slideshow... I suppose if you *happened* to be sitting close by, you might *accidentally* see some images...'

The mischievous gleam in her eye was irresistible. He knew he ought to be looking at his speech, but his curiosity about her was getting the better of him. She struck him as talented and he wanted to know if he was right. He sat beside her then opened up his speech and smoothed it out on the table. There was something joyful about the little conspiracy they were sharing and when he spoke he couldn't keep the smile out of his voice. 'I'll just work on my speech...'

She turned to face him, eyebrows arching. 'And I'll go through the pictures I took this morning...'

For a long moment he held her gaze. He noticed the curve of her cheek, the wisp of hair falling against her neck, the sweet shape of her mouth and he noticed the way her expression was changing, how the light in her eyes felt like a soft pocket of warmth—felt like home. Confused suddenly, he forced himself to look away and concentrate on the screen.

Her pictures were good! Sharp, clear, well-composed. The leaning shot made him laugh—Lucas was going to love it. She'd caught some great candid moments on the terrace too. When he saw a familiar little face with thick dark lashes the breath caught in his throat.

'Stop!'

'You want to see this one?'

He nodded.

With a click, she enlarged the image so that his daughter's face filled the screen. He stared at the photograph. Alessia was wearing her mother's secret smile. She was a happy little girl but he'd never seen that smile on her face before. Suddenly he felt disorientated, stranded between the past and the present.

Olivia leaned back in her chair. 'She's lovely, isn't she? Is she a relative?'

'Yes.' He swallowed hard. 'Alessia is my daughter.'

'Oh!' She looked shocked then a little embarrassed. 'I didn't know she was yours…'

Two spots of colour were blooming on her cheeks and instantly he felt guilty. She hadn't seen him with Alessia. His mother had been babysitting all day, and Alessia had been taking a nap while the family photos were being taken. Olivia knew nothing about his situation. All she knew was that he'd been catching her eye all day, smiling at her, receptive to her flirting. Maybe he'd even encouraged it. He'd have to think about that later, but right now he owed her an explanation.

'Her name is Alessia.' He swallowed. 'The way you've caught her—her smile. She looks just like her mother.'

He noticed Olivia glancing at the gold band on his left hand, noticed a new flush of colour creeping upwards from the base of her throat.

'Is your wife—?'

'No! She isn't here.' With difficulty, he held her gaze. 'She passed away two years ago.'

Olivia's face crumpled. 'Oh, no. No! I'm so sorry.' Her words escaped in a gasp and she lifted her hand as if she was going to touch him, but she didn't, just held his gaze with glistening eyes. 'Alessia must have been a baby.'

He nodded slowly. 'We'd just celebrated her first birthday…' In his mind he could see Izzy holding the lemon birthday cake she'd made, icing sugar in her hair and on her nose, and that scary moment when Alessia had reached out to touch the single burning candle. He'd blown it out just in time.

Olivia turned to look at the screen. 'If Alessia looks like her mother, your wife must have been beautiful.'

'She was…' He watched her, staring at the screen, chewing her lip. He supposed she was taking it all in, feeling foolish perhaps… He couldn't tell her he was feeling foolish too. He'd never expected to feel attracted to his brother's wedding photographer, never expected to be sitting beside her, breathing in the scent of her perfume, telling her about his wife and daughter.

The mounting noise of footsteps and voices in the hall outside seemed to draw a line under the moment and it was a relief. He ran a hand through his hair. 'I'd better go… Everyone's coming in…' He folded up his untouched speech. 'Looks like I'm going with the speech as it is.'

'I'm sure it'll be great!' She smiled. 'Actually, it better be great because I'll be taking pictures during the speeches—you need to give me some good moments!'

There was something reassuring in her gaze, something that bolstered his spirits. He got to his feet, slipped the pen into his pocket. 'I'll do my best.'

Olivia adjusted her ponytail and fanned her face with her hands. The great hall was warm in the aftermath of dinner, but it wasn't the only reason her cheeks felt hot. She was still reeling from everything Zach had told her, felt so stupid for thinking…for imagining… *How* had she managed not to notice his wedding ring? So much for supposedly having an eye for detail!

She looked across to the top table. He was scribbling furiously on a piece of paper—revising his speech after all. His mother was sitting in the next seat with Alessia on her knee. Alessia was clasping a crayon, bent over a colouring book, concentrating hard, except for the moments when she stopped to look at Zach. Alessia was copying him and he had no idea. Fathers and daughters… She pushed the thought away, lifted the camera and snapped a lady in a pink hat blowing bubbles from a tiny bottle.

Zach had let her down gently she supposed, but the more she thought about it, the more she realised that he'd been at it too with his lingering looks and little smiles during the family photos—it definitely wasn't her imagination.

She scanned the room for more photo opportunities, snapped a man putting on his wife's hat, acting the fool. She looked at Zach again. His lips were moving, rehearsing the new words he'd written, her silver pen glinting in his hand.

Maybe the truth was that they were attracted to each other, but a random wedding day crush wasn't going to lead to anything, especially since a widower with a daughter was the last thing she was looking for.

Too complicated!

She didn't like loose ends. She liked things cut and dried, wanted someone she could build a life with, not someone who had a life she'd have to fit into. She glanced at Alessia. She knew nothing about small children, didn't see herself as a stepmother. She was only twenty-four; she was still carving out a career. Emotional entanglements would only take her eye off the ball. She had to push forward, seize opportunities…

She scanned the room, saw Ralph talking to a young couple then discreetly handing them a business card. Networking was easy for him—he had a good reputation, a solid client base. If she started up on her own she'd have to break in and that was difficult, especially since she wanted high-end clients.

Yet again she found her gaze drifting back to the top table. *Zach* had really liked her photographs. He might recommend her to people he knew. The Merrill family owned a hotel chain after all… Suddenly he looked up, straight into her eyes and there it was again, that feeling that there was something between them. She smiled back quickly and looked away. No! She wouldn't be able to ask Zach for any favours. He only had to look at her and her head started to spin.

When she saw the Master of Ceremonies approaching the top table to announce the speeches, she lifted her camera. Photographing the speeches was another concession Ralph had made to her. She needed to focus on getting great pictures because, until she found the courage to break out on her own, she needed this job.

CHAPTER TWO

Six weeks later...

OLIVIA MADE HER way down the aisle of the bus and sank into a seat. She hefted her camera bag onto the vacant seat beside her and rummaged in her other bag for her sunglasses. In spite of the tinted windows, it seemed too bright. Bright and sunny and warm. Deliciously warm!

As she watched the other passengers piling aboard with belongings of all shapes and sizes, she had the urge to pinch herself yet again, just in case she was dreaming. Was she really here in Italy, on the final leg of her journey to start a new job in Ravello?

The bus belched, lurched then pulled away from the airport bus stop, cruising slowly to the exit before joining a busy road. The sun glinted off the chrome of unfamiliar cars, dappled through the leaves of unfamiliar trees and she felt her lips curving into a smile. It *was* real, and it was all because of what had happened after the Merrill wedding...

They'd been driving back to London when Ralph had suddenly announced that he was letting her go.

She couldn't believe her ears. 'You're letting me go!

Why? Because I took a few photographs of the groomsmen? For goodness' sake, Ralph.'

'It's not that.'

'What then?'

He threw her a sheepish look. 'Because you're after
my job!'

'I'm not!'

He pulled up at a set of traffic lights and turned to
face her. 'Okay, I'm not saying you want *my* exact job,
but you want more than I can give you. I'm not looking
for a partner, Liv. I want an assistant. At the very most
I want someone who's happy shooting the flowers and
the frilly bits—a few guests now and again. You, my
darling, want to be *the* photographer with a capital F.'

'It's P! And yes, I won't deny that I want to be a wedding photographer…one day…but I'm not ready.'

'You're more than ready.' The traffic light changed
and Ralph drove on. 'I watched you working with those
boys today and you were great. You get on with people,
your technical skills are top-notch. It's time for you to
fly the nest.'

She felt as if the air was rearranging itself around
her. Ralph had been getting on her nerves for ever, but
this wasn't what she'd planned—she didn't have a plan.
Maybe that was the problem. She'd spent most of her time
with Ralph just simmering with frustration, but she'd
never done anything about it. She hadn't imagined that
he would be the one to push her off the plank.

'Don't look so glum, darling. You can have some of
my old gear as a leaving present.' He tipped her a wink.
'You're going to be a big success. Just make sure you're
not a big success on my patch!'

After the initial shock, she realised that he was right.

Letting her go was a backhanded compliment. Although the thought of launching herself as a wedding photographer was scary, she knew she had the skills, and handling Ralph's admin had given her a good insight into the business side of things. Her biggest challenge was going to be finding the right clients, but then...

On her very last afternoon Ralph muttered something about having left some kit for her as promised, then he'd shot off to some 'important' meeting which didn't seem to be marked in the diary. When she went into his office and saw what he'd put out for her she was overwhelmed. Some of the gear had hardly been used, just mothballed in favour of something newer or fancier. She was looking at everything he'd given her, feeling a bit emotional about it, when the telephone had rung.

'Good afternoon. Holdsworth Photography.'

'Hello. Is that Olivia Gardner?'

The man's voice was familiar. Probably one of Ralph's bridegrooms. 'Yes. Can I help—?'

'I have something of yours...' Little pause. 'It's got your name engraved on it.'

'Something of mine?' A rapid clicking sound filled her ears and suddenly she knew why she'd recognised his voice. 'Zach Merrill! You've got my pen!'

'I forgot to give it back... I'm so sorry.'

She could hear the smile in his voice, momentarily lost herself in a memory of intent blue eyes. 'There's no need to apologise. You were stressing about your speech, if I remember rightly. In such circumstances, petty theft is excusable.' She couldn't stop smiling, couldn't help feeling a little glow at the thought of him, even if he was absolutely not her dream man. 'It was very good, by the way—your speech, and I've heard lots of speeches—'

'Thanks! I'm not so sure, but I'll take your word for it.'

His voice in her ear sounded warm, intimate some-how. She was blushing, glad that he couldn't see her face. She cleared her throat, tried to sound blasé. 'So—about the pen. It was a twenty-first birthday present—can I have it back?'

'Of course. You might even want to collect it in person…'

His voice was playful. She felt her forehead creasing, a smile lifting the corners of her mouth. 'Okay, you've got my attention.'

'Actually, this isn't just about the pen—' His tone downshifted, became serious. 'I need to talk to you about something. Calling you at work was the only way I could reach you, but it's not a conversation we can have if Holdsworth's about.'

'He's not here—but it wouldn't matter anyway. It's my last day today.'

'Your last day! You've got a new job?' He sounded disappointed.

She chewed her bottom lip. She was growing more confused by the second. 'No.' Deep breath. 'Actually, I'm going out on my own.'

'Ahh.' He was smiling again, she could tell. 'Well, in that case I'll get straight to the point. You may remember that my family owns a chain of hotels.'

She could feel her heart thumping. 'Yes.'

'In addition, I own an exclusive wedding venue. High-end. We look after everything: accommodation, catering, ceremony and…photography.' His voice tightened. 'I've just come off the phone with my photographer, Michele. Some idiot knocked him off his moped, fractured his leg. Poor guy's going to be out of action for at least six weeks.' He sighed. 'So, here's the thing… I'm booked

solid and I need a wedding photographer to fill in—
someone I can trust.'

Olivia's head began to spin so fast that it took a moment for everything to sink in. Was Zach Merrill offering her a succession of high-end wedding clients on a
plate? She felt her spine tingle. This was her moment, her
chance to prove herself. She tried to calm her galloping
heart with a slow, measured breath. 'You're asking *me*
to step into your photographer's shoes?'

'Yes. I've seen the quality of your work, the way you
interact with people. You'd be perfect, I know you would.
Is there any way you could help me out?'

Ah—let me see...

'Yes! That is, I want to say yes, but I have so many
questions! I mean—I don't even know where your venue
is—although I've worked in a lot of places with Ralph
so I might know it.'

He'd laughed then. 'I doubt it. Casa Isabella is in Ravello.'

'As in—Italy?'

'That's right.'

'Wow!'

After his call, she'd looked at Casa Isabella online,
scrolled through the website pages with wide, excited
eyes. It was a grand old *palazzo*, slightly faded but elegant. Its secluded hillside setting above Ravello offered
spectacular views of the Tyrrhenian Sea from its terrace
and balconies, but it was the garden that had taken her
breath away. Ancient cypress trees on terraced lawns, a
stone pond with a sparkling fountain, arches leading to
secret garden rooms with weathered statues. Achingly romantic, it was a wedding photographer's dream venue...

And now she was here, all set to photograph six weddings in a prestige venue—in Italy! Portfolio couples! She felt sick with nerves, a little dizzy, high on adrenaline, still incredulous but happy and excited too. No wonder she kept wanting to pinch herself.

She pulled a bottle of water from her bag and took a steadying sip as the poor dwellings on the outskirts of Naples gave way to hillsides covered in olive trees. The bus trundled through small towns with narrow streets, screeched to a halt more than once to avoid scooters weaving through the traffic. She gazed at the sun-baked terracotta roofs, so different to roofs in England. She got her phone out, took pictures through the window— ancient churches, walls covered in brightly scrambling bougainvillea. She watched people going about their day-to-day business, saw people sitting at roadside cafés reading the papers or chatting with friends. Between the towns, she glimpsed lemon groves behind crumbling walls and then, on the skyline, she saw the mighty Vesuvius, its peak rising into a smear of hazy cloud.

She sipped her water again and thought about Zach. Now that he was going to be her boss, it was inappropriate to think about him in anything other than a platonic way, yet when she pictured his eyes, recalled how handsome he'd looked at Lucas and Sophie's wedding, she felt a little glow of anticipation that made her lips curve upwards into a secret little smile.

Zach Merrill leaned against the wing of his convertible, pushed his sunglasses onto his head and looked along the valley, searching the twisting road for signs of Olivia's bus. He couldn't believe how things had worked out. After Michele had called him from the hospital, he'd contacted some photographers he knew, but none of them were free. Calling Olivia had been a long shot, but he'd seen that she was tired of working for Holdsworth, had hoped that she would consider his offer. How lucky that she'd been free to come.

His fingers closed around the pen in his pocket. He remembered the look in her eyes when she'd handed it to him, warm light pouring into him, making him dizzy. He'd had to look away, force himself to concentrate on the pictures filling her computer screen, but it was lucky too that he'd seen those photographs, seen the quality of her work. If he hadn't—Alessia's face captured so perfectly—he might not have thought of her as a replacement for Michele at all.

He pulled the pen from his pocket, ran his finger over the inscription. He hadn't meant to steal her twenty-first birthday pen. He hadn't been himself that day…noticing Olivia with her bright brown hair and warm smile, liking the way she was looking at him, the way she was flirting, and then he'd been remembering Izzy and worrying about his speech. Emotions piling up, layers of confusion, his feelings all over the place…and then seeing Alessia's face in the photograph…so like her mother's.

And now Olivia was on her way to Ravello, as if some invisible ink was drawing them together.

He slipped the pen back into his pocket. His mother-in-law, Lucia, had questioned why he was bringing an untested photographer all the way from England—'Couldn't you get someone from Naples?'

He'd told her that the decent people were already booked for the summer. He'd pointed out that Olivia was a native English speaker, which was perfect because their clients were mostly English-speaking. Besides, he'd added, wasn't it the decent thing to do, to give a talented person a break? She'd agreed but she'd had a knowing look in her eye which bothered him. Maybe she thought that having Olivia to stay at Casa Isabella was going to change things. He could understand that in a way.

Turning the faded *palazzo* into an exclusive wedding venue had been Izzy's idea—their dream project. They'd started on the interior renovations and then Izzy had found the original landscape plans in the attic. After that, she'd worked closely with the gardeners to restore the old pathways and formal beds, breathing life back into the neglected garden. She'd get so excited about the smallest thing: new shoots on old wood, some jaded creeper bursting into flower... He'd loved Izzy with all his heart. He missed her every day. But he didn't appreciate his mother-in-law dissecting his motives for bringing Olivia here. It was a business decision. He needed a wedding photographer and Olivia was talented, professional and discreet. Plus, she was available. That was all there was to it.

When the bus finally came into view he rocked forward off the car and lowered his sunglasses, trying to ignore the little knot of excitement tightening in his stomach. After she'd agreed to come he'd phoned her a few times to discuss practical matters like getting her a computer. He'd enjoyed their conversations. He'd liked her enthusiasm, but talking to her, hearing the vitality in her voice, had made him realise how jaded he felt. He was married to the business, worked like a dog, but he didn't feel fulfilled. He felt restless.

When the bus pulled in and Olivia bumped down the steps with her camera bag he almost didn't recognise her—she looked so different to the way she'd looked at the wedding. She was wearing blue sneakers, faded jeans and a white top which was slipping off her shoulder. Her hair was twisted into a loose knot and most of her face was hidden by a very large pair of sunglasses. The sight of her made him ridiculously happy. He had to fight the urge to pick her up and swing her around. Instead he held out his hand. 'Olivia! Welcome to Ravello.'

She pushed her sunglasses up and stretched her hand to his. 'Zach! It's so nice to see you, and please—call me Liv. Everyone else does!'

'Okay, Liv.' He smiled. The sunlight catching her eyes made them look lighter than he remembered, like amber, and for the first time he noticed the darker ring around the edge of her irises. When he realised he was still holding her hand he let it go quickly and reached for her camera bag. 'How was your journey?'

'It was great, although I can see how Michele got hurt. The roads here are challenging, and as for the way people drive—'

The bus driver set down a modest suitcase and another big camera bag. Zach handed him a tip then picked up her other bags. 'You see a lot of dented cars around here, that's for sure! Is this the only luggage you've got?'

'I travel light.' She widened her eyes. 'Except for the camera gear!'

'I suppose it's just as well…' He motioned to his car.

'Nice!' She walked over, ran her fingers over the silver paintwork. 'It's not even dented!'

She was teasing him, laughing, and he couldn't help laughing too. 'I don't get out much.' He put her bags in the back and opened the door for her. 'Ready?'

'Absolutely!' She slipped her sunglasses over her eyes and beamed.

She felt the sun warming her face as Zach drove them up into the hills. It felt so good to see him again. As the bus had pulled in, the sight of him waiting for her had set her heart going—she'd been glad of her dark glasses. He'd looked handsome at the wedding, but today, casually dressed in a pale blue shirt and navy chinos, he looked even better. More relaxed. From behind her sunglasses she took in the golden skin at the base of his throat, the nice shape of his mouth, the straight nose. His dark hair had been combed back at the wedding, but now it was blowing every which way in the breeze, dishevelled, touchable.

He glanced at her and smiled. 'What do you think so far?'

Gorgeous.

She blushed, wondered if he'd noticed her checking him out. She turned to look at the view. 'It's lovely, greener than I imagined and so warm.'

'I'm sorry I couldn't pick you up in Naples. I had a meeting sprung on me at the last minute.'

'That's okay—the bus ride was an education.'

His shirt sleeves were rolled back. It was hard not to notice his forearms. Tanned, muscular. She forced herself to concentrate on the view: slopes thick with sturdy shrubs and olive trees, a pair of donkeys in a paddock, tails flicking. She adjusted her sunglasses, glanced at him again. How old was he? Early thirties perhaps—at least six years older than she was—and married.

Widowed.

She wondered about his wife. He'd had so much to cope with: grief, a young baby and a business too. *'I don't get out much.'* Did he ever get lonely?

On a tight bend thick with trees he steered the car into a concealed entrance and stopped in front of tall iron gates set into a stone wall. Engraved on a simple plaque fixed to the wall were the words *Casa Isabella*.

He pushed his sunglasses up, turned to face her. 'Isabella was my wife's name—Izzy.' She noticed the way he drew in a breath. 'When we get to the house you'll meet my mother-in-law, Lucia. She helps me with Alessia.'

Olivia sensed that she didn't need to reply.

'Lucia's a strong woman, an incredible person, and I couldn't have coped without her these past two years.' A shadow crossed his face. 'She's grateful to you for coming at such short notice but…she's a little unsettled… maybe because this was Izzy's home.' He turned to press a button on the dash and the gates started to move. 'I wanted to tell you, just in case you pick up a vibe…' He met her eye again and suddenly he smiled. 'I'm probably worrying too much. You're really good with people—it won't be a problem.'

As he slid the car through the gates she tried not to think about Lucia, the admirable but possibly hostile mother-in-law. Instead, she looked back at the gates closing behind them. 'Do you need such tight security here?'

'Not really, but we had a celebrity wedding last year— they insisted on gates.'

She wanted to know more, but she didn't want to seem star-struck so she nodded and tried to look blasé as he drove them through a terraced vineyard and onwards through an ancient olive grove. Under the shade of the olive trees the light was blue-green, thick as gauze. She made a mental note to go back with her camera some time, try to capture it.

Emerging into the sunshine, the road continued through an area of rough pasture, then turned sharply to the right. As Casa Isabella came into view, framed by an avenue of tall cypress trees, she gasped softly. White-washed in pale ochre, roofed with weathered pantiles, the ground floor windows were tall and shuttered, arranged at identical intervals along the length of the house. In the centre, an imposing double stairway led to a vast oak door. She knew from the website that on the other side of the property, facing the sea, was a long, arched veranda opening out to the wide terrace where the wedding ceremonies took place. Beyond the terrace, over the stone balcony, and all around the property lay the enchanting garden.

'Papà! Papà!'

Olivia watched Alessia run into Zach's arms, watched him swing her up, cuddle her in. He rattled off something in Italian then lowered his voice, adopted a coaxing tone until Alessia turned dark eyes towards her. He cautioned gently. 'In English, remember…'

Alessia licked her lips. 'Hello, Olivia. Welcome to Casa Isabella.' She smiled quickly then buried her face into Zach's shirt, giggling.

Olivia stepped forward hesitantly. Photographing kids at weddings was one thing; conversing with them was quite another. 'Hello, Alessia. I'm very pleased to meet you.'

Alessia jerked her head away from Zach's shoulder and eyed her again, frowning a little.

Zach tickled her under the chin. 'Do you remember Olivia from Uncle Lucas's wedding? She took your photograph.'

Alessia began to writhe and giggle. Olivia took a few steps back. Watching Zach with his daughter, hearing the unfamiliar words pouring from his mouth so easily, was bringing her down to earth with a bump. She'd never thought about it before but of course he could speak Italian. He *lived* here. His *wife* had been Italian. Conscious suddenly of being the outsider, she turned away, hitched up the neckline of her top to cover her bare shoulder. Flirting, imagining—it had to stop here. He was embedded in a life that had nothing to do with her—a life she could never see herself being part of.

'Nonna!'

Alessia's cry broke into her thoughts and she turned to see an elegant woman walking down the grand hallway towards them.

'Lucia!' Zach shifted Alessia to one hip and held out his arm. 'Come meet Olivia.'

As she drew closer, Olivia could see strands of silver in the older woman's hair, sense the reticence in her slow smile. She was glad that Zach had warned her.

'Welcome, Olivia.' Lucia leaned in to air-kiss her cheek. 'Thank you for coming.' Another kiss. 'We are very grateful.' She stepped back, eyes searching Olivia's.

Olivia smiled. 'No, I'm the one who's grateful!' She couldn't read Lucia's expression and it was unnerving, so she tried to visualise the older woman as a reluctant wedding guest facing the camera. She'd found the trick to getting people on board was to be bubbly, to distract them in some way, so she stepped into the middle of the wide hall and looked up at the glittering chandelier suspended from the ceiling. 'This is astonishing!'

She'd been so mesmerised by Zach and Alessia that she hadn't properly looked at her surroundings, but now she took it all in. The patina of the wooden floor beneath their feet, the chalky yellow walls, the twin gilt-edged mirrors hanging over the console tables positioned on either side of the grand door. Beyond the vestibule where they were standing the floor of the wide inner hallway was laid with pale polished stone. The walls were hung with paintings and below the paintings there were more console tables, and occasional chairs.

When she finally looked round to smile at Lucia she wasn't faking her delight. 'It's so beautiful... Italy... Ravello! This house...everything! I'm over the moon!'

Lucia was looking at her with wide eyes and at the edge of her vision she could sense Zach stifling a laugh. Perhaps she'd overdone the enthusiasm, but then Alessia suddenly wriggled out of Zach's arms and came to stand by her side. She looked up, took a deep breath and said, 'This is *as-ton-ish-ing!*'

As Lucia and Zach burst out laughing, she breathed a sigh of relief. Never had she been so grateful to a child in all her life. She looked down at Alessia and grinned. 'I'm so glad you agree!'

Casa Isabella really *was* astonishing. As Zach showed her around, Olivia could feel herself falling in love with it. The rooms were large and airy, high-ceilinged, flooded with light. The décor was a mixture of antique and contemporary. What she liked most was that Casa Isabella felt like a home—a big home certainly, but every space was inviting.

Outside on the terrace, the view over the grounds to the sparkling sea took her breath away. She wanted to explore the garden straight away, but Zach said they weren't finished inside yet. He led her back inside and along another wide hall on the ground floor.

'Your rooms are along here.'

'Rooms?'

'Of course! It's a small suite, a bit rustic—we haven't got as far as renovating this part of the house yet—but

I think you'll be comfortable.' He opened a door off the hall. 'The kitchen's here.'

She stepped into a small, high-ceilinged room. It might have been a laundry room once, but now it was equipped with a fridge, a kettle, a two-ring hob and a microwave.

He smiled. 'It goes without saying that you can eat with us whenever you like…'

She tried to imagine eating dinner under Lucia's watchful eye. 'It's very kind of you to offer, but I'm sure your family time is precious.'

His eyes narrowed and he looked as if he was about to say something but then he stepped back into the hallway and opened a set of double doors on the opposite side. 'The rest of the suite is in here.'

She stepped through a small lobby and into a large comfortable sitting room. In one corner there was a desk with a computer and hard drives, but the rest of the room was set out for relaxing. A sofa and chairs were loosely arranged in front of a marble fireplace, lamp tables and other occasional tables scattered in between. The French windows overlooking the garden were open, white muslin curtains lifting in the breeze. She gazed at the view, all smiles. 'This is lovely.'

'It's a doer-upper, but I'm glad you like it. The bedroom's through there, and there's an en suite bathroom—it's old-fashioned but it works.'

She pushed open another set of doors and smiled again. The bedroom was spacious. The walls were whitewashed, yellowing in places, but the effect was charming. A huge antique bed was made up with white bedlinen, a blanket folded over the mahogany footboard. She noticed that her suitcase had already been brought in and left on a rack between a large wardrobe and a large chest of drawers. Everything in the room seemed large. She peeped into the en suite bathroom and smiled again. Claw-foot bath, huge porcelain sink and a separate shower recessed so deeply that there was no need for a screen.

She turned around. 'It's lovely, Zach.' The dark serious eyes she'd seen in the car had been replaced with twinkling blue ones and she was glad. Perhaps now that she'd cleared the hurdle of meeting Lucia he would relax. 'I don't know what I was expecting, but it wasn't this—I mean, a whole apartment to myself?'

'You'll need somewhere to hide from the mayhem.'

She sat down on the bed and gazed around the room. 'Is that what it's like?'

'It can get crazy sometimes. We've only got fifteen guest bedrooms, but we're filled to capacity every weekend and, as you know, weddings are demanding. There's all the coordination beforehand, then when the wedding party arrives it's busy. There's always an army of beauticians and hair stylists in tow, then caterers, florists—you know the score. After the wedding we have to keep going. Breakfasts, checking out the guests, arranging transport, room cleaning, maintenance, then it begins all over again.'

'Do you ever get time off?'

'Not much.'

She ran her hand over the quilt, felt its silky cotton softness. Eight-hundred thread count.

Nice.

She looked up, found that he was watching her. Little butterflies started up in her stomach. 'So, why put yourself through it? Weddings, I mean. You could run yoga retreats instead—far less demanding!'

'Lower income too—this place costs a lot to run.'

Suddenly, his eyes took on a faraway look and he turned away, walked to the window. For a few moments he gazed at the view. 'Actually, it's not about the money. It's because we fell in love…'

Silhouetted against the window, he cut a lonely figure. Olivia felt a shiver travelling up her spine, an urge to go to him, but instead she folded her hands in her lap.

'When we came to view this place we'd been looking for a going concern, a boutique hotel—something that we could just take over. But then this place came up. It was in a bad state. The interior was shot, the garden was a jungle. Everything was wrong with it, but it had good bones and as for the location… I remember we stood out there on the terrace as the sun was going down and it was romantic.' She could hear the smile in his voice, his evident fondness for the memory. 'Then Izzy looked at me and said, *"We should turn this into a wedding venue."* It was an inspired suggestion… I bought it the next day.'

Olivia imagined standing on the terrace with Zach, a fiery sunset over the sea, his body warm and close…but that was Isabella. He was in love with Isabella, he'd made his vows to Isabella, built a life and a home with Isabella.

Suddenly, he spun round and smiled. 'Impressive speech about gratitude, by the way. Not at all over the top.'

She could feel the warmth in his smile, felt that they really were becoming friends. She pulled a face and laughed. 'I was trying to be amenable. At least Alessia appreciated my performance.'

He laughed. 'Yes, thanks for that. *As-ton-ish-ing* is going to be her new favourite word.'

'Well, it's a good word.' She got to her feet and joined him at the window. 'It sums up Casa Isabella perfectly.'

CHAPTER THREE

FROM HIS OFFICE BALCONY, Zach could see Olivia working with the bride and groom in the garden. Over the hubbub of wedding guests on the terrace below, he could hear the occasional burst of laughter from the couple as she directed them through a walking sequence. She looked confident and relaxed, demonstrating to the bride how to hold the bouquet as she walked, adjusting the flower on the groom's lapel. He remembered the way she'd tidied his own buttonhole at Lucas's wedding, standing so close to him that he could smell the lingering fragrance of her shampoo. She'd taken him by surprise, or rather he'd taken himself by surprise, noticing things about her, like the way her smile reached all the way to her eyes, and the graceful way she moved.

He retreated into the room and poured himself a glass of water from a jug on the table. He'd thought she might be nervous about today—her first wedding at Casa Isabella—but he'd been watching her discreetly all day and she'd been every bit as polished and professional as he'd hoped. If she was nervous, she'd certainly kept it under wraps. He sipped from his glass, felt the cool liquid sliding down his throat. Soon her working day would be over. The wedding breakfast and speeches were finished.

There was only the first dance left for her to shoot. Michele usually took a little break before photographing the first dance, but she was out there with the couple, taking pictures in the mellow evening light. Just yesterday she'd been telling him all about the golden hour, how it was the most beautiful light for romantic pictures, but as she'd been talking all he'd been able to think about was how much he liked the light in her eyes.

She was a breath of fresh air, a little breeze stirring his senses around, blowing through the veil of sadness that had settled over him since Izzy's death. As soon as he'd finished showing her around the house on the day she arrived, she was off exploring every inch of the grounds and formal gardens. All week she'd been out there, taking test shots, assessing the light at different times of the day.

Dedication!

Only this morning she'd suggested some adjustments to the ceremony layout on the terrace which would give her better shooting angles. 'The pictures are what the couple take away with them,' she'd said. 'We need to give them the best possible images, and that works for your business too because those pictures on your website gallery will help sell the venue.'

It was nothing he didn't know already, but although he was always busy and involved with things, of late he'd lost that intimate connection with the business that he'd had at the beginning. Olivia's energy and enthusiasm were challenging him, reminding him just how emptied out he felt.

Izzy's death would have finished him if it hadn't been for Alessia. Alessia was his reason for living, the reason why he'd needed to achieve Izzy's dream of turning this place into the perfect wedding venue. He was well aware that throwing himself into the renovation, driving himself day and night to push the project forward had been his way of coping with the grief. Eight months after Izzy's funeral, Casa Isabella had opened for business. Merrill Hotels now had a destination wedding venue in its portfolio, a database of eager couples looking for a romantic wedding venue in Italy. The first year had been a huge success. Five-star testimonials had led to a rush of forward bookings so that now he barely had time to breathe. When Olivia had asked him if he ever took time off, he'd wanted to laugh. Lucas's wedding had been his first weekend off in over six months.

Olivia threw herself onto the bed and exhaled a long, happy sigh. Her first solo wedding—in the bag! She smiled at the ceiling.

This morning, when she'd tapped on the bride's door, she'd been jittery with nerves, but after shooting the first few pictures the butterflies in her stomach had vanished. Now she was exhausted, but euphoric too. She was so glad she'd taken those last romantic pictures in the low light, got that little flare at the side of the frame. Stunning!

As she slipped out of her dress and pulled on her old jeans and a tee shirt, she was thinking about Ralph, how touchy and difficult he used to be during a wedding. After today, she could understand him a little better. The pressure had been relentless, not only because of the responsibility, but because she'd spent the day pushing herself, chasing the perfect shot—what Ralph used to call the money shot.

She freed her hair from its clip and shook it loose. She knew she should chill out, but she was buzzing.

She simply had to download the pictures, take a look at what she'd got.

In the sitting room she switched on the computer. Zach had bought the best equipment for her, top quality hard drives, the latest graphics tablet. With sixteen hundred photographs to turn around in a week, she'd told him she would need a fast system and thankfully he'd listened. She started downloading the pictures then crossed to the French windows and flung them open. Instantly she could hear the muffled bass beat of the wedding band playing some lively number in the function room, snatches of chatter and laughter from guests relaxing on the terrace above. She stepped outside, breathed the fragrant evening air. The statues and fountain were lit up and there were more tiny lights twinkling amongst the leaves of the trees closest to the house. Everything looked magical. Isabella's dream brought to life.

Was running a wedding venue Zach's dream too? She couldn't help wondering...

He'd been on the go all day, on hand for the wedding planner, quietly making sure that everything was running smoothly. He seemed to drive himself hard, had admitted that he didn't take much time off, but it didn't make sense to her. The Merrill family was wealthy. There was the UK hotel chain and now this Italian wedding venue. She'd looked at the marketing brochures and the rate card. She knew how much it cost to have a wedding at Casa Isabella, and the place was booked solid! Even if her estimation of running costs was wildly inaccurate, she figured that Zach could easily afford to employ a manager. He employed other staff after all: a housekeeper, several cleaners, a secretary, two gardeners and a maintenance guy. Perhaps it was none of her business, but it bothered her that in the short time she'd been here she'd never seen him take Alessia out or play with her for more than five minutes at a stretch. It was clear that he adored his daughter, yet Alessia seemed to spend nearly all her time with Lucia. Olivia couldn't help feeling that if he didn't make time for Alessia now he would regret it later.

She massaged the back of her neck, felt memories unspooling. Her relationship with own father wasn't great, but at least she could look back at the happy times they'd shared...the way his eyes used to twinkle. *'Let's go adventuring, Liv!'* That always meant they were going to do something special—wild swimming, long walks, campfires and marshmallows. He was an ecologist—passionate about nature. He knew bird calls and the proper names of all the insects and plants. For the longest time she'd admired him. The way he stood out from the crowd—not just because of his height and his ponytail, but because he was outspoken. She remembered the primary school parents' night when he'd challenged her teacher about letting kids use plastic straws for a collage on the classroom wall, other parents and kids looking on, whispering.

She'd modelled herself on him. During a class session on religion and ritual across different cultures she'd proudly told the class that her parents weren't married, that marriage was an outdated ritual that had nothing to do with love and fidelity. She'd been defiantly vocal, just like he was—and then he'd left, moved to Wales.

She felt as if he'd hung her out to dry.

It hadn't helped that her three best friends all had parents who were happily married, ticking off anniversaries year after year. Celebration cakes, little weekend breaks, family get-togethers. No wonder she'd become fixated on a fantasy of perfection.

At university she'd tried to wean herself off the idea, tried to be more casual about relationships, but she'd failed. Now she knew her own mind. She wanted to do things by the book. A ring on her finger, total commitment, no loose ends. She wanted someone who would promise to love and cherish her for the rest of her life— someone who wouldn't leave like her father had. The trouble was, no one had ever come close.

'Hello?'

A voice from inside startled her. She listened again.

'Liv—?'

Zach!

She stepped back into her sitting room to find him standing in the doorway with a tray of food balanced on one arm and a bottle of wine in his hand. When he saw her, he lifted his eyebrows and put on a waiter voice. 'Room service for Olivia Gardner.' And then he came forward and set the tray and bottle down on a low table. He drew back to his full height and smiled. 'I also wanted to say thanks for doing such a great job today.'

He looked tired, she thought, strained around the eyes in spite of his smile. 'That's so nice of you, Zach, thank you.' She looked at the tray. It was filled with a selection of delicious-looking dishes from the wedding buffet, and a bowl of fat green pitted olives. All at once, she felt ravenous. She popped an olive into her mouth, then offered the dish to him. 'Will you join me?'

'I can't. I need to get back— Besides, I'm sure you could do with some peace and quiet.' She could see tension in his eyes and suddenly she really wanted him to stay, wanted to see him relax.

'Actually, I'm feeling a bit wired and I could use some company. I'm downloading today's pictures—if you stay you could look at them…'

His eyes darted to the computer. She could see he was tempted. She pushed a little harder. 'Look, I don't want to drink alone. Please, stay for a little while. I'm sure the wedding planner can cope without you and, to be honest, you look like you need a break.'

For a moment his expression clouded and she wondered if she'd crossed a line, but then slowly he smiled. 'I *would* like to see your pictures, and you're right! A glass of wine would really hit the spot right now. Is there a corkscrew in the kitchen?'

'Second drawer on the left.' He lifted an eyebrow and she laughed. 'The garden isn't the only place I recced thoroughly.'

He loved the photos and she was relieved; he'd brought her here to do this job after all. He liked the ceremony shots taken from the new angles, and he raved about the way she'd captured the atmosphere of the wedding— tiny details and big, happy smiles. He'd looked a little wistful when they got to the last photos of the couple in the garden at sunset and she wondered if he was thinking about Isabella.

Now she was curled up on the sofa with a second glass of wine, a little mellow buzz thrumming through her, and he was sitting in an armchair with his legs stretched out. He'd taken off his jacket and loosened his tie. She tried not to notice the dark hair at the base of his throat, the little hollow that she wanted to touch with her fingers and her lips. She imagined pulling his tie right off, reaching for the buttons of his shirt, undoing them one by one, feeling the delicious heat of his skin, the scent of him as she pressed her lips…

What was she doing? Zach Merrill didn't fit the profile of her ideal man. It didn't matter that his eyes seemed to run right through her, that she couldn't look at him without wondering what it would be like to touch him, but he could never be hers. He was still in love with his wife and he was her employer and he had a daughter *and* she was living under his roof alongside his mother-in-law. She forced herself to concentrate on his face.

He was looking around as if he was noticing the room for the first time. 'I haven't spent a lot of time in this part of the house. It's nice in here—like a little sanctuary.'

'That's it exactly! When I come in here and close the door, I forget I'm in a great big house. I love it!'

'What else do you love?' Smiling blue eyes. 'I'm curious.'

She felt herself blushing. 'You mean raindrops on roses, whiskers on kittens… That kind of thing?'

'It'd be a start!' He sipped his wine and suddenly his eyes grew more serious. 'What I mean is, here you are, helping me out, doing a fantastic job too, and I've suddenly realised that I don't know anything about you.'

She felt the breeze from the open window rippling over her bare arms, goosebumps prickling her skin. She didn't like talking about herself. With a camera around her neck she knew who she was, but without it, when the lens was focused on her, her instinct was to hide. She rubbed at her lower lip with her thumb, tried to sound casual. 'What do you want to know?'

He laughed. 'Don't look so terrified. We've both spent the day looking after people, being polite…careful about what we say. I just want to have a normal conversation, like, I don't know… Did you always want to be a wedding photographer?'

An image slipped into her head: herself clambering over a stile with her dad, big binoculars swinging from her neck. Suddenly she was laughing. 'No—for a while I wanted to be David Attenborough.'

His eyebrows lifted. 'You're a nature-lover?'

'I guess…' She smiled. 'My dad was—*is*—an ecologist. We used to go out a lot when I was little—bird-watching, deer-stalking. Lots of hiking! I had this huge pair of binoculars and I used to love looking through them, seeing things so close. It was like watching my own little wildlife film.'

'And now you spend your time looking through a camera lens. I can see a pattern.'

'Maybe I like spying on people—or maybe I like controlling the view…' She sipped her drink, lost herself for a moment. 'You can make things look perfect when you control the view.'

'So, you're either a spy or a control freak and your father is responsible?'

She shrugged. 'Well, you know what they say about formative influences—maybe I just like taking pictures.' He was looking at her, gently inquisitive, but she didn't want to talk about her dad. She remembered what she'd been thinking earlier, about Alessia. Perhaps she could steer the conversation in a different direction.

'Fathers and daughters—it's a special bond, don't you think?' She searched his eyes, wondering if he was hearing what she was saying to him. 'I see it at every wedding… *Who giveth this woman?* The little private looks, all that emotion.'

He looked down at his glass. Perhaps she'd struck a

nerve. He got to his feet, retrieved the wine bottle from the table and topped up their glasses. 'I suppose so—but weddings are emotional events from start to finish. I can see *you* love it all.'

'Why wouldn't I? Weddings are very photogenic, especially in a venue like this.'

'So, you're all about the photo opportunities then?' He grinned. 'No misty eyes during the vows…?'

She felt a blush creeping over her cheeks. 'You were *watching* me during the vows?'

He was laughing now. 'I might have noticed you dabbing your eyes.'

She liked the way his face shone when he laughed, as if someone had switched a light on. She couldn't help smiling too. 'Okay, so I'll admit I get caught up in the ceremony. I find it moving, the idea of pledging yourself to another person for ever, being so sure that you've found the right one.' She sighed. 'Doesn't it get to you too?' His eyes darkened and instantly she regretted her question. 'I'm sorry—that was thoughtless—'

'It's okay.' He ran a hand through his hair, looked down at his glass. 'I don't usually watch the ceremony—but I do know this. When I saw Izzy walking towards me on our wedding day I felt…emotional…joyful. When you find the one you want to spend the rest of your life with, getting married feels like the most natural thing in the world. It was for me—I didn't have to think twice.' He looked up and suddenly his eyes were full of concern. 'Hey! You mustn't get upset.'

She hadn't noticed her eyes welling. The purity of his feelings had touched her, stirred an ache deep within her. It was as if he'd read out loud the script of her private fantasy. She wiped her tears away with her fingers and laughed to hide her embarrassment. 'I'm sorry...' She shook her head. 'How did we even start talking about this?'

'Binoculars, camera lenses, weddings...'

She shifted her position on the sofa and sipped her drink. 'Okay, change of subject. When you're not working, which is hardly ever, I've noticed, what do you like to do?'

He settled back in his chair and smiled slowly. 'I like playing the guitar.'

'You're a musician?'

He nodded, smiled sheepishly. 'A failed one. A million years ago I was in a band, but then I grew up.' He sipped his wine. 'I still dabble though. There's a bar in Ravello—I play most Thursday evenings—keeping my hand in.'

So, there was another side to Zach, something that was just him, something that wasn't connected to Casa Isabella. She felt as if she'd found a pearl in an oyster. 'That's amazing! What kind of music do you play?'

'Mostly classical these days, but sometimes I play with other guys, sort of improvised folksy stuff.'

'Could I come to watch you play?'

'Sure—if you want.' He looked shy suddenly. 'It's low-key, not very rock and roll.'

She smiled. 'I like low-key.'

He drained his glass and stood up. 'Okay then. It's a date—so to speak.'

She felt a blush warming her cheeks. Had she been too forward, inviting herself along? She hoped he was okay with it. Maybe he wouldn't want her there, invading his private world. If only she could see inside his head, know what he was thinking.

He was doing up his tie. 'I better get back.'

She rose to her feet, reached for his jacket just as he did. For a long moment she felt trapped in his gaze, felt the heat from his hands radiating through the fabric, and then somehow she made her feet move. She stepped back quickly, busied herself with tidying the used plates and glasses onto the tray. 'I'll wash these and bring them back tomorrow.' When she looked up again, she had to pretend that her heart wasn't beating like a drum. 'Thanks for the food and the wine—and the company.'

He seemed preoccupied as he shrugged into his jacket and walked to the door, but when he turned and smiled there was something in his eyes that made the breath catch in her throat. 'It was a pleasure. Goodnight, Liv.'

Zach walked slowly towards the reception hall. From the grand sitting rooms he could hear the hum of voices, the occasional burst of laughter—wedding guests enjoying time away from the dance floor. He envied Olivia, tucked away in her little suite. How peaceful it had felt there. It had been hard to make himself leave. That moment with the jacket, the way she'd been looking at him and the warmth of her hands so close to his, the sweet curve of her mouth. He'd felt a momentary madness, a desire to step closer and touch her lips with his own, and now he couldn't figure out if wanting to kiss someone who wasn't his wife was reprehensible or not. In two years he'd never so much as looked at another woman, but then there she'd been, at Lucas's wedding, Olivia Gardner! And he'd borrowed her pen and forgotten to give it back, and Michele had had his terrible accident and she'd stopped working for Holdsworth, and now she was here, under his roof, as if fate had somehow...

'Zach!'

Lucia was walking towards him, a look of slight consternation on her face. 'Alessia said you didn't read all of the story—'

'She fell asleep before the end.'

'Well, she must have woken up again.' Lucia sighed. 'The little monkey told me she was cross with you.'

He pictured his daughter's face, her cheeky smile, the way she frowned at him sometimes. 'She's always cross with me.'

Lucia's eyes grew serious. 'You need to spend more time with her, Zach.'

He pushed a hand through his hair and waited for two giggling guests go by. 'I know. Maybe tomorrow I'll take her somewhere.' He touched Lucia's arm. 'I'm sorry. I know you could do with a day off.'

'I don't mind looking after Alessia, you know that, but she needs you, Zach. You don't have to take her anywhere. Just give her some of your time. That's all she wants.'

What had Olivia said? *Fathers and daughters—it's a special bond, don't you think?* In the glow of the nightlight, he watched Alessia sleeping. Such thick dark lashes, just like Izzy's. He smoothed one of the little eyebrows with a gentle finger and she stirred for a moment before falling back into her dreams. He leaned in, kissed her forehead then quietly slipped from the room.

Lucia was right; he needed to spend more time with Alessia. He loved Alessia with all his heart, had never intended to step back, but in the months after Izzy's death, finishing the renovations and bringing her dream to life was all he could think about. If Alessia couldn't see her mother, he'd made up his mind that she would feel Izzy's presence everywhere: in the house, in the garden, all around. And then Casa Isabella had taken off and he'd been consumed by the demands of the business. Making it better. Making it even more perfect, always striving. Work had turned into a habit he couldn't shake because his feelings for Izzy were tangled up inside it.

He kept telling himself he'd get a manager, but it hadn't happened yet. Perhaps if Lucia hadn't been a widow—perhaps if she hadn't been willing and able to step into the breach so completely—he would have been forced to balance his time better—would have been a better father.

He knew that it was time to cross that bridge, time to cultivate a special bond with Alessia before it was too late. She was growing up fast, becoming a proper little girl now. Soon she'd be laying down memories which she would take into adulthood, like Olivia's recollections of nature walks with her dad—big binoculars, little adventures. It was time for him to create adventures for Alessia.

He felt tired. He knew he ought to crash but instead he lifted his guitar off its stand and dropped onto the sofa. He tuned it by ear, little plucks of the strings until it sounded right, then absently he strummed a melody he'd been working on. He'd enjoyed being in Liv's apartment. She hadn't brought much with her, yet somehow she'd made the space her own… Flowers from the garden arranged in a jug on the mantelpiece, a scarf draped over a chair back, a small pile of books on a side table. And it had been nice just talking… He could tell that she found it hard to talk about her father and he was curious about that, but he hadn't wanted to ask…and then there'd been all that stuff about marriage and finding the perfect person, Liv almost in tears. But he hadn't minded talking about marrying Izzy. She'd been the love of his life.

He changed key, started playing the melody again. But it was confusing, the way he felt when Olivia looked at him, how he'd wanted to kiss her. Did it mean he was healing? Most days it didn't feel like that, but lately... He stilled his fingers, picturing Olivia earlier in the day, darting about with her cameras, so lively, so lovely in her summer dress. So off-limits.

His fingers started moving again. No matter how much he wanted to, he could never kiss her. She was here to work for him. Kissing her would be crossing a line—and what would he say afterwards? It was clear that she had romantic notions in her head, clear that she was looking for the kind of commitment he couldn't see himself giving again. Izzy had been the one and she was gone. He strummed a final chord then put the guitar back on its stand. He and Olivia would just be friends. That was as far as he would ever let it go.

CHAPTER FOUR

OLIVIA BLINKED AND pushed back her chair. She needed to take a break from the computer screen, stretch her legs. She supposed the wedding guests had all checked out by now. From mid-morning, through the open windows, she'd heard the sound of cars drawing up, the rise and fall of voices, doors sliding, tailgates banging and then it had gone quiet. Once again, clear as a bell, she could hear the tinkle and gush of the fountain in the garden, the chatter of birds in the trees.

She pushed her bare feet into her sandals and stepped through the French windows into the warmth of the afternoon sun. The informal garden at this side of the house was laid out in a series of shady rooms, like secret gardens, and she wandered from one to another until she came to a stone bench positioned to make the best of the sea view. She pressed her hand to the stone. It felt cool and inviting so she stretched out along its length and stared up at the infinite blue sky. For the hundredth time she thought about the night before, the way Zach had looked at her as they'd both held onto his jacket. He'd glanced at her mouth, a flicker of something in his eyes which had caused her heart to bang like a drum. Had he been thinking about kissing her?

She threw an arm over her face and closed her eyes. She'd thought about kissing him plenty of times, imagined what his lips would feel like on hers, but if it came to it, would she let it happen? *'I didn't have to think twice.'* That was what he'd said last night about marrying Isabella; it was obvious that he was still in love with his wife.

Suddenly the stone beneath her felt too hard and she pulled herself upright. He might have thought about kissing her, but it didn't mean anything. It couldn't mean anything because of Isabella. So…it must have been a reflex…because they'd been standing so close and because they'd had a glass or two of wine. The thrill of the moment tingled through her again. His eyes on her mouth, the ache in her veins…

She had to stop thinking about it! A casual fling with Zach, even if she was into that kind of thing, could only end in disaster. He was her employer and she needed this job, needed the portfolio she was going to create by working here. Jeopardising that would be madness.

She got to her feet, brushed herself down then paused. Even if Zach *did* like her, even if he wanted a proper relationship, would she dive in? As she turned it over in her mind, she was seized by an uncomfortable realisation. She couldn't help it—she wanted the fairy tale— the thrill of starting out together with everything ahead. Like that Carpenters' song about white lace and promises, new horizons…

Zach had had his beginning with Isabella. He had a daughter, a living, breathing part of Isabella who looked just like her mother he'd said… Olivia sighed. She couldn't see herself fitting in with a child, with Zach's readymade life. She'd always see ghosts in the shadows, so no matter how much she liked him, no matter how much she fantasied about kissing him, she could never let anything happen. Being his friend would have to be enough.

Slowly, she retraced her steps through the secret gardens then took a path which led to the formal garden. This was the garden with the best view of the sea. She gazed at the vast stretch of blue, watched the sparkling yachts and gleaming motorboats trailing white plumes of surf, their paths crossing and fading like chances. No wonder Zach and Isabella had wanted to buy this place—the location was perfect.

When she felt the sun burning her bare legs she turned back towards the house, pausing to take in the golden glow of its stone walls against the deeper greens of the surrounding trees and shrubs. She was about to walk on when she suddenly noticed that Lucia was waving at her from the terrace. She waved back, smiling, but as she got closer she realised that Lucia wasn't waving, she was beckoning. Perturbed, Olivia hastened up the three flights of stone steps to the main terrace, wondering why she was being summoned.

She'd barely spoken to Lucia since she arrived. She'd been busy, recceing the gardens, planning the best angles, taking test shots. She'd been terrified of making a mistake, of not being properly prepared for that all-important first wedding, and anyway, after Zach's warning, she'd decided it would be best to keep out of Lucia's way.

She cleared the final steps with a pounding heart, but when she looked across the terrace she couldn't help smiling. Alessia was splashing about in a little paddling pool, a big pair of green sunglasses perched on her nose. Lucia was hovering nearby with a towel over her arm and a slightly harassed expression on her face. She looked rather overdressed for poolside duties, Olivia thought.

As she approached, Lucia looked up and beamed. 'Olivia! I hear the wedding went very well yesterday.' The older woman pulled her into a surprisingly warm embrace, kissed each cheek in turn. 'Zach told me you took wonderful photographs!'

'He said that?' It felt nice, hearing Zach's praise from Lucia's lips. 'I was a little nervous, to be honest, but it went well. The bride and groom were lovely—'

'Nonna! *Guarda cosa so fare?*' Alessia was pouring water out of a plastic teapot onto the terracotta setts.

Lucia turned and smiled. 'Very clever, my darling, but please speak in English—for Olivia.'

Alessia lifted her chin and peered over the sunglasses, which had slipped halfway down her nose, then she giggled and plunged her teapot back into the water.

Lucia turned back apologetically. 'I'm sorry to ask you, Olivia, and I wouldn't be asking at all if I hadn't seen you walking in the garden, but I'm meeting a friend in Ravello…'

That explained the outfit.

Lucia rolled exasperated eyes. 'Zach was supposed to be here but he had to take a phone call…and it's lasting a long time…' She lifted the towel off her arm, dangled it in her hands. 'So, I was wondering…'

Olivia could feel perspiration blooming on her back.

'Would you please stay with Alessia until he comes? It won't be long—it could be just for one minute, but I really have to go now…'

Lucia was holding out the towel, her eyes imploring. Olivia glanced at Alessia, felt her stomach kink. She had no experience of looking after small children. What if something happened whilst she was in charge? Lucia's eyes were warm, expectant, pleading.

Olivia nipped at her lower lip with her teeth and glanced at the pool again. *Six inches of water!* Alessia seemed to be perfectly happy, playing with a family of yellow ducks. Maybe Zach *would* be right down and perhaps babysitting Alessia would earn her some favour, ease Lucia's misgivings about her, whatever they might be. She sucked in a big breath and took the towel from Lucia's hands.

'Okay, I'll keep an eye on her until Zach comes back. It'll be…fun!'

Zach put down the receiver with a sigh. His father was hard to shake off when he was talking business, thought nothing of interrupting his son's Sunday afternoon to discuss marketing strategies and balance sheets. He was amazed that his father still had that fire in his belly, admired it in a way. Of late, his own fire had dwindled to barely a glow. He switched off his computer, tidied his papers into a pile. Lucia was going to be cross with him for taking so long, but this was how it always was for him. Work first!

As he walked through the house, listening to the echo of his disenchanted footsteps, he pictured himself at twenty-one, arriving in Rome with a rucksack on his back and a guitar case in his hand. He'd fallen in love with Italy during a family holiday and had always wanted to return, wanted to learn the language. So, after he'd finished his music degree, he'd bought a ticket…

He'd got a job in a pizza place, spent his evenings working in a bar, playing sometimes. In those days he'd fancied himself as Joe Satriani. He'd met other musicians, joined a band, spent two years gigging all over Europe. They'd got decent reviews, made enough money to keep body and soul together; they'd even started talking to record companies. They thought they were going places, believed they'd break through…but instead they broke up. They'd been in Naples when their charismatic lead singer suddenly announced he was going solo. Zach hadn't seen it coming. None of them had. They'd tried to find a new singer, but the glue was loosening. The band fell apart.

And then he'd met Izzy. Her family owned a restaurant in Naples and she'd been his waitress. He'd gone back night after night, just to see her, but soon he'd realised that he'd need to offer her more than his love, and his disillusionment with the music industry. He went back to England and joined the family business. His father had been delighted. Playing music was all very well, he'd said, but he thought Zach should have another string to his bow—his father used to like that joke! Ironically, another string to the Merrill Hotel group's bow was exactly what Zach achieved. He spearheaded a profitable new enterprise—Merrill Select—specialising in exclusive luxury boutique hotels. He was enjoying his success but Izzy owned his heart and soon his flying visits to Naples weren't enough. He'd come up with an idea. The Amalfi Coast was a burgeoning tourist spot—a prestige boutique hotel could do very well. It was the best compromise he could think of, running a Merrill Select hotel in Italy with Izzy. They'd been looking for a suitable place when they'd found Casa Isabella…

He'd traded music for the hotel business, traded the

hotel business for an exclusive wedding venue, and then he'd lost his guiding star. If he felt adrift sometimes, perhaps it was understandable...

As he neared the terrace the sound of frenetic splashing and happy laughter interrupted his train of thought. He paused to listen. The voice he could hear with Alessia's wasn't Lucia's... He felt a smile coming as he softened his tread and moved closer. Beside a stone pillar he stopped and gazed across the terrace.

Olivia was standing in the paddling pool holding Alessia's hands. Alessia was jumping up and down, Olivia lifting her higher than she could jump on her own. They were both laughing and Alessia was shouting, 'Again! Again!' The area around the edges of the little pool was mottled and damp, littered with toys—yellow ducks, assorted buckets and a plastic teapot. It was a lovely scene, one he didn't want to interrupt, so he leaned against the pillar to watch. Olivia's legs were bare, glistening wet. There were splashes on her shorts and tee shirt, drops of water clinging to her face and hair. When Alessia stopped jumping Olivia helped her to sit down, then stepped out of the pool and knelt on a towel.

'Alessia, I'd like a nice cup of tea!' Olivia handed Alessia the plastic teapot and held out a little blue cup. 'Could you please pour me some?'

Alessia screwed up her face in concentration, dunked the teapot into the pool then looked up, spied him against the pillar and started to scramble to her feet. 'Papà!'

Olivia's hands shot out to steady her.

Zach wished he could have watched them for longer, but he'd been rumbled. He strode across the terrace. 'Hey! You look like you're having fun.'

Olivia looked up and smiled. 'We're having the best time ever, aren't we, Alessia?'

'Sì, sì, sì!'

Alessia reached for him and he lifted her into his arms. He felt the coolness of her little body, wetness from her swimsuit seeping into his shirt.

'Lucia had to go out.' Olivia was swiping water from her legs. 'She asked me to babysit.'

'I'm sorry—she should have brought Alessia to me.'

Olivia stood up straight and met his gaze with a little wide-eyed shrug. 'Alessia was playing! Lucia probably didn't want to spoil her fun. Anyway, I didn't mind.'

'Well, thank you—I appreciate it.' He sighed, tidied wet strands of hair from Alessia's face then kissed her little nose. 'My father decided that today would be a good day to catch up on business. It's hard to get away once he starts talking.'

Olivia bent to pick up the ducks then launched them into the water. 'At least you still catch up—'

'Paparelle!'

Alessia was struggling in his arms so he put her down.

She squatted next to Olivia, picked up two of the ducks and pushed their beaks together. *'Bacio!'*

Olivia laughed, touched Alessia's shoulder. 'That's a kiss! Are the ducks kissing?'

Alessia giggled. 'Kiss!'

Light was bouncing off the water, reflecting on his daughter's face, dancing in Olivia's eyes. Watching them, Zach felt an unexpected swell of happiness. He was used to seeing Alessia with Lucia but, for some reason, the way she'd taken to Olivia pleased him beyond measure. He dropped down beside her and dipped his hand into the water.

'Do the ducks love each other?' Olivia was asking and Alessia returned a deep nod, her eyes dark and wise. She lifted one of the ducks to Olivia's mouth and Olivia laughed. 'You want me to kiss the little duck?'

Alessia giggled, pressed the duck's beak to Olivia's lips. 'Mwah!'

Alessia lifted the duck to his lips. 'Papà, you kiss the duck.'

Olivia was laughing at him now, eyes shining. He looked at Alessia then planted a kiss on the wet plastic beak. Alessia giggled again, her cheeks round and smooth as apples. Then he was laughing too. Perhaps the bridge he needed to build with his daughter wasn't so wide after all. He pulled her onto his lap and pressed his lips to her damp hair. When he looked up, Olivia was gazing at him softly.

She moistened her lips, shot him a little smile. 'I should go.'

Alessia wriggled backwards against his stomach, the sweet smell of her skin reminding him of vanilla. The warmth of the sun, the warmth of his daughter's body nestled against him felt so nice that he didn't want to spoil the moment with goodbyes, but how could he make Olivia stay? She was getting to her feet. He hesitated for a scant second then leaned in to his daughter's ear, stage-whispered, 'We don't want Liv to go, do we?'

Alessia tipped up her face to look at him then scrambled off his knee and put her hand into Olivia's.

Olivia smiled down at her. 'But I have to go. I've got to work.'

Zach watched a familiar frown appearing on Alessia's face. It was the frown she used whenever he told her he was too busy to play.

She tugged on Olivia's hand. 'Why?'

Olivia looked at him, widened her eyes. She was trying not to laugh, he could tell.

'Because I work for your daddy and if I don't do my work he will be very sad.'

Zach dipped his hand into the pool again, ran his fingers back and forth. He could feel a smile growing on his lips. Using Alessia as a go-between was ridiculous. If he wanted Olivia to stay, there was only one thing for it. He cupped his hand to make a scoop and suddenly hurled a handful of water out of the pool. As it splattered over Olivia's legs, she shrieked, Alessia shrieked, then both of them laughed. Olivia fixed him with a look that made him jump to his feet and step back.

'Alessia! Can you please pass me the teapot? I think your daddy would like a nice cup of tea…'

Olivia pressed the towel to her face then blotted her hair. The puddles from their water fight were evaporating quickly in the late afternoon sun. She watched Zach drying Alessia, towelling the little legs and arms, turning her this way and that, pulling a little tunic dress over her head. He was a good father, she could see that. She looked away, gazed at the boats criss-crossing the blue expanse of sea below. She remembered days at the beach with her dad, the way he'd throw a huge towel around her when she came out shivering, enfold her in his big, warm bear hug. And then he'd make a fire on the beach by rubbing two sticks together, which was the coolest thing ever, and he'd cook something he'd brought for them and always there'd be toasted marshmallows afterwards. She smiled at the memory then let it fade as she felt an incoming tide of pain.

'Who's hungry?'

She turned, saw that Zach had finished with Alessia and was rubbing at his wet hair with the towel. She couldn't resist a victory smile. Her revenge for the splashing he'd given her had been swift and satisfying. A pot of 'tea' over his head, with Alessia laughing so much she'd got the hiccups. Then there'd been chasing, water being flung from buckets, a game of catch the duck: total mayhem. Good fun. But she couldn't stay—she hadn't meant to stay this long.

She slipped on her sandals. 'Thanks, but I should go.'

He dried his face and smiled. 'Eat with us, Liv. Please… It's nothing fancy—just pizza. You can work later…'

She could see in his eyes how much he wanted her to stay, but there was something else too, something in his gaze that was making the ground shift beneath her feet. She felt her stomach tilt. The problem was that she *wanted* to stay, *wanted* to share whatever it was they'd been sharing all afternoon but she was torn, confused by a blurring of lines which she thought she'd drawn in permanent ink.

Suddenly an irresistible little hand pushed its way into hers. She looked down to see Alessia looking up at her through thick, thick lashes. 'Don't you like pizza?'

She smiled and threw Zach a helpless look. 'I like it if it doesn't have pineapple on it.'

Zach flung his arms out, mimicked a strong Italian accent. 'Theze eez *It*-aly! Pineapple is for-*beeden*.'

He looked so comical that she couldn't help laughing. She looked down at Alessia, squeezed the little hand. 'Okay, in that case I'm in!'

Zach's ground-floor suite was located at the opposite end of the house to hers. There was a large open-plan

kitchen/sitting room, flooded with light from two sets
of French windows. The décor was neutral, the furniture
comfortable, but Olivia got the impression that it was a
work in progress. Bare wires poked through one of the
walls in the kitchen—'Waiting for wall-lights,' he told
her. There was a collection of pictures propped against
the wall in the sitting room—'Waiting to be hung,' he
said. She noticed his guitar, sleek as an amber jewel,
parked on a stand in the corner.

Alessia took her hand, tugged her through the apartment to her own little bedroom. In contrast to the living
area, Alessia's room was finished to the highest degree:
brightly painted walls in a delicious shade of mango,
colourful pictures, a blue toy box and bookcase, a white
wardrobe and chest of drawers. Alessia shifted a row of
teddy bears so that Olivia could sit on the bed then she
knelt in front of the toy box, pulling out dolls and plastic
ponies, chattering away, half to herself and half to Olivia.

As she looked around, Olivia could feel Isabella…
could read the past as if it had been written on the wall.
They must have been working on the renovation, discovered that they were expecting a baby. She could hear Isabella's voice: 'There's mess everywhere, Zach. We need
this room to be perfect for the baby…'

A photo frame on the bedside table caught her eye
and she picked it up.

Isabella!

A lovely face framed by straight dark hair, cheekbones
defined by the makings of a smile. Her eyes sparkled
with a warm, mischievous light, as if she had a secret
she was dying to tell.

Olivia stared at the photograph, losing herself in the
eyes of the woman who'd captured Zach's heart, until a

clatter of toys on the floor jerked her out of her trance and hurriedly she put the frame back.

She watched Alessia trotting a pair of white ponies with long pink manes across the floor, making little clicking noises with her tongue. She *was* like her mother— would look more and more like Isabella as she grew up.

Olivia wondered what Zach had told her. *Mummy's in heaven...?* It was what she would say if Alessia was hers. *Mummy's in heaven but she's watching you all the time, sending her love to you on...sunbeams.* Something like that...something Alessia could see.

She heard approaching footsteps then Zach appeared in the doorway, waving a bottle. 'Glass of wine?'

Alessia looked up, carried on clicking her tongue.

'Sounds great!' Olivia put the jumbled teddy bears back into line then stood up. When she caught Zach's eye she could see amusement on his face and she felt her cheeks creasing into a smile. 'What? It's how I found them.'

He shook his head a little and smiled, then dropped to his haunches. 'Alessia, why don't you bring Poppy and Wizard into the sitting room for a gallop?'

Alessia rocked back on her heels, pushed the hair out of her face. 'Okay.'

Olivia followed Zach through the apartment. She liked the way he walked, the way his hair grazed his collar at the back of his neck, dark and soft. She liked the shape of his shoulders, broad, dependable-looking. Behind her, she could hear Alessia's tongue still clicking furiously and it was hard not to laugh. She liked Alessia, found her sweet and comical. That she could find a child fascinating was a revelation. She'd never spent a lot of time with small children. As an only child, she'd been surrounded by adults most of the time. She had a vague recollection of the kids at nursery school, but that was different—they'd all been kids together then. Alessia was the first youngster she'd spent proper time with, and she'd enjoyed every moment.

In the kitchen she watched Zach checking the temperature of the oven and deftly adjusting the shelves. She was so busy admiring the graceful way he moved that it took her a moment to notice the little piles of neatly sliced onions and peppers, the stack of grated mozzarella and thinly sliced Italian sausage arranged on the large marble island unit. Two large pizza bases were arranged on baking trays—floury. Freshly made!

'You *make* your own pizza from scratch?'

He poured the wine and handed her a glass, a mischievous glint in his eye. 'Yeah! Doesn't everyone?'

She laughed. 'No—o!'

'To be fair, I don't make it often these days—' He picked up his glass, touched it to hers. 'But since Alessia woke me up at stupid o'clock this morning I thought I'd make some dough—to get into her good books. She *loves* my pizza!' He sipped his wine, smiling. 'It's not a big ask. I've had plenty of practice. I worked in a pizza place for a while, when I first came to Italy.' He parked his glass on the side, started spooning tomato sauce over the bases and smoothing it out with the back of the spoon, then he looked up. 'That was in Rome…a long time ago.'

The intensity of his gaze was disconcerting. She groped for the backrest of a tall stool, pulled it out and seated herself as casually as she could manage. 'Were you studying Italian? Is that why you came here?'

He scattered toppings over the pizzas with a practised hand. 'No! I studied music, but I've always loved Italy and I wanted to learn Italian, so after my degree I came over…and, apart from a shortish stint in England, I've been here ever since.' He pulled open the oven door and threw the two tins inside, then picked up his glass and drank. 'Right! There's a bowl of salad in the fridge. If you could grab it and give it a toss that would be great. Dressing's over there.' He smiled. 'I'm going to get Alessia washed and then we can eat.'

'So, what's the story with your dad?'

Olivia spluttered into her glass and swallowed hard. She was glad that he was putting the leftover salad into the fridge and couldn't see her reaction. The remark about her dad had fallen from her mouth accidentally when he'd been telling her about his own father. She thought he hadn't noticed, was glad that he hadn't picked up on it, but he'd obviously been biding his time, waiting for the right moment to come back to it. Was there ever a right moment for that conversation? Fathers… Daughters… She glanced at Alessia, who'd fallen asleep on the sitting room sofa—out for the count. 'I… Erm—'

Zach was leaning over the island unit now, refilling her glass. 'I'm sorry if that was a buzzkill—you don't have to answer.'

There was a gentle light in his eyes and for a moment she felt the tug of it, as if he was guiding her to a safe haven, a place where she could open up and talk. She pressed the tip of her tongue against her teeth. The thing was, her feelings about her family were such a muddle, she wouldn't know where to begin. *No!* She'd have to give him the brush-off.

She reached for her glass, took a hefty sip. 'It's nothing really. We used to get on; we don't any more.' She'd managed to sound blasé, but inside she was breathing through the pain she felt, consciously smothering the little judder in her heart.

Zach put the bottle down and settled himself onto a chair. He was looking at her intently. She looked away, fingered the stem of her glass. She wanted to drink the lot, but it would only make her feel worse.

He sighed. 'I shouldn't have asked—I'm sorry. It's just that when we were talking last night I got the impression you were close to your dad, so I was surprised about what you said this afternoon, about not catching up with him…'

'It's the way things go sometimes…' Olivia sipped her wine again, held it in her mouth for a few seconds before swallowing. What did it matter anyway? Maybe telling Zach about her dad would make him see how important it was to stay close to Alessia, to not let work come between them. As long as she kept her tone matter-of-fact, she'd manage—it was only conversation, after all.

She looked up, met his gaze squarely. 'I told you that Dad's an ecologist. What I didn't say was that he's rather unusual.' *Breathe.* 'Both of my parents are unusual.' She gave a little shrug. 'Mum used to wear these long skirts, jumpers knitted by yaks—are you getting a picture?'

Zach nodded.

'And Dad's tall. He's got a ponytail and big feet in big boots. You might say that my parents stood out in a crowd.' She sipped her wine again. 'They never got married. They didn't see the point! They weren't into all that. They were into conservation. When I was growing up, Dad was involved in a lot of environmental campaigns. He thought nothing of berating my teachers for "ecologically unsound" decisions in the classroom. He tended to draw attention to himself—and there was a knock-on effect…'

Zach's eyebrows lifted in a question and she forced herself to continue.

'At school I used to get teased a bit—nothing drastic—but I was marked out because of my parents, and…well, because of myself too. Back then I was just like my dad. I was outspoken. I challenged people about things, set myself up for—' she fingered her glass through a hazy memory of taunting faces '—but you know I was okay with it because I was proud of Mum and Dad. I respected them. Dad was my absolute, total hero—better than all the other dads by a mile.' She could feel a bubble building in her chest but Zach was looking at her, eyes so blue and clear and kind that she wanted to go all the way. She swallowed hard.

'So…not long after my thirteenth birthday, Dad came into my room one morning and told me he was leaving… he said he was moving to North Wales… He'd been offered this Field Ecologist's job, something that would really make a difference, he said, and he couldn't turn it down…

'I didn't understand why he kept saying that *he* was leaving, not *we*.' She could feel a hot glaze of tears at the edges of her eyes and swallowed hard again. 'But you see that was the second bombshell. Unbeknown to me, their relationship had *run its course*—that's what he said!' She blinked, felt a wet trickle sliding down the side of her face. 'Then Mum came in. She said it had been a mutual decision. She didn't want to move to Wales. She said that she and Dad would still be friends…that there was nothing for me to worry about—' The empathy she could see on Zach's face was suddenly too much to bear.

She closed her eyes, swallowed the lump that was thickening in her throat. 'But there was! Because for years I'd been telling everyone at school that marriage was pointless. I was very vocal about it…so you see…' she dropped her face into her hands '…lots to worry about.' Tears were sliding freely down her cheeks now, winding through her fingers, and she didn't want to be crying like this in front of him but she couldn't stop. She tried to speak, big wet gulps of words. 'I felt—so—stupid.' And then, through a haze of tears, she sensed him standing, moving towards her.

'Liv. You were thirteen.' His hand was on her shoulder, he was coaxing her up, smoothing the hair away from her face. 'I can't watch you crying and not put my arms around you.'

And then she was melting against him, drawn into his warmth, and it felt like hours before the tears began to subside. His hand was gentle at her back, a little rigid at first, then softer until she could feel a gentle pressure from his fingertips. She could feel the damp crush of his shirt against her cheek, his heart beating, and slowly, almost imperceptibly, a steady heat began to flow through her veins, a new kind of awareness. He was feeling it too, she could tell. The moment was heavy, so heavy that it felt like a weight pressing down on her. He shifted on his feet and she sensed him looking down, waiting… For what—for her to lift her face? The thought of it made her dizzy.

'Papà…'

'Alessia!' He breathed his daughter's name and Olivia felt his arms slackening around her, a cool invasion of air between them as he stepped back. He was looking at her, a strange hazy light in his eyes. 'Are you okay?'

She swiped at her eyes and her cheeks. 'Yes—I'm sorry.' Her words were tumbling out in a rush. 'Thank you for holding—I must look a state—I should go.'

He put a hand on her arm. 'You don't look a state and you don't have to go—there's more to talk about.'

'Papà, *dove sei?*' The voice from the other room was sleepy.

'I'm right here, Alessia. I'm coming!'

He was still holding her in his gaze, a weight of kindness in his eyes that was making her bubble up again and she couldn't bear it. She took a step towards the door. 'Go to her. I'm fine, really. You don't have to worry about me.'

CHAPTER FIVE

OLIVIA SUDDENLY REALISED that she'd been staring at the same photograph on her computer screen for ten whole minutes. She pushed her chair back, walked to the open windows and looked out. Today the view reminded her of a holiday postcard: harsh light, saturated colours, zero charm. She slumped against the casement, felt the restless curtains brushing her bare feet.

Zach had come to see her the morning after her meltdown. She'd smiled, apologised for crying all over his shirt then told him she was really busy. She hoped he could see that she didn't want to talk. She couldn't. Not until she'd untangled the knot inside her head. It was what she'd been trying to do for the past three days, but everything was mixed up: feelings about her dad, feelings about Zach and Alessia. For every thread she managed to straighten out there was another one twisting itself even tighter.

Perhaps she should have left the terrace the moment Zach arrived that day, but she'd been enjoying herself with Alessia more than she could ever have imagined and Zach had seemed so pleased, had looked at her with such a happy light in his eyes that she couldn't bring herself to walk away. She'd been mesmerised by him, by how he was with Alessia. The way he'd drawn Alessia into his lap, the way he'd kissed her head…it had made her think about her dad, churned her up about it all.

Her mum used to smile at her, tell her she was a daddy's girl. She loved her mum but spending time with her dad always felt special. He was her best friend! She closed her eyes, trying to see beyond…

Zach smoothing Alessia's wet hair away from her face, kissing the plastic duck because she wanted him to… *'Why don't you bring Poppy and Wizard into the sitting room for a gallop?'* He knew the names of Alessia's little ponies…because he was interested…because he loved her…because to him Alessia was the most special little girl in the world…

Olivia sank to the floor and wrapped her arms around her knees. She could feel the ache of tears behind her eyes again. Her dad had been like that…with her. She was an only child, his only daughter… Had he found *her* interesting? Had he wanted to spend time with *her* as much as she wanted to spend time with him? It had never occurred to her before, but had she been *his* best friend too?

And now she remembered the pain in his eyes when she told him he'd let her down. He'd sat on her bed, reached for her hand but she'd pulled it away. 'Liv, I'm moving out, that's all. I'm not abandoning you… There's a room for you in my new place…you're still my girl. Didn't I bring you up to be a free spirit?' She hadn't been able to speak, to fit words to the confusion in her head, so she'd twisted her fingers in her lap and stared at the carpet.

He'd put a hand on her shoulder. 'I'm not letting you down. I love you. I'm here for you. I'll always be here for you... But sometimes life leads you onwards, you know. You can go with it or you can stick...' She'd felt the pressure of his fingers on her shoulder, a little squeeze. 'I have to go with it... I thought you of all people would understand.'

She'd tried to understand but her relationship with him had changed after that. There was something unhealed between them, something she couldn't push past. Her role model, her hero, had flown off into the sunset to fight the good fight somewhere else. He'd found something more important than his family. More important than *her*. That was the way it had felt to her thirteen-year-old self.

The start-up kick of a lawnmower broke into her thoughts—the gardeners getting everything ready for the next wedding. She let her knees drop out and sat cross-legged. She wished she hadn't told Zach about her dad. Digging through old memories, delving into deeply personal stuff was tipping the scales too far. He was her boss! She pictured the mischief on his face as he'd hurled water at her legs, felt a smile tugging at her lips. Okay, maybe he was also a friend, becoming one anyway. But then, when he'd been holding her, there'd been that moment...

She got to her feet, poured herself a glass of water. In a moment of weakness he might have given her the impression that he wanted to kiss her...but maybe she'd misconstrued things. She'd been upset and it had felt so nice being held in his arms, all warm and safe, and there'd been that lovely subtle scent of his cologne, the rise and fall of his ribcage, the steady beat of his heart... Easy to get things muddled up with all that going on. Muddles and tangles and confusion, Zach whirling around in it. She couldn't stop thinking about him, couldn't stop wondering why his arms had felt like home when the home she'd sold herself looked so different.

She sipped her water.

Free spirits—that was how she'd seen her parents when she was growing up, but after her dad left she'd questioned the whole ethos. Suddenly all that freedom seemed like a messy way to live, and she didn't want messy. A clean start with someone demonstrably committed to her—that was what she'd set her heart on. Good times, bad times, making a home and having a family, growing closer, working things out, weathering the storms. With Zach, she'd be stepping into Isabella's shoes and maybe she wouldn't fill them properly. Maybe she wouldn't live up to *his* expectations and he'd end up disappointed, the way she'd been disappointed in her dad. She pressed the cold glass to her forehead. She was getting ahead of herself, thoughts running away with her, getting tangled up again. *Stop it!* Nothing had happened with Zach.

As she sat down at her desk and reached for the computer mouse, Alessia's face shimmered in front of her eyes, trotting the little ponies, tongue clicking nineteen to the dozen… She sighed. Any kind of relationship with Zach Merrill was bound to be complicated, and she wasn't at all sure that she had the heart for complications.

Olivia pulled the USB stick out of the computer and fitted it into its box. *Done!* Eight hundred wedding photos edited, processed and ready to send to her first bride and groom! She wanted to run upstairs and tell Zach, but she could hardly do that when she'd been avoiding him for the past three days. Her jubilation evaporated instantly. Hiding away had felt right at the time but, thinking about it now, she wondered if her behaviour had been a little childish. What must he have thought when she turned him away from her door? Had he been hurt?

The sound of voices broke into her thoughts—a familiar little giggle then a knock. *Alessia!* Her mouth went dry. *Zach?*

She hurried to the door but, when she opened it, it was Lucia who was standing there, holding Alessia's hand. Alessia was jiggling up and down and as soon as Lucia let go of her she rushed forward and wrapped her arms around Olivia's legs.

'Well, this is a lovely surprise!' Olivia bent down, hugged the little body, kissed the top of her head. Alessia's hair smelt sweet and clean. She had the urge to lift her up and cuddle her in, but Lucia was watching, waiting to talk to her.

'Hello, Olivia. I'm sorry if we are disturbing you but Alessia wanted to say hello.' The older woman kissed her on both cheeks then stood back and smiled. 'We haven't seen you in the garden for a few days. You're just like Zach—always working.'

Olivia felt her heart skip at the mention of Zach's name. 'I've been busy. Erm…would you like to come in?'

'If it's okay, we'll come in for just a minute.' Lucia smiled apologetically. 'Alessia wanted to see your room…'

'Well, I suppose that's fair.' Olivia stepped aside for Lucia to enter. 'Alessia did show me *her* room, after all—' For a moment her words seemed to hang in the air above them and she faltered. Did Lucia know that she'd spent an evening with Zach and Alessia? *Probably! Definitely!* She sucked in a deep breath and followed Lucia into the sitting room, Alessia dancing and hopping at her heels. 'Can I get you some tea, or some lemonade?'

'No, thank you.' Lucia was looking around then met her eye and smiled. 'Are you happy down here? It's a quiet part of the house…'

'I love it, maybe because it *is* so quiet.'

Lucia's eyes glowed warmly. For some reason Olivia found it hard to hold her gaze so she glanced at Alessia, who was examining her computer desk from a safe distance. She'd clearly been instructed not to touch anything. When she turned back to Lucia, she suddenly noticed the older woman's well-fitting white dress with navy topstitching, the red glossy nails, freshly painted. She wondered if Lucia was going on a date. It was hard not to smile at the thought of it. 'You look very nice, Lucia. Are you going out?'

The older woman coloured slightly. 'Yes—I have…a thing…in town—'

Definitely a date!

'Is Alessia going too?'

Lucia shook her head. 'No…she's staying here… Maria's going to keep an eye on her until Zach's finished his meeting with the accountant.'

Olivia pictured Maria, the housekeeper, a bustling, slightly breathless middle-aged woman who always seemed to be busy with laundry. Would Maria have time to play with a three-year-old child? It seemed unlikely, whereas Olivia herself happened to be free.

Olivia glanced at Alessia, who was now peering closely at the scarf she'd draped over the back of a chair—a present from her dad—navy silk printed with bumblebees and dragonflies. She smiled. 'Lucia, would you like me to look after Alessia?'

Lucia's eyes widened. 'No, no, no! I wouldn't want to impose—'

'But I'd like to—I've just finished editing my first wedding and I was about to go out for a walk.' She turned to Alessia. 'Would you like to go for a walk with me, Alessia? We could go adventuring…'

All smiles, Alessia bounded over and reached for her hand. *'Sì!'*

Olivia laughed. 'I understand *that* word.'

Lucia smiled hesitantly. 'Well, if you're sure…it would be very nice for her.' She lifted an eyebrow. 'She seems to have taken to you, Olivia.'

Olivia grinned, squeezed Alessia's little hand in hers. 'And I've taken to her too.'

Lucia beamed. 'I'll tell Maria then.' She turned to Alessia. 'Now, be a good girl for Olivia.'

'Sì, Nonna.'

'Oh, and Olivia? Could you please tell Zach that I'm having dinner out, but I'll be back before he has to go?'

'Of course.' Olivia wondered where Zach was going. Perhaps he had a date. A little knot started twisting in her stomach just thinking about it. She was so distracted that she didn't notice Lucia walking towards the door until the older woman turned around and looked at her. It was a long look, wistful.

'You know, in this light you remind me a little of my daughter.'

Olivia gripped Alessia's hand. She didn't know how to respond.

Lucia smiled. 'I hope you have good adventuring, as you call it.' She winked at Alessia and then disappeared through the door.

For a long second Olivia didn't move, then suddenly

she became aware of Alessia staring up at her. She looked down, caught a fleeting impression of Zach in Alessia's eyes which took her by surprise. She smiled. 'Shall I bring the camera? I could take some nice pictures of you for your daddy and for Nonna—would that be nice?'

Alessia nodded enthusiastically.

'Okay then, let's go!'

The light had mellowed and the day looked softer now, the colours richer. Olivia wanted to explore the outer reaches of the property, but soon discovered that walking with a three year-old required an unhurried pace. Alessia kept stopping to examine the smallest things: a fallen leaf with curly edges, a hairy caterpillar looping along the ground… But it was nice listening to Alessia's chatter, pointing things out to her. Olivia realised how often she was repeating her dad's words, telling Alessia the proper name for the cloud they could see, or the name of a flower…smothered memories unfolding like petals as they walked.

By the time they reached the dark hush of the olive grove, Alessia was flagging. Olivia picked her up, felt the little arms snaking around her neck. 'Shall we have a rest?' Alessia nodded and suddenly she felt guilty for bringing her this far. There was an old bench under a nearby tree and she carried Alessia there, put her down then sat down beside her. Within moments, Alessia was scrambling onto her lap. For a second Olivia hesitated, then she slipped her arms around her. It felt nice, a little strange.

She'd started noticing things about Alessia that reminded her of Zach—like the way she walked and the way she looked when she was concentrating on something. As she held Alessia, she got the strangest feeling that she was holding Zach too, and it felt like a little release, like an outlet for all the confusion in her head. She lowered her face, felt the softness of Alessia's hair against her cheek and pulled her a little closer.

Zach switched off his computer and stretched. His meeting with the accountant had felt interminable. He'd struggled to concentrate because he'd been thinking about his set for the evening. Playing in the bar was the highlight of his week, the only time he could forget everything and lose himself in music. He got to his feet and walked over to the window. The view was spectacular. He could see the formal garden with the craggy Amalfi Coast beyond—blue sea and sky—but he wasn't really looking at it. He was wondering what to do about Olivia.

He hadn't seen her all week and that was fine. He understood. If she didn't want to talk about things, he could respect that. But he couldn't help wondering if she was avoiding him because of the other thing that happened—or rather the thing that hadn't happened. It had confused him too, sent his own thoughts wandering into unfamiliar territory.

Their afternoon by the paddling pool had reminded him of how joyful life could be. Alessia and Olivia seemed to have an easy compatibility and he'd been drawn into it, hadn't wanted Olivia to leave because it felt right. It felt like the way things were supposed to be.

When Izzy died, Alessia had barely started walking so they'd never had that kind of family time together. The paddling pool afternoon had been a new experience for him, and he'd loved every minute of it. He could still hear Alessia's laughter as Olivia poured the water over his head, still see the way Olivia had been looking at him, her eyes shining with mischief. And then later when she'd been crying, and he'd held her, there'd been that moment when he'd started noticing how good her body felt pressed against his, and he'd realised how much he missed being warm and close to someone who was not his daughter. He'd wanted to tilt Olivia's face to his, kiss her, lose himself in her warmth and her softness.

He didn't know what to make of his thoughts. For so long he'd been putting one foot in front of the other, not really thinking about anything except achieving Izzy's dream. Working long hours, not spending enough time with his daughter. And now Olivia was here, bailing him out, messing with his head. Was there a way to put things straight, to draw a line in the sand? It should be easy. Liv was working for him, which meant that their relationship ought to be strictly professional, but she was living in his house, and Alessia liked her. *He* liked her—and he got the feeling that she liked him too.

He walked slowly out of his office and closed the door behind him. Avoiding each other wasn't going to solve anything. He needed to see her, be friendly with her. That was the only way he'd be able to put things back on the level. She'd told him she wanted to watch him play at the bar. Maybe he could ask her if she still wanted to go. Hopefully, if he made it sound casual, it would break the ice.

He was heading down the stairs when two figures caught his eye through the half-landing window. One tall, one small, walking down the cypress avenue. *Olivia and Alessia!*

He wondered where Lucia had gone, hoped that Olivia

wasn't feeling put upon—he hadn't brought her here to be his daughter's babysitter. He took the stairs two at a time, plunged through the grand doors and hurried down the stone steps.

'Papà!'

Alessia started running towards him, a happy smile on her face. 'Hello, monkey!' He scooped her up then turned to Olivia and smiled cautiously. 'Babysitting again?' She looked pale, he thought, a little tired.

'Lucia had a…thing…in town.' He saw a hesitation in her smile, which bothered him. 'Maria was going to mind Alessia but, since I was going for a walk anyway, I offered to take her with me.' She stepped closer, touched Alessia's cheek. 'We had a nice time, didn't we?' Alessia nodded, let her head drop against his. Olivia looked at him apologetically. 'She's tired. I probably walked too far… I'm not used to kids.'

'You could have fooled me!' He stroked Alessia's hair. 'You're really good with her.'

'That's because she's adorable. She's easy to lo—' She stepped back, fiddled with the camera around her neck. 'I was going to take some pictures, but it never happened…' A smile played on her lips. 'We found a butterfly…'

'And some ants, Papà!'

Olivia laughed, warm light filling her eyes again. 'Yes! Lots of ants—and we sang the song!'

'The song?'

Olivia giggled, looked at Alessia and started to sing. '"Now the army ant did say…"'

Zach felt his cheeks creasing into a smile as Alessia joined in.

'"I don't want to march all day…"'

As the words of the old song came back to him, he

couldn't resist singing too. '"I want to dance not drill, tap my feet until, I'm a true formicidae."'

He was laughing hard now; so were Olivia and Alessia. When Alessia warbled the last line again, he laughed even more, joined in with the next verse, widening his eyes, acting the fool, being utterly, joyfully silly. When he noticed that Olivia had stopped singing, he looked around then laughed all over again. She was standing a little distance away, taking pictures.

'Now *that* was a golden moment!' She widened her eyes, shot him a cheeky smile. 'I couldn't resist.'

It felt so good to see her, so good to see her smiling again that Zach only realised he was staring when she looked down, clicked a little switch on the camera. She took a step backwards then lifted her hand. 'Oh! Lucia said to tell you she was having dinner out but she'll be back before you have to go…'

For some reason his pulse was climbing. 'Right. Thanks…' She was gazing at him and he could tell she was about to walk away. He'd intended to throw the bar invitation into the conversation casually but the ant song had stolen his thunder. Now he was going to have to invite her more formally. He drew in a breath. 'I'm playing at the bar tonight… I told you about it, remember?'

She lifted her chin. '*That's* where you're going!'

'Where else?' He smiled. 'Do you still want to come?'

Her expression softened. 'Well, I *have* finished editing the Hadleigh wedding so I'm free…'

He could feel Alessia's fingers twirling in his hair, hear her giggling in his ear. 'So that's a yes?'

Olivia smiled, eyes full of light. 'Yes—I'd like that, thank you.'

'Great! We'll leave at half-eight. I'll meet you out

here.' Alessia's fingers were raking his hair upwards now. He grinned. 'That's assuming my hairstylist has finished by then.'

Olivia pulled back the doors of her wardrobe and gazed at the contents: three summer dresses suitable for wedding days, a pair of faded jeans, two pairs of smart shorts, one pair of denim cut-offs, assorted tops, a pair of white crops and a denim jacket. Three pairs of sandals and a pair of blue sneakers were arranged at the bottom. She hadn't brought much, intending to buy anything else she needed locally, but that hadn't happened yet. She ran a hand over the hangers. The choice of outfit was important. She wanted to look nice, but not done up.

Seeing Zach again, singing the silly song, laughing together—it had felt so right. She'd missed his smile, the kindness in his eyes… She reached for the white crops and a black V-necked tee shirt. Going to see him play this evening, spending time with him on her own would be good for her, would give her a chance to redraw the boundaries in her head. She laced up her sneakers, pulled on the denim jacket. She considered lip gloss, decided against. It was going to be hard, but somehow she had to plant Zach firmly in the friend zone.

As she walked through the house she felt a little surge of happiness. Getting away from Casa Isabella for the evening was just what she needed. A change of scene. She was dying to see Ravello, dying to see Zach in a different environment, playing his guitar. He'd looked a little wistful when he told her he played, called himself a failed musician. He'd studied music so he must have been serious about it once, but now he was running a wedding venue and playing in a bar once a week…

'Hi!'

She stopped in her tracks. He was walking along the hall towards her, guitar case in hand. He was wearing jeans, not chinos, and the kind of tee shirt women like to steal: faded, butter-soft. Sexy. She swallowed hard, reminded herself about the friend zone. 'Hi!'

He smiled. 'Ready to go?'

There was an energy about him—like electricity. He couldn't wait to play, she could tell. She smiled. 'Yes—I'm excited!'

'Don't be, please.' He grinned. 'I couldn't stand the pressure.' He opened the door and she stepped outside into the mellow dusk. The scent of roses and oleander flowers drifted on the air as they went down the steps towards the waiting car. He put his guitar case on the back seat then opened the door for her. 'I was going to drive with the hood down, but I'll cover up if you think you'll be cold.'

'No, down's good.' She smiled. 'I'm a sucker for a convertible…'

'Me too—obviously!' He smiled and closed her door, strode round the car and slipped into the driver's seat. 'So, thanks again for looking after Alessia—and *huge* thanks for teaching her that song.' He shot her a mischievous smile as he started the engine. 'I now have the mother of all ear-worms playing in my head. There's every possibility that a few chords of the ant song might make it into my set tonight.'

She laughed. That song… All afternoon, memories had been trickling back, things her dad used to say escaping from her own lips as she'd walked with Alessia. It was still so strong inside her, the good stuff, that for a while she'd let go of her pain. *'You were thirteen'*—that was what Zach had murmured as he'd pulled her into his arms. At twenty-four, could she sift through those feelings again, find a grown-up perspective on things? She looked at Zach, his face shadowy in the twilight. It was unlikely that he'd bring up the subject of her family again in case it upset her, but she needed him to know that she *could* actually talk about her dad without turning into a snivelling mess.

'My dad taught me that song.' Zach threw her a glance and she gave him a little smile. 'We were camping one time and we found an ants' nest in the woods, just like Alessia and I did today. I was worried that the ants would come into the tent. I kept thinking I could feel them crawling on me, so my dad taught me the song…and I didn't mind the ants after that.' She could tell that he didn't know what to say. She took a deep breath. 'You know, they weren't even arguing… I had no idea they were planning to separate…so that morning, when Dad told me… I was—' She closed her eyes. 'You've no idea how angry I felt, with Dad especially, because he'd been my rock and I felt like he'd left me in the lurch… I'm sorry I wasn't able to talk to you about it the next day, especially after—'

'You've got nothing to be sorry for.' Zach drove through the gates then stopped the car. 'I understand everything. Your parents' split was a massive shock. On its own it would have been bad enough but facing down those kids at school—'

A deep, dark ache stirred inside her, spreading upwards until she could feel it at the base of her throat. She swallowed hard, whispered, 'Kids at school?'

He frowned. 'Yeah…isn't that at the heart of everything?'

She stared at him.

'The teasing… Sticking up for your parents' choices… Fighting their corner… Then having the rug pulled, just like that! It would make anyone angry.'

A car spun past, catching them in its headlights. Olivia looked down at her hands. How could it be that Zach had shone a light into shadows she didn't know existed? She felt his eyes on her, a little unravelling of something deep inside herself. She looked up, noticed the illuminated clock on the dashboard. 'We should go or you'll be late.'

He looked at her for a long second then threw the car into gear and pulled onto the road, accelerating hard. After a few moments he said, 'Are you okay?'

She stared ahead at the darkening valley, at the lights glinting from the houses scattered over the slopes. 'Yes— or at least I think I will be.'

'*Salve,* Zach!'

Smiling faces turned towards them as they stepped through the doorway. Olivia hung back. This was *his* night. She didn't want to saddle him with tedious introductions or with having to translate for her. In a corner there was a chair with a microphone stand set at guitar height. She threaded her way through the dark wooden tables and flickering tea lights until she found an empty seat close by, then she sat down and looked around.

It was an interesting interior, dark and intimate. In the past it might have been a wine cellar. The ceilings were arched, the walls were rough stone, illuminated at intervals with projector slides of music notes. *Cool!* She looked over to the bar, caught Zach's eye. He smiled at her, motioned to the beer bottles in his hand—one was for her—and carried on talking to a good-looking man in a pale linen jacket. The place was filling up fast. She figured that most of them were locals, the way they came in and sat down, the way they ordered without looking at the drinks list. She looked over at Zach again. He was talking to some other people now, trying to demonstrate some musical chord, struggling because of the beer bottles in his hand. He was animated, into it, she could tell. As she watched him, she couldn't stop her eyes travelling down… His jeans looked soft. They hung from his hips in just the right way. She should see the shape of his behind, wondered how it would feel to slip her hand into his back pocket.

Friend zone!

She shifted in her seat, slipped off her jacket, draped it over the back of her chair. When she looked over again he wasn't there and then she saw him making his way through the tables towards her, smiling.

'Sorry that took so long—I got caught.' He handed her a beer. 'I start in ten, so I'm going to go tune up. I've told Mario not to let your drink run dry.'

'Thanks, but I'm here for the music, not the drinks!'

He took a swig from his bottle. 'Now I'm nervous.'

'Why?'

He smiled, lowered his voice. 'Because I want you to like it.'

Those eyes…that smile… Impossible… 'I'm going to love it. Now, go on… Break a leg!'

She watched him walk away, watched him tuning his guitar, that same look of concentration on his face which she could see on Alessia's face sometimes. He was born to this, she could tell. Such fluidity in his shoulders and arms as he moved his hand along the fret, plucking strings, listening to the sound of the notes, little adjustments, listening again. He looked as if he was in another world; he looked at home there.

Someone behind the bar made an announcement she didn't understand, but there was a ripple of applause followed by a gradual hush. Zach caught her eye briefly, then bent his head and began to play.

She hadn't known what to expect, but from the first note he had her. Zach could *really* play. The agility of his fingers on the strings was hypnotising: fast, slow, teasing, spirited. And the way he cradled the guitar, moved his shoulder in and out as he played, it seemed as if he was physically connected to the melody. The combination of the music and the way he looked in his tee shirt and jeans, the way his hair touched his neck, the little contortions of his face as his fingers slid up and down the fret, took her breath away. She was unravelling, spiralling into a blissful kind of ache. More than anything she wanted to touch him, to feel his fingers on her skin, his body against hers. When he got to the end of his final piece and the bar filled with applause, she was a mess of hot tears and burning desire.

'Isn't he just brilliant?' A voice in her ear took her by surprise and she turned to see the good-looking man in the pale linen jacket, who'd been talking to Zach earlier. She hadn't noticed him sitting down beside her. He was clapping enthusiastically, smiling, leaning in so she could hear him above the noise. 'He is *so* talented. I love to hear him play.'

'That was my first time actually.' She pressed her fingers to her eyes and laughed, slightly embarrassed. 'I'm feeling a bit emotional…'

'Me too.' He smiled. 'I'm Milo, by the way. Milo Beneventi.'

'It's nice to meet you. I'm Olivia.' She smiled and sipped her beer, then she looked over at Zach. He was surrounded by friends and fans, but he must have sensed her somehow because suddenly he looked up, straight at her. He mouthed an invitation for her to go over, but she couldn't. She didn't trust herself not to throw her arms around him and press her lips to his. She needed to keep her distance, so instead she smiled at him then went to splash her face.

CHAPTER SIX

ZACH PUT HIS guitar case on the back seat, toyed with the key fob in his hand. He wondered what was going on with Olivia. She seemed quiet, preoccupied somehow. 'Do you want to go for a walk?'

She glanced at her watch. 'It's late.'

'That's a statement, not an answer.'

Her mouth quirked. 'I'll rephrase. Don't you think it's a little late for a walk?'

'No—not for me.' He ran a hand through his hair. 'Would you mind, Liv—please? It's just that I always feel restless afterwards...'

She held his gaze for a long moment then smiled. 'Okay. It's a lovely night.'

Yes! He pressed a button on the dash, watched the hood lifting up and over, then he locked the car. He threw her a smile. 'So...we'll begin our nocturnal wanderings in the very heart of Ravello. Are you ready?'

She lifted an eyebrow, looked as if she was stifling a giggle. 'I think so.'

He slid the key into his back pocket and led the way along a narrow street which opened into Piazza Centrale. The bars were closed, awnings pulled up, chairs and tables stacked. He spun round, walked backwards so he could see her face. 'This is the main square. It's heaving with tourists during the day. The cafés do a roaring trade.'

She turned a slow circle, looking at everything. 'That's a big church.'

'Duomo di Ravello! Strictly speaking, it's a cathedral.' He wondered if she'd say anything about his set. He'd felt her watching him while he was playing, had glanced up a couple of times, seen a depth of emotion in her eyes that had taken him by surprise, but she hadn't said anything yet and it seemed out of character somehow, especially when she'd been so excited about the gig. Maybe she was thinking about her parents again…or—he felt a knot tightening in his stomach—maybe she was thinking about Milo Beneventi.

After the show he'd been pulled into his usual crowd. He'd caught her eye, beckoned her over, but she'd held back. The next time he looked he'd seen her talking to Milo. Milo had fluent English so he supposed it made sense, but for some reason it bothered him, the way they seemed to be getting on so well. Suddenly, he'd wanted to be away from the crowds and the noise. He'd wanted to be with Olivia on her own, wanted to hear her thoughts about the music and about his playing, but ever since they left the bar she'd been quiet, a little distant, and he didn't understand why. Now he was wondering if she'd wanted to stay—because of Milo…

He watched her as she walked up the cathedral steps, noticed her slender calves in her white cropped jeans. He remembered the way she'd looked in the paddling pool, bare-legged, water drops glistening on her skin. He looked at his feet and swallowed hard. He couldn't let himself think about her like that, and he couldn't ask her what she thought about his playing either because that would seem needy. He sighed, followed her up the steps and turned to look across the square. The lights glowing from the houses on the opposite side of the valley looked like strings of fairy lights. He'd never noticed that before.

'I love those trees.' She was looking into the branches of the umbrella trees. Her hair was loose, falling at the side of her neck in gentle waves. When she pushed it away her perfume reached him on the air.

'They're called umbrella trees… Did you like my set?'
Damn!

She seemed to hesitate, then turned to look at him. 'Very much.' She smiled softly. 'You blew me away, Zach.'

He dropped his gaze, felt a tiny, powerful rush of joy. 'And you were going to mention this, when?'
Ouch!

'I mean, I'm glad you liked it—but you've been so quiet… I thought you might have been all over it—you know, giving me a full crit.' He flashed a smile. Perhaps he could claw back a shred of dignity by being light-hearted.

She started down the steps, then stopped to look back at him. 'You want a full crit?' Her smile was mischievous. 'Let's walk and I'll tell you my thoughts.'

'Okay.' He dived down the steps after her, then led her onto the Via del Episcopio. He felt like a cat on a hot tin roof. He had no idea why her opinion mattered so much, but it did.

'I don't know anything about music in a technical sense…' She threw him a little hopeless look. 'But honestly, I was mesmerised from the start, and that last piece you played…'

'Fauré's *Pavane*.'

'It made me cry.'

'I'm sorry—'

She nudged his shoulder playfully. 'Happy tears! I found it moving…haunting. Just lovely. Listening to you play, seeing the feeling you put into it and how good you are, I just kept wondering…'

'Wondering…?'

She stopped and gazed up at him. 'I just kept wondering why you're in the wedding business when you have such talent, such an obvious passion for music.'

As he held her gaze he remembered his father's words on the phone the day he'd broken the news that the band had split. *'So you'll come home now…apply yourself to something more worthwhile?'*

He shrugged. 'Music's a tough business. I gave it my best shot, but I had to move on—I had to "come to my senses" as my father used to say.'

'Give up, you mean?'

'Whoa! I haven't given up! I still play.'

'Once a week—in a bar.'

'It's enough.'

'Is it?'

He stared at his feet. Somehow the conversation had taken a serious turn. He couldn't see why it mattered to her anyway. She was a swallow, passing through for the summer. Why would she even care about his music and what he did with it? When he looked up again she was gazing at him, her eyes all softness and warm light. A small breeze lifted her hair and he couldn't help noticing her pale skin, the swell of her breasts in the low V-neck she was wearing.

She took a little step towards him. 'I'm sorry. It's not

my place, but you said you wanted a full critique.' She seemed to be taking in every detail of his face, reading every line and all the lines in between. 'I think you have an amazing talent, Zach. I'm not qualified to know if you're up to playing Carnegie Hall, but I can see how much you love music and I think that's why you feel restless after a gig… I think you should do more with it, chase the thing you love…'

Her words were making his head spin. He'd buried his ambitions a long time ago and now she was stirring the old dreams around, looking at him with such belief in her eyes and something else too which was drawing him like a magnet. He caught himself looking at her mouth, the soft fullness of her lips, and he felt himself drifting towards her, moving in triple slow motion, losing himself in her eyes and the shape of her mouth, the curve of her cheek, and there was heat rising through his body, his hand reaching towards her face—

'Excuse me! Is this the way to Piazza Centrale?'

He snapped back to the moment, dropped his hand. An elderly man was looking at him. He took in the pale blue eyes, the checked shirt, the smiling grey-haired woman standing at the man's side. 'Er…yes! You're on the right road; just keep going down there and you'll come to it.'

'Thank you so much. Goodnight.'

As they strolled away, he became aware of his heart bumping against his ribs. What was happening to him? If the old couple hadn't interrupted him, he might have kissed Olivia. He probably, definitely would have kissed her, and then what? He felt a wash of relief. She'd taken him by surprise, caught him off-guard with her flattery, her enthusiasm for his playing and he'd felt young and free and he'd been about to…

Disaster!

He raked a hand through his hair and looked around. She'd walked a little distance away, seemed to be scrutinising something on the wall of a house. He wondered what she was thinking, hoped it wasn't going to be awkward between them now. She turned to look at him, smiled her usual warm smile.

'What does this say…? Something about André Gide and E M Forster—?'

He went over. 'It says they were guests here once.'

'Oh!' She walked on. 'Like me.'

Olivia poured herself a glass of water, added a chunk of lemon then went back to the computer. She studied the thumbnails on the screen. Saturday's bride had been beautiful. The groom had been handsome. Everything had looked perfect. And yet, as she scrolled through the pictures, she knew there was something missing. She'd had to work a bit harder with this couple, coaxing them into romantic poses. Perhaps they'd been camera shy, or perhaps they weren't naturally demonstrative, or perhaps it was just that they weren't really in love…

She lifted the glass to her lips and took a long sip, contemplated the gap between seeming and being… What *was* perfection anyway? She'd spent that day making perfect pictures of something that hadn't been perfect at all. She pushed her chair back and walked to the window. Her thoughts were tangling again…

She couldn't stop thinking about Zach and that night in Ravello. The way his fingers had caressed the strings, the way he'd looked in his tee shirt and jeans… She'd tried to hold her feelings in, but without realising it she must have been sending out signals because he had definitely been going to kiss her. His eyes had gone all hazy and he'd been leaning in, stretching his hand towards her face, and her heart had been going nineteen to the dozen and she'd wanted it so badly, that kiss…and then the tourists had arrived.

Since that night she'd been telling herself that not kissing him had been for the best. She'd repeated all the usual mantras. He might be attracted to *her,* but he was still in love with his wife. He was her boss and there was Alessia, and this whole life he'd built here. Everything about Zach was complicated and *she* didn't want complications. She wanted a new beginning, a perfect man, a perfect wedding…to prove…what? A kaleidoscope of memories shattered into shifting circles—her dad, campfires and hiking, loading his belongings into the car, and the kids at school teasing and taunting. She squeezed her eyes shut. She couldn't think straight any more.

A knock on the door startled her and then she smiled when she remembered her last visitors—Alessia and Lucia—Lucia dressed to the nines, blushing about the 'thing' she was going to in town.

Boyfriend!

Maybe Lucia was bringing Alessia to say hello again—that would be nice—but when she opened the door, it wasn't Lucia.

'Zach!'

'Hi! I hope I'm not disturbing you…'

Jeans, white shirt, tiniest delicious waft of cologne.

'No! Come in. I'm only editing—'

'Good pictures?'

'No—they're rubbish.' He lifted an eyebrow and she laughed. 'Of course they're good. Can I get you something—a glass of lemon water?'

'No, I'm okay, thanks.'

She sat down on the sofa, hoping he couldn't tell that her heart was racing. 'So—?' She saw him noticing her legs in her denim cut-offs, golden-brown now instead of milky-white. He didn't sit down.

'I've just had a call from Milo Beneventi.'

He was studying her face as if he was looking for something, expecting a reaction. She didn't recognise the name. 'Okay...'

'From the bar—you were talking to him.'

'Erm...' Her mind was blank. The night at the bar, her head had been full of Zach and his playing. Music and longing. She could feel herself blushing, tingling at the memory...and then an image came to her: handsome face, pale linen jacket. He'd been sweet, could speak English. 'Ah—*that* Milo. Yes, I remember now.' She smiled but for some reason Zach didn't.

'He's an architect. Did he mention that?'

She tried to remember, drew another blank. 'No, I don't think so.'

'He's been involved with a property on Capri. It's nearing completion and he needs someone to take pictures. He wondered if you'd be interested.'

'Yes!' She parked her glass and stood up. 'I would be... Absolutely! I *love* architectural work, especially interiors. Before I started working for Ralph, I used to do bits and pieces for an arts magazine—galleries, places like that...'

She suddenly noticed the wariness in Zach's eyes and toned down her enthusiasm. Maybe he was worried she'd leave him in the lurch. He should know she would never do that; she'd committed herself to him for six weeks. She tried to warm him with a smile. 'What do *you* think?

I mean… I'm here to work for you—I wouldn't want you to think—'

'I'm not thinking anything… It's absolutely fine, if you want to do it—'

'I do! It's a good opportunity! When I go back to London, I'm setting up on my own, shooting weddings, but I might have to be flexible at the beginning. A varied portfolio is currency. It'll help me to get other work while I'm building up my weddings.' She smiled. 'I'm grateful to you, Zach—you do know that?'

His eyes softened. 'I'll give you Milo's number. Have you got a pen?' Suddenly he broke into a smile and it was the old smile.

She laughed. 'I've heard that line somewhere before!' She picked up a pen and notepad from her desk and handed them over. 'Did he mention a timescale?'

Zach was mouthing the numbers as he wrote, little movements of his lips, the same lips that had come so close to kissing…

'As soon as possible, I think.' He placed the notepad and pen back into her hands.

'I'll need a decent tripod.'

'Michele will lend you one—he said if there was anything you needed—'

'I remember.'

'I'll speak to him, sort it out.' He took a step towards the door, then stopped. 'Milo said he'd pick you up in his boat—' She felt her eyes widening. This was getting better by the second. 'But I'll take you—'

'*You* have a boat?'

He nodded slowly. 'Yes. It's been laid up for a while.' His eyes were clouding over again. She wished she knew what he was thinking. 'I've been meaning to take it out for ages, but you know how it is—work gets in the way.' He seemed to drift for a moment, then he collected himself. 'Anyway, I'll take you.'

'Only if you've got time—I know how busy you are, Zach, and I don't want to put you to any trouble.'

'It's no trouble.' He shifted on his feet, fixed her with an even gaze. 'Like I said, the boat needs a run anyway.'

There was something bewitching about the light under the olive trees. The canopy was dense, the groundcover sparse. She thought that the trees must have gone feral a long time ago. She liked sitting here, wrapped in the mysterious blue-green light. She liked the emptiness, the silence that was barely threatened by the breeze whispering through the branches. It was a good place to think about things.

She lifted the camera to her eye, then put it down again. She wished she could see inside Zach's head. Ever since that night in Ravello he'd been acting differently. She'd done her utmost not to let the almost-kiss spoil their friendship, had tried to act as if nothing had happened, which it hadn't. Just like the other time nothing had happened.

So confusing.

The first time, he'd been holding her. She could see how physical proximity might have fuelled…but the second time they'd been standing on a narrow street, and she'd taken a step…and he'd taken a step…and she'd been feeling…but what about him? What did Zach feel? She sighed.

On the surface everything was normal, but she could tell he was preoccupied and it was bothering her. Perhaps he was reflecting on what she'd said about doing something with his music. Reaching back into the past, trying to pull old dreams into the present—that kind of thinking could fill your whole head, especially when you had a business to run, a daughter to think about… There would be other pressures too. Casa Isabella was a solid business—stepping away from it wouldn't go down well with his father, she supposed. Perhaps she should have kept her thoughts to herself, but watching him play, seeing the way he poured his heart into the music, realising how talented he was… It had moved her deeply and he *had* asked her what she thought. She'd had to tell him.

She wandered through the trees, little clouds of dust whirling around her feet. Parched earth, silence, mysterious light. She dropped to her knees, lifted the camera. Chinks of sunlight, bright rays piercing the gloom—light on dark—an interesting composition. She fired the shutter, listened to the sound of it reverberating.

She lowered the camera. At least the plans for her photoshoot on Capri had fallen into place. She'd made the arrangements with Milo, and Zach had secured the use of a tripod. He'd been seeing to his boat, getting it seaworthy, he said, but when he smiled at her there was no twinkle in his eyes. She'd tried to lighten his mood by offering to scrub the decks, but he'd said there was no need. He wasn't exactly shutting her out, but it felt as if he was stepping away. She remembered how she'd needed time to work through the stuff about her dad and it wasn't over yet—she was still trying to sort out her feelings. If Zach was preoccupied with his thoughts, there was nothing she could do except offer him a shoulder if he wanted it. He'd been there for her after all.

She got to her feet and brushed the dust off her knees.

The next day he was taking her to Capri. Being alone with him on a boat might be the perfect opportunity for a heart-to-heart.

Zach checked the mooring rope then walked slowly down the jetty. He hadn't been onto the boat since Izzy died—hadn't been able to face it. They'd had such good times on *Django*—on their own, with family and with friends. Coming onto the boat again—checking things over—was something he'd needed to do for a long time. It had felt like his final frontier and it had drained him emotionally. The next day there'd be a new passenger, a new voyage to make.

His car was parked close by but he walked past it and onwards into the narrow streets of Minori. He needed a coffee, some time to think things through. Since that night in Ravello with Olivia, his emotions had been all over the place and he had to get a grip.

At a small café he took a seat outside and ordered an espresso. He gazed along the street, but it was Olivia's face he could see—her eyes... Twice, he'd come close to kissing her, which was confusing enough, but it wasn't only physical attraction he was feeling and that was confusing him even more. He liked that she was so fond of Alessia. He liked how much she'd been moved by his playing. He liked her warmth, her sense of humour, the way she was so easy to be with...

He sipped the strong bitter coffee, felt his mood darkening.

He wished he'd never told Milo what a great photographer Olivia was, that night in the bar. It had been hard enough watching them chatting together, but he'd never expected Milo to suggest a photo shoot! This Capri caper was *his* fault, and the whole thing was messing with his head.

He felt the sun on his face and closed his eyes.

Olivia!

He had no claim on her so whatever it was that was churning him up about this trip, he'd have to get it under control. Maybe it was a protective thing…

That's it!

He'd taken his boat out of dry dock because he wanted to make sure she'd be safe. It was only natural, he told himself. She'd come to Ravello to work for him after all, and therefore she was *his* responsibility. He pictured Milo—that handsome face, that white smile, that irrepressible charm. He opened his eyes and reached for his cup. Milo seemed like a nice guy, but at the end of the day he knew nothing about him, and for that reason there was no way on earth he was letting Olivia go to Capri alone.

CHAPTER SEVEN

SHE WAS WEARING jeans and a white sleeveless shirt, sneakers and sunglasses. He couldn't detect any make-up, not that she needed any. Her hair was drawn into a ponytail, loose strands flying in the breeze. Her face was a picture—all smiles. He turned his gaze back to the sea, felt the power and thrust of the engine, the thrill of speeding through water. He'd missed this!

He looked at her again, felt a smile tugging at his lips. It was idiotic, he knew, to be analysing the nuances of her appearance, but the fact that she looked so...unadorned, pleased him. It meant she wasn't trying to attract Milo's attention, and for some reason that made him ridiculously happy. He leaned towards her, shouting over the engine noise. 'What do you think?'

'Fantastic!' she yelled back. 'I don't want it to end!'

'Want to drive?'

She widened her eyes, excited. 'Can I?'

'Sure!' He slowed right down and slipped out of the helmsman's seat.

She glanced at him, then gingerly took his place and put her hands on the wheel.

'What do I do?'

Her face and arms looked tanned against her white

shirt. He noticed a sprinkle of tiny freckles on her nose, caught the scent of her perfume as he stepped in again to steady the wheel.

'It's easy.' He pointed to a distant buoy bobbing on the water. 'See the marker up there?'

She turned to look at him, her face so close that he couldn't stop himself glancing at her mouth, that soft little pout, the briefest dart of her tongue as she concentrated on what he was saying.

'Just aim for that, keeping left.' He smiled. 'Ready?'

'I guess!'

He dropped the throttle and she gave a little shriek as the boat ploughed forward. She was sitting bolt upright, eyes fixed on the buoy, arms flexing as she handled the wheel. It was hard not to laugh. 'You're a natural!'

She grinned, not taking her eyes off the water. 'You think so?'

'Oh, yes!' Suddenly, he had an idea, leaned in. 'Will you be okay for a moment?'

Head rigidly pointing forward. 'Don't leave me...'

'I'm not leaving you... I'm just going onto the foredeck.'

'Why?'

He laughed. 'Never mind why—just keep steering!' He moved away, found a position on the bows and took out his phone.

When she saw what he was doing she started to laugh, yelling, 'No! Don't you dare!'

'Keep your eyes on the road!'

She looked so great, so happy steering the boat, that he had to take a picture...and he could tell she didn't really mind. She started pulling faces, striking poses—looking for land, doing Jack Sparrow—then she took

her hands off the wheel and stretched out her arms—
Titanic!

He was laughing so hard that he only noticed the
buoy when they were twenty metres away. 'Olivia! Go
left!'

He leapt to the helm, throttled back then seized the
wheel, steering clear of the marker with metres to spare.

'Did we nearly hit—?'

'No! Yes! Possibly—but it wasn't your fault.' He
grinned. 'I was distracting you and, to be fair, I told
you to aim for the marker!'

She grimaced. 'I almost crashed.'

'Just like *Titanic*!' He laughed and nudged her shoulder. 'Forget about it.' He dropped the throttle and the
boat took off again. As the wind whipped at her hair he
saw her cheeks lifting into a smile. He leaned in. 'Want
to go faster?'

Wide eyes. 'It goes faster?'

He put his hand on the throttle, smiling. 'Hold on!'
He pushed the lever and the boat surged forward, ripped
across the water, bouncing hard then flying, bouncing,
flying—and she was squealing with laughter, gripping
the rail so tightly that he couldn't help laughing too. It
was the best he'd felt for days…this joy of being on the
water, the speed, the sunshine, her laughter… It felt like
freedom.

He followed the coast so she could see the towns—
pastel houses crammed onto impossible slopes—then
he turned west. As they approached Capri, he slowed
down. Milo was meeting them at the property, a secluded
place with a private mooring on the eastern side of the
island. Olivia had pushed her sunglasses onto her head
and was gazing at the craggy slopes of bleached rock,

marvelling at the tufts of trees and shrubs which grew on the inhospitable cliffs.

She caught his eye. 'Don't you find this amazing?'

'Every time!' He took off his sunglasses and slipped them into his shirt pocket. 'There are some underground caves on Capri that you really should see. You'd love the light! Emerald, turquoise. It's stunning.'

She turned, studied his face for a moment then shot him a little smile. 'You seem happier today…'

'Happier?'

She nodded. 'You've seemed preoccupied recently. I've been worrying that it's got something to do with what I said…about your music. I didn't mean to upset—'

'You didn't upset me.' He looked along the shoreline, trying to spot the mooring. 'You were very enthusiastic. I was pleased that you enjoyed my playing, flattered that you think I could do something with it…'

She was still looking at him, a little frown on her face. 'So—if it's not anything I said, what is it then—what's wrong?' She nudged his shoulder. 'I mean, fair's fair! I cried all over *your* shirt—the least I can do is listen if you want to talk…' She tucked some loose strands back into her ponytail and smiled, eyes wide and gentle, drawing him in again. He looked away, scouring the shoreline. Perhaps the mooring was on the other side of the outcrop. Her eyes on him, searching his face, wanting an answer. He couldn't tell her that he was a ball of confusion and that she was rolled up in it. Maybe he could tell her about the boat, about the sadness it had stirred up inside him. If he told her, maybe she'd be satisfied and wouldn't dig any deeper. He dropped the throttle a little more so that the boat was barely moving.

'It's the boat.'

Her forehead creased. 'The boat?'

He nodded. 'I haven't been on it since Izzy died. We both loved this boat, had great fun with it, but after she passed I couldn't bring myself to… Besides, I had other priorities. Getting *Django* out of dry dock has been hard—'

Her face fell. 'I feel bad now—for putting you through that. Milo could have picked me up—'

'No!' He checked himself. 'What I mean is, I couldn't let him do that when I have a perfectly good boat. I *wanted* to get it back out on the water, and you needing a ride was just the push I needed. I knew I'd have to face it some time and now I have, thanks to you!' He smiled. 'If I look happy it's because I am.'

'So you're okay, really?'

'Yes! Really!' The throaty burble of the engine, the sloshing of waves against the hull filled a long, silent moment. She looked as if she was about to say something but suddenly, up ahead, he caught sight of Milo's boat moored at the end of a long jetty, the man himself waving.

'Wow, Milo! This place is amazing.'

'You like it? That's good. If you like it, it will make your photographs *splendide*.'

Olivia couldn't help liking Milo. His accent was charming, *he* was charming. Warm brown eyes, thick dark hair. He was tall, his body well-honed under his expensive shirt and designer jeans.

As he showed them around, he explained that the property had been designed as a deluxe holiday let for couples. 'So… I started with a traditional structure then incorporated modern elements, like steel for the canopy and lots of glass—to make the most of the view.'

Zach ran his hand down a steel column. 'I like this—it's unexpected.'

Milo smiled. 'Thank you, Zach. Architects enjoy playing with expectation.'

The interior was modern and minimalist—pale marble floors, white walls. There was a magnificent master bedroom with luxury en-suite bathroom, a sleek white kitchen with brushed steel appliances and slate worktops. The spacious sitting room, furnished with white leather sofas and a black marble coffee table, opened to an al fresco dining area which overlooked the sea.

'It's romantic—' Olivia conjured an image of Zach walking across the room towards her—faded jeans, shirt unbuttoned one notch lower than decent, those eyes. 'But it's also got a calm, timeless vibe, like a sanctuary.'

'Exactly!' Milo smiled. White teeth. 'Calm, romantic, secluded—that's what the client wanted, so if that's what you are feeling then I have succeeded!' He had such a sunny smile…delightful.

She spun around slowly, assessing the ambient light, thinking about shooting angles, when she caught Zach staring at her. He looked preoccupied again. She wondered if he was thinking about the boat, memories of Isabella…

Milo was extracting a silver ice bucket from a length of bubble wrap. 'So, we'll begin shooting outside while we have the morning light, then we'll come inside, okay?'

'Sounds good to me.' She knelt to open her camera bag, taking out the things she needed. When she looked up, Zach was leaning against the wall, examining a painting.

Zach!

This shoot was going to be so dull for him. She glanced outside. Milo was polishing two glasses with a cloth, carefully arranging them on the table next to the ice bucket. She stood up, kept her voice low. 'Listen, Zach…you're going to get so bored. Seriously! Watching this kind of shoot is like watching paint dry. You don't have to stay. I'll be fine with Milo, really!'

He came towards her. 'I don't mind staying.' He looked at her evenly then shifted his gaze to the man outside. 'I mean, how long will it take?'

Why was he so distracted? She cleared her throat to get his attention. 'Two or three angles per room, exteriors from all sides, I guess, maybe some shots of the view—' She gave a little shrug. 'A couple of hours, probably.'

'You don't want me to help with anything?' He turned to look at Milo again, and Olivia followed his gaze. Milo had moved on to wiping the chair backs with a cloth, his movements deft, his face tense with concentration.

She couldn't help smiling. 'I think Milo's got it covered.'

'Okay.' Zach's smile didn't reach his eyes. He slipped his sunglasses from his shirt pocket and put them on. 'If you think you'll be okay, then I'll take the boat for a blast.'

She pulled a cross-eyed face. 'I'm only trying to save your sanity.'

'It's probably too late for that.' He smiled softly. 'You've got my number, yeah, just in case?'

She nodded. 'Are you *worried* about me?'

He seemed to falter. 'No—not worried. I'll see you in a while.' He turned away, walked towards the terrace.

'Have fun!'

He threw up his hand in a backward wave.

She watched him pause to speak to Milo, and then he was striding towards the cliff steps. Moments later he was gone.

Distractedly, she opened up the tripod and attached the camera. Zach had been through a great sadness in his life but he was sociable, likeable, an easy-going person. Yet, minutes after they'd arrived, he'd become withdrawn. Something was eating him up and she couldn't figure it out. She looked up, saw Milo beckoning from the terrace. She waved back and picked up the tripod. She'd have to forget about Zach for a while. She needed to concentrate on the shoot.

Milo was easy to work with. He positioned things without her having to ask, styled the shots with an expert eye. The props he'd brought were tasteful: cashmere throws, pillar candles, crystal glasses. As they worked, he chatted about architecture, art and music…

'Zach is very talented with the guitar…' He smoothed a throw across the bed, turning back an edge to show the fringe. 'Sometimes when he plays, I feel a sadness in his heart…' He stood back. 'How's that—do you need me to pull it back a little more?'

She looked through the viewfinder. 'No! That's perfect.' She took three shots, different exposures. She thought about the boat, the sadness Zach had talked about just hours ago. 'I suppose, on some level, playing gives him an outlet…' She detached the camera from the tripod, gave it to Milo so he could check the last few shots.

'Olivia, these are perfect! It's a wrap!' He flashed his white smile. 'We're a good team! How about a glass of wine?'

It was a relief that Milo was pleased with her work. She smiled. 'A glass of wine sounds like a very good idea.'

He handed her the camera. 'Can I help you pack up?'

'No, thanks.' She gave him a little shrug. 'I count it out and count it in again—force of habit, so I know I've got everything.'

'Okay. *I* will go and open the wine!' He left the room and she smiled to herself. The wine he'd brought as a prop had been chilling in an ice bucket on the dining table for over an hour. It would be perfect by now, and didn't she deserve a little celebration? Her first overseas commercial shoot! Milo was happy, and *she* had more classy photos for her portfolio. She folded the tripod and packed away her kit. When she went through to the sitting room Milo handed her a glass, then raised his own.

'Thank you, Olivia, for a successful shoot. Here's to many more in the future!'

She touched her glass to his and took a long sip. It would be great to shoot more Italian interiors. Milo would be a good contact. She suddenly realised he was watching her, a smile in his eyes.

'You like?'

'Mmm—it's delicious.'

He looked pleased. He motioned to the sofa. 'Let's take the weight off. Is that what you say?'

'Yes! Your English is very good.' She dropped onto the long sofa, ran her hand over the leather. It felt soft, yielding. Expensive. Milo sat on the sofa too, a little distance away. He took a sip from his glass, crossed one leg over the other.

'So, forgive me, but what did you mean by *an outlet* when you were talking about Zach's playing?'

'I meant that maybe playing gives him a way of expressing his grief…'

'Grief?' Milo frowned. 'What grief?'

'I…thought you knew…about his wife… She died.'

Milo's face blanched. 'I had no idea…' He shook his head a little. 'I don't know Zach very well… I only moved here a year ago. What happened to his wife?'

'I don't know. I haven't wanted to ask—but I do know she passed a couple of years ago.'

'Oh, dear.' To her surprise, Milo's eyes began to fill with tears. 'This sad news is setting me off…'

She leaned forward. 'Are you all right?'

He put his glass down, wiped his eyes with his hands. 'I'm sorry; forgive me. I get emotional because I lost someone too—it's why I came to Capri. I couldn't stay in Naples after Sergio died…'

Sergio!

'He had a cancer of the pancreas… We found out too late.' He sniffed, took a drink from his glass. 'I keep myself to myself most of the time, so no one knows. I don't socialise much…but I like the bar, listening to the music. It's nice.'

She thought of Zach on the boat that morning—*'If I look happy it's because I am.'* Was that the truth or had he been trying to make her feel better about the boat? Was he still trapped in his grief like poor Milo? That night in Ravello, when he'd reached out to her, that look in his eyes. The threads inside her head were tangling again.

She took a small sip of wine then set down the glass. 'I suppose it must be hard to move on when you've lost the love of your life…'

Milo's eyes filled with fresh tears. 'It's not hard, Olivia. It's im-pos-sible.' He began to sob and for a moment she felt completely helpless, then she did the only thing she could think of. She moved along the sofa and wrapped her arms around him.

Zach began to untie *Django* from her mooring then stopped and re-tied the rope. He couldn't leave. He'd brought Olivia to Capri so he could keep an eye on her—on Milo. Jetting off around the island would defeat the object. He sighed, scaled the short ladder and jumped aboard. He yanked a bottle of water from the fridge near the helm, took it onto the foredeck and sank onto one of the sun pads.

When they'd set out this morning he'd felt great. He'd worked through his sadness about getting the boat out, had loved every minute of their little voyage to Capri. And Olivia had loved it too—the views, the speed, the feeling of flying across the water. Her face had been a picture, glowing, full of life.

Alive!

It had been a long time since he'd felt like that. But then somehow, up there, looking around the property, he'd started noticing little looks between Olivia and Milo.

Noticing or imagining?

He swallowed hard. And then she'd said he could go, that she'd be fine with Milo. He snapped the cap off the bottle, swigged down an icy mouthful of water. Had she really been trying to save his sanity or was there another reason she'd wanted him to leave? He looked up at the house on the cliff, and suddenly an image came to him—Olivia in Milo's arms. As his stomach churned, he suddenly realised that he was sick with jealousy.

He dropped his head into his hands and groaned. He

liked Olivia—liked her so much that the thought of her being with anyone else was driving him crazy. He hadn't realised until this moment how far gone he already was… She was doing something to him, making him think about things that were too difficult to think about…like caring for someone again. But he was stuck. How could he think about moving on when he'd hadn't said goodbye to Izzy? Her face that night, laughing… *'I'm fine, Zach. Stop worrying.'* The aftershock, the dazed limbo and always Alessia's tragic eyes, looking for her *mamma*, crying for a loss she couldn't articulate. He'd fallen on the renovation of Casa Isabella like a half-starved animal, worrying at it like a dog with a bone. He never thought he'd step back, begin to see a wider view. But it *was* happening. Olivia was making it happen, and she had no idea what she was doing to him. Instead, she was in the house on the cliff with Milo Beneventi.

He pressed the cold bottle to his forehead. He was scared to look back, scared to look forward. He didn't know what to do… All he knew was that he had two hours to talk himself off the ledge.

'Zach!'

It took him a split-second to take in the open wine bottle, the two empty glasses, her hands wrapped around Milo's. Her eyes. Milo's eyes. His gut twisted tight. Just minutes ago, on the boat, he'd reminded himself that Olivia was a free agent, but he hadn't expected to walk in on something like this.

Breathe.

'Hi! How did it go?'

Smile.

She was standing up, smiling. 'Really well.'

Milo was standing up, smiling. 'Olivia is a joy to work with!'

The pair of them, smiling at each other, exchanging little looks. It was an effort to control his voice. 'That's great! I'm glad it went well.'

Milo motioned to the wine bottle. 'Would you like a drink, Zach?'

He couldn't imagine anything worse. All he wanted to do was escape. He spied Olivia's bag and tripod in the corner.

'I'm sorry, Milo, but we have to get going.' He gave a little shrug. 'Something came up.' He turned to Olivia. 'Are you good to go?'

'Yes.' He could tell she was trying to read his thoughts. 'The gear's all packed.'

He went for her bag and tripod. When he looked up, she was giving Milo a hug.

'I'll send the photos as soon as I can.' She stepped back, looked deeply into Milo's eyes 'You take care now. I'll see you soon.'

Zach realised he was grinding his teeth. 'Liv, I'm sorry, but we really *do* have to go.' He leaned forward, shook Milo's hand. 'Sorry, Milo. I'll see you around some time…'

He started walking towards the terrace, heard Olivia's quick footsteps behind him. He didn't look back but hurried down the steep winding steps which led to the jetty. He stood aside to let her onto the boat first, then handed her the tripod.

As she took it from him, her eyes locked on his. 'What's happened?'

He fought back a wave of guilt for dragging her away on false pretences. 'Nothing's happened.'

'You said, *"Something came up"*—what came up? Is everyone all right—Alessia?'

Her sweet concern for his family increased his misery. He picked up the camera bag, handed it up to her. 'Everyone's fine.' He attempted a reassuring smile, then untied the boat, threw the rope on deck and jumped aboard.

'So, what's up then?'

I think I might be falling for you.

He broke away from her gaze, took the wheel and turned the key in the ignition. The engine kicked and slowly he backed *Django* away from the jetty.

She came to sit beside him at the helm. 'What's going on, Zach? I feel like you're mad at me and I don't understand…'

He throttled forward slowly, pointing the boat towards the open sea. When he turned to look at her, he hated the bewilderment he could see in her eyes, hated himself for being the cause of it. He sighed. 'I could never be mad at you, Liv. I just need to get back, that's all. I… I've got a meeting.'

'Oh! I didn't know.' She dropped her sunglasses over her eyes. 'You didn't mention it before.'

She was staring into the distance, her lips pressed together, a small frown creasing her forehead. He wished he could tell her what he was feeling, but he was a mess and he knew that whatever he said would come out all wrong. He pushed the lever, felt the boat lifting in the water, but this time she didn't laugh and squeal.

The wind tugged at his hair, the growl of the engine filled his ears and in his head, over and over again, he replayed the scene he'd just witnessed. He'd walked in on something. They hadn't tried to hide it… Their hands had remained clasped, their affection obvious. He felt his jaw tighten as he tried to bury his anguish. Olivia was single and he had no right to feel put out if she liked Milo. He glanced at her, noticed goosebumps on her bare arms. He rummaged under his seat for his old hoodie and handed it to her, raising his voice over the engine noise. 'You're cold—take this!'

She gave him a little smile, eyes hidden by her shades. 'Thanks!' She pulled it on, wrapped it tightly around herself. Out of the corner of his eye, he saw her drawing the hood against her cheek, breathing in the scent of the fabric, and for some reason the small action seemed to ground him.

He thought about the night in the bar, what he'd seen in her eyes as he was playing, the way she'd looked at him on that narrow street in Ravello. It felt wrong that she could like Milo. How could she like Milo when, from the very first moment she'd looked at him, he'd felt something between them?

How could she like Milo?

Suddenly she was pushing her sunglasses up, leaning in so he could hear her voice. 'Zach! How much do you know about Milo?'

Was she tapping him for information? A fresh wave of misery crashed over him and he swallowed hard. 'Virtually nothing.'

She stood up and pressed her back against the windscreen so she was facing him. The breeze was buffeting her hair, loosening it from her ponytail, but she didn't seem to notice. She looked at him squarely, raised her voice above the engine. 'So…you don't know that he moved to Capri after his partner, Sergio, died?'

It took a moment for her words to sink in. 'Sergio?'

She nodded, shouted, 'Sergio was the love of his life! Had pancreatic cancer… They found it too late.'

In his head, images scrolled in slow motion. Milo's eyes filled with—sadness! Deep looks… Clasped hands… Liv stroking Milo's shoulder as she was saying goodbye. He could see it all so clearly now. She'd been comforting Milo, not… He groaned inwardly—he'd been such a fool, blinded by jealousy, and she'd worked it out, seen right through him. She was gazing at him, hair blowing all around her face, and he could hear all the words she wasn't saying.

He shook his head, spoke half to himself. 'I've been an idiot…'

'What?' She was frowning. 'Can we please stop the boat? I can't hear you!'

He throttled down, switched off the engine. The boat reared and fell back into the dark shifting water, rolling and pitching, little sloshing sounds framing the fresh silence. He dropped his hands from the wheel, moistened his lips.

'I've been an idiot… I thought—'

'I know.'

She was looking at him, reading him like a book, he felt, but he didn't mind. It was a relief to be found out. He smiled, gave a little shrug. 'I suppose I've blown my cover…'

Her eyebrow lifted, warm light playing across her irises. 'Probably.'

He took a step towards her, wished he could stop his heart banging against his ribcage. 'I like you, Liv.' Another step forward. 'I didn't realise how much until today…'

Her eyes were holding his, hair softly blowing across her cheek.

'So…?' Her voice sounded husky.

He reached a hand to her face, felt her melting into his touch, and then slowly he lowered his mouth to hers. Warmth…softness…the taste of wine on her lips… For a moment he lingered there, letting the sensation wash over him, and then he was pulling her closer, desire catching him like a wildfire, torching every nerve in his body.

He pulled her hard against him and she sighed, slid her hands over his shoulders and up into his hair. Her lips were parting and he was taking everything, kissing her deeply, losing himself in her. It had been so long since he'd had this—felt this—he couldn't stop. He worked his hands under the hoodie, under her blouse, senses swimming as his fingers connected with the warm smoothness of her back. He could feel her hands sliding into the back pockets of his jeans, drawing him closer, and it was almost too much. It occurred to him that he could anchor the boat, take her down into the cabin—but was he ready? She was here to work for him…and there were things he needed to get straight in his head. He liked her so much, wanted her so much, but he had to slow down, take a moment.

He took her face in his hands and broke off breathlessly. Her eyes were hazy, her cheeks flushed, lips swollen. He steadied himself, pressed his forehead to hers. 'Wait—'

'Wait?'

'Just for a moment…'

He felt her arms sliding around his waist, the softness of her hair on his neck as she laid her head against him. He wrapped his arms around her, buried his lips in her hair. 'I'm sorry.'

'You don't have to be sorry.' She pulled her head away

from his chest, looked into his face. 'It must be hard...
after losing...' She pressed her lips together. 'Milo says
it's impossible for him to move on...'

He studied her face, seeing little glimmers of light
in his eyes. What was he seeing there? Fear? Longing?
Something else...?

He sighed. 'I don't think it's impossible... It's just
that everything feels so new...like uncharted waters.'
He smiled. 'Maybe I need to stay in the shallows for a
while. Can you understand that?'

She touched his cheek, smiled. 'The shallows are
warm and safe. They're a good place to start.'

CHAPTER EIGHT

OLIVIA WATCHED ZACH and Alessia romping around in the water. Minori beach was a world away from the sands of West Wittering and those shivery mornings with her dad. *'Come on, Liv. It's bracing.'* That cold slab of wet sand under her feet which made her arches ache, that breathless tiptoe advance, the icy creep of water up her legs, her dad laughing. He used to pull her in. The breath would freeze in her lungs as the waves closed over her shoulders. She'd come up kicking and gasping, then laughing because it wasn't so bad after all. *'You've got to dive right in.'* That was what he used to say.

She drew her legs up and hugged her knees. Over the past couple of weeks she'd found herself thinking about her dad quite a bit, teasing out all the little knots in her head. Since the day he left, she'd been blaming him for everything. But Zach had been right. The real feeling of betrayal had sprung from the years she'd spent rebuffing jokes about her family from the kids at school. She'd felt so small and stupid when it came out that her dad had left. Not that they'd joked about that exactly, but she'd seen it in their eyes, she'd felt the warm breath of their whispers. That was when her self-confidence had evaporated and that was when the fantasy had started. Her fixation with finding a perfect man, a man whose heart belonged only to her. A man who wasn't afraid to commit. A man who wanted to marry her.

Zach had Alessia on his shoulders now, holding her hands, scuffing through the little waves. Olivia couldn't help smiling as she watched them. Since arriving in Italy, her narrow view of perfection seemed to have expanded. Being with Zach was helping her to see things differently. That day on the boat, when he'd kissed her for the first time, she'd been filled with dismay when he pulled away. She'd thought he was changing his mind. She'd given him a get-out, told him what Milo had said about moving on, but he'd taken her by surprise with his answer and then he'd said, *'Everything feels so new...like uncharted waters...'* She'd never looked at things that way before. She'd focused so much on what he'd had with Isabella that she'd never thought that there could be anything new for him to discover. His words had bolstered her spirits that day.

'Hey!' He lifted Alessia off his shoulders and dropped to his knees on the sand. 'Why didn't you come in?'

Blue eyes, still giving her butterflies. She reached a towel out of the bag and wrapped it around Alessia tightly. 'What have I got here? A bug in a rug?' Alessia giggled, shrugged out of the towel and plonked her bottom onto the sand. She picked up a little spade, started to fill a yellow plastic bucket.

Zach was rubbing his shoulders with a towel, smooth golden skin, biceps flexing as he worked the towel over his body. She released a slow breath. How could she tell him she was getting tired of life in the shallows?

She smiled. 'I was happy watching.' He had just the right amount of dark hair, well defined abs, the dusky trail leading… 'Besides, it's nice for you two to be together on your own.'

He laid his towel on the sand. 'It was lovely in the water, wasn't it, Alessia?'

Alessia looked up, quirked her mouth. 'It was *as-ton-ish-ing.*'

Olivia laughed. 'I'm never going to live that down, am I?'

He stretched out beside her. She felt his hand on her bare back, his fingers moving slowly up and down. Her stomach clenched. Did he have any idea what he was doing to her? She felt his lips on her shoulder. 'What about dinner tonight?'

She turned to look at him. 'You mean, *going out* for dinner?'

He nodded, fixed her with a darkening gaze. 'Somewhere nice…'

She smiled. 'Somewhere nice sounds…very nice!'

His lips grazed her shoulder again. 'I'll pick you up at seven.'

She could feel his fingers at the base of her back tracing warm circles round and round and, as she held his gaze, she could see a steady heat building. She swallowed hard, forced out an even breath. 'I'm looking forward to it.'

'Zach, this is beautiful!'

Happy light in her smile, eyes sparkling. It's what he'd been hoping for. He tugged her close, kissed her hair, breathed in the soft musk of her perfume. The warmth of her body flowed into the hand he'd pressed to her waist and he could feel it moving through his veins, transforming itself into the stirrings of an immeasurable want. He released her quickly, stepped back so she could follow the waiter who was leading them across the terrace to a balcony table overlooking the sea and the tangerine heat of the sunset.

He'd never been to Ambruosi, the restaurant at the Palazzo Broccardi. That was part of its appeal—he'd wanted to take her somewhere that would be new for both of them. More than anything, he wanted some time alone with her, away from work, away from anything familiar, and this was perfect! A sunset, a balmy evening, candles on the table and Piazzolla's *Oblivion* playing in the background. He ordered wine, watched as Olivia looked around delightedly. Such a lovely face, little gold studs glinting in her earlobes, her neck smooth and lightly tanned.

Two weeks had passed since the shoot on Capri. Two more weddings had taken place at Casa Isabella plus a last-minute renewal of vows celebration that had disrupted their routine. Both he and Olivia had been busy. He'd managed to spend some time with Alessia, and Olivia had accompanied him to his gigs at the bar but, apart from evening walks in the garden and the occasional sundowner on the terrace, they hadn't seen much of each other.

In truth, he'd been preoccupied with business matters. His father had floated the idea of a second wedding venue in Italy, wanted Zach to start searching for a suitable property. For some reason it had felt as if the walls were closing in.

He'd needed their afternoon at the beach…time with Alessia and Olivia, living in the moment. The memory of Liv in her swimsuit, smooth skin on her arms and legs, the way her back had felt, warm and silky… He hadn't wanted to stop his fingers moving over her skin, and now she was sitting here in a soft dress that skimmed in all the right places, her face glowing. It was hard to keep focus.

When the waiter had poured the wine he lifted his glass. 'Here's to freedom!'

'Freedom?'

'Getting away from the grind...'

She lifted an eyebrow. 'I'll drink to that.' She took a sip from her glass and set it down. 'It's relentless, isn't it...running a wedding venue. I thought wedding photography was demanding but at least it's just one day—' She pulled a thinking face. 'Followed by three days on the computer, admittedly, but the venue thing, dealing with people all the time—that's full-on.'

He took a long sip of his wine, held it in his mouth for a moment. *'It's relentless.'* She was reading his mind! He pictured his father at the other end of the phone. *'Casa Isabella's been a huge success. We should repeat the winning formula with a new venue.'* He pushed the thought away—dwelling on it would only make him morose.

She toyed with the stem of her glass. 'Zach, why don't you employ a manager?'

His heart caught. A tiny needle-prick. He picked up his glass again. She was looking at him, eyes keen, endlessly curious. That feeling again, walls closing in. He sipped his wine then drew a measured breath.

'I suppose it's got a lot to do with Izzy...the fact that she loved it so much. I've felt a responsibility for...' His eyes drifted to the sun, fading to a blush on the horizon. Unpacking the past. Maybe he should talk about things more. Open up. He turned back to Olivia, met her gaze.

'Izzy's family had a restaurant in Naples. She grew up with it, helped out, but she was ambitious. She had big plans! She studied hospitality and business at university. After she got her degree, she found an investor, persuaded her family to renovate the restaurant, take it more upmarket. That's where I met her.' He smiled. 'I'd been bumming around Europe in a band, playing little gigs, deluding myself that we were going places. We got to Naples and our singer bailed, then the band split and I was killing time, wondering what to do... I went into Izzy's restaurant one night and she took my order... I went back the next day, and the day after that...' He leaned back in his chair. 'I suppose we had a lot in common, my family being in the hotel business...

'I wanted to stay in Naples but I needed a career change, needed to make some money, so I went home, started working for Merrill Hotels. Dad was thrilled—his son and heir was finally on the right track. I started a new line of boutique hotels, high-end places. It was going well but I wanted to marry Izzy and live in Italy, so I decided to buy a hotel here. Dad liked the idea of a European expansion, said he'd invest. So I moved to Italy and started looking, but then Izzy's father died and Lucia didn't want to carry on with their restaurant any more. Izzy and I were married by that time. It seemed like the perfect moment for us to find a hotel we could run together...

'We did a road trip, viewed a lot of places that didn't quite hit the mark, and then Izzy found Casa Dorato—that's what it was called then—it means "Golden House".' His mouth suddenly felt dry and he picked up his glass, took a slow slip. 'It wasn't the going concern we'd been looking for. It was in a terrible state but we saw something in it and Izzy said we should turn it into the most romantic wedding venue on the Amalfi Coast.'

He smiled. 'My father took some persuading because of the renovation cost but Izzy could be very persuasive…'

'And then you lost her…' Olivia's eyes were glistening.

He swallowed hard. 'Aside from the grief, I felt… stranded. Does that make sense?' It suddenly occurred to him that Olivia, of all people, would understand. 'Like when your dad left—that feeling of the rug being snatched from under your feet. I had a half-renovated *palazzo* and a baby. The only thing I could think of was finishing what we'd started. Knowing how much Izzy had wanted it was reason enough for me to do it…and then, when it was finished, I wanted to make sure it was a success—for her.'

He smiled. 'I know I *should* get a manager. For one thing, I need to spend more time with Alessia but letting go isn't all that easy.'

'Maybe it's because you still feel stranded—' Olivia was gazing at him over the rim of her wine glass. 'I mean, if you let go of the reins, what comes next? It's a scary thought.' She sipped her wine. 'I think it's why I stayed with Ralph for so long. The alternative seemed so much worse—striking out on my own again—maybe failing again. In the end he forced my hand. Did I ever tell you that?'

'No! You said you were going out on your own.'

She laughed. 'Well, the truth is that Ralph gave me a little push, and then you called and offered me this great opportunity—I mean, what are the chances?' She smiled. 'Maybe that's all *you* need—a little push.'

As the waiter set out their entrées he turned her words over in his head. Letting go…*what comes next?*… chances… Could Olivia be his second chance? Maybe it was time to come out of the shallows…

* * *

Zach reached for her hand. 'Dance with me…'

They were walking along a tree-lined path that ran below the restaurant terrace. Small footlights illuminated the tree trunks, fairy lights twinkled in the branches. She recognised the music drifting down from the restaurant, eddying around them like little waves. She smiled hesitantly. 'Here?'

'Why not…? There's music!'

There was something in his eyes that told her resistance would be futile, so she smiled and stepped into his arms. He pulled her close, started to move her around in a slow circle. His hand at her back felt firm and warm.

She looked into his face. 'I know this music…'

'It's famous! *Gymnopédies* by Eric Satie. I play it sometimes…' His eyes went hazy and he leaned in, brushed her lips with his, then he straightened and spun her around quickly, as if she wasn't already dizzy enough. 'Satie was very eccentric. He only ate white food, and he had a whole wardrobe of identical suits so he didn't waste time choosing what to wear.'

She smiled. 'You know so much!'

His eyes locked on hers. 'When you have an interest, you tend to absorb details…'

'Mmm…' She was thinking about the beach, details like the curve of his shoulder as he'd dried himself, the defined abs, the trail of dark hair leading… He chose that moment to pull her closer, pelvis to pelvis. She swallowed a little gasp and closed her eyes. Thighs, hips, torso— moving against her—steady heat flowing from his body into hers. She could feel desire guiding his every move and it was what she'd been waiting for—wasn't it?

His hair skimmed her cheek as his lips touched her

neck. She melted into his warmth, the sensation of his mouth on her skin. She couldn't fight this—she didn't want to fight it. She tangled her fingers into his hair, tipped her head back as his lips grazed the skin at the base of her throat, and it was like falling…letting go… but could she really let go without knowing what was going on in his head?

'Zach, please stop…'

He pulled away, eyes burning into hers. 'Stop?'

Her ribs felt tight. She couldn't pinpoint the exact moment she'd fallen in love with him, but ever since that moment her lines had blurred. She wanted this…wanted him, but she needed a moment to think… If he was coming out of the shallows it had to mean something… Something real. And if he was ready then she was too, but she had to know what he was feeling. Her words tumbled out in short breaths. 'If this isn't…if you can't…then please stop because I need more of you…'

He took her face in his hands. 'I can give you more…' Then he kissed her softly, deeply, and she was unravelling, losing herself in the perfect taste of his kiss, and when she thought she was about to die in his arms he pulled away breathlessly. 'Let's go home!'

She watched shadows weaving and dancing on the walls, felt his fingers tracing a slow, meandering journey along her inner arm, a sequence of little presses against her skin. She felt a glow of recognition. 'What are you playing?'

His lips touched her shoulder. '*Pavane*. You liked it, remember…?'

She rolled over to face him. His gaze was soft in the candlelight, hazy from their lovemaking. 'I don't know which one I like best… I love *Pavane*, but now there's the dirty dancing one…'

'The dirty dancing one!' He laughed. 'I'll never play *Gymnopédies* again without remembering…'

His gaze held a trace of heat, something else too which reached right into her heart and nestled there. She touched his shoulder, ran her fingers over the smooth arc of muscle. In this moment she felt so close to him, felt as if everything had opened up between them. The way he'd told her about Isabella, how they'd started out together…all that history…but there was something left, something she needed to know.

'Zach, what happened—to Isabella?'

She saw the light drain from his eyes, heard the little catch in his breath and then he was rolling onto his back. He stared at the ceiling for a long moment and she wondered if she'd pushed too hard, but then he started to speak.

'It was a brain haemorrhage—very sudden.'

She reached for his hand, felt him folding it into his. He closed his eyes, as if it was the only way he could see into the past.

'We'd gone for dinner at friends'… It was a lovely evening so the plan was to eat outside. I was on the terrace with the guys, having a beer, and Izzy was inside, catching up with the girls. She was bringing a bowl of salad out and she must have caught the heel of her shoe somehow… I heard a crack, then a smash and when I looked up Izzy was on the ground… I ran over. For a moment she looked dazed, then she laughed, called herself a *klutz*. I helped her up. I was worried because she'd hit her head but she said she was fine, that it was just a bump. She was more worried about the broken salad bowl. She was picking up the pieces, apologising. I took her aside, asked her if she really was okay and she told me to stop worrying…'

He fell silent for a moment. Olivia felt his fingers tightening around hers.

'An hour later when we were eating, I felt her touch my hand suddenly, like she was trying to grab it, and then she collapsed, fell against me. I went crazy. I was holding her, calling her name, trying to wake her up, yelling for someone to get an ambulance, and it seemed to take for ever to come… They tried so hard to bring her back, but she didn't wake up again.'

Olivia tried to imagine it. One moment sitting there at the table, the next moment everything sliding away into darkness. Zach, floating in a vacuum of disbelief, the shock repeating like a mirror reflecting itself—on and on and on. She couldn't find the words so she squeezed his hand softly. 'Thank you for telling me.'

He turned to face her, traced the line of her jaw with his fingers. 'I've lived it a thousand times and every time it's the same. No warning. No time for saying…'

'Goodbye?'

He hesitated for a moment then nodded and as he looked at her she could see a glow there, kindling his eyes back to life.

'What do you say to Alessia…?'

He drew a wretched kind of sigh then seemed to steady himself. 'I put a photo of Izzy on her bedside table… I tell her that Mamma's with the angels, that she watches over her all the time, that she loves her…' He swallowed, shook his head a little. 'What can you say…? Alessia doesn't remember and maybe it's easier that way.' Lines appeared on his forehead. 'She sees the world with a child's eyes; she isn't burdened with sadness. If you have to lose a parent maybe it's easier if you never got to know them.'

He sat up suddenly, ran a hand through his hair. 'The only way I could think of to make Alessia feel Izzy's presence was to make this place everything Izzy had wanted it to be. Every piece of furniture, every paint colour…everything has Izzy's stamp on it. When Alessia's older maybe she'll feel her mother here somehow…' He picked up his watch from the bedside table and slipped it on, then swung out of bed, reaching for his trousers.

She sat up, holding the sheet against her body. 'You're not staying…?'

He turned around to face her. 'I'm sorry. Believe me, I want to—but I can't.' He was pulling on his shirt now, buttoning it up. 'Lucia's babysitting. I'm already later than I said I'd be.'

It was perfectly reasonable, so why did she feel a spike of desolation?

He pushed his feet into his shoes then came to sit beside her. He wrapped his arms around her, cool clothes against her warm skin. He kissed her softly. 'I'll see you tomorrow, okay.'

'Yes, of course…' She smiled. 'Sleep well, Zach.'

His eyes flickered with something she couldn't read, then he left the bedroom, closing the door quietly behind him.

She fell backwards and stared at the ceiling. He was in the east wing and she was in the west wing. Between them lay the house: everything with Isabella's stamp on it.

She took her coffee with her, walked barefoot through the dewy grass until she came to her favourite bench.

There was a cool stillness in the garden, a peachy glow of dawn on the horizon. The day still felt like a figment of someone's imagination, like an idea not fully formed, and she wanted it to wash over her, clear her mind, suggest a direction.

The way he'd been last night…that slow dance, the way he'd held her against him, his hand at her back, fingers slowly circling… Just thinking about it, and what happened afterwards…the delicious heat of his skin against hers, slow, deep kisses, the ache of longing, the blissful ache of release… The sweet intimacy of it had stolen her breath away, otherwise she might have whispered her secret, told him that she was in love with him. She'd seen the light in his eyes too and she'd dared to hope… But then he'd left, and she'd had the whole night to think.

She sipped her coffee, stared at the old house glowing golden in the sunrise. It was his Taj Mahal, his monument to Isabella and a legacy for Alessia. It was unreasonable, illogical of her to feel threatened by it, but she couldn't switch off the feeling that this place would always stand between her and Zach. She felt the old demons awakening inside her—that yearning for total commitment, that yearning to be at the centre of someone's universe, not just a satellite passing through. And even though she could trace its origins to the thoughtless taunting she'd endured at school, and even though she'd learned that she had room in her heart for a widower with a daughter, somehow, the house and everything it stood for felt like too much. She'd never expect him to give it up— that would be selfish—but she needed something for herself. Some proof that she mattered as much—more.

The problem was, she didn't know what that proof could be or how to find it.

The sun was climbing slowly, throwing shadows across the formal garden below. She got to her feet, wandered through the secret garden rooms she loved. Pale statues, enigmatic smiles. She ran her fingers over the smooth cold arm of a cherub and fought back a wave of sadness. Her time here was running out. Two more weddings to shoot and then Michele would be well enough to come back. So many things crowding into her head at once. What would happen in two weeks? What did she want to happen? Her feelings for Zach were undeniable, but this thing they'd started…was it all just a massive mistake? Was he going to shake her hand at the airport and say goodbye?

'You're up early!'

Startled, she looked up to see Lucia strolling towards her through the stone archway of the ancient folly. She was wearing a light summer dress and sandals, a cardigan draped over her shoulders.

Olivia tightened the belt of her robe, felt its wet hemline catching her ankles. 'I woke up early. Couldn't go back to sleep.' She smiled. 'I thought I might as well come outside.'

Lucia's eyes held her in a warm gaze. 'Ah! Well, it's the best time of day for a walk. So quiet, so cool. I always find it a good time for thinking about things…'

Olivia saw a glint in the older woman's eye, remembered Zach telling her how Lucia had seemed *'a little unsettled'* about her being here. Strange! Apart from the very first time they'd met, she'd never found Lucia to be anything other than warm and friendly. It flitted through her mind that perhaps it had been Zach himself who'd felt unsettled. She looked down at her feet, gave a little shrug. 'I wasn't expecting to bump into anyone…'

Lucia waved a dismissive hand, chuckled. 'It's fine! There was a time I'd walk barefoot in the grass too.' She brushed an insect off her shoulder. 'How was your dinner?'

'It was…lovely.' She felt a blush creeping over her cheeks. Lucia had been babysitting last night, would have been there when Zach got back—very late. 'The hotel is magnificent—we had a balcony table, a thousand feet above the sea.'

'Ambruosi's very famous and of course the gardens are delightful.' She plucked a bougainvillea blossom from a swinging stem, twirled it in her fingers. 'It was nice to see Zach going out on a date… He works too much.'

Olivia felt a swell of gratitude followed by a crushing desire to cry. The older woman seemed to be bestowing a kind of blessing on her. In the wake of her uncharitable feelings about Isabella, how thwarted she'd been feeling by Isabella's invisible presence, it was humbling. She swallowed hard. 'Yes! He does.'

'You've got two more weddings, two more weeks with us, yes?'

Olivia nodded.

'It'll be gone before you know it.'

She nodded again, folded and unfolded her arms. 'I was thinking the same thing this morning.' She felt her lips wobbling into a lopsided grin. 'Feeling a bit sad about it, you know.'

Lucia swished past her then turned around, fixed her with a level gaze. 'You must make the most of the time you have… That's all any of us can ever do.' She smiled. 'Enjoy the rest of your walk.'

Olivia stared after her until she'd disappeared from view and then she wrapped her arms around herself and walked slowly towards the stone arch. Lucia seemed to be encouraging her—to do what—get closer to Zach? She leaned against the cool stone and sealed her eyes shut. It wasn't that easy, especially when she was on the verge of thinking that last night had been a terrible mistake... She'd wanted him so much, but she should have thought it through a bit more. What had happened between them hadn't felt like a casual thing, but what it was exactly she didn't know and, until she did, she couldn't let it happen again.

Such a mess!

She took a deep breath and opened her eyes. Maybe he'd say something, tell her he wanted her to stay...and then at least she'd have something to work with.

If he didn't say anything—she sucked in another deep breath—if he didn't, then maybe she'd have to keep in mind what Lucia had just said about time. Her last two weeks were going to fly by. Maybe she should stop worrying about where things might go with Zach... Maybe she needed to dig out some of her old resilience, concentrate on getting out more, seeing things, having fun. Two weeks left—she had to make them count.

CHAPTER NINE

ZACH WATCHED OLIVIA squinting at the screen of her mobile, her face contorting with concentration. 'I don't know why you're bothering—you'll find it on Google Images. It's the most photographed tree in the whole of Italy, apparently.'

She tapped the screen, frowned, tapped it again. 'Rightly so! It's magnificent and completely lovely. As to why I'm bothering—I just want my own souvenir of the Rufolo umbrella tree. At least I'm not dragging you into a selfie.' She looked at him, a flicker of uncertainty in her eyes, and then she turned away to look at the view. 'I can't get over how blue that sea is.'

'Hopefully, it'll cheer up soon.'

'Ha ha, very funny!' She pocketed her phone then stepped close, wrapped her arms around his waist and huffed a little sigh. 'I keep thinking I should've brought the proper camera but after yesterday—ugh! Just the thought of tugging that thing about in this heat—'

'You need a break.' He kissed the tip of her nose. 'Ready to move on?'

'Yes! What's next?'

He slung an arm around her shoulders, started walking. 'The gardens at Villa Cimbrone. The Terrace of Infinity.'

She peeked at him from under her sunglasses. 'It sounds very romantic.'

'It'll be heaving with *turisti*—'

'Of which I am one.' She mock-frowned, quirking her lovely mouth. 'Is it painful, doing the tourist thing with me…? It's just that I want to see everything before I leave.'

Before I leave.

Her words struck him like a body blow, but he smiled. 'Of course I don't mind. You know I like…being with you.'

'Ditto.' She smiled then looked away.

He steered her back through the gardens, past the Moorish Tower with its famous fresco and along a shady path which led back to the Piazza Centrale, then he took her hand and led her through the crowds towards Cimbrone.

He couldn't believe that over a week had passed since they'd had dinner at the hotel, since they'd danced on that twinkling walkway, since they'd made love for the first—and only—time. He'd been mesmerised that evening, had felt so close to her, so…*found*.

But something had changed. She'd started speaking to him in exclamation marks. Colourful, upbeat tones, the joviality in her voice never quite reaching her eyes. Yet when he touched her she melted into him just like before, and when he kissed her he knew her truth. She wanted something from him, and the imminence of her departure was making everything worse.

After yesterday's wedding, her penultimate, he'd hoped for a quiet day but she'd asked him to take her sightseeing in Ravello because *'I'll be leaving soon'*. Lucia had told her she ought to see the gardens at Rufolo and Cimbrone, and they were the last places he wanted to go because of the crowds and because Izzy had loved the gardens so much.

As he dodged and weaved through the ambling tourists, pulling her along in his wake, he was fighting the urge to sit her down in some quiet bar, tell her he'd fallen in love with her. But what would he say after that? When he imagined the scene it was the part that always tripped him up. Falling in love with her was easy, but he wasn't a free agent. He was tied to the business, and there was Alessia to think about. If she wanted to be with him she'd have to slot into this life he'd made, take on his daughter, and he wasn't at all sure if that was what she really wanted. And there was something else too…

He still dreamed about Izzy. Did that mean he hadn't let go enough? How could he know how much letting go was enough? It wasn't as if he'd been a widower before. He had no experience of how grief worked. There seemed to be an aching gap between himself and the person he wanted to be, and he didn't know how to bridge it. Most importantly, he didn't want to hurt Olivia, so he'd followed her lead—kept things light and breezy—but it didn't feel real and it was killing him. He *had* to talk to her, find a way somehow. In the meantime, he was condemned to plodding beside her on the narrow pathway to the gardens behind a group of shuffling tourists. He watched her feet, tuned in to the soft slap of her sandals on the stone path.

When they struck a patch of shade she pushed her sunglasses up. 'Lucia was telling me that the Bloomsbury Set used to come to Villa Cimbrone.'

More chit-chat.

'That's right! It's attracted a lot of artistic types over the years.' He threw her a smile. 'Greta Garbo stayed here back in the thirties, but she didn't come *"alone"*!'

'You're on fire today!' She was laughing, that familiar warm light shining in her eyes, and for a moment everything felt perfect.

He put on a tour guide voice. 'The gardens were extended and improved in the early twentieth century by Ernest William Beckett. In later life, he was saddled with the unfortunate title of Lord Grimthorpe but, on the bright side, he *was* a friend of Vita Sackville-West, so he probably got a bit of free gardening advice…how to prune his roses—'

She was properly laughing now, dimples in her cheeks, eyes shining. Her face looked so sweet and happy that he couldn't help laughing too. 'I've probably got all that wrong. Izzy was the one who knew…'

Her laughter faded and the glow in her eyes dimmed a little bit. He cursed under his breath. He'd have to stop doing that…mentioning…and yet he couldn't switch Izzy off like a tap. She'd been a massive part of his life. Maybe coming here had been a mistake, but Ravello was a small town; there wasn't much in it that he hadn't seen or experienced with his wife.

They queued at the kiosk, sun beating down. She pulled on a sunhat. He wished he'd remembered to bring one. He paid, shoved the tickets into his pocket. He showed her the cloisters, watched her taking in the pale stone arches, the mullions twisted like sticks of barley sugar. The courtyard space was filled with glinting sun, pockets of shade. Ivy grasped at the walls, reaching past other climbers which he couldn't name.

On the Terrace of Infinity she gazed at the view, examined the busts, giggled at one with a broken snub nose. He watched boats streaking across the sea, remembered kissing her for the first time. She stuck her feet through the railings at the lookout point, gazed down at the scalloped terraces and tiny white houses. 'You should try this—it makes you feel dizzy!'

You make me feel dizzy.

He led her along a covered walkway, wishing the wisteria was still in bloom so she could see it, the clusters of petals rippling like confetti. On through the rose garden, heady with scent, past statues to the Temple of Bacchus, then more paths, worn steps and everywhere splashes of colour, fat, bristling yew trees, slender cypresses and the tall umbrella pines.

On the lawn she took out her phone, aimed it at the view and tutted. 'I know *I'm* a tourist so I have no right to get impatient, but I *wish* all these people would vanish so I can get a clean shot.'

He wished all the people would vanish too. He stepped behind her, wrapped his arms around her shoulders. She sank back against him, warm and damp. He kissed her neck, tasted the saltiness of her skin. 'I think we should find a quiet bar, grab a cold one...'

She swivelled to look at him, a wicked gleam in her eye. 'You mean you're not enjoying the *turisti*?'

'I want to get out of here—' he released her, grabbed her hand '—and I'm taking you with me!' He started running across the lawn and she was running beside him, holding onto her hat, laughing. Then she was tugging at his hand, breathless, giggling.

'Zach, stop! What about the gift shop?'

He looked back, saw that she was teasing and pulled her on. 'Don't even think about it!'

* * *

Off the main drag, away from the crowds, he spotted an arched doorway, heavy doors pinned back with iron bolts, black and white floor tiles. A big green pot plant squatted in the entrance lobby, its fronds disturbed by the slight breeze. It looked cool, inviting but, most importantly, it was unfamiliar.

'This place looks promising.'

She pushed her sunglasses up, smiled. 'Okay.'

The interior was unexpected. A domed skylight in a high ceiling funnelled light into the centre of the room but the light fell away sharply so that the tables clustered around the walls were crushed into semi-darkness, brightened only a little by the tea lights flickering in amber glass lanterns. More amber lanterns were suspended at intervals over the long mahogany bar, and at the end of the bar, in a corner, gleamed a baby grand.

'Where is everybody?' Olivia's voice was hushed.

He'd been about to say the same thing. The place was deserted. He squeezed her hand, called out, 'Hello? Is there anybody here—?'

So quiet. He let go of her hand, walked to the bar and called out again. No reply. He looked at the piano, wandered over, lifted the lid carefully. He pressed middle C, heard the note ring out clear and true. He smiled. He hadn't touched a piano in quite a while. He tried a scale.

Nice!

'You play the piano too?' She was walking towards him, eyes curious.

He ran a hand through his hair, smiled. 'A bit. I had lessons—it's how I started really. Then I got into guitars and left the old Joanna behind.' He played a few one-handed notes. '*This* is a lovely instrument.'

'Play something—please.' She was smiling. Properly happy.

He pulled out the stool and sat down, tested the pedals. It had been so long since he'd played. He looked at her, lifted an eyebrow. 'This might well be a catastrophe...' Then he ran his fingers over the keys, took a deep breath.

Focus.

The first notes sounded clumsy, and then it came back. *Für Elise*, his grade seven piece, the notes rising and falling, that moment of teetering on a brink then filling out, swelling into the bolder melody. He glanced up. She'd rested her cheek into her hand, in her eyes a look of... He looked down, watched his fingers on the keys, losing himself...

As he played the final note a voice ballooned through the room. 'Bravo!'

Startled, he swung round, jumped to his feet. Behind the bar stood a middle-aged man, slightly balding, with dark eyes, grey smudges underneath, a gap between his two front teeth.

'Thanks! I hope you don't mind. We came in for a drink, but there was no one...' He shrugged. 'I saw the piano...'

'It's absolutely fine! I just opened up, then had to go out for a moment. I'm sorry I wasn't here.' He smiled. 'I'm Marcello. What can I get you?'

Zach looked at Olivia.

'Frascati, please.' She smiled. 'And a glass of cold water.'

'I'll have the same, thanks.'

Marcello reached for glasses, twisted the caps off two bottles of water and set them on a tray.

Zach stepped up to the bar, pulled out his wallet. 'It's

funny, I haven't noticed this place before. Have you just opened?'

Marcello's eyes snapped up. 'Yes. Last week.' He poured two glasses of wine.

'Ah…' Zach looked around. It had a nice vibe, a bit different to the other bars he knew. 'It's great!'

Marcello put the wine glasses onto the tray. 'It is—although, sadly, I might have to give it up.'

'Why?' Olivia had parked her elbows on the bar.

Marcello glanced at her then looked at Zach. 'Let's just say that my brother let me down. We were supposed to be business partners.'

Olivia frowned. 'I'm sorry. That's terrible.'

Marcello shrugged. 'Where would you like to sit?'

Zach looked around, pointed to a random table. He was curious about Marcello's predicament but he didn't want to press him. 'So, do you play the piano?'

Marcello laughed roundly. 'No! It's my brother who plays but we wanted to have a piano in the bar, for people to play if they want… You play very well…er…?'

'Zach! I'm sorry. I should have introduced myself. This is Olivia.'

Marcello nodded at Olivia then decanted their glasses and water bottles onto the table. 'It's nice to meet you both.'

A group of four were drifting in. Marcello acknowledged them with a nod then turned back to Zach. 'Let me know if you need anything else, and please—if you want to play the piano again, feel free.'

'Thanks!'

When he turned to face Olivia he found her watching him with a bemused expression on her face. He picked up his glass, smiled. 'What—?'

'Just you.'

'Me?'

She took a drink of water then picked up her wine glass. 'You love playing so much. I could watch you all day.'

He laughed. 'Hmm—I think the novelty would soon wear off.'

'Why do you always do that?' She was frowning at him.

'Do what?'

She leaned forward on her elbows, fixed him in her gaze. 'Whenever you talk about your music, you downplay it. You say you *dabble,* or that you played *little gigs.* Or you say you were *deluding yourself.* What's that all about?'

He drank from his glass, let the cool wine slip down and hit the sweet spot. 'It's terminology, that's all.'

'What did Isabella think about your playing?'

'She—' He drew a momentary blank, shrugged. 'I was finished with music when I met her. I was ready to move on. I didn't play much. We had other things going on.'

She sat back in her chair and sipped her wine. He wished he could see what she was thinking. He'd wanted to have a heart to heart but playing the piano for her seemed to have jinxed everything.

'Liv, you mustn't read too much into the music thing...' He leaned across the table, held her in his gaze. 'I love music. I always have, I always will, and I do think about it sometimes, but it's a cruel business and being good isn't enough. You need to be lucky, connected maybe, you need to give up everything and even if you do that there's no guarantee of success. By the time the band split I was happy enough to walk away, to move on with my life. Maybe my dreams of rock superstardom died, but other dreams came true. I fell in love, made a home in Italy, had a beautiful daughter and then…'

I fell in love with you.

He held the words in his mouth, rolled them around on his tongue. Somehow, this didn't feel like the right moment.

'And then?'

He shrugged, moistened his lips. 'And then the dreams change.' He grinned. 'You dream of cold Frascati in a quiet bar, a dip in the sea with your daughter—stuff like that.'

He watched her gazing around.

'Well, whatever you say, I can see something in you when you're playing that feels… I don't know…like you're at home in your skin.' She turned, met his eyes, her expression soft. 'Have you ever thought about something like this?'

'What do you mean?'

'Like running your own music bar?' She smiled. 'I think you'd be in your element, being around musicians more, playing gigs yourself, bringing guest musicians in. Ravello's the city of music, after all!'

He shook his head. It was a ludicrous idea. He was too busy with Casa Isabella to even consider it, and there was the new venue his father wanted him to find.

He glanced at the piano then drained his glass. 'In another life, maybe. In this one, I've been tasked with finding a second wedding venue on the Amalfi Coast. A new sister for Casa Isabella. Merrill Hotels is expanding its Italian interests! How about another drink?'

She shook her head. 'No—no, thanks.' There was

something in her eyes. She seemed upset. 'I… Do you mind if I abandon you for a little while…?'

'I thought we were having a drink…?' Suddenly it felt as if everything was crashing around his ears. 'Is it something I said?'

She was reaching for her bag, standing up. 'No, nothing like that. It's just that I wanted to get some postcards and some tourist trash to take home.'

He couldn't let her leave. He started to stand up. 'I'll come with you…'

'No!' She put out a hand to stop him. 'You'd hate it, poking around crowded shops.' She glanced at the piano. 'You should stay here, play some more… I'll be back soon.'

She didn't give him time to reply, just turned away and hurried towards the door.

The light outside seemed too bright. It was prickling her eyes, making them water, or maybe it wasn't the light. She slipped on her sunglasses and walked quickly down the narrow street towards the town centre.

Why was everything such a mess?

The morning after their dinner date, after they'd been so tender with each other, he'd been tied up with meetings and when they did see each other he hadn't said anything about wanting her to stay on after her wedding shoots were finished, so she'd decided to be light and breezy about everything, not wanting him to think that she expected anything—and the whole week had felt weird, and today had been weird too. There'd been moments when things had felt normal, but at other times…

She stopped walking, fell back against a shady wall. The problem was they were skating around a conversation they needed to have, stuck in a pathetic limbo because neither of them wanted to say *What happens now?*

What happens now?

That he could play the piano had been a revelation. She loved watching him, listening to him, the way he seemed to become this other person, as if the music was freeing him. And when he'd looked up at her something in his eyes had made her ache with longing, reminded her of how intimate they'd been, how much she wanted to feel that closeness again.

And then, as she'd looked around the bar, it had come to her that his music was her proof. She loved his playing, treasured it like a precious thing, because it was all him, the purest expression of his spirit, the thing about him that had nothing to do with Isabella or the growing aspirations of Merrill Hotels. She wasn't asking him to forget anything in his past but she wanted some part of him that was hers alone to take forward into the future. And so she'd suggested a music bar.

'In another life, maybe.'

His words had cut her down, because that was exactly what she wanted. She wanted him to have another life, not this one where he was married to Casa Isabella, sidelining his talent, enduring long Sunday phone calls with his father. She wanted to hear him play his music, she wanted him to have time for paddling pool afternoons with Alessia, for making pizza from scratch, for dancing…

She pushed herself away from the wall and walked on. But how could she say those things to him? She had no claim on him, no say in how he lived his life. They'd spent a night together—not even a whole night—and the next morning it was as if too much time had passed and there'd been a gap between them that should have been filled with light and love and laughter, but wasn't.

In the town centre she crossed the *piazza*, wandered through the crowded alleys on the other side, past little shops and bars. She stopped to take a photo of some grapefruit-sized lemons in a basket, all pale and knobbly. Her dad would have laughed, would have picked one up to feel the weight of it. She squeezed into a busy gift shop, bought postcards—a nice one of the 'most photographed tree in Italy' with that blue sea beyond. Others of pretty pastel towns teetering on craggy cliffs. Several of the Cimbrone Gardens, then some random views: narrow streets with peeling doors…the cathedral. Pictures she would have taken for herself if she'd brought her proper camera. In another shop she bought souvenir bottles of Limoncello and a leather purse for her mum, then she retraced her steps to the *piazza* and sat on the warm cathedral steps with a hundred other tourists.

She gazed across the square, remembered the first night she'd seen it—the cafés and bars all closed, Zach fidgety because she hadn't said anything about his playing. It had mattered so much to him what she thought, and now he was trying to convince her that his music had been a young man's dream, something he'd cast aside quite happily. She didn't believe him.

She pulled out her phone, looked at the photo of the giant lemons. Idly, she drew eyes on them, little shocked mouths, added a caption: *Massive mutant lemons caught in the wild!* She thought about her dad again, what he'd said about bringing her up to be a free spirit. She'd felt like a free spirit when he'd been there for her, watching her back, and then, after he left, she'd turned into this other person. A person who needed everything to be squared off, a person who was uncomfortable with loose ends. Someone who was frightened to speak out. She turned the phone over and over in her hands. Her parents had been wrong not to include her in their decision to separate but maybe she'd been too hard on them, too hard on her dad especially. He was only human; everyone made mistakes. She'd made hers, with Zach.

Her dad was just at the other end of the phone if she needed him, probably up to his oxters in a river, but there all the same and thinking about that made her feel better. She attached the silly lemons photo to a text and sent it to him. What would he think when he got it? He'd be pleased. Maybe he'd feel a change in her—sense a return of the old Liv. She wondered what he'd advise her to do about Zach. He'd probably shrug, say he was the last person to ask and she'd laugh and tell him he was right. Her phone buzzed. He'd texted back! Laughing icon, thumbs-up icon, blowing kiss icon. Three symbols which felt like diamonds in her hand—symbols which proved that he was right there if she needed him. She swallowed a little sob of relief, wiped her eyes under her sunglasses.

Zach would be wondering where she was. Imagining his eyes, his smile, she drew in a long, slow breath. She'd taken a wrong turn after her conversation with Lucia in the garden that morning. Instead of talking to Zach, she'd buried her head in the sand, turned into an avatar, some upbeat version of herself—a sightseer, for goodness' sake!

She picked up her bags, threaded her way down the steps through the tourists sitting enjoying the late-afternoon sun.

Telling Zach what was in her heart wouldn't be easy—she might well lose him—but she couldn't put it off any longer. In a week she'd be shooting her last wedding and a few days after that she'd be leaving. She needed to talk to him. Ask the question: *What happens now?*

Her phone buzzed—Zach was texting.

Where are you?

She tapped out a reply.

On my way.

She walked along the narrow street, past the pale lemon walls of a smart hotel then onwards into a narrow pedestrian alley with grey crumbly-looking walls. In front of her a small knot of tourists melted away and then she saw him leaning against a wall, his phone in his hand. When he spotted her his eyebrows lifted and he broke into a smile—a smile that made her heart quicken.

'Did you get what you wanted?'

'Yeah…'

He was searching her face, his eyes so clear and blue, so intense, that she wanted to look away, or fall into his arms. She fiddled with the bag in her hand, wondering how to begin, when suddenly he said, 'Liv, we need to talk.'

She swallowed hard, met his gaze again. 'Yes.'

Silently, he took her hand, led her up the walkway and into a small public garden which overlooked the sea. There was a green bench with a curved back, happily vacant. He sat down and she sat beside him. It was a sheltered spot. The late afternoon sun was throwing long shadows, playing with texture in the pale stone walls and in the leaves, and the grass and the railings.

He released her hand, smiled awkwardly. 'Where to begin…?'

She looked at him, tried to read the tiny fluctuations of light in his eyes, watched him drawing in a breath and letting it out again.

He ran a hand through his hair. 'I want to say sorry for the other night… I should never have—'

'You regret what happened?' The words had sprung from her mouth—defensive. She could feel her heart going fast.

Breathe.

'No!' He shook his head. 'You must never think that.' His eyes softened. 'Olivia, my feelings for you… It's not a question of regret… But I didn't think things through. Leaving you afterwards—it felt so wrong, but I had to get back for Alessia, and then the next day I wanted to talk to you, but you seemed different. All week you've been different, and I haven't known what to say to you or what you're expecting from me.'

'Expecting?' She looked at her fingers. 'You make it sound as if everything's down to me.'

'Liv, please look at me.'

She lifted her eyes to his.

'Can't you see that I'm in love with you?' The light in his eyes, enfolding her, making her heart stop and start and quicken. 'But I'm worried that I'm not what you want. I'm a fixed entity. I have a business, a child, a life here—' He reached his hand to her face, stroked her cheekbone with his thumb. She felt her senses swimming, an ache of longing building deep inside. 'I never expected to feel this way about anyone again and I'm floundering because where we go from here is up to you.'

A little breeze caressed her neck and it seemed to

steady her. 'I don't think it's up to me, Zach.' She lifted his hand away from her cheek. 'You say you're a fixed entity, but none of us is fixed.'

She turned her gaze to the sea, examined the blur of sea and sky on the horizon. 'For a long time I had this fixed idea about what I wanted in a relationship. A perfect love, starting out together, all the boxes ticked. No loose ends. The opposite of my parents. And then you came along and all those rigid ideas of what makes perfection started to crumble. My frame widened.' She turned to face him. 'I was falling in love with you, then I discovered I had room in my heart for Alessia as well.'

He was looking at her intently, eyes filling with a hazy kind of light.

'But one thing hasn't changed. I don't like uncertainty. I want commitment and I don't know if you can give me that.' He opened his mouth to speak but she had to finish. 'You say you're in love with me, but how can you be in love with me when you haven't said goodbye to Isabella?'

'Izzy's gone—'

'She's gone, yes, but at the same time she's everywhere.' She felt tears gathering behind her eyes, swallowed hard. 'On your boat, at Villa Cimbrone today. She's probably here in these gardens too… At the house, every colour on every wall, every piece of furniture— her choice. And I understand, I really do. Surrounding Alessia with all the things her mother loved… I wouldn't have expected anything less from a devoted father. But you must see that you're wrong about everything being up to me.' She saw his eyes cloud. 'What I want, what I need from you is something that feels like a beginning.'

'So you want me to…what—put the past behind me?'

He slumped backwards. 'I can't do that. Izzy's inside me—she'll always be there.'

'I'm not asking you to forget the past, or your wife—I would never ask you to do that—but I need to feel that you can widen your frame too. Go forward…'

He was shaking his head. 'How?'

'I'm talking about—' she couldn't bring herself to mention his music again '—being true to yourself. You joined the family business to make your father happy, you bought a wedding venue because Isabella was ambitious, and you've devoted yourself to making it everything she wanted it to be and more. And I'm not saying that those were bad decisions, that you weren't happy to make them at the time, but the look on your face when you told me about the new wedding venue—it wasn't the look of a man who wants to build a wedding empire.'

He held her gaze then looked away across the sea.

'You're holding on so tightly, Zach, and I don't know why. You won't hand things over to a manager, not even so you can spend more time with Alessia, and if you won't do it for your daughter there's no hope for me. If you can't let go of your old life then I can't build a new one with you.'

He turned to face her, eyes more grey than blue, shut down somehow. 'So that's it then.'

CHAPTER TEN

THE ROAD WAS quieter than he'd thought it would be and he was glad. Driving the coastal route towards Sorrento could be slow. It was usually clogged with tourist buses and local traffic, pedestrians walking, shrinking back as impatient scooters zipped through gaps. Carefully, he passed a line of dusty cars parked tightly against the kerb, impossibly close to one another, dents and scrapes in doors and wings. He accelerated out of the town, felt a flicker of elation.

Driving! This sensation of forward motion, of clearing the bends and twists in the road with the sea at his shoulder and the sun on his face was exactly what he needed after days behind his desk, working with his father on the viability of a new wedding venue. He'd hardly seen Olivia. She'd cloistered herself away, editing, and he'd kept his distance because he couldn't think of what to say to her.

He'd felt bruised by her words in the Giardini Principessa di Piemonte. Chastened because she was right about Izzy being everywhere. He'd stood in those same gardens with Izzy, his arms wrapped around her, watching the sun sliding into the sea. And when she'd said, *'You haven't said goodbye to Isabella'*, she'd unwittingly hit another nerve. A sigh shuddered through him. Losing someone so suddenly left no time for goodbyes, left no time for saying all the things you should have said, like—*I'm sorry.*

He'd told Olivia what happened the night Izzy died, but he hadn't told her everything. He hadn't told her that on the way over to their friends' house they'd had a disagreement about a fountain for the garden. He hadn't flat out refused, but what Izzy had wanted was out of budget—although he'd bought Casa Dorato, Merrill Hotels was funding the renovation and he was under pressure to prioritise the internal work so they could start forward booking. They'd both been overtired—Alessia had been teething for weeks, waking them up at night. In the car, things had got a little heated and when they arrived they'd gone their separate ways. Him onto the terrace for a beer with his friends, Izzy into the house to chat to hers. And then she'd brought out the salad.

After the funeral the first thing he did was put in the fountain, and then he'd kept going—doing everything she'd wanted. Trying to make amends. Guilt and sorrow bound up with atonement. It was a hard habit to break, but if he didn't want to lose Olivia he would have to try.

For days he'd been thinking about all the things she'd said, and she was right: building a wedding empire wasn't his dream, but it was his family's business and if Merrill Hotels wanted to expand then he was obliged to facilitate that. It was why he was making this trip—to view a prospective acquisition.

At a junction he took a right and drove up a steep winding road until he arrived at a pair of stone pillars. A black sign with gold lettering confirmed that he was in the right place: *Villa Fiori.* He liked the look of the entrance: classy enough for Merrill Select. As he drove down the long shady driveway and parked the car he felt a lightening of spirit. Maybe running two venues would give him the push he needed, compel him to delegate the day-to-day running of things in both venues, and that would give him more time for Alessia. More time for living.

Villa Fiori was completely different from Casa Isabella. The manager, Lorenzo, was very accommodating and showed him around with pride. It was a modern boutique hotel with pale marble floors, lots of glass and chrome—the kind of thing that Milo might have designed. The sea views were spectacular, the bedrooms and bathrooms large and luxurious. The function room had a glass ceiling and shutters which opened onto a terrace laid with wooden decking, sheltered from the wind by glass panels, stainless-steel rails running along the top. Zach liked the contemporary vibe, could see the kind of clients who would be attracted to such a place.

The manager left him to go ahead and look at the grounds on his own. There was a large rectangular formal garden, well laid out with areas of cool shade under the mature trees. Olivia would know how to improve it for photography and thinking about her made him realise how much he was missing her, how much he liked being with her. He wondered what she was doing at that moment. Was she thinking about him? He felt a stab of anguish and walked on.

There was an old lemon grove adjacent to the main garden, a suggestion in the sales particulars that the land could be developed for guest chalets or a gymnasium, but he already knew that if he bought Villa Fiori he would never destroy the lemon grove. He'd never shaken off the Englishman's thrill of seeing lemons dangling from branches and as he walked through the trees, treading a path through a froth of groundcover, he thought about his wedding day... They'd got married in a place just like this. He looked up into the branches, caught little glimpses of the blue sky above, and for a moment he could feel the shape of her hand in his, see her eyes shining for him, full of love.

They'd written their own vows. He'd made his pledge to her in Italian; she'd spoken to him in her faltering English. *'We will make mistakes, Zach, and there will be days which are not easy but I vow that, whatever happens, I will hold you in my heart for ever.'*

He swallowed hard, pictured her face, the way she'd look at him with her sweet secret smile. He closed his eyes, listened to the sound of his own breathing and the sound of the leaves rustling in the breeze.

And I'll hold you in my heart for ever too, Izzy... I'm sorry we never got the chance to say goodbye, but I have to say it now. I've got to start again... I think I've been given a second chance, and I've got to find a way to take it.

'So, you think it's an option?'

'Definitely! It's classy, well maintained, well situated and it's completely different to what we've got so we'll be widening our client base.'

'I like the sound of that. What about the lemon grove, the potential?'

'Forget it! If we're selling weddings, the lemon grove's an asset. It needs tidying up, but with some TLC it'll give us another option for the ceremony. We can make all the outdoor spaces flow together. That means maximum flexibility in terms of what we can offer our clients.'

'You don't think guest chalets—?'

'No, Dad! If we buy Villa Fiori, the lemon grove stays. It's special! And we don't need guest chalets—there are twenty-eight bedrooms!'

'Okay.' Cynical sigh. 'If you say so. What about staff?'

'The manager thinks the staff will stay.'

'Will *he* stay?'

'Yes. I spoke to him about that. He's doing a great job there. He's invaluable and he knows it. If we buy the place, I suggest we give him a salary increase to keep him sweet—I'd be in trouble if he decided to leave.'

'Fine! Right then, I'll instruct our people to make an offer and we'll see what happens. Have a safe drive back, son!'

'I will. Bye, Dad.'

Zach stared at the phone in his hand, felt a little wash of relief. If the sale went through his father would get the business expansion he wanted, and if Lorenzo stayed on as manager his own role at Villa Fiori would be minor once the restructuring from hotel to wedding venue had been achieved. And he'd saved the lemon grove, at least for now.

He rolled the phone around in his hands, then tapped the screen, opened his photos. Olivia on the boat. He felt his lips twitching upwards into a smile. Her face tense with concentration then laughing, clowning about, doing Jack Sparrow... They'd narrowly missed that marker but it had felt so great, just having fun, and he wanted to feel like that again, make things right somehow. If only there was a way to show her... He closed the screen, threw his phone onto the passenger seat and started the engine.

The drive back to Ravello was slow. Outside Praiano, traffic was tailing back from the tunnel. He switched on the sound system, listened to Pablo Sáinz Villegas playing the adagio from Rodrigo's *Concierto de Aranjuez*.

He remembered an interview he'd seen, Pablo talking about music being an extension of his soul, an expression of his spirit, and he could hear it in every note Villegas was playing, could relate so strongly to that feeling. He shifted in his seat. What had Olivia said to him in Marcello's bar? *'I can see something in you when you're playing that feels... I don't know...like you're at home in your skin.'*

He smiled, remembering the way she'd watched him playing in the bar that first time, tears welling in her eyes when he'd played Fauré's *Pavane*…and afterwards on the street, her expression so soft and earnest… *'I'm not qualified to know if you're up to playing Carnegie Hall, but I can see how much you love music and I think that's why you feel restless after a gig...'*

That she'd been moved by his playing had touched him deeply, had made him want to kiss her, fuse his spirit with hers. He shifted in his seat again, realised he was chewing his thumb nail. The way he felt on Thursday afternoons—looking forward to playing. It was only a little set in a little bar but playing freed him in a way that nothing else did, and she could see it, had seen in it in him straight away. *'You should do more with it, chase the thing you love...'*

The traffic was moving now and as the car crawled through the tunnel he was breathing in fumes and Pablo's haunting guitar was echoing all around him and thoughts were flying through his head so fast that he almost couldn't keep up. As he drove out of the tunnel into the fresh air and blinding sunshine everything fell into place.

Liv wanted commitment, but she wanted something for him too. He could see it now—what she'd been trying to say. *'I'm talking about being true to yourself...'*

She wanted him to free himself—through his music. Not because she wanted him to forget Izzy or the past, but because she felt the greatest connection with him when he was playing—that was where she wanted them to begin. He'd been so blind. In Marcello's bar she'd even suggested he could run a similar place and he'd dismissed the idea out of hand. He'd upset her! That was why she'd left so suddenly.

This was something he could fix but words wouldn't be enough. He needed to make her feel it, needed to make a grand gesture…and then suddenly he couldn't stop himself from smiling because he knew exactly what he was going to do.

Olivia stared at the cardboard box on her bed. It had arrived a couple of days ago. She knew what was inside but she hadn't been able to face opening it until now. She cut through the plastic binder and slid the inner box from its cardboard sleeve. Slowly, she lifted the lid, felt a little gasp escaping from her lips. It was perfect. A whitewashed oak frame, four photographs side by side in sequence. Zach and Alessia singing the ant song! Animated faces, shining eyes and, in the last photo, eyes half-closed, both of them laughing hard. Just one of many happy memories of her Italian summer.

She closed the box, pressed her palms to her eyes. She hadn't seen much of him since their sightseeing day in Ravello. Instead of bringing them closer together, their

talk in the gardens had driven a wedge between them.
She'd been over their conversation a hundred times in
her head, realised how intractable she'd sounded, as if
she was delivering an ultimatum. She hadn't meant to
sound that way. When she'd said that she couldn't build
a new life with him if he was hanging onto the old one
it had been more a statement of fact than anything else,
but he'd clammed up after that and they'd driven home
nursing a troubled silence.

In the house he'd taken her hands in his, kissed her
on the cheek then walked down the hallway towards his
apartment. There'd been finality in that kiss, the sense
of a wall between them that she couldn't breach. She'd
turned and walked down the opposite hallway to her own
rooms, crying the whole way.

East. West. The house in between.

When she'd cried herself out, it came to her that at
least she'd spoken her mind, told Zach what she needed,
and there was something in that realisation that gave her
strength. Whatever happened next would be down to
him, and in the meantime there was work to do.

But work didn't stop her heart aching, didn't stop her
missing his smile. She took to meandering around the
house, hoping to run into him, but he was never around.
In a bolder moment she'd run upstairs to his office, was
about to knock on his door when she'd heard his voice
and realised that he was on the phone. She'd retreated,
taken herself for a walk in the garden and bumped into
Lucia. Lucia had told her he was busy making plans for a
new wedding venue and the news had lowered her spirits.

Perhaps she'd got him all wrong! Maybe he *was* a
businessman above everything else and she'd been reading things into his music because it was the only toehold

she could find, the only piece of him that didn't belong to Isabella.

If he was going ahead with a new wedding venue it meant he was choosing business over music; it meant that if she wanted to be part of his world she would have to fit in. She tried to imagine it but drew a blank. She would never be happy, never feel important enough if she was just another card slotted into the pack.

She picked up the cardboard box. The walls in his apartment were bare, pictures waiting to be hung. Perhaps he would put this one up at least. She'd take it to him. If he was there, maybe they could mend their fences, agree to be friends.

There was a heavy stillness in the house. A hush in the hallway. She tuned in to a far-off noise in the garden— a wheelbarrow moving over gravel. She could feel her heart drumming against her ribs, her stomach churning. If she was resigned to being just friends, then why was her heart beating double time at the thought of seeing him?

She stopped at his door, swallowed hard and knocked. She heard a door bang somewhere but it hadn't come from inside. The apartment was deadly quiet. She licked her lips and knocked again, harder this time, straining to hear any movement inside, but there was nothing. Deflated, she turned around and froze.

He was walking along the hallway towards her. He was wearing jeans and the tee shirt she liked and—he was smiling. 'I've been looking for you!'

She felt her heart exploding softly in her chest. She shifted on her feet, tried to breathe calmly. 'I was looking for you too…obviously…since I'm standing outside your door.' She gave a little shrug, held the box out towards him. 'I've got this. It's for you…and Alessia.'

His eyes were so full of light and warmth that it was hard to hold his gaze. 'A present? I'm excited—can I open it now?'

She couldn't help smiling. 'Of course.' She stepped aside so he could unlock the door then she followed him inside.

Alessia's doll's house was spread open on the sitting room floor, a clutter of miniature chairs and beds and dolls strewn around. Still no pictures on the walls. His guitar wasn't on its stand.

'Mind your feet. Tiny dolls are the choice weapon of any self-respecting three-year-old!' He flashed her a smile, put the box down onto the sofa. 'Now, what have we got here?' He seemed ridiculously happy. Surely it couldn't be just her present… Maybe he'd pulled off some big business deal.

She watched him lifting the lid, heard him catch his breath, watched his eyes flit along the row of pictures, and then he was turning to her, the look in his eyes making her dizzy.

'It's beautiful.' His voice sounded hoarse. He cleared his throat. 'I never expected…' He lifted the frame out of the box, held it at arm's length, looking at the pictures, smiling, just smiling.

She struggled to find her own voice. 'I'm glad you like it. I hope Alessia likes it too.'

'She'll love it, I know she will.' He put it down on the sofa. 'Thank you, Liv. It's such a lovely gift. We don't have many pictures taken together.' He looked around the room. 'You'll have to tell me where to hang it. I'm useless at things like that—it's why the walls are bare.'

She didn't need him to say the rest, that Isabella would have known where to hang their pictures, which light fittings would have looked best on the walls.

He ran a hand through his hair and stepped towards her. 'I was looking for you because I wanted to say sorry about the other day...'

'You don't have to be sorry.' She shrugged. 'We had to talk it out...' She felt his hands closing around hers, warm and tight. It wasn't what she was expecting.

'Sometimes words mess things up, don't you think?'

There was a mischievous glint in his eyes, something that was making her feel tingly inside. 'I suppose, but sometimes—' She felt his finger on her lips, a little warm pressure. She stopped talking, fought the urge to kiss his finger. He was looking at her and she could see a secret burning in his eyes, a little smile lifting the corners of his mouth.

'I want to show you something and, until I've shown you, will you promise not to say a word?'

The way he was looking at her was turning her inside out. She couldn't have said a word even if she'd wanted to. She nodded.

He smiled. 'Okay then... Let's go.'

As he drove she found it hard not to stare at him. She could feel the energy thrumming through him, see it in the way he was holding himself and in the way he moved. Shifting through the gears, steering around the bends. He was on fire and she was beside herself with curiosity, tingling from head to toe.

In Ravello he parked the car and took her hand. He led her through the narrow alley where she'd seen the lemons, past the tourist shops with their racks of postcards and shelves bursting with limoncello bottles. He sidestepped tourists, not hurrying, not dawdling but pulling her onwards. In the *piazza* someone stopped them to ask for directions and she caught herself chewing her bottom lip with frustration.

'Good luck. I hope you find it,' Zach was saying and then he looked at her, a twinkle in his eyes. 'Sorry about that…' His hand closed around hers again and he pulled her on across the *piazza*, then turned left, striding up a familiar road. Where the road forked, he led her onto the narrow walkway, the one next to the gardens where they'd had their talk and then a little distance beyond that he stopped. He was smiling at her, a little glint in his eye. She looked around, not sure what she was supposed to be looking for, and then she noticed a pair of heavy doors with a canopy above, folded back. She stepped closer. It looked like Marcello's bar, all closed up. She turned to face him, felt a frown creasing her forehead. Why had he brought her here?

He held her gaze, then slowly he pulled a key from his pocket and stepped towards the door. For some reason she was starting to cry and then she was laughing, and she wanted to say something but the words wouldn't come out, so she let him lead her inside and, inside, she could hardly believe her eyes. Thousands of tea lights were flickering on the tables in the dark recesses of the bar, and in the centre of the room, under the dome, there was a single chair, a microphone stand and his guitar.

He seated her at a table, touched her face gently. 'Don't say a word, remember,' and then he was settling himself onto the chair, lifting the guitar onto his lap. He plucked the strings softly, strummed a chord, then lifted his eyes to hers.

'Olivia Gardner, in this bar, which I now own jointly with Marcello Moretti, I am literally going to play my heart out for you.'

As his fingers moved over the strings, as she heard the first notes of Fauré's *Pavane*, she felt goosebumps rising on her arms and a hot thick mess of tears behind her eyes and she could hardly breathe because the music was so beautiful, and because her heart was so full of love for him.

As he played he was picturing her face the first time he'd seen it. She'd been looking down at him from the balcony at Kensall Manor. He could see in his mind the way her cheeks had lifted into a smile, that little blush, the way her eyes had glowed. Trapped in her gaze he'd felt at home, would have happily stayed there in the hall, just looking at her, and then he remembered her face as she got off the bus in Ravello, excited eyes, wide smile... running her hand over the wing of his car, mischievous... and their water fight, that demon glint in her eye as she'd stepped towards him with the brimming plastic teapot, Alessia's throaty laughter echoing off the walls. The way she'd looked on the boat, hair blowing, her eyes laying him bare...their first kiss.

He put it all into the music, felt as if he was playing his own heartstrings, and he wanted her to feel it in the depth of her soul because the music could say it so much better than his words ever could. When he played the final note and lifted his eyes, her hands were pressed to her face, which was wet with tears. Perhaps she'd heard every word he'd been playing. He put the guitar down and stood up.

She was getting to her feet, wiping her eyes with her

hands, smiling through a fresh wave of tears. 'I don't know what to say, Zach. That was so beautiful—all of this is beautiful.' She stepped closer, looked around then turned back to him. 'You actually *bought* the bar?'

'Half of it, strictly speaking—Marcello's brother's share.'

'When?'

He smiled. 'The day before yesterday.' She started to speak, seemed to be struggling to find words so he carried on. 'It took me a while to work everything out—but what you said to me in the gardens, about running a wedding empire... Well, you were right! It doesn't excite me—'

'But... Lucia said you've bought another wedding venue!'

'We are—in the process of, anyway, but if the sale goes through there's a manager in place. My involvement will be minimal.' He took a step towards her. 'I was on my way back from the viewing when I started thinking about music and all the things you said—and all the things I said—and I started to see that maybe there was a way to have it all.' He closed the distance between them and took her hands in his. 'You reminded me how alive I feel when I'm playing. It's a feeling I don't get from running the business, but I'm never going to play Carnegie Hall and I wouldn't want to anyway. I like my life here.'

He felt a smile tugging at his lips. 'But Ravello *is* the city of music—and, as I was driving home, I remembered Marcello saying he might have to give this place up—and suddenly I had this crazy idea. So I stopped in to have a chat with him and, before I knew it, we were planning a guest list of musicians, talking about adding a mezzanine floor. With such extensive plans in place, it seemed only proper to make him an offer for his brother's half.'

'Zach, please tell me that you haven't done all this for me.'

Her serious tone threw him for a moment and then he saw in her eyes what she was saying. He lifted a hand to her face, traced his thumb over her cheekbone. 'No, I did it for myself because music is what I love, and I did it for you because you asked me to be true to myself.'

She leaned in to his hand, smiled softly. 'That's the right answer.'

He gazed at her, saw the love light in her eyes mingling with the flickering flames of a thousand tea lights, and he knew that this was the right moment. 'Liv, I know we haven't known each other that long, but from the first moment I saw you I felt a connection.' He smiled. 'I know things haven't been easy but I think we've got potential, don't you?'

'Potential?'

'I want you to stay… I want you to help me hang my pictures, I want you to teach Alessia more silly songs, and I want to play my guitar for you every night.' A tear was rolling down her cheek. He followed it with his thumb, gently pushed it away. 'I love you. I want you to marry me… Will you marry me, Olivia?'

Her eyes were glistening now…and she was pressing her lips together, and then a little smile broke through and she was laughing and crying… 'Yes, yes, I will.'

He felt a wave of relief followed by a wave of euphoria. He pulled her into his arms, swung her around and laughed. 'You've really got to stop crying now because I want to kiss you.'

CHAPTER ELEVEN

Eight months later...

'STEP AWAY FROM the window, darling—the light's too harsh.'

'I told you it would be—it always works best over there, near the wardrobe.'

Ralph lowered his camera and mock-scowled. 'And so the pupil becomes the master!'

'You were a good teacher.' She spun round, took up position in front of the large mahogany wardrobe and struck a pose. 'Thanks for stepping up, Ralph. I'm no good on this side of the camera and if I have to go through it I'd rather go through it with you than anyone else.' She looked down at the bouquet in her hands then looked up and smiled.

'Keep it! Don't move, darling—you look amazing.'

She laughed. 'I know for a fact you say that to all your brides.'

'Ah! But today I mean it. You *do* look amazing—but you need to stop talking so we can get the job done.'

She smiled, turned this way and that, lifted her chin, dropped her shoulder, perched on the bed, looked lovingly into the lens, laughed over and over again, mostly for real because it felt weird.

He put the camera down, glanced at his watch and wiped his forehead on his shirt sleeve. 'Where's your father?'

'He's on his way.' She put a hand on his arm. 'Ralph, I want you to relax. It's a very informal wedding—just take happy pictures, okay. They don't need to be perfect.'

A knock on the door made her jump.

Ralph lifted an eyebrow. 'It looks like you need to take your own advice!'

She couldn't deny that she was jittery. If she wasn't such a bag of nerves she'd have been laughing at herself. All those years dreaming of this day, and now all she wanted was to skip to the part where Zach was beside her, holding her hand. She crossed the room and opened the door.

'Dad!'

He seemed to sway a bit at the sight of her and then she could see a tell-tale glisten at the edge of his eyes, could feel her own welling up.

'Oh, Liv...' His mouth was wobbling. 'You look—'

She swallowed hard, flowed into his arms. 'Dad, will you stop it—you're setting me off.' He was holding her in his big bear hug and even the new fabric smell of his wedding day suit couldn't mask the comforting scent of him that she remembered from childhood, from all the times he'd held her like this before. She closed her eyes, let the moment linger...

After the dust had settled from Zach's proposal and after she'd completed her last wedding shoot, she'd gone back to England to tell her mum and dad she was getting married. She'd spent time with her mum in Sussex, then stayed for a week with her dad in North Wales.

Mending their fences had been easier than she imagined. They'd talked about the past, but mostly they'd got on with living in the present. He'd taken her swimming in another freezing sea, and afterwards there'd been hot chocolate out of a dented old flask. He'd marched her to the top of Mount Snowdon and back down again. In the pub he'd got steamed up about plastic pollution and global warming, talked about petitions and about what was going on in the Green Party and she'd listened, felt his passion and fury, potent as ever.

Suddenly she became aware of Ralph clicking away and she stepped out of her dad's arms, but he kept a hold of her shoulders, looked at her with a little glimmer of inkling in his eyes. 'You're glowing, Liv,' and then he beamed, dropped his hands and rifled in his pockets for a handkerchief.

She felt a little colour rising in her cheeks, glanced at Ralph, but he was busy positioning her bouquet on a table near the window so he could take a picture of it. 'It's my wedding day, Dad—of course I'm glowing. I'm happy!' She smoothed the front of her dress, cleared her throat. 'Now, are you absolutely sure about walking me up the aisle? I know it's not really your bag.'

'It's what you want that counts.' He mopped his eyes and smiled. 'It's your day, and I'm here for you... I'll always be here for you.'

She could feel a lump thickening in her throat, laughed as she snatched a tissue from a box on the table. 'You're going to have to stop saying things like that or I'll have to get the make-up artist to come back.'

The door rattled, opened jerkily and Alessia's face appeared in the gap. Her little mouth stiffened for a moment, eyes widened, and then she ran over, wrapped her arms around Olivia's legs.

'You look *so* pretty!'

'And so do you! Very pretty. Has Daddy seen you in your dress yet?'

Alessia shook her head, spoke in a theatrical whisper. 'No! Nonna said it had to be a surprise.'

Olivia laughed, bent down to kiss her. As she felt Alessia's arms sliding around her neck she thought about Izzy, how she had never felt her own daughter's embrace, and she closed her eyes to let the sadness wash over her and subside. It was strange, she thought, how much she'd opened her heart and mind to Izzy after Zach had made his grand gesture, after he'd asked her to marry him. The house had settled into being a home, no more east and west.

Absently, she started pulling out the skirt of Alessia's dress, the pale lemon silk rustling in her fingers. She'd found little soft shoes to match and Alessia had declared that they were *dancing shoes*. Now Alessia was busy pointing her toes, sketching out a little dance on the spot as Olivia fanned out the skirt and pulled the petticoats straight. The hairstylist had woven the same little yellow flowers and Gypsophila into Alessia's hair that she was wearing in her own and the final result was perfect. Zach was going to be even more smitten with his daughter than he already was.

Zach! The love of her life. Just the thought of him was enough to make her heart leap with joy. She pictured his face, the way the little lines around his eyes crinkled when he smiled, the blue of his irises sparkling like sunlight and starlight mixed together.

He and Marcello had done so well with the bar. They'd commissioned Milo to design and put in a mezzanine, and they'd added a few other refinements: a new canopy for the entrance, adjustable lighting. They'd rebranded the place, called it Pavane, which had made her smile. She'd taken the photographs, built a website, while they focused on forward-booking a succession of guest musicians. The official launch had been a nerve-racking success and Zach had been walking on air ever since...

Suddenly she realised that Alessia had stopped dancing and was staring at her. She smiled, checked the sash at the back of Alessia's dress and stood up.

Ralph had her bouquet in his hands, passed it to her. 'Right, you two, let's grab some pictures and then it'll be show time.'

'Today, Olivia, I join my life to yours, not only as your husband but as your friend, your lover and your confidant...' His voice was clear, self-assured. She could feel the warmth of his hands around hers, the warmth of the spring sunshine on her back, and in his eyes she could see so many things—love, trust, honesty. Desire. 'I want to be the shoulder you lean on, the rock on which you rest, the companion of your life.' She watched his lips moving, felt his words settling into her heart. He paused, smiled softly. 'From this day forward I will walk beside you. My path is now your path. I am yours, for ever.'

The celebrant was turning to her now, giving her a little nod. She felt a smile tugging at her lips, a little lump in her throat as she fastened her eyes on his.

'Zach...what can I say that I haven't already said? What can I give to you that I haven't already given? My body, my mind, my soul and my heart. They're all yours.' His eyes were glistening. She felt a tear sliding down her cheek. 'Everything that I have. Everything that I am belongs to you from this day forward.' She had to stop again. The depth of emotion she could see in his eyes was almost too much to bear. She felt his hands squeezing hers and she took a big breath. 'And I promise that I shall be yours for ever. I will follow you anywhere you go, everywhere you lead me to. Hand in hand. Heart in heart.'

For a moment she lost herself in his eyes and then the celebrant was asking for the rings and Zach was gazing at her, sliding a ring onto her finger, and then she was pushing a ring onto his and there was a blessing, and she could smell the scent of fresh cut grass and the fragrance of the flowering wisteria but all she could see was him... and then he was taking her face in his hands and she felt his mouth on hers, warm and perfect, and he didn't pull away but kissed her slowly, a long kiss that made the ground sway beneath her feet, and she could hear the guests clapping and laughing, a random 'whoop' and then he broke away, still gazing at her. She saw his lips moving silently, 'I love you,' felt her heart caving in her chest, her cheeks aching with a smile.

And then suddenly Alessia skipped forward and looked up. 'Papà. That was yucky!'

Zach walked to the edge of the terrace and leaned on the parapet. He needed a moment to take it all in, to acclimatise to his happiness. Somehow he was here again on his wedding day, surrounded by family and friends. He looked down at his left hand, rotated the new platinum ring on his finger. Married! He'd thought it would never happen again. He felt a little smile growing on his lips and looked up. Olivia was mingling with their guests, her eyes glowing, cheeks dimpled in endless smiles. He watched her, bathed in the surge of love and admiration he felt for her.

She was talking to Milo. She had her hand on Milo's arm and their faces were animated, and then Milo was pulling her into an embrace, kissing her cheek, and she was laughing, kissing him back. He remembered how mad with jealousy he'd been when he'd thought... That seemed such a long time ago. He shifted his gaze to the man at Milo's side. His name was Luca, a musician Milo had met at Pavane. The bar seemed to bring people together somehow...

Going into business with Marcello had been a good decision. He was playing more regularly now—playing with other musicians too—living just enough of the old dream to feel energised. And the bar was getting great reviews on the Web, becoming known for its eclectic mix of acts, for being a platform for up-and-coming musicians. It felt great, giving new people a chance to be heard. Ravello—the city of music—the perfect place for a music venue. He was so grateful to Olivia for giving him a nudge in the right direction.

Lucia was walking towards his parents, her new friend Massimo at her side. Zach looked down at his feet to hide his amusement. Liv had guessed ages ago that Lucia had a suitor but she'd kept it to herself, dropped mischievous hints now and again. He'd been the last to know.

He looked up again. Lucia was talking to his mother. His father was sitting in a chair bouncing Alessia on his knee. She was showing him her dancing shoes, talking nineteen to the dozen he could tell. He liked seeing them together, could already see how Alessia could wrap her grandfather around her little finger. It made him chuckle. He'd never learned that art, but at least his father was delighted with Villa Fiori, pleased with the manager, Lorenzo. The bookings were promising for the coming year and the next year would be even better. Casa Isabella was already booked to capacity—that was why he and Olivia had set a date at the end of March—it had been the only free Saturday in spring.

He'd half-expected her to choose somewhere else to get married but, if anything, she seemed fonder of the house now than she'd ever been. It was as if she'd bonded with Izzy somehow—and she'd melted his heart when she'd said that Izzy was family, that if they married somewhere else then it would be like shutting Izzy out.

They'd had their ceremony in the garden, not on the terrace. Olivia was especially fond of the shady little garden rooms, the arched folly with its rampant clambering wisteria, and they were a small gathering of immediate family and friends so the space had felt intimate. Perfect.

'Are you okay, Zach?'

He turned and smiled. Lucia had joined him, elegant in her red dress. 'Yes. I'm happy—what about you? Are you okay?'

She linked her arm through his. 'Yes. I'm fine. A little sad, but I'm very, very happy for you and Olivia. She's… she's good for you, Zach, and Alessia loves her so much.'

He felt a lump rising in his throat and nodded.

Lucia drew in a breath, looked over the terrace then lifted her eyes to the house. 'I think Isabella is at peace now, knowing that you are loved and that Alessia has a mamma. I feel her, you know…and I think she's happy today.'

Zach looked down, saw that Lucia's eyes were wet. He put his arm around her shoulders, pulled her against him. 'I couldn't have managed without you, you know that, don't you? You've been a tower of strength for me and for Alessia and I want to thank you from the bottom of my heart.'

She sniffed, sighed a little. 'You helped me too, Zach. Letting me stay here, letting me look after Alessia—it helped. Being useful took my mind off things a little bit...'

He shifted his gaze back to the terrace, watched Olivia talking to her mum and dad. Family. It was so important. He was glad she'd made up with her dad. He could see how close they were, could see it in their eyes and in their body language as they chatted.

Olivia turned her face, caught his eye, lit up as if she had a little beacon inside. The way she looked in her ivory silk dress, the simple neckline sitting just below her collarbone, the soft fabric flowing around her legs as she moved. He wanted to take her into a quiet part of the garden, pull her close, kiss her slowly, deeply, feel her body pressed against his. The thought of it was making him dizzy.

'You should go to her, Zach. I can tell you want to... and the way she's looking at you—she wants you too.' Lucia patted his arm. 'Go...go!'

He kissed Lucia's cheek then walked to Olivia's side. He slipped his arm around her waist, leaned in to her ear. 'I'd like to spend some time alone with my wife.'

Her breath warmed his cheek. 'You must have been reading my mind.'

'Let's go!' He lifted two glasses of champagne from a passing tray, handed her one and led her into the garden, through the shady rooms she loved. At the folly where they'd exchanged their vows he stopped, turned to face her.

She had the strangest look in her eye, a warm, glowing, secret look which was turning him inside out. He reached for her hand. 'Have you any idea how lovely you look? How happy you've made me today?'

She smiled. 'So you couldn't be happier…?'

'No! I absolutely couldn't.' He lifted his glass, touched it to hers. 'Here's to you, my beautiful, amazing wife.' He put the glass to his lips, felt the cool champagne tingling on his tongue, then realised suddenly that she hadn't moved. She was looking at him, glass in hand. He felt a frown creasing his forehead. 'What's wrong, Liv?'

She looked down at her feet, seemed to be smiling, and then she looked up. 'I can't drink this.'

'Why—?' The word escaped from his lips a nano-second before the penny dropped and then he was staring at her, looking into her eyes, just to make sure he'd got it right. He swallowed, found his voice. 'You're—? No! We're—?'

She was smiling and nodding, her eyes sparkling. 'Yes!'

He felt the glass slipping from his fingers, heard it land on the grass. 'When did you—? How…?'

'A couple of days ago—I've been so busy with the wedding that I hadn't noticed I was late.' He watched as she put her glass down on the folly step. 'I'm only six weeks. As to how—' She pulled a thinking face. 'I think you know!'

'So you couldn't be happier?'

Just moments ago she'd asked him that, and now he thought he might actually burst. Slowly, he reached his hands to her waist, looked at the way her dress fell straight down over her flat stomach. He dropped to his knees, kissed the place where the new life was growing, whispered, 'Hello, baby.'

And then he felt Olivia's fingers in his hair and he remembered why he'd wanted to be alone with her.

He stood up, cupped her face tenderly in his hands and kissed her slowly, deeply. He felt her body rising to his and then he was losing himself in the warm smell of her skin, the scent of her perfume and the fragrance of wisteria drifting on the gentle breeze.

* * * * *

HER HOMECOMING WISH

JO McNALLY

To first responders everywhere
who balance family and personal lives against
their stressful jobs, and who carry the weight
of people's expectations every day.

Thank you.

Chapter One

How could a liquor store owner not have any booze
in his house?

Mackenzie Wallace kept opening and closing her
dad's kitchen cabinets as if she hadn't searched each
and every one already. Hell, she'd even checked the
bedroom closets and the cabinet in the laundry room.

She did *not* want to go downstairs to her father's
liquor store in the middle of the night.

But she *did* want a glass of scotch.

And Dad's apartment was dry as a bone.

There was no sense procrastinating. She grabbed
the keys hanging by the back door. Dad's old gray
hoodie also hung there, worn and faded. Mack
looked down at her purple pajama shorts and green
cotton camisole. No one would see her in the dark,

wee hours of the morning, but she was still a little *too* naked for venturing outside. The hoodie barely fell past the hem of her shorts, but at least it covered her almost see-through top. And it would protect her from the cool night air. It might be the end of April, but in the Catskill Mountains of New York, that could mean snow flurries as easily as daffodils.

If nothing else, she'd have a great story to tell Dad when she visited him at the hospital tomorrow morning. No, later *this* morning. Ugh. She needed some serious sleep after too many hours packing, driving and unpacking in one day. Surely a glass of Dad's top-shelf scotch would do the trick. All she had to do was let herself into the liquor store and find it.

She'd watched her brother do it dozens of times when they were kids. As much as she'd tried to distance herself from Ryan's bad behavior, he'd pressed her into lookout duty more than once—a nervous ten-year-old standing outside the door, praying no one would come by. *Especially* Mom and Dad. Young Mackenzie could never bear the thought of disappointing her parents. And look at her now—slinking back to her childhood home as a bitter divorced woman in need of booze.

She side-eyed her reflection in the small mirror by the back door—put there by her mom, who'd never had a hair out of place when she left the apartment. Mom, who'd been gone so many years now, would definitely *not* approve of Mackenzie's appearance *or* her behavior. Mack raised her chin. As much as Mack had adored her late mother, she didn't want to

be her. Not anymore. Her days of living up to someone else's standards were *over*.

She tucked her unruly hair behind her ears and
slipped her feet back into her bright red leather flats.
If the ladies of Glenfadden Country Club could only
see her now. Mack snorted, talking to the large orange tabby cat watching her from the armchair, "As
if we care what that group of two-faced Connecticut
snobs think anymore, right?"

Her cat, Rory, meowed in response, casting a ma-
levolent gaze around the apartment. He was clearly
ticked off about being stuffed into a canvas cat car-
rier for the four-hour drive from Greenwich. Mack
walked over and scratched the top of his head. The
Maine coon cat was as big as a small dog. Her ex-
husband hated him. But it was Rory's attitude of
fierce independence that drew Mack to him in the
shelter two years ago. Maybe she'd had a premoni-
tion that she'd need a tough friend, and Rory was
it. He tried to ignore her touch in true Rory fashion, but he couldn't disguise the purr that rumbled
in his chest. She grinned. "You stay here and guard
the place. I'll be right back."

The closest full-time residents in the row of shops
and apartments in downtown Gallant Lake lived
three doors down and were surely sound asleep. Still,
she tiptoed down the stairs outside the back door. The
metal fire escape stretched the length of the block
on the second level, connecting the buildings. Stairs
to the parking lot were spaced along the walkway.
She was going to a ridiculous length for a drink, but

now that it was on her mind, she couldn't turn back. It would only take her a few minutes to grab a bottle of Macallan and get back upstairs.

She used the back door to the store, knowing she'd be able to find her way through the familiar space without needing to search for any light switches that might attract attention at 2:00 a.m. The door opened easily, letting out a low groan as it swung closed. She waited, then let out a long sigh of relief at the silence that followed. Didn't look like Dad ever installed that alarm system he kept threatening to buy.

She'd just let herself into her father's store without permission, barely dressed, sneaking around as if she was some kind of thief. She couldn't help feeling a little thrill at doing something so out of character. She had every right to be here, of course, but it still felt deliciously naughty.

She used the flashlight app on her phone to work her way around the boxes in the back hall and into the store itself. And that's where her plan took a turn. Her father may not have installed an alarm, but he'd completely rearranged the store in the year since she'd been home. There were three café tables and a bunch of stools pushed together in the back corner of the store, and the display shelves had been rearranged. More space was devoted to wine now, which was a change she definitely approved of, but where was the top-shelf liquor that used to be displayed back here?

Working her way down the aisle with her phone light, she found the gin and vodka. She wasn't looking to make cocktails, so she kept going, being careful not to bump into the displays on the endcaps. A car drove by slowly outside—probably some poor soul heading home from working the night shift somewhere. She found the good stuff behind the checkout counter.

"Sorry, Dad," she whispered. Hopefully, he'd forgive her for helping herself to store inventory. It was a small price to pay for bringing her back to Gallant Lake ahead of schedule. She'd really been hoping for a few weeks on a beach somewhere before she swallowed her pride and moved back home with Dad to figure out her next steps. It wasn't as if Dad planned on falling off that ladder, but it *had* succeeded in giving him what he'd wanted—one of his children running the family business. At least for now.

Well played, Dad.

She tore the wax seal from the bottle and tugged the top off. Reaching under the counter, she found the heavy crystal tumblers Dad always kept handy for after-hours tastings with friends. Her phone sat on the counter near the cash register, light shining upward, casting soft shadows, but the old-fashioned streetlights on Main Street spread enough light into the store that she didn't need it. Those lights were new, and she liked the quaint atmosphere they created in the village. The rim of the glass had just touched her lips when she heard the muted groan of the back door closing.

No. It couldn't be. She'd locked it. She was *sure* she'd locked the door. But that was definitely the same sound the door made when she'd come into the store. A hot flush of adrenaline washed under her skin, spiking her heart rate to the point where it threatened to jump straight out of her chest. Would the intruder be able to hear it? Because there was no doubt in her mind—there *was* an intruder. Someone had just let themselves into the store in darkness. Time seemed to slow as she listened to what were definitely soft footsteps coming down the hall.

Now what? Hide? Run? Scream? No. She'd vowed to herself on the drive over here from Greenwich that she was done acting meek and playing nice. This was Wallace Liquors. She was Mackenzie Wallace, and she wasn't going to let some low-life criminal mess with her family's business.

She swallowed the scream still threatening to break free. She needed a plan. A fast one, because there was another footstep. Damn it, she wasn't good at thinking on the fly. Good girls who never got in trouble didn't need escape plans. Her shoulders straightened. Good thing she wasn't a good girl anymore, wasn't it? She took a quick inventory.

Her phone was only a few feet away, but with the flashlight app still on, it would send a beam of light moving around and draw the intruder's attention to her location. Calling 911 would mean speaking aloud, again exposing her to the bastard who'd dared to enter her father's store while Dad was lying in a hospital bed. Fear began to morph into rage. She pulled the hood up over her long blond hair and toed off her shoes for silence. Logical or not, she couldn't help thinking the element of surprise was her greatest advantage.

What would Dad do in this situation? She reached under the counter and smiled. There it was. Dad's old baseball bat, suspended on brackets. He'd always called it his "burglar alarm." Mack slowly lifted and removed the bat. This would at least give her a chance. If she scared him away, or even incapacitated him a little, she'd have time to call for help. Or run.

She crept toward the back corner by the hallway. This was just the perfect end to a far-from-perfect day. *Focus, Mackenzie.* She heard one footstep. Another. He was at the end of the hall. The beam of a flashlight cut into the darkness. If she didn't move now, he'd see her with his next step. She raised the bat, breathed a quick prayer and stepped forward, swinging with every ounce of strength she had.

There was a sharp, shouted curse, and the next thing she knew, she was being slammed against the wall so hard she saw stars. The bat was wrenched out of her hand, her body spun to face the wall, her arm twisted so high behind her back she was sure it was going to break. Something hard and cold touched her neck, directly under her ear. Her bad day just got a whole lot worse. For the first time, it occurred to her that this could be her *last* day.

Was this really what her final moment on this earth would be like? Half-dressed, defending her dad's liquor store in freaking Gallant Lake, New York? It hardly seemed fair. Her vision blurred, but she refused to pass out and let this jerk have his way without a fight. *Focus!*

In between some of the harshest swear words she'd ever heard, she heard some others that refused to compute.

"Don't move, you son of a…"

Swear. Swear. Swear.

"Give me your other hand."

Swear. Swear. Swear.

"You're under arrest, pal."

Wait.

What?

She tried to make eye contact, but he had her face pressed so tightly to the wall she could hardly breathe, much less move.

"*Arrest?* Wait, no… Are you…a cop?"

There was no humor in his responding laughter. "Yeah, it's your lucky night. Breaking and entering *and* assaulting a police officer. You picked the wrong town…"

Mack gathered the deepest breath she could, blinking back tears at the pain in her arms.

"I'm not a *thief*! This is my *father's* store! I didn't break into anything. I used a *key*!"

A thick, tense blanket of silence fell on the hallway. Not a sound. No breathing. No movement. Finally, the pressure on her arms and against her chest eased. He stepped back half a step. The man's voice went from cold and commanding to incredulous.

"Mac*kenzie*?"

Deputy Sheriff Dan Adams willed his heart to fall back into a steady rhythm again, but the damn thing wouldn't cooperate. He'd expected to confront some dumb-ass teens looking for trouble in Carl's store. The whole town knew about Carl's fall from a ladder. The popular local businessman had ended up with broken ribs and a badly broken ankle. Dan figured some punk was taking advantage of Carl's situation to get some free booze or easy drug money. The one thing he didn't expect? Seeing the distinctive dark shape of a baseball bat whipping toward his face.

At that point, his training took over. He went through the motions without a lot of thought. Other than thinking he was royally pissed off.

Disarm the perpetrator. Subdue him. Restrain him.

Express extreme displeasure with the perp's behavior.

Throw him in the car and haul him to jail.

And then the perpetrator spoke. A *woman* spoke. And claimed to be Carl's daughter.

Well, son of a…

Carl only had one girl.

Dan reached up and tugged at the hood, uncovering a tumble of thick blond hair.

Mackenzie freakin' Wallace.

He'd just held a nightstick to the head of Mackenzie Wallace. Little Mack. The sweet baby sister of his best friend in high school. She was still faceplanted against the wall, probably afraid to move, even though he'd released her. That was when the old protective feeling kicked in, along with a flood of horror at how many ways this could have gone seriously wrong.

"Jeez, Mack, what the hell?" Dan turned her around. "I could have *killed* you. You know that, right? What the fu...what are you doing here?"

She stared at him, wide-eyed. "*Danny?* Danny Adams?"

He spread his hands. "I go by Deputy Sheriff Adams these days."

That didn't seem to compute.

"You're a cop? *You?*"

As Dan studied the look on her face, he couldn't blame her for whatever mix of anger and shock she was feeling. If he'd seen teenage him do some of the things she had seen growing up, he wouldn't believe it, either. But that was a different time. A different Dan. He took another step back, but he had to ask.

"Mackenzie, seriously." He looked down at long, bare legs. "Are you *naked* under that hoodie? What are you doing in here at two o'clock in the morning?"

Her voice chilled. "What are *you* doing in here at two o'clock in the morning, Deputy Sheriff Adams? Besides assaulting innocent women on their own damn property?"

He understood why she was ticked off. He'd scared her. But he hadn't done anything wrong. "I drove by, saw someone moving around in here with a flashlight and investigated. Your dad gave me a key years ago. I had no idea you were back in town."

"I didn't know I had to check in with the sheriff when I arrived." Sharp words, but some of the fire left her voice. Mackenzie rubbed her wrist, and Dan felt a stab of guilt.

"I'm sorry, Mack. You had the hood up, I had no way of knowing..."

"Was that a gun I felt against my neck?"

"Was that a baseball bat I saw swinging at my face?"

She gave a short laugh, and Dan felt something shift a little in his chest. It was the husky laughter of a grown woman, not the giggle of the cute little pig-tailed girl from his memories. She nodded, running her fingers through her hair to push it off her face.

"Fair enough. I couldn't get to sleep, and Dad didn't have any good stuff upstairs. So I figured I'd pull a Ryan and help myself."

"That's definitely something your brother would do." Dan frowned into the darkness. Ryan and Mack had always been as different as night and day, with Mackie being the Goody Two-shoes to Ryan's wild ways.

"I don't suppose you can join me while you're on duty?"

"Join...?"

"There's an open bottle of very expensive scotch on the counter, just waiting for someone to enjoy it." She laughed again, softly this time. "And I'd *really* like to hear the story of how Danger Dan turned into a lawman."

Dan grimaced. He hated that stupid nickname Ryan made up, especially coming from Mack. Even if he *had* earned it back then.

"Is your husband waiting upstairs?" Dan wasn't sure where that question came from, but, to be fair, all Mack ever talked about was leaving Gallant Lake, having a big wedding and a bigger house. The girl had goals, and from what he'd heard, she'd reached every one of them.

"I don't have a husband anymore." She brushed past him and headed toward the counter. "So are you joining me or not?"

Dan glanced at his watch, not sure how to digest that information. "I'm off duty in fifteen minutes."

Her long hair swung back and forth as she walked ahead of him. So did her hips. *Damn.*

"And you're all about following the rules now? You really have changed. Pity. I guess I'm drinking my first glass alone. You'll just have to catch up."

He frowned. Mackenzie had been strong willed, but never sassy. Never the type to sneak into her father's store alone for an after-hours drink. Not the type to taunt him. Not the type to break the rules.

Looked like he wasn't the only one who'd changed since high school.

Chapter Two

Mack willed her hand not to shake as she poured two fingers of Macallan into a second glass and slid it across the counter in Dan's general direction. He hadn't moved from his spot at the end of the hall, where he stood—watching. *Damn.* Danny Adams.

Danny, of the dragon tats, hard-drinking and wrong-side-of-the-law escapades in high school. Danny, who'd spent most of his waking hours upstairs with her brother, Ryan. Smoking pot and playing stupid video games in Ryan's room. If they weren't hanging out upstairs, they were racing around the countryside in Ryan's souped-up Nissan, looking for trouble. And one night, they'd found it. At least, Ryan had.

She'd lost track of him after the accident. Ryan

had been in the hospital for ages, and she didn't remember Dan coming around much. Then there was the trial. Then Mom got sick. And the life hits just kept on coming, until Mack finally made her escape from Gallant Lake, burning all her bridges on the way out.

Now she was back. And there was Dan. In a sheriff's uniform. Never saw *that* coming.

"Are your fifteen minutes up yet?" She gestured toward his glass. "I doubt your boss is wandering the streets to check up on you…"

Dan held his wide-brimmed hat in one hand and ran the other through his sandy brown hair. He stared at her like he'd just stumbled across a unicorn.

"It's not about getting caught, Mackie. It's about being responsible. If I get a call in the next few minutes, I need to be ready." Well, wasn't he a good little scout? He looked around the store. "How's your dad?"

"Tired and grumpy, but on the mend. You're really going to count down to your quitting time before you drink? The Danny Adams I knew would have crawled over broken glass to get to alcohol."

A weird shadow crossed over his face before he leveled a pointed hazel-eyed gaze at her. This was clearly his stern law enforcement officer face. "One—I'm *not* the Danny Adams you knew. High school was over twenty years ago. Two—don't call me Danny. Ever. Three—I'm a sheriff's deputy, and I take my job seriously. I'd like to keep it. Of *course* I'm not going to drink on duty."

She leveled a gaze right back at him, but her fingernails were tapping rapidly on the counter. She'd known Dan since she was in grade school. Hell, she'd *crushed* on him back when his hair was long and shaggy and his attitude had been pure bad boy. But he'd never stopped being Danny, the kid who'd roughed her hair and thrown popcorn at her during movie nights. Cop face or not, he wasn't going to intimidate her now. She took a long, slow sip of scotch. "Tell you what—I'll try not to call you Danny if you'll promise not to remind me how long ago we met."

He nodded, his mouth sliding into a half grin. Some of the tension left his stance, and she realized her own fingers had stopped their nervous tapping. The adrenaline rush of their violent encounter was fading for both of them. Dan walked toward the counter, his eye on the very expensive scotch. He glanced at his watch, then up at her.

"It really has been a long damn time since we first met, Mack. A lifetime ago. You were just a kid."

"So were you. And you just failed your promise… *Danny.*" He rolled his eyes, reminding her again of that high school kid he'd been. He and Ryan met in freshman detention and became fast friends. Mack was in…she paused to think. "Oh, my God, I was in fifth grade when you and Ryan became partners in crime. How is that even possible?"

Dan propped his hip against the counter across from her. Now that they were closer and the lights were on, she could see the deep lines next to his eyes.

As if he'd seen a lot of sun. Or a lot of trouble. He was looking at the counter, but she had a feeling he was a million miles away.

"Are you okay?"

His head rose sharply at the question. "Why do you ask?"

"I don't know. You look tired or stressed or something."

Dan grunted in response. "Or something." He looked at his watch, closed his eyes briefly, then reached for the glass of amber liquid. He downed it in one gulp, then gave a loud sigh of satisfaction. "Not my usual end-of-shift choice, but you can never go wrong with Macallan." She held up the bottle to pour a refill, but he shook his head. "I may be off shift, but I'm in uniform."

With a start, she realized she had no idea what kind of life Dan Adams lived these days. He wasn't wearing a ring, but that might be an in-uniform thing. The guy had to be almost forty, so he probably had a wife and family. She took in his intense composure, his square jaw, broad shoulders and calm—if tired—eyes. Yes, this looked like a man with a Sunday school teacher of a wife, a couple kids and probably a dog, too. She couldn't help thinking that was a damn shame. She splashed more scotch in her own glass and lifted it in a mock toast.

"I don't have that problem, since all I have to do is crawl up the stairs. Did you settle down with anyone I know?"

He lowered his brow. "Settle down? Oh, you mean

family? I married Susanne Buckley. You might have known her—she was between our grades, a couple years behind me. Cheerleader. Class president. Homecoming queen."

Mack started to laugh. "*You* landed a homecoming queen? With your reputation? How did her parents let *that* happen?" She had a vague memory of Susanne—cute, perky and popular. No match for Danger Dan.

That odd shadow crossed his face again. He didn't seem to like being reminded of his teen adventures. "We didn't get together until after college, so her parents couldn't do anything about it." His voice dropped so low she barely heard him. "But it didn't stop them from trying."

Silence fell in the store again. Her long day started to catch up with her, and she couldn't stifle the yawn that came out of nowhere. Dan straightened with a smile.

"It's late…or should I say early? Between our little adventure and the booze you've had, I'm guessing you'll get to sleep now." He started to turn away, then stopped. "It wasn't a gun, by the way."

"What?"

"You asked me before if you felt a gun to your head. It was my baton. Cops don't make a habit of blowing people's heads off for burglary."

She considered that for a moment before nodding solemnly. "Good to know. But that *was* a baseball bat I was swinging."

He huffed out a laugh. "Never thought I'd see the

day when sweet little Mackie would try to take me out with her daddy's bat."

"I'm done being sweet little Mackie, Dan. Being sweet got me nowhere."

The truth was, she hadn't ever *been* sweet. She'd acted the part, but only as a means to an end—to make other people think better of her. Being that calculated couldn't really be *sweet*, could it? It certainly hadn't made her a lot of friends. And it didn't help her hold on to a husband.

Dan studied her, and she had a feeling he was trying to put together a profile, cop-style. Trying to figure her out. *Good luck with that.* His slanted smile returned. "It got you back to Gallant Lake, helping your dad. That's exactly what I'd expect from the sweet little Mackie I knew."

She grimaced. It wasn't like she'd had anywhere else to go. Mason had kept both the house and the condo in the divorce. She hadn't had the stomach to fight him. She'd taken the cash and left. She lifted her chin. "I'm turning over a new leaf. One that doesn't include 'little.'" She gestured down to her well-rounded figure. "And especially doesn't include 'sweet.'"

He pursed his lips, tilting his head to the side with a skeptical grin. "Yeah. Okay. Whatever you say. Get some sleep, and don't forget to lock up after I go. In fact..." He picked her phone up from the counter and handed it to her. "Unlock it." She followed his order without question, not realizing she'd done so until he was taking the phone back from her and started tapping. "Here's my number. Text me when you're locked in upstairs."

"Yes, sir. Officer, sir." She gave him a mock salute, realizing the scotch might just be kicking in. "Say hi to Susanne for me."

He'd started walking away but hesitated on that last line. He gave a quick shake of his head, then kept on going. The back door gave its usual groan as he left. It wasn't until then that Mack noticed the atmosphere change. Dan seemed low-key, but his presence had still brought a definite energy to the place. Energy that evaporated as soon as he left. She thought about that for a minute, then dismissed it as nothing more than her adrenaline letdown from being shoved hard up against the wall by a guy she'd once known as a pimple-faced kid. She closed up the store and headed back upstairs.

She shoved the still-annoyed cat off her bed pillow and crawled under the covers after sending a quick text that all was well. Mack had a hunch her dreams were going to be filled with golden-green eyes that had more of a story to tell than just "I'm not that Danny anymore." And damned if she didn't want to know more about it.

"So let me get this straight." Asher Peyton turned away from the dresser he'd been building and sat on the bench next to Dan. His best friend looked puzzled. "You knew Carl's daughter when she was a kid? And you accosted her last night in Carl's store?" Asher chuckled, rubbing the dark beard he was sporting these days. "Good luck getting any more first-responder discounts from Carl, man."

"I hope to God she doesn't tell him." Dan took a swig of the cola Asher had given him. He was on duty soon, so he'd had to turn down the beer he'd been offered. Asher always had a supply of both on hand for him. "But I didn't accost her. There was a person with a flashlight in Carl's store in the middle of the night. I *apprehended* her, at best." Sure, he'd been rough with her, but damn. He gave Asher a pointed look. "And let's not forget that baseball bat she swung at my head."

"Yeah, that would have hurt. Makes total sense you'd have a drink with her after."

Dan didn't respond. Mainly because he couldn't explain it. He'd seen Mack a few times since high school, but not up close and personal like last night. Probably the closest they'd been as adults was when he shook her hand at her mom's funeral years ago, but she'd been a shell-shocked college freshman with hollow eyes that day. She probably didn't even remember him being there. Once in a while he'd seen her in the liquor store, visiting with her dad. But Dan had never stopped by. Why would he? He was part of the reason her family—the family that for years had felt like it was *his*—had spiraled into tragedy. He'd supplied the alcohol the night Ryan and Braden crashed, and Braden had died. It was just dumb luck that Dan hadn't been in the car with them.

"Hello? Earth to Dan?" Asher's voice broke into his thoughts, almost making him flinch. But Dan had learned long ago not to show that kind of reaction to anyone around him. Calm and steady was the lawman's mantra. *Never let them see you blink.* He held in a steadying breath, then released it slowly, grinning at Asher.

"Sorry, man. My little run-in with Mack aside, last night was a hell of a shift. Stupid kids drag racing out on Hilton Road. And another damn overdose. It took two doses of Narcan to bring the guy back." The nasal spray superdrug made him feel like some kind of god, bringing the dead back to life. But there was something about the look in the person's eyes when the Narcan kicked in and jolted them back to planet Earth. They'd taken the opioids to escape, and here they were, waking up to flashing lights and yelling voices and all the chaos they'd been trying to get away from. In last night's case, Kyle Alderwood had OD'd in his car, sitting in his parents' driveway in one of the nicest neighborhoods in town. His mom, Barb, was screaming and crying in a panic in the front yard while neighbors tried to comfort her. What a scene. He'd felt everyone's eyes on him. This scourge had come to Gallant Lake under his watch.

"He made it?" Asher asked. Dan nodded, staring into his glass and wishing it was something other than soda.

"How many overdoses does that make in the last month or so?" Asher looked up as a customer walked in.

"Too many." Dan answered. "Too damn many." He needed to figure out who was distributing opioids laced with Fentanyl in Gallant Lake, and why they'd

picked his quiet little town, but he hadn't managed
it yet. The stuff was everywhere all of a sudden, but
the path back to the suppliers was a cleverly knotted mess he hadn't been able to unravel. He just had
to hope the new interdepartmental task force would
figure it out. Soon.

Asher spoke with the woman who'd come in to
check on a sideboard she'd ordered the previous
week. He explained that the curly maple she'd re-
quested hadn't even arrived yet. And there were three
orders for his custom-built furniture ahead of hers.
But he promised her she'd have it in time for her
daughter's wedding shower in two months. Reas-
sured, the woman left. Asher stood at the café table
he used as a checkout counter, looking out the window at downtown Gallant Lake.

"Does Carl's daughter have lots of blond hair?
And a bang-out figure?"

Dan stood, scowling at his friend. "Maybe. Why?"

"I think she just bought out the sports section at
Nate's hardware store. She must be into hiking and
stuff, huh? Like you?"

Dan ignored the speculative look Asher gave him.
Ever since Asher married Nora Lowery, he'd turned
into Cupid, trying to help Dan's nonexistent love life.
But Dan had two strikes against him with the ladies.
He was a cop, with all the stress and weird hours that
entailed. And he was a single dad.

He walked toward the window. "Can't be Mack if
she's buying hiking equipment. She never did anything that might get her nails dirt—" His voice trailed

off. Because hell if that wasn't Mackenzie talking to Nate Thomas on the sidewalk outside Nate's store. She was holding hiking poles under one arm, with a biking helmet dangling from her fingers. Her other hand was holding a... Was that a *kayak paddle*?

"So that isn't your girl?" Asher asked.

Dan pressed his lips together. "You've been watching too many of those mushy movies with Nora on the romance channel." He looked back out the window. "No one is 'my girl.' But yeah, that's Mack."

There was no mistaking her figure, full and curvy. And that thick mane of blond hair, pulled back into a ponytail instead of being carefully styled as usual. She was wearing jeans and a T-shirt. Back in the day, Mack always looked like she was ready for tea with the queen, no matter what she was doing. He couldn't remember the last time he saw her in denim. Not even in high school. Dan stiffened at the sight of Nate's hand on her shoulder as they laughed about something together.

Naturally, Asher picked up on his body language. "Nate's quite a catch, you know. Maybe not the most exciting guy in town, but he's steady and reliable and single..."

"I don't see a hardware store owner as Mack's type."

Asher's shoulder rose. "You didn't see her as an adventurer, either, but it looks like she's ready for hiking, biking and kayaking all in one shopping trip. Either Nate's more of a master salesman than I gave him credit for, or you don't know Mackenzie Wallace as much as you think you do."

Mack turned and walked across the street toward the liquor store, loaded down with shopping bags and supplies. "I knew her as a skinny, stuck-up kid who liked to follow her brother and me around and lecture us like she was our grandmother. But somewhere in the last twenty years, she's clearly blossomed."

Asher scoffed as they walked to the back of the shop again. "Blossomed, huh? Now who's been watching girlie movies? And FYI—you can laugh at that romance channel all you want, but they have some pretty deep stuff, and it puts Nora in the cuddling mood, which suits me just fine." He held his hands up at Dan's expression. "Okay, I'm dropping the subject. How's Chloe doing with school?"

Dan took a sip of soda and smiled. His daughter was a topic he was always happy to discuss. He told Asher how the eight-year-old was acing her grades. Her teacher, Sarah Conway, regularly sent emails saying what a delight Chloe was to have in her class.

Now that he thought about it, Chloe was a little like a young Mack—always eager to please and striving to be the best at everything. The only difference was Chloe was a tomboy through and through and had the scrapes and bruises to show for it. Just this week, she'd tried to slide down the banister in his renovated Victorian house and nearly broke her arm when she tumbled off halfway to the ground floor. His ex-wife, Susanne, had a fit when she saw Chloe's puffy wrist, but the doctor confirmed it was just a minor sprain.

Asher finished his lunch and moved to the unfinished dresser on the work table, and Dan knew it was time to go. He had shift in a few hours. He'd usually spend his extra time with Chloe, but Susanne had taken her into the city to shop this weekend. He could probably use a nap after working overtime last night to help out another deputy. That's what a smart man would do.

But Dan wasn't all that smart, because he headed right down Main Street toward the liquor store.

Chapter Three

Mack sat behind the counter and stared at the hiking poles leaning against the back wall, right between the cognac and the whiskey. She shifted on her dad's weathered old stool, and her hiking boots clunked against the counter. Damn, these things were bulky. Nate had told her they were the highest-rated hiking boots on the market, and that she should wear them a few hours at a time to break them in and get used to them. So here she was, clumping around Dad's liquor store in boots that would horrify the ladies back at Glenfadden Country Club. She grinned. That just made her like these boots all the more.

Her dad's friend Bert Jenkins worked in the store part-time. He'd been covering full-time since Dad's fall five days ago, so she'd given him a couple days

off. It was weird being back in Gallant Lake, working
the store on a Saturday. Everyone wanted to know
about Dad, who had been grumpy as hell when she'd
seen him this morning. But everyone also seemed
a little hesitant to start up a conversation with her.
Most of them had watched her grow up in this place.

To be fair, she hadn't been much of a social butterfly those last few years she'd lived here. It felt
like half the town hated them back then because of
Ryan's accident and Braden's death. Then Braden's
family sued. And lost. Ryan was a mess. Her mom
was sick. Dad did nothing but work. And Mack had
spent her days tap-dancing like crazy to keep everyone happy at home and get good enough grades to
earn a scholarship to a college as far away from Gallant Lake as possible.

She slid off the stool and walked to the back of
the store, where the café tables and chairs sat in dis-
array. The stroll down memory lane wasn't doing
a thing to make her feel better about coming home
again. She started arranging the tables and chairs.

Dad had told her he'd read an article about having
wine tastings to draw in new customers, though he
hadn't gotten around to having one yet. But he *had*
ordered the furniture. And rearranged the store to
shift the wine section toward the back wall, where
the tables were. It was an interesting concept, since
wine was his biggest seller. Forcing people to walk
past the bottles of vodka and gin to get to what they
came for probably led to some impulse purchases.
Dad had owned this liquor store for thirty years, but

he never stopped trying to make it better. She slid two more chairs over to a table. She'd been to her share of fancy wine tastings back in Greenwich and could probably bluff her way through a wine night or two. If she was going to run the place, she should try to contribute something.

Dad had seemed more than happy to give her free rein over the store this morning. It used to be strictly his domain, but he'd shrugged off her news of taking a bottle of scotch last night—she skipped over her run-in with Dan. He told her it was a family business and she was family, so she could make her own decisions. Maybe it was the pain meds making him so amenable. He'd seemed resigned to spending a little more time at the hospital and then going to the rehab center as his ankle healed.

The bell over the front door chimed. She turned with a smile, but the smile faltered when she saw Dan Adams standing there. Her skin warmed at the memory of him pressing her against the wall last night after she'd tried to bash his head in. He was out of uniform now, in jeans and a well-worn henley. But he still sported the slanted smile she was beginning to think was a regular feature. It made him look perpetually amused, but his eyes were watchful. As if the half smile might just be a mask he wore to make him look nonthreatening. For some reason, she wanted to rattle him out of that disguise.

"What can I help you with, Officer? Looking for another Macallan?"

His smile deepened. "In the middle of the afternoon? Seems a little indulgent. I think that's a drink best saved for evening hours." He walked to the back, spotting the chairs and tables she'd set up. "So Carl's going through with his plan for wine tastings?"

Mack shrugged. "I think he's a little intimidated by the idea, since he's not a huge wine drinker himself. But he was all for it when I told him I might give it a try. He has to call the licensing commission to make sure I qualify as a legal agent of the store so it's all on the up-and-up." She stepped back to inspect the tables, trying to determine if they were spaced far enough apart and making sure they weren't blocking access to the wine displays.

Dan gave a low whistle. "Those are some pretty fancy boots you got there, Mackenzie."

She looked down at her sturdy footwear. "I'm breaking them in. Nate Thomas says they'll keep me warm and dry when I hit the trails."

"Hit the trails? You could climb Everest in those things. I watched you grow up, kiddo, and I never once saw you on any trails around here." Dan pulled out a chair and made himself at home.

Mack lifted her chin with a sniff. "I grew up a long time ago. I've changed."

"Yeah? Is this part of that new-leaf thing you talked about last night?"

Her chin rose. "As a matter of fact, yes. It is. I'm tired of the sweater-set-and-pearls crowd."

Dan shook his head. "I don't know what that means, but the Mack I knew wore nothing *but* sweater sets."

She studied him for a moment, tipping her head

to the side. "That's the whole point of a new leaf. I think I made it clear last night that I'm not the Mack you knew."

He looked around the store, showing no signs of responding. Was he ignoring her? Dismissing her? Taunting her? Insecurity made her chest go tight. She'd vowed not to give a damn about how anyone judged her, but old habits died hard. Her fingernails dug into her palms. She turned away and straightened some wine bottles, refusing to speak before he did. She could wait him out. Out of the corner of her eye, she saw his slow smile return. Instead of reacting to her comment, he jumped to a new topic.

"You said you weren't married anymore. What happened?"

She huffed out a surprised laugh. "Nice segue, Danger Dan. Just dive right into the deep end, why don't you?"

A flicker of uncertainty passed over his face before he composed himself again. "Sorry. Sometimes I fall into cop mode with the tone of my questions. It's just…" He ran his hand through his hair, leaving finger trails in the short, thick locks. "The last I knew, you were living your dream life over in Connecticut. Big house. Rich investor husband. Queen of the country club crowd. At least, that's the way Carl made it sound." He looked down at her feet again. "And now you're clumping around your dad's liquor store in hiking boots. I'm curious how that happened."

She turned back to the wine display, fussing with

the same bottles she'd just straightened, doing her best to keep her voice steady. "Well, you know what they say—be careful what you ask for. Some dreams aren't all they're cracked up to be. So I'm starting a new dream, here in Gallant Lake. And nowhere near my ex-husband and his social circle."

Gallant Lake might not be where she'd planned to be living at this point in her life, but it was where she was needed. It wasn't easy to think about facing everyone and explaining her failed dreams, but she'd just have to suck it up. Hopefully, she hadn't burned *all* her bridges with her *Mean Girls* act in high school. She stared blankly at the bottle of merlot in her hand. It would serve her right if the whole town shunned her.

Dan's voice went hard. "Did he hurt you?"

It made sense that a law enforcement officer would go there first, but the question still made her look up in surprise. The memory of how her marriage collapsed still stung.

"Not the way you're suggesting, no. But it wasn't fun." She'd left everything she'd known behind in Greenwich, including her so-called friends.

Dan sat at one of the tables with a sigh. "Divorce is never fun."

She spun on her heel, which wasn't easy in those boots.

"You, too?"

"Three years ago." He nodded, staring at the floor. "Susanne and I were able to keep the focus on what was best for our daughter, but it still feels like a failure, you know? You don't have kids?"

Her heart pinched tight. "No. No kids. And yes. Feels like a failure." She gave him a thin smile. "But I did get custody of our giant grumpy cat."

Dan chuckled. "I can't tell from your tone if that's a win or a loss."

She thought of how Rory had tried to smack Dad's bowling trophies off the shelf one by one that morning while she scrambled to catch them like a juggler, cursing the cat the whole time.

"I'm not sure, either," she laughed. "He's a pain in the ass. But he keeps the bed warm." *Oh, damn.* She waved her hand in dismissal. "Well, crap. Talk about oversharing."

Dan gave her a quizzical look. "Don't take this the wrong way, because it's not a criticism, but… I don't remember you swearing. Like…*ever.*"

She gestured to herself. "New leaf, remember? This is new and improved Mackenzie, with no mouth filter. And hiking boots."

And twenty extra pounds since high school. She cringed inside. He must think she'd just let herself go entirely.

"Hey…" Dan's voice was soft as he stood and took a step toward her, forehead furrowed. "New leaves are supposed to make you feel *good*. What's wrong?"

Her breath caught as she tried to steady herself. She could not have a postdivorce meltdown right now. Those were reserved for late evenings, when she was alone and in the dark. She bit her lip hard to bring herself back under control.

"Like you said… Divorce is a failure, and mine's officially only a month old. And look at me. I'm an overweight mess dressed in combat boots." She blinked, willing this pity party to go away. Dan's gentle laughter helped.

"Okay, let's break down that comment. I said divorce *felt like* a failure, not that it *was* one." He ran his eyes up and down her body. "I don't see a mess, or anything wrong with your weight. I see a woman who's just as beautiful as ever, in a very grown-up way." A funny vibration started low in her abdomen. He thought she was beautiful? His hand touched her upper arm gently. "And if you want to call those combat boots, you go right ahead. You'd make a kick-ass soldier, and you're gonna knock the hell out of this new leaf of yours."

Dan sat in his patrol car a few nights later, thinking about that conversation with Mackie. She considered herself a hot mess, but all he could see was her sass and sharp humor. The new fighting spirit she seemed to have. She'd stood her ground that first night, wielding a baseball bat. Every inch of her was an intoxicating, curving temptation. If that was a hot mess…he was into it.

He shifted on the seat, glancing at the radar as a sedan rolled slowly and carefully by. He'd intentionally parked so he'd be easily visible to drivers. Anyone who whipped by him tonight over the speed limit was literally begging for trouble. But he was really hoping no one would. He was worn-out and looking forward to a few days off. The swing shift schedule was a killer, but he didn't have much choice.

When Gallant Lake decided it couldn't afford its own police force ten years ago, the county sheriff's office had taken over. Dan was a wet-behind-the-ears rookie back then, but the town and county made an agreement. They made a position for him as a deputy sheriff, along with the former police chief, Mike DiNofrio, and gave Dan and Mike the Gallant Lake district to cover. It was the county's way of reassuring the locals that they'd still have coverage by guys they knew.

But they were stretched thin these days, thanks to budget cuts. If there was something going on elsewhere in the county, Gallant Lake was out of luck, with the nearest on-duty sheriff up to twenty miles away. The state troopers helped with coverage, but again, it depended on who was where. There were too many times when there wasn't a law enforcement officer anywhere near Gallant Lake, much less patrolling its streets on a regular basis.

And now that the Gallant Lake Resort was expanding and bringing a lot more tourists and workers to the area, the town needed *more* law enforcement coverage, not less. There'd been some talk about restarting the local police force, and the new mayor was behind the idea. But it wasn't going to happen anytime soon, thanks to politics—one of the few things Dan hated almost as much as he hated the cheap, deadly drugs coming into this area lately.

Several more vehicles meandered past his post. The last one gave him a glare and jumped on the gas shortly after passing him, as if taunting him. He was too tired to play games today. He didn't hit the lights right away, watching to make sure the guy wasn't stupid enough to stay at the high speed. Sure enough, the truck slowed back down again. Good thing. He was in no mood to deal with some hotshot kid in a jacked-up truck.

When Dan picked up his daughter the next morning, after far too little sleep, Chloe had enough energy for the both of them. As usual, she was the life force that kept him going.

"Dad! Oh my *God*! Did you *hear*? There's a fashion show at the resort and Mom said I could be in it! I'm gonna be a *model*! In a real fashion show!" Chloe grabbed his hand on the sidewalk and tugged him toward Susanne's house. Which used to be *their* house. Back when they were a family. His daughter's words didn't sink in until they were walking inside.

"Wait…did you say you're going to be in a fashion show, Chloe? Is it a contest or something?"

"I don't think it's a contest. But Miss Mel at the shop said she'll order me something special to wear, and she said it could be purple!" Dan couldn't help smiling, despite his confusion. Chloe's entire room was purple, from walls to curtains to carpet. At both houses.

Susanne stuck her head out of the kitchen doorway and waved at Dan. "Hey! Come have a cup of coffee while she gets her stuff ready. I'll fill you in on the big fashion show." She winked. "No reality TV stuff, I promise!"

While Susanne was pregnant, she and Dan had made themselves a few promises, as all new parents do. They'd provide a united front at all times. They wouldn't be overprotective helicopter parents, but they wouldn't be free-range parents, either. And they'd never push their child to do something they didn't want to do. No screaming stage mom. No cursing hockey dad. No unhealthy competition of any kind. They'd let their child *be* a child. No overwrought reality show parenting.

That became their mantra for all of it. *No reality shows!* Susanne had a particular hatred for the cable shows that seemed to glorify horrid parents exploiting their children, who were pushed to win dance contests or kiddie beauty pageants or whatever. After Chloe was born, they realized parenting—not to mention *marriage*—was a lot more complicated than they'd ever anticipated. When one of them thought the other—or Chloe—might be getting a little too carried away, they'd remind each other there were no cameras around. No need for drama.

A fashion show? That one sounded straight out of reality show land.

"I *swear* she's only doing it for fun," Susanne said as she handed him a mug of coffee. "No competition. It's part of the big charity fund-raiser the resort does for that veterans' group every year. You know,

with the golf tournament and the fancy gala? Samir
is on the board this year, with Amanda Randall. She
said they were going to be looking for local fashion
models, including children. So he suggested Chloe."

Dr. Samir Badawi was Susanne's fiancé. He'd
come to the country as an orphan from Sudan, spon-
sored by a church in Gallant Lake, and was now a
dermatologist in White Plains. He was a good guy
as far as Dan could tell—soft-spoken, kind, smart.
Chloe seemed to like him. And Susanne was over
the moon for the guy.

It made sense—Samir was everything in a mate
that Dan wasn't. Wealthy. Didn't have a dangerous
job with crazy hours. Susanne probably didn't text
Samir all day just to make sure he was okay. She
didn't have to worry that he might die on his shift.
Her fears over being a cop's wife had been a big
factor in their divorce. He'd tried to explain that her
fretting distracted him and actually put him at more
risk, but that argument just made things worse. So
yeah, Samir was probably a better fit for Susanne.
Dan wasn't sure how he felt about the guy making
decisions about Chloe's activities, though. He also
wasn't sure he wanted his eight-year-old daughter
parading around in front of strangers.

"I thought you and I were still making decisions
about Chloe as a team." He sounded more resentful
than he'd intended. Dan usually swallowed pesky
things like emotions to keep from showing them.
Susanne's eyebrow rose.

"Samir is going to be Chloe's stepfather in six

months. I think that makes him part of the so-called team, Dan. And I *did* text you yesterday to call me, which you never did." She had a right to be ticked at him. He drained half his mug of coffee and reined in his annoyance. She knew he didn't answer her texts during shifts unless she said it was urgent. Call me wasn't urgent. But there was no sense in both of them getting mad.

"I get that, Suze. I do." He splayed his hands in surrender. "And I like Samir. But Chloe's still *our* daughter. A heads-up would have been nice, even if you didn't think my opinion was required." He'd tried to sound reasonable, but he could hear the resentment in his voice, and so could Susanne. Instead of challenging him, she bowed her head and sighed.

"I'm sorry if it felt like a blindside, but I did try. I can't help it that you were working. And we just agreed yesterday after we took her to Five and Design to talk to Mel, and Chloe got so excited about it." She gave him a smile. "As you may have noticed. She'll be wearing a modest party dress. No self-respecting reality show would be interested in this. I promise."

Dan chuckled despite himself, tension leaving his shoulders. Melanie Lowery—no, Melanie *Brannigan* as of last month—owned an upscale women's boutique on Main Street. Mel had married sports agent Shane Brannigan on St. Patrick's Day at the resort, and it had been a blowout of a party. The former fashion model had settled in Gallant Lake to be close to her Lowery cousins, including Asher's wife, Nora.

Their other cousin, Amanda Randall, was the wife of the owner of the Gallant Lake Resort, the town's biggest employer and tourist draw. And a fourth cousin, Bree Caldwell from North Carolina, had founded the veteran support charity with her husband. It seemed unlikely that this was some mad plot to corrupt his daughter. He reached out and clinked Susanne's mug with his.

"If the Lowery women are involved, I'm sure Chloe will be fine. And she's definitely excited." He straightened at the sound of his daughter galloping down the stairs. "Sorry if I overreacted. It's been a tough couple of days."

Susanne nodded. "You look beat. I heard there was another overdose. Are you any closer to finding the bastards selling the stuff?"

His shoulders slumped under the weight of what was becoming a familiar question. "Nothing yet. We need more dedicated investigators, but the department is stretched too thin on this new budget. We don't have the manpower to do the job right."

She put her hand on his shoulder, and he could feel her tension. Talking about understaffing was probably making her even more nervous about his job. "Has there been any more talk about reestablishing a Gallant Lake police department?"

Dan turned to wash his mug in the sink. Treating this little house like home was a tough habit to break after sharing years of family life there.

"The politicians are talking, but that doesn't mean

anything. They're *always* talking." Dan hated politicians and their verbal gymnastics.

Susanne watched him dry the mug and put it away in the cupboard. "If you're that understaffed, do you think you'll have to work the night of the gala next month? Chloe will want you there. And she has a fitting at the boutique in a couple weeks. I'll text you once we have a time." Susanne knew he had little control over his schedule. It wasn't as if he ever *wanted* to miss family events. She cleared her throat. "Rumor has it Blake Randall is pushing hard for a local police department, and he has some clout as the owner of the resort. And didn't you say Asher was on some committee about it?" She hesitated. "If you were chief…"

If he was the police chief of Gallant Lake, he'd probably be working even more hours than he was now. Chloe dashed into the kitchen, school backpack over one shoulder and a purple duffel bag over the other. He glanced at his watch. She'd be late for school if he didn't get moving.

"Kiss your mom goodbye, baby, and let's go." He looked back at Susanne as he headed out. "Honestly, Suze, I don't get into what the committees and politicians are up to. It's all just noise until a decision is made." He held the door open for his daughter. "I'll have her back here by Sunday night."

Dan dropped Chloe off at school and drove to the small Victorian house that was his home now. It was just a few blocks from Susanne's place in one direction and the elementary school in another. Close enough that Chloe could ride her bike back and forth between her parents' houses. He crawled into bed to catch as much rest as he could before picking his daughter up later. These swing shifts were going to be the death of him yet.

As usual, every worry from every corner of his life rushed through his mind as he lay there, trying to fall asleep. Among them were the usuals—who was selling drugs in his town? What would happen once Susanne and Samir married? The house Dan and Susanne had bought right after they'd married was a little humble for a doctor. Susanne was still in her thirties. Would she and Samir have children? How would Chloe deal with that?

But today, as had happened every day this week, his last thoughts before closing his eyes were of a sassy blonde standing in her father's liquor store wearing those ridiculous hiking boots with a smile that wasn't quite as sugar sweet as it used to be. Mack now had a daring smile that teased of adventure. And the light in her brown eyes teased at even more. Or maybe he was just imagining that. After all, she'd been Perfect Mackenzie back in school— perfect grades, perfect clothes, perfectly angelic behavior. She'd been the sugary counterbalance to all the trouble her brother and Dan managed to find. Determined to leave Gallant Lake in her rearview mirror, she'd gone off to college in California, then married a banker and moved to a mansion in the wealthiest enclave of Greenwich, Connecticut. Dan had been happy for the kid when he'd heard.

But she wasn't a kid anymore. And he had a feeling she might not be all that angelic, either. And that's the thought that kept him awake the most.

Chapter Four

"Welcome to your first Women in Charge meeting, Mackenzie!" Nora Peyton raised her foam-topped mug of cappuccino in Mack's direction. "The only rule for our meetings is that there *are* no rules. We just brainstorm and try to help each other. There are no bad ideas, because even the worst idea might lead to something brilliant."

Nora's Gallant Brew coffee shop was closed for the evening on Thursday, and the front row of lights was off. There were five other women gathered at the table nearest the coffee machines—Nora, petite and smiling, with her brunette bob tucked behind her ears. Nora's two cousins were there—Mel Brannigan, owner of the Five and Design boutique, and Amanda Randall, whose husband owned the Gallant Lake

Resort, and an interior designer in her own right. While the Lowery cousins were new faces to Mack, the other two were much more familiar: Cathy Meadows, the former owner of the coffee shop and current part-time employee there, and Thea Winters, who'd owned the Gallant Lake Flower Shop for at least fifty years.

"So glad you could join us, Mackenzie." Amanda leaned forward. She was petite like Nora but had long blond curls that made her look a bit like Little Bo Peep, especially with the pink polka-dot top she was wearing. Amanda was full of restless energy, shifting in her chair and tapping the side of her mug with her spoon. "The female business owners of Gallant Lake need to stick together!"

"My friends call me Mack. And I don't actually own anything. My dad is the boss…"

He'd surprised her a few times this week, though, repeatedly hinting that he wanted Mack to take a more active role in the family business while she was here. She got the feeling he wanted her staying a lot longer than just to regroup from her divorce. But she wasn't ready to consider a permanent move to Gallant Lake just yet.

Mel put her hand on Mack's arm. "How *is* Carl? I meant to get over to see him last week, but I had an awful spring cold and didn't dare risk making him sick."

"He's good, Mel. Rarin' to go, but the doctors are still worried about his ankle." She'd met with the doctors that morning and had been dismayed at what they'd had to say. Before she could explain, Cathy—of all people—spoke up.

"The doctors think they'll have to do more surgery to repair the tendon." Cathy shook her head, pushing her braid of gray hair back over her shoulder. "If they do, Carl won't be able to put an ounce of weight on it for *weeks*. Silly old goat, climbing on ladders at his age…" She looked up and noted Mack's raised eyebrows. How did Dad's former neighbor know all this when Mack had just heard it a few hours ago? Cathy blushed and rushed on. "I just…happened to stop by…before I came here…to say hi to my old friend Carl…because I was in White Plains to…"

The three Lowery cousins exchanged amused glances. Mack wasn't sure what she was missing. Nora coughed and began nodding quickly.

"I sent Cathy to White Plains to pick up an order and told her she should stop and see her…old friend." Dad had told Mack that Cathy had semiretired a few years ago. She'd sold the shop to Nora but stayed on as a part-time employee. Nora shifted in her chair, then straightened and grinned brightly. "So anyway, we started this group last fall, half as a joke, but we're actually starting to get some things done here in Gallant Lake. We have more members, of course, but this was an impromptu gathering to meet you, and some ladies couldn't make it. Including our esteemed mayor, Margie Malone."

Thea harrumphed, her mouth twisting into a scowl. Mack had known the woman all her life, and she wasn't sure if she'd ever seen her smile. Such an odd personality for a florist.

"Esteemed to *you*, maybe," Thea said. "The jury's still out on her. After all these years, she's—"

"She's making great progress." Amanda finished, but probably not the way Thea would have. "She secured a grant to fix up the park, and she's working with Nate at the hardware store to finish the waterfront project and the boardwalk that runs behind the shops over there."

Thea rolled her eyes but didn't respond, pressing her mouth into a tight, thin line.

"As I was saying," Nora continued, "we started meeting monthly, or as needed, to discuss how our businesses are doing and come up with ideas for promotions and stuff. And we encourage each other."

"Why do you call it Women in Charge?" Mack asked.

"That started at my wedding a few years ago," Amanda laughed. "It was a small wedding…"

"In a castle…" Mel muttered. Mack knew Amanda and her husband lived in the historic old castle named Halcyon, just outside town. The place had been vacant for ages. In fact, when Mack was a teen, the rumor was that the place was haunted.

Amanda lifted a shoulder at her cousin's comment. "Anyway… I didn't want a big wedding party, and there's no way I could choose one cousin over the others, so Blake and I dubbed them the Women in Charge for the day. My friend Julie was my attendant, but these ladies, along with my other cousin

Bree, organized every little detail for me." Amanda sat back, sipping from her coffee. "I was recovering from an…accident. And I was pregnant, which my cousins didn't know at the time. It was such a relief to hand off the worries to them. We figured if *we* could help each other like that, imagine if the women in town started lifting each other up? And since we're all involved with businesses here, it just kind of grew from there." She grinned at Mel. "That whole pregnant-at-the-wedding thing seemed to have caught on."

Mack looked at Mel in surprise. "You're expecting?"

Mel used to be a famous fashion model. She went by the name Mellie Low back then. It was easy to see how that career came about—the brunette was tall and striking, even without a bit of makeup on. Her dark hair was pulled back into an artfully messy twist, and Mack suspected Mel's casual slacks and sweater sported expensive designer labels.

The woman's face went pink as she patted her flat stomach. "One month married and three months pregnant. Not the way Shane and I planned it, but we're happy. And terrified."

Nora smiled. "You'll be perfect parents." She patted Cathy's hand. "Even though Cathy isn't a business owner *now*, she was one for years, and knows everyone and everything involving Gallant Lake. We're newcomers, so we rely on Cathy and Thea and some of the other women to keep us from rocking the apple cart *too* much."

Mack nodded. Cathy hadn't changed much through

the years—she'd always been such a free spirit. Her hair, now pewter instead of the auburn Mack remembered, was still as long as ever, pulled back in that signature heavy braid. Mom used to call Cathy a "hippie girl who never grew up," but they'd been close, if unlikely, friends. Cathy used to live in the loft over the coffee shop, and Mack's parents were just two doors down. Mack used to run over to Cathy's shop for hot cocoa after school, and Cathy always tossed extra marshmallows on top. When Mom got sick, Cathy was there every day, bringing meals or magazines or just sitting and holding Mom's hand. But Cathy seemed to be having a hard time maintaining eye contact across the table. Maybe the memories made her as sad as they did Mack.

"So…is your dad really going to have wine tastings at the store?" Amanda winked at the women around the table. "That would be so much fun! We could promote it from the resort as something guests could attend, and maybe encourage other shops to stay open later that night. With a little wine to loosen the purse strings, people might spend money more freely."

Thea surprised them all when she agreed. "I'm not sure how ethical it is to rely on booze for business, but we need more bodies downtown before we *all* go belly up." She glanced out the windows to a quiet Main Street. "We need more businesses, too."

It seemed the number of boarded-up storefronts increased every time Mack came home. Dad told her it was better now than it had been, but not by much. Most of the businesses they'd lost during the recession and the resort's struggles twenty years ago were gone for good. Main Street had no bakery, no restaurant, no gift shops. There wasn't even a *bar* downtown. Everyone went to the Chalet for drinks and music. The pizza place and townie bar just outside the village center had been there forever. It was where all the cool kids used to hang out after school, but that had never been Mack's crowd.

"If we get more people," Nora said, "the businesses will follow the money. But I think plying people with alcohol may not be the way to go. I think Sheriff Dan will have something to say about that. And if Dan doesn't want it to happen, it won't."

Mack frowned. Dan was a sheriff, but he wasn't going to tell her what to do with her father's business. Along with the bad news about Dad's foot, they'd had good news today, too—she *was* an official legal agent for the store and *could* host wine tastings there.

"I have no intention of letting people get drunk. If I decide to have wine tastings, Danny Adams can't tell me not to." A strange quiet came over the table, and eyes went wide. Okay, maybe she'd sounded overly defiant, but she was tired of people telling her what to do.

Nora spoke first. "Dan is my husband's best friend, and I've never *ever* heard him called Danny." She grinned. "But I'm thinkin' I'll be doing it from now on. Do you *know* him, Mack?"

Not as much as she'd like to. She held in a little shiver. Where did *that* thought come from? Probably from the same place that wouldn't let her forget how it felt when Dan had her pressed against the wall in the store last week. She gave as casual a shrug as she could manage.

"I've known Danny since I was in fifth grade." There was a delighted intake of breath from the cousins. "He and my brother were best friends in high school. I was four years behind them and pestered them all the time. And by *pestered*, I mean *tattled on*. They got in more trouble…"

Cathy laughed. "Oh, those two boys had more energy than brains, didn't they? Remember when they spray painted all the senior names right down the middle of Main Street before graduation? And they took the principal's car and put it out on the old pier, and everyone was afraid the pier would collapse before the police could get the car off there."

"That wasn't funny," Thea said with a frown. "That little escapade could have cost their parents a bundle. I don't know how those two didn't end up in jail…" Her voice trailed off. She looked at Mack and had the good grace to show regret, remembering one of *those two* was Mack's brother. "I mean, not that they were bad kids…"

Nora's mouth had fallen open. "Are you telling me that straight-arrow Dan—I mean *Danny*—Adams was a wild child? I don't believe it! He's so quiet and honorable and heroic. He helped save my Asher when he was in a bad place a few years ago, before we met. I mean…he's our Sheriff Dan. He's literally run into burning buildings to save people. He climbs trees to rescue kittens. He's a local legend. Our hero."

It had been enough of a shock to see Dan in uniform the other night. But a *hero*? Well, maybe that shouldn't be a shock. At heart, Dan had always been *good*. She thought of the time she'd fallen off her bike when she was twelve. She'd been bruised, bloody and in tears when she got home. Dan—who was *always* at their house—was the one who'd dried her tears, joked around until he got her to laugh and bandaged her cuts. That day was probably when her girlish crush on him really began.

But oh, he'd been wild. Much too wild for wearing a law-enforcement uniform. Yet here he was, twenty years later, the *hero* of Gallant Lake. Her chest warmed. Good for Danny. While she'd been screwing up her life, he'd been rebuilding his. And she shouldn't be doing anything to tarnish that. She reached for one of the ginger cookies Nora had set out.

"No, they *weren't* bad. They were…energetic." She heard Cathy give a soft huff of laughter. "And yes, they were rascals, but they were just kids back then." She bit into the cookie. "Just a couple of active, adventurous boys."

That was a stretch. The two of them had more than one run-in with the old police chief, Mike Di-Nofrio. Chief DiNofrio had developed a soft spot for Ryan and Dan for some reason. Mack realized she *still* had a soft spot for Dan. And maybe a little bit of that girlish crush, too.

"Daddy, come *on*. We'll never get to the top if we don't hurry!"

Chloe was running ahead on the path up the side

of Gallant Mountain, zigzagging around trees and in and out of his view. Oh, to have that child's energy.

"I'm coming, sweetie. Daddy's a little tired today." He tried to pick up his pace, ignoring the protest from his aching body. Nothing like wrestling with some guy who outweighs you by forty pounds *and* is amped up on meth to make it clear you're getting older. Pete Malteer had taken his mom's front door right off its hinges last night. Not the screen door— the solid wood front door. The guy had been out of his mind, furious that his poor mother refused to give him any more money, knowing he'd just spend it all on drugs and booze.

When Dan responded to the call, Karen Malteer had been cowering in the garage, hiding from Pete while she called 911. Shaneka at the 911 call center kept Karen on the line until Dan pulled in. He could hear Pete inside the house, trashing the place. Idiot. No, that wasn't right. It was the drugs making Pete that way. Shaneka told him where to find Karen, and he got her safely over to the neighbor's place before returning to deal with Pete. Dan called for backup, but there'd been an accident up on Route 28 and a shooting in the southern part of the county, so everyone was busy. He was on his own.

Dan was good at talking people down, but Pete wasn't in the mood to talk. He'd taken one look at Dan in the doorway and charged. They'd landed on the sidewalk three steps below, with Dan generously absorbing Pete's impact. Because he was a good guy like that. Pete started swinging, but Dan had the advantage of *not* being higher than a kite. Pete only landed a few blows before Dan had him cuffed and cursing on the ground a few minutes later. He was paying the price today, though. His ribs were covered with bruises. So were his knuckles, because Pete wasn't the only guy who could land a punch.

A few minutes later, Chloe came back down the trail, running straight at him instead of her usual meandering. He automatically went on alert, looking for other hikers or an animal that might have startled her.

"Dad! There's a lady up there dancing in the clearing! She's barefoot and she's *dancing*! Do you think maybe she's a fairy? Or maybe it's the ghost from Halcyon!"

Halcyon was a local landmark—an actual castle over a hundred years old. Blake and Amanda Randall lived there with their family. And yes, it was rumored to be haunted, but Dan doubted very much that a ghost was tripping the light fantastic on Gallant Mountain. His first guess? Sounded like someone high on something.

Damn it, he couldn't even enjoy a hike with his little girl without those freakin' drug dealers spoiling his day. And here he was with no gun, no radio, no nothing. Just cargo shorts, a T-shirt and sneakers. And his daughter. Dan hesitated, considering whether to go forward or get Chloe back to the car. If it *was* someone high, they could easily tumble over the ledge and fall several hundred feet down the side of the mountain. Or they could put another hiker in danger.

"Okay, Chloe. We'll go check out your dancer. But you have to promise to stay right with me, okay? And don't say a word until I know it's safe."

Chloe rolled her eyes dramatically, hands on her hips. "Dad, it's just a dancing lady. Of course it's safe."

He felt a sharp regret that his little girl would someday have to know that people were seldom "just" anything, and were too often *not* safe. As a cop, it had always been a tough balancing act for him to maintain—seeing the worst of people on the job and trying to shield Chloe from that when he was home.

"You're probably right, but humor me, okay?" She nodded and followed him up the path. He'd explained more than once that sometimes she and her mom just had to let him be who he was—a man determined to keep them safe, even if it meant he worried too much. Chloe had accepted it more readily than Susanne, who didn't like him scaring Chloe with the way he acted.

The clearing just below the famous Kissing Rock near the top of Gallant Mountain was about an acre. Dan suspected someone had cleared it decades ago, but local lore said the grassy plot was a natural little oasis in the middle of the forest. It was anchored on one end by the legendary bus-size boulder and at the other end by a sharp drop-off with a spectacular view of Gallant Lake and the Catskill Mountains. It was privately owned, but the no-trespassing signs meant nothing to locals who'd been coming up here for generations to make out on the famous Kissing Rock.

Not that Dan would ever ignore the signs. He had explicit permission from the owner, Blake Randall, who owned much of the mountain these days. Blake had bought up a ton of property around the lake a few years ago to protect it from development, and he'd held on to the mountain land.

Dan could see the clearing just ahead, and Chloe was tugging his hand to get him to hurry. Knowing he wanted her to be quiet, she whispered, but in a voice that probably carried halfway up the mountain.

"See, Daddy? See the dancing lady?"

He stopped at the edge of the woods, figuring he could tuck Chloe behind a tree if there was trouble. But he hadn't anticipated *this* kind of trouble.

Mackenzie Wallace was twirling in the center of the clearing, blond hair swinging. She was wearing jeans and a dark blue shirt advertising Nora's coffee shop, the Gallant Brew. And her feet were indeed bare. With fire engine–red polish on her toes. She had earphones on—he could see the bright pink cord leading from her ears to her back pocket. Whatever music she was listening to had made her completely uninhibited. Her hands were up in the air, her eyes were closed and she was lost in herself and in the moment. She swung her arms out and spun again, then started jumping to the beat of the silent song. The sight made his chest go tight. She was beautiful, and it had nothing to do with physical appearance. It was her *spirit*—she was beautiful in her freedom.

Dan felt as though he was intruding on something important. Something deeply personal. As much as he wanted to know what she was doing barefoot in a clearing that was just showing the bright greens of spring, he didn't want to intrude on her moment. He should walk away. But his feet were rooted to the ground as securely as the trees around him. Chloe's attention span was substantially shorter than his, though, and she forgot to even try to whisper.

"See, Dad? I *told* you it was a barefoot lady dancing on the mountain! Isn't she pretty? Can we dance, too?" Chloe's high voice must have broken through whatever music was playing in Mack's ears, because she stopped dancing and started looking around. She froze when she saw them, then squinted. Dan realized they were in the tree shadows and might look threatening, so he stepped into the sunlight.

"*Dan?* What are you doing…?" She yanked the ear pods out and stared, her mouth falling open but no more words coming out.

His smile was automatic. That seemed to be how it worked around her. "I think the bigger question is what are *you* doing? Having a little *Sound of Music* moment up here, Mack?"

Her face went bright red, and she quickly ran her hands over her hair, pushing it back over her shoulders. "I… I'm…hiking. It's been a long time since I saw the Kissing Rock, so…"

His right brow shot up. "So you figured you'd celebrate the occasion with an interpretive dance?"

Mack's laughter was quick and full. "Yup. That's it. You caught me honoring the mountain gods." Her head tipped to the side. "Is that not still the tradition?"

"The tradition these days is for people to honor the no-trespassing signs on the trail." He was still smiling, so she didn't even pretend to take him seriously as she walked their way.

"Looks like I'm not the only one breaking the rules, Officer." Chloe giggled at Mack's observation. Mack looked down at her and grinned. "*And* you're corrupting the town's youth. Who is this pretty lady?"

Chloe jumped forward, her hand extended. "I'm Chloe and this is my dad. Why are you barefoot? Why were you dancing? Do you live here? Are you the ghost?"

Mack's eyes went wide at the barrage of questions, then she gave Dan a quick wink before answering.

"I'm Mackenzie Wallace, but you can call me Mack. I grew up here a long…" She glanced up at Dan. "…*long* time ago. I'm definitely not a ghost. I'm dancing because Whitney Houston was telling me she needed to dance with somebody, and I figured I'm somebody, right?" Chloe nodded enthusiastically in agreement.

But there was one question left unanswered. Dan gestured to her feet. "And where are your shoes, dancing queen?"

Mack's face twisted. "Those weren't shoes. They were torture devices." She held up one foot to expose the ugly, open blister just below her ankle. "The other foot is just as bad. I couldn't take one more step in those things once I got up here."

"Let me guess," Dan said with a chuckle. "You decided to hike up the mountain in those heavy boots you just bought this week."

"Well, I wore them around the shop for a few days to break them in."

"Because you do so much walking in a liquor store. What did you wear for socks, Mack?"

"Um…my gym socks. You know, tighty-whities?"

He closed his eyes tightly. "That is *not* what tighty-whities are. And those socks are no match for a mountain and a brand-new pair of hiking boots. Where are they now?"

Chloe raised her hand to get their attention. "Wait. Do you guys *know* each other? Daddy, do you know Mack? Did you arrest her or something?"

Mack started laughing again. The sound of her laughter, so deep and free, did something weird to Dan's chest cavity. It resonated there and made him relax somehow. Mack leaned over to face Chloe.

"Actually, your daddy *did* try to arrest me, but it was a misunderstanding. We've known each other a long time. Since I was a little girl not much older than you are, I'm guessing. Are you ten? Twelve?"

Chloe straightened, looking very pleased at those guesses. "I'm *eight*, but I'll be nine in November. What was my daddy like as a kid?"

Mack's eyes flickered up to his face, and she must have noted his tension. Chloe was bound to hear stories of Dan's misspent youth eventually. But not today. Mack flashed him another wink.

"Your daddy was my big brother's best friend, and

they did a lot of…fun…things when they were boys. How about you? What do *you* like to do for fun?"

As easily distracted as ever, Chloe launched into a list of all the things she liked to do. Mack seemed to be listening closely, and Dan appreciated that she didn't talk down to Chloe or treat her as less than a person. He'd dated a few women who seemed to see his daughter as an unfortunate intrusion on their time. Dan followed the two females walking hand in hand toward the Kissing Rock at the base of the mountain peak. Didn't really need to be thinking about *dating* and *Mackenzie* in the same breath. That was a nonstarter for a couple of reasons. But most importantly for how their pasts were tragically entwined.

She'd never blamed him for Ryan's accident, probably because she didn't know—or forgot—that he was the one who'd stolen the gin they were drinking that night. Maybe she'd forgotten his involvement. But Dan never would.

Chapter Five

Mack smiled at the sight of Chloe's small hand in hers as they walked. The little girl had short brown hair just a shade darker than Dan's and wide brown eyes full of interest and energy. She reminded her of Dan's and Ryan's restlessness that always seemed to lead them to trouble. But Chloe seemed to have plenty of positive outlets for that energy, from all the things she was listing as her favorite things to do. Maybe if Ryan and Dan had had those kinds of outlets as kids, they wouldn't have been so bored and drawn to mischief.

"…and I take dance class and piano lessons and I play soccer and I like to ride my bike…"

It was mortifying that Dan Adams had caught her dancing all by herself up here. She hadn't been able to resist, though, especially once she'd kicked those god-awful boots off at the base of the Kissing Rock, vowing to never wear them again. The newly grown grass had felt so cool and soft under her feet.

"…and I like to read! I'm reading a book about a girl who builds a submarine…"

Mack hadn't even made it halfway up the mountain path earlier before she knew those boots were a mistake. It started as an irritating burn, but once the blisters broke, every step was painful. She'd been in tears when she reached the clearing, and she'd immediately plopped down in the grass and pulled off the boots and the cheap socks that had wadded themselves around the arches of her feet.

Then she'd stood in her bare feet and took a step toward the vista of Gallant Lake and rows of blue-tinged mountains marching off into the distance. The dirt and the grass and the wildflowers were cool and soft under her feet. Running around without shoes wasn't something she'd done as a child, any more than climbing a mountain was. She'd been a good girl who wore nice clothes and didn't get into trouble. But her good girl days were over, and she was barefoot on a mountainside on an early-May morning. It felt amazing. Freeing. Exciting. When Whitney's song came up on her playlist, there was nothing else to do but dance.

"…and I like to make jewelry with beads and string, but Mom says I just make a mess. I only knocked over the tray of beads one time, but boy, was she mad. I'll make you a bracelet if you want one, but I'll have to do it at Dad's house. What color would you like?"

It took Mack a second to realize Chloe had stopped for a breath and was waiting for an answer.

"I'm sorry, honey…what am I picking a color for?"

Chloe raised her arm straight up, pointing to the beaded and knotted purple bracelet she wore. "A *bracelet*, silly! *My* favorite color is purple, but you can pick a different color as long I have beads in that color. And I have a lot of beads…"

Dan put his hands on his daughter's shoulders. "I knew letting you have those chocolate caramel pancakes at the diner this morning was a mistake. Why don't you go burn off that sugar high by picking some wildflowers for Mack? See how many different kinds you can find. Just stay away from the cliff."

Chloe took off like she was shot from a cannon, making Mack laugh.

"The apple didn't fall far from the tree with that one. She's as restless as a teenage boy I used to know." She met Dan's gaze. "She's adorable."

Dan looked back at his little girl, darting around the mountainside. Mack could hardly believe Dan was really a *dad*.

"Yeah, I think I'll keep her," he said. "Now, where are those boots? You can't go back down the trail in your bare feet."

"Actually, that's exactly what I plan on doing. There is no way I'm shoving my feet back in those torture devices." She walked over to where she'd thrown them, along with the fancy telescoping walking stick, and handed them to Dan. "Ever again."

He studied her for a moment, his face serious. "What are you doing, Mack? What's with the hiking boots and the biking helmet and the kayak paddle? You were never one for the great outdoors, unless maybe you were playing tennis or snow skiing down the bunny hill, and now I find you *dancing* on Gallant Mountain. Barefoot! I didn't think you even knew about the Kissing Rock or the old trail."

"Oh, please." She waved her hand. "Just because I was too much of a Goody Two-shoes to walk up here, didn't mean I hadn't *heard* about it. It was the most infamous make-out place in town, except maybe for Gilford's Ridge and the old ski place on the other side of the lake. Is that still open?" He shook his head in the negative, and she frowned. "That's a shame. I don't know how you heard about the biking or the kayaking—which I haven't done yet—but I *did* tell you I was turning over a new leaf. Anything old Mackenzie wouldn't do, *I'm* doing. And I started with Gallant Mountain." She held up one foot and wiggled her toes. "And dancing barefoot. Which was unplanned, but also un-Mackenzie-like. So that gets bonus points."

Dan glanced toward Chloe, who was staying a safe distance away from the cliff edge, running in and out of the trees on the edge of the opening with a fistful of flowers in her hand. He looked back to Mack, his brows bunched together.

"I don't think you've told me what exactly was

wrong with the *old* Mackenzie." He sat on a smaller boulder at the base of the cliff and patted the stone for her to join him there. "I kinda liked her, except when she squealed on my best friend and me."

"Oh please," Mack scoffed as she sat. "You didn't know her… I mean…me. You and Ryan were off doing your thing and barely knew I existed. No one knew I existed back then, except my teachers and the church ladies and Mom. I made them all so proud…" Her voice trailed off. Approval had practically been an obsession back then. Having people see her as the opposite of Ryan. Having people tell her parents they were lucky to have such a good, sweet child as Mackenzie. The more she'd heard it, the more she'd believed it, and the more determined she was to meet those expectations that everyone placed on her. "You might think it was easy being Gallant Lake's sweetheart, but it wasn't, Dan. It was hard, and it messed me up."

"Messed you up how?"

She sighed, leaning back against the rock wall behind her and closing her eyes. The air was sharp and clear up here, and it felt good in her lungs. She inhaled deeply and imagined it cleaning away the past few years. Her thoughts drifted to Greenwich. The way everyone watched her perform her perfect-wife act for years. The cool admiration in their eyes until she flipped the script and told them all what she really thought of their little games.

"Mack? What happened to you after you left Gallant Lake?" Dan's voice was firmer now, and she opened her eyes to find him leaning toward her in worry.

"*Nothing* happened. That's the point. For years and years, not one damn thing happened in my life that meant anything. And I'm ready for something to *mean* something, Dan. Hell, even these blisters *mean* something. They mean I *did* something. I *felt* something. You have no idea what a big deal that is to me right now. How much I need it." Her fervency surprised her as much as it did him. It was the first time she'd really articulated those feelings out loud since her divorce from Mason. Another milestone. She bumped her shoulder against him. "You told me you're not Danger Dan anymore. That's too bad, because I'm going to give Danger Mack a try."

Dan leaned back next to her. She didn't miss the way his eyes quickly found his daughter before he relaxed. "A couple of blisters don't exactly make you dangerous. If they make you happy, fine. But I can't let you walk down the trail in your bare feet. That's just begging for tick bites and open cuts that could get infected. It's bad enough you've got those blisters to worry about. We don't need you *and* your dad laid up right now." He reached into her boots and pulled out her sweaty white socks. "Let me tie these *tighty-whities* over the blisters to protect them, then you can wear the boots as far as your car."

"Wow. You went from Danger Dan to Captain Responsibility. Impressive. And dull."

He glared at the ground in silence. Before Mack could ask what was bothering him, Chloe ran up, breathless and clutching a handful of flowers. "Here, Mack! I found eight different kinds of flowers and two types of grass. Does that count? Aren't they pretty? Have you picked a color for your bracelet yet?"

"If I remember correctly," Dan started, "Mack's favorite color used to be mint green or anything pastel. That's all she used to wear."

Chloe grinned widely enough for Mack to see she'd recently lost a tooth. "I have pastel colors! Grandma Buckley asked for a bracelet like that. I'll just make two!"

Terrific. Mack and Grandma liked the same colors. She narrowed her eyes when she heard Dan's choked laughter. He wouldn't look up, concentrating *very* hard on wrapping her ankles and sliding those infernal boots on her feet. He wasn't wrong. She'd been the queen of buttery-yellow sweater sets and powder-blue skirts. She carried her tendency for soft, safe, ladylike colors to Greenwich, too, with a few touches of classic black for trips to New York. But to get the same color as Chloe's *grandmother*? Nope. She took the flowers from Chloe and pointed to the girl's sparkly bracelet.

"Actually, Chloe, that's not true anymore." Mack glanced at Dan before smiling at his daughter. "My favorite color these days is the same as yours—purple! Can you do that? A bright purple glittery bracelet?"

"Oh, yes! I have new glitter beads that will be perfect! Daddy, can I make Mack's bracelet at your house?"

Dan's eyes were on Mack. "Sure, baby. Make it as big and bright as you want. Because apparently I don't know Mack as well as I thought."

Mack dipped her head in acknowledgment of his confession. She was no longer a woman of pastel good behavior. And Dan was no longer a guy looking for danger. She couldn't help thinking that was a pity. She was going to be in Gallant Lake awhile— forever if Dad had *his* way—and Danger Dan would have been a fun diversion. But Dudley Do-Right Dan? Not as tempting. Or so she kept telling herself.

Mack stared at the doctor in shock. "Six *weeks*?"

The doctor, who seemed barely old enough for medical school, much less practicing medicine, nodded with a bright smile, as if having no idea what his words were doing to her. She'd figured Dad would be home in a week or two. Hobbling around on crutches, maybe, but home, so she'd be free to figure out *her* life. But now he was having *surgery*?

"Yes, Miss Wallace…"

Dad interrupted with a grumble. "It's Mrs. Burns."

"Actually, Dad…" She gave him a warning look. "It's not anymore. You should be *happy* I took your name back." It was frustrating that her own father refused to accept her divorce. He was still in the *Did you try hard enough?* phase. But then again, Dad had no idea what Mason had done. She looked back to the young doctor, determined to focus on the present, not the past. "You're saying he can't put weight on that foot for six weeks? Not even…?"

The young doctor knew how to scowl. "No weight *whatsoever*. Not a single step. That tendon was hanging on by a thread, and if we don't give yesterday's surgery time to take, it won't heal at all. And there are very few options at this point if it doesn't." He brightened. "But we'll give Carl a scooter to use so he'll still be mobile."

"But his apartment is upstairs." She turned to her father. "Did you *know* this, Dad?"

He was sitting up in his hospital bed. Even in his pea-green hospital gown, he looked surprisingly robust and completely unconcerned at the prospect of not being able to access his home of thirty years. He gave a sharp nod.

"It's okay, Doc. We'll figure something out."

"We *will*?" she asked after the doctor left them alone in the room. "You say that like you have a solution in mind, but I'll be damned if I can see one."

Her father gave her a sharp look. "Watch your language, young lady. And yes, I have options, but I need to talk to some folks first. How's the store doing? Is Bert covering enough hours for you? What were your numbers for last week?"

She followed his lead and talked business until it was time for her to go, but the whole time she was wondering where Dad was going to live. She looked at the hulking shape of Gallant Mountain looming over the town as she parked behind the store. Despite her worries, it made her smile.

Hiking had been fun last weekend, but the blisters *still* hadn't healed, and her feet were too tender to wear those damn boots for a while, even with the extrathick wool socks Dan had dropped off for her yesterday. He'd had a good laugh when he walked into the store and saw her soaking-wet hair and foul mood. She'd discovered shortly before his arrival that kayaking was *not* going to be one of her adventures.

Nate Thomas had loaned her a small kayak and tried to show her how to use it shortly before Dan showed up, but she and kayaks just didn't get along. Maybe it was a balance thing, but she'd wobbled and shaken so much that she couldn't manage to stay upright. And when the kayak flipped, she'd panicked every time. It wasn't the water as much as her claustrophobia—being upside down in the lake while strapped into a vessel determined to hold her there. Nate was a patient soul, but even *he* suggested she might want to try another hobby.

So this weekend, she was going to take her brand-new bicycle and she was going to hit the roads. It wasn't a mountain bike, but she figured one step at a time. Besides, it would help her get in shape, and biking was something she hadn't done much as a little girl. Her bike had been for riding back and forth to school or over to her friend Shelly Graber's to do homework when they were twelve. So pedaling through the hills around town would be fun and at least a *little* adventurous.

She had Shelly Graber—now Shelly Markson— on her mind this week. Shelly had actually walked into the liquor store the other day. Mack wanted to hide behind the counter. She'd left Shelly in the dust back then after Ryan's accident. Things had been chaotic at home, and Mack had started down her path of people pleasing. Or parent pleasing. And teacher pleasing. Not so much friend pleasing. Friends couldn't get her into college and out of the little town that was suffocating her.

But she didn't hide. She'd looked her onetime best friend in the eye and asked her how she could help. Shelly hadn't changed much. Tall, athletic and devil-may-care, wearing jeans and a Gallant Lake sweatshirt, with her long brown hair tucked into a ball cap. Shelly laughed at Mack's expression and asked for two bottles of Mack's best cheap wine. Then she'd invited Mack to join her and her friends at the Chalet. Mack stared in stunned silence at the question until Shelly set the bottles down on one of the café tables and gave her a warm embrace. She said of *course* she'd forgiven Mack for ghosting her all those years ago. Shelly reminded Mack that neither of them were in high school anymore. She told Mack about her four children—four!—and invited Mack to country music night at the Chalet.

She said her older brother might join them for a drink. Mack remembered Owen Graber as a handsome boy who always had an easy smile and a mischievous gleam in his eye. Owen had been part of Ryan and Danny's wild bunch, but Shelly said he was settling down after sowing many years' worth of wild oats, including a short stint in jail a few years back. Shelly warned that Friday-night crowds could get a little rowdy, but Mack waved off her concern. Rowdy was definitely *not* Old Mack's style. Neither were ex-cons. Her heart beat a little faster. Maybe Owen was just the bad boy she needed right now. Maybe Owen's company would keep her from wondering what Danny Adams was up to on a Friday night.

Chapter Six

"Why are we doing this again?" Dan asked as Asher parked at the Chalet. "Like I don't see enough drunks when I'm on the job, you're bringing me to a *bar* on my first full weekend off in ages? Besides, it's late. Why can't we just drink at your shop like we used to…?"

"Whah, whah, whah." Asher slammed his car door. "Will you stop whining? You're not having your wisdom teeth extracted, for Chrissakes. You're going out for a drink to celebrate your friend's engagement. I'm pretty sure it won't kill you." They started walking across the lot. Asher looked over at Dan, then shook his head. "And the only reason we're late is because you were dragging your feet trying to beg off. You used to rag on me about becoming a hermit, but look at *you*. When's the last time you had social interaction with someone that didn't involve handcuffs, Sheriff Dan?"

Dan thought about Mackenzie dancing on the mountain last weekend. Mack didn't seem terribly impressed with his status as Sheriff Dan, Hero of Gallant Lake. Maybe she hadn't heard the wondrous—and often exaggerated—tales of his derring-do. The truth was, he'd never been that comfortable with the title, and he resented the pressure it put on him. The folks new to town knew him as the lawman. A benevolent good guy keeping them safe. And the folks who'd lived here awhile looked at him as the bad boy who'd turned his life around. Both versions of the story ended up with him on some sort of pedestal, and that was a very narrow place to build a life.

When Asher opened the door to the Chalet, noise poured out—laughter, shouting, music, glasses clinking together. A typical Friday night at a townie bar, and the partying was in full swing. It was too late to turn back now.

Shane Brannigan and Nate Thomas were drinking at a booth by the windows. Shane, a sports agent, was married to Melanie, the owner of the upscale boutique in town who was helping Chloe pick out a dress for that gala. Dan spotted Blake Randall at the bar. The owner of the Gallant Lake Resort, with two restaurants of its own, didn't spend a lot of time hanging out at the Chalet. But his wife, Amanda, had insisted that he and the guys celebrate Nick West's engagement to Cassie Zetticci somewhere other than the resort where Nick and Blake worked.

The man of the hour, Nick, was standing next to Blake, accepting well wishes from the crowd. Nick had come to town the previous summer as Blake's director of security. He'd been a police detective in LA before making the move, and he and Dan had become good friends.

Nick saw Dan standing there and waved him over as Asher moved on to the booth. "Hey, look, it's Sheriff Dan in the flesh!" Nick announced loudly. "Let me buy you a beer, Dan-o."

Dan hated that name, but Nick had clearly had a few beers already, so he let it slide. He accepted the beer and shook Nick's hand.

"Stop reminding everyone of my profession tonight—it's a buzzkill." He clapped Nick on the back. "Congratulations, man. Have you and Cassie set a date?"

Nick shook his head. "I've promised to show up at the appointed time, but the rest of the details are up to her." He took a long swig of his beer. Nick was lean and tough—a rock climber and white-water kayaker. Blake's build was broader and taller. And he had that air of being in charge, even leaning on the bar at the Chalet. Blake bumped Nick's shoulder.

"How is it that I know more about your nuptials than you do? You're getting married in September. At Halcyon. On the veranda if the weather's nice. Inside if it's not. The women are all over it."

"Nice." Nick raised his glass, which seemed to

have magically refilled itself. "Married in a castle. Who'd have thunk it? Come on, let's get back to Shane and Nate." Nick wavered on his feet, making Dan wonder A—how much had he had to drink? And B—who was driving this crew home? As if reading his mind, Nick gave him a lopsided grin. "Relax, Officer. Shane's our designated driver tonight." They approached the table. "See? He's drinking soda. Or something. What the hell *are* you drinking?"

Shane lifted his glass of ruby liquid. "Cranberry juice. You'd think I'd be sick of it by now, with Mel wanting nothing but for the past month or so, but my pregnant wife has me hooked on the stuff. Although I'll admit, I generally add lots of vodka to mine at home. But not tonight." He drained half the glass and sighed. "Tonight I'm sober. I promise, Sheriff Dan."

"Christ, will everyone stop calling me that?" Dan sat down with a growl. He glared at Asher. "*This* is why I don't go out. Between everyone calling me Sheriff Dan like I'm some kind of cartoon character and then not being able to get respectably drunk in the same town I'm supposed to be protecting." His glass of beer was still distressingly full. He'd be nursing that one all night, or at least until he got home to have a whiskey—or three—in private.

"Yikes." Shane laughed. "I thought my *wife* was hormonal. What's got *you* in such a twist?"

Asher chuckled. "More like *who* has him in a twist. A ghost from his past has him shook."

Nick set his glass down, his smile fading. "What kind of ghost? Someone you arrested?"

"No," Asher replied, more than happy to speak for Dan. "A *lady* ghost. Carl Wallace's daughter is here to help run the liquor store while he's laid up." Asher gave Dan a speculative look. "And it turns out our buddy Dan went to *school* with Mackenzie Wallace."

Nate Thomas's head bobbed up and down. "We *all* went to school together, but she was a few years behind…" He snapped his fingers. "That's right—you and her brother, Ryan, were best buds! It was you two who tore up the football field doing doughnuts with your dirt bikes, right? Hey, did you know she's…"

"Wait…" Blake held up his hand. "*Sheriff Dan* got in trouble in school? Please, tell us more!"

Nate interrupted. "Dan, she's h—"

Asher jumped in. He knew about Dan's past and knew why Dan didn't want to talk about it. "What are we, a bunch of gossiping old women? We *all* had adventures in high school. And I imagine we all had some girl we'd like to see again…" He glanced at Dan. "Or not. So give the guy a break. Nate, how's business been?"

Music swirled around them. Country wasn't Dan's thing, but judging from the crowded dance floor, people were into it. There was a lot of hooting and hollering involved, which meant Nate had to practically yell to be heard.

"Business sucks, as usual lately. But Mackenzie…"

Asher tried again to distract Nate. "And that stupid parrot of yours—how's he doing?" Nate's parrot, Hank, was a minor tourist attraction. He lived in a large cage in the hardware store and liked to swear. A lot.

"Still likes to curse a blue streak." Nate shrugged. "Might be why business is so bad, but what can I do?" He leaned toward Dan. "She's here."

"Who's here? Your *parrot*?" Nick looked around, as if Nate would actually bring Hank to a bar like some pirate.

"No, you idiot." Nate looked straight at Dan. "Mackenzie Wallace. She's over on the other side of the bar, with Shelly Markson and Kiara Kelsoe. Shelly's brother was over there, too."

Dan went very still. Mack was *here*? With Owen Graber? Christ, he knew she wanted to find her adventurous side, but hanging out with Owen Graber wasn't a great idea. His friends moved on to discussing baseball, which was normally a conversation Dan would gladly be a part of. But he couldn't focus on anything other than Mack being in the bar. With Owen.

Back in high school, Owen had been part of their group of troublemakers. Outsiders on the far edge of polite society. Punks thinking they were clever rebels of some kind. They'd never met a rule they didn't want to break, and Dan really couldn't remember why, or what the point was. Attention? Danger? Fun? For him it was probably just an escape from his parents' divorce and all the tension at home. His father was angry and distant, and often drunk. Dan's friends became his family, even if they were often drunk, too.

Dan outgrew his rebel phase in the span of one awful night, when Ryan Wallace wrapped his car around a tree and Braden Michaels died. It could have been him. He was supposed to be with them. More than once he'd thought it *should* have been him. He'd decided after that night, with a little tough love from Chief DiNofrio, that he was done with the whole criminal-in-training routine.

But Owen hadn't learned his lesson nearly as fast. He'd bounced around from job to job, living with his parents, getting high every weekend, playing video games in the basement. Then he was arrested in White Plains for possession, but Owen always insisted it was a setup. The only reason Owen hadn't done serious time was because the detective screwed up the chain of custody and the case got tossed. Because of that arrest, Owen was one of the names on Dan's short list of suspects for being involved with the recent influx of opioids.

Mack said she wanted a walk on the wild side, but Dan didn't think she wanted to get quite *that* wild. He stood, getting the attention of his friends. He flipped his thumb toward the back of the bar, where the restrooms were. But that's not where he went.

He walked around the bar to the group of tables on the other side. It didn't take long to find Mack. Her golden hair was loose and full, catching the lights from the dance floor. She was in jeans, with a snug black knit top cut just low enough to be interesting. She and Shelly were laughing at something Kiara was saying. And sitting there, with his arm over the back of Mack's chair, was Owen.

Dan wasn't sure what this emotion was flaring

up inside of him or where it was coming from. He only knew his fingers curled and his pace picked up as he headed to their table. Was it knowing Owen's shady past that bothered him? Or was it the way Owen was leaning toward Mack, his fingers touching the back of her neck? Whatever it was, it had Dan burning inside.

Mack sensed Dan's presence before she saw him. She was laughing with Shelly, and just like that, she knew Dan was there. They'd just sat down from dancing to a bunch of pounding songs about bonfires and girls dancing in pickup trucks, and Mack had drained her frosty glass of beer. So *not* a country club thing to do. They were laughing at some of the lyrics when she lifted her hair away from her neck to cool off. Owen reached over to "help," and she didn't miss the way his fingers lingered on her skin. He'd been flirting lightly all night, but she had a hunch his heart wasn't in it. He was smooth, but it felt like he was on autopilot. Still, it was fun to be on the receiving end of a man's attention.

She looked up and looked straight into Dan's eyes as he rounded the bar. He was wearing well-worn jeans and a plaid shirt with the sleeves rolled up. And a scowl. What was *that* about?

Giddy from alcohol and adrenaline from all the dancing, Mack jumped to her feet and threw her arms around Dan's neck, surprising everyone including herself. "Danny! What are you doing here? Pull up a chair! We've got a big head start on you, so you have a *lot* of catching up to do, mister."

As she heard the heightened pitch of her voice, Mack knew she'd had too much to drink. But the bar was hot and the beer was cold and had gone down much too easily. Dan set his hands lightly on her waist, his scowl deepening. "I think you might be too far gone for me to catch up, Mackenzie. How many have you had?" She just shrugged, because she wasn't really sure anymore. She smacked his shoulder playfully.

"I'm a big girl, Danny. I don't need some guy with a badge watching out for me."

Dan tensed, his eyes growing hard. "I'm more than a guy with a badge, Mackie."

Was he? She'd yet to see it. Even with his daughter on Gallant Mountain, he'd been cautious and protective. The ultimate good guy. The opposite of what she was looking for. His eyes were darting around the room, as if he was casing the place, looking for trouble so he could rush in and prevent it. A pretty young waitress came over to take Dan's order. He looked at the pitcher of beer on the table and ordered a cola. *Ugh.* Even on a Friday night, he was still Mr. Straight Arrow. Dan's expression cooled even more when Owen stood to hold a chair out for Mack. Was he...*jealous*? Dan grabbed a chair from a neighboring table and slid it close to Mack as she sat down between them.

She pretended to fan herself. "Is it just me or is there a lot of testosterone in the air all of a sudden?"

Shelly giggled. "I should get a pic of this. It's like you have a devil on one shoulder and an angel on the other."

Owen laughed. "And which is which?"

He was just as good-looking as ever, with auburn hair falling across his forehead and a wicked, fun-loving glint in his brown eyes. Looking for laughs, just like in high school. He'd been cracking jokes and buying drinks all night. But, like Dan, he was drinking cola. Kiara, whom Mack had never really known that well, had filled her in earlier that evening on Owen's brush with the law. Kiara told it as a cautionary tale, warning Mack that a lot of people thought Owen was trouble. Which was interesting, because Kiara, with her skinny purple braids pulled high on her head and looking like an African queen, hadn't taken her eyes off him all night. Maybe that was why Dan was all bristly and broody at her side. The lawman versus the lawbreaker.

Mack pretended to consider Owen's question. "Well, you were both devils in high school, but now? I guess I'd need to do more research with each of you to know for sure."

Dan was silent, while Owen just laughed harder, resting his hand on her shoulder. Kiara's face fell just enough to confirm Mack's suspicion that the woman had a mad crush on Owen. Owen's shady past didn't bother Kiara one bit. Owen was either completely clueless or was willfully ignoring Kiara's attraction to him. He was treating Kiara the same as his sister—teasing and...brotherly. Kiara hadn't exactly been welcoming to Mack, but she still felt a stab of pity for her.

Shelly asked Dan about his daughter, which seemed to cool some of the edginess he'd brought to the table. The two of them settled into a conversation about something happening at school. Kiara wagged her eyebrows, looking between Dan and Mack, and Mack shook her head. It would be convenient for Kiara if there was something between Mack and Dan, but it wasn't going to happen. Mack had already lost her trophy husband and all her so-called friends in Connecticut. She didn't dare set her sights on Gallant Lake's local hero. Kiara gave up, then put her hand on Owen's arm and laughed loudly at something he said about the pitcher being empty again.

Mack couldn't remember the last time she'd hung out with friends and shared laughs over a pitcher of beer like this. She sighed. There was a good reason for that—she'd *never* hung out at a bar, drinking beer with friends. Good girls didn't do that. Good girls sipped martinis while squeezed into torturous support garments under their cocktail dresses at parties where a sense of competition lay just under the surface. Who was skinnier? Who had the newest fashion? The most expensive jewelry? The most successful husband? The most interesting lover?

How in the world had fun-loving ten-year-old Mackenzie Wallace, with her pigtails and scuffed-up sneakers, turned into a country club diva? It was a long, gradual descent into living a lie, but she hoped the path back to finding herself wouldn't take nearly as long. And she was determined to make it as interesting a journey as possible. And one without making new enemies. She grabbed Kiara's hand when another fast tune started blasting over the sound system. Kiara hesitated, then nodded and stood. Mack leaned forward when they got to the dance floor and winked.

"Don't worry, I'm not interested in Owen."

Kiara's eyes went wide. "Why are you telling *me*? He's not my guy."

"But you'd like him to be."

Kiara stopped moving and almost got knocked off her feet by some guy behind her. She moved closer to Mack and started dancing again. "Is it that obvious?"

"Well, I don't think *he* has a clue, but yeah, I could see it. Have you told him?"

"No way. We've been friends forever, and I don't want to screw that up." Kiara's eyes clouded. "Besides, it's strictly one-sided." Mack couldn't argue, since Owen had been paying more attention to Mack all night. Kiara glanced over at their table. "Why do you care, anyway?"

Mack missed a step. "Ouch. Why wouldn't I?"

The volume rose on the pounding song they were dancing to, and someone in the crowd whooped, making everyone around him laugh. Mack had to lean in to hear Kiara's answer.

"I don't know," Kiara said, glancing away. Then she looked straight at Mack. "You were kind of a bitch in high school. You acted like you were too good for Gallant Lake or anyone who lived here. Everyone called you the ice queen."

Mack's face felt like it was going up in flames. "I know. I had a lot going on at home, and..." She spread her hands and lifted her shoulders. "I was trying to be the perfect kid. Instead of being a happy kid. Or a nice kid. I'm sorry if I ever treated you bad."

Kiara didn't answer. They kept dancing, but the song soon ended. They headed back to the table, but Kiara stopped Mack at the edge of the dance floor.

"Nothing specific happened with us, but everyone said you were a stuck-up snob." Then Kiara smiled and bumped her shoulder. "You seem cool enough now."

It wasn't exactly a ringing endorsement, but at least it left room for hope. And maybe friendship. If she stayed around for any length of time, Mack would definitely be making more apologies like this. She'd left Gallant Lake after high school in a self-important blaze of glory, doing all but writing the words "See ya, suckers!" on the back of her car. People weren't likely to forget stuff like that, even if it was twenty years ago.

Kiara tipped her head toward the table. "What about you and Dan? Did I pick up on some chemistry there?"

"No, thanks. He's too... I don't know... Mr. Lawman these days. Maybe if he was still the Danny Adams we knew in school..."

Mack's gaze met Dan's as they approached the

table, and he gave her a quizzical smile. Kiara was trying to say something, but the music was too loud. They moved closer.

"That bad boy might still be in there. You just have to coax him out!"

"And how do you suggest I do that?"

"Dance with the man!"

Dance with him?

Mackenzie hadn't danced with a man in a long time. Mason would never risk looking foolish dancing to a fast song. He'd told her he couldn't afford to have someone video him and embarrass him with his investors, as if his dancing was really memorable. It wasn't. He'd occasionally oblige her with a slow dance, but in the last few years of their marriage, it had never felt like he was *there*. Even with her in his arms, his mind seemed elsewhere.

Kiara was saying something else, and Mack leaned in and turned her head to try to hear her. Her gaze landed on Dan again. He was looking straight at her. Again. They were almost at the table, and Kiara's voice dropped.

"…hasn't taken his eyes off you. I think you should dance with the guy and see what a little body contact does!"

As enticing as *a little body contact* sounded, it was a bad idea. If she really wanted to move forward and start fresh, dancing with her high school crush wasn't the way to do it. Especially since he'd turned into Captain Responsibility. She wanted an adventure with someone who wasn't afraid to break a few rules, and that wasn't Danny Adams.

Dan leaped to his feet to hold Mack's chair, and Owen scrambled to match his chivalry by holding Kiara's. Then Owen refilled Mack's glass of beer from the new pitcher, smirking at Dan as if he'd just won extra points in some competition. Dan glowered in return. If Kiara wasn't so into Owen, Mack might have flirted back more aggressively, just to see where it might lead. And what Dan would have done. She frowned. All her thoughts seemed to circle back to him.

"How many have you had again?" Dan's brow arched as she took a drink. She set the glass down and met his gaze, refusing to be intimidated.

"I don't see where that's any of your concern, Officer." Mack pulled her hair up and pressed her cool, damp napkin on the back of her neck. "I'm not driving, so put your badge away."

He scowled. "I'm not flashing a damn badge. I'm asking as a friend."

"Is that what you are? A friend?"

"What else would I be?"

They stared at each other in silence, although the din of the bar was pounding around them. People talking, shouting, laughing. Music throbbed, acting as the drumbeat beneath the action. With a start, Mack realized she was starting to lean closer to Dan. *Don't mess with the local lawman, remember?*

"Would you excuse me for a minute?" She stood, and Dan leaped to his feet again to hold her chair.

Mack needed to do two things—visit the ladies' room and put some space between her and Danger Dan. She'd felt slightly off balance from the moment he walked over to their table, and she didn't think it was all due to the beer.

She was mortified at her appearance in the ladies' room mirror. Her hair was wild, her face was shimmering with sweat and her eyes were bright. Too bright.

She put a cold, wet paper towel on her face and ran wet fingers through her hair to settle it down. When she came back out into the bar, Dan stood again. He sure was Mr. Manners tonight. But there was a heat there in his eyes that made her wonder if Kiara was right. If Danger Dan might still be in there.

In an unplanned act of bravado, she grabbed Dan by the hand before he could sit back down.

"Come on, Danny boy, let's dance!"

Kiara and Shelly let out catcalls from the table as Mack led a bemused Dan to the dance floor. A fast song was blaring about country boys and back roads.

Dan protested he didn't know much about country music, but Mack ignored him. Then he spun her effortlessly and she realized he was actually a good dancer. His eyes never left hers as she bounced to the song's beat, but she couldn't read his expression. All those years of law enforcement had taught him how to hide his feelings well.

The next tune slowed to more of a two-step. It was one of those stereotypical country songs—the singer was crooning about how jealous he was of the beer his girlfriend put to her lips. Dan twirled Mack around again, leaned close and said, "Did that singer just say he wanted to check his girl for *ticks*?"

Mack threw her head back and laughed. "Sure— but he wants to do it in the moonlight. That makes it romantic, right?"

"I'd never thought about it, but I can see how that might be fun." Dan flashed Mack a smile that almost made her heart stop. Her smile faltered, but she forced herself to respond lightly.

"It's every country girl's dream."

"Okay, hold still then…" Dan grabbed her tightly by the waist and they both started laughing as his hands moved lightly up and down her back, making motions to check her for pests as she swatted at him.

Then the song stopped, and a slow song came on. Dan pulled Mack close and there they were, locked in an embrace in the center of the floor, swaying gently against one another as the singer crooned about blue not being a good color on his girl.

Back when she'd been a teenager, she'd privately dreamed of slow dancing with Danny Adams. It was surreal to actually be doing it so many years later. As the song continued, she found herself relaxing into his arms. Whether it was the alcohol, the song or his embrace, Mack felt a flood of emotions as they swayed together. She'd spent so much time being angry about the failure of her marriage, but some of that anger was beginning to ease. She rested her head on Dan's shoulder and felt tears threatening to spill. She'd been without a man's caring embrace for too long. She hadn't realized until that moment how very lonely she'd been.

Dan seemed as unprepared for the intimacy the song invited as she was. His hands fell to her waist. She could feel him hesitating, debating with himself. But as Mack snuggled closer, his arms tightened reflexively. One hand moved up her back. When she laid her head on his shoulder, he slid his hand to the back of her neck and dropped his cheek to the top of her head. It was intimate and private and lovely.

The music built, and Dan spun across the floor without releasing her. She moved with him as if they were one, hip to hip, head on his shoulder, secure in his arms. For a moment, the rest of the world fell away. When the music stopped, they stayed locked in their embrace in the center of the dance floor. Mack finally blinked and looked up, surprised to see the floor crowded with other couples. It felt as though they'd been dancing completely alone.

Dan took a deep breath, and his arms loosened enough for her to step back and look up into his eyes. They were dark and intense and were locked on her. His guard had dropped, and she was surprised to see sadness there, and longing. And there was also heat. She felt suddenly sober and stepped away abruptly.

"You know, I'm thinking it's time for me to head home." Mack glanced away to break the intense moment. She'd wanted this, but now that she was confronted with the chance to be a little wild, she felt panic bubbling up.

Dan's brows rose. "You haven't finished your beer."

"I think I can do without more beer, don't you?"

But she followed him back to the table. She tried to avoid Kiara and Shelly's speculative expressions. After that slow dance, she and Dan were going to be gossip fodder in Gallant Lake for sure. When Dan leaned over to answer something Kiara said, Shelly grabbed Mack and started whispering.

"That man has the hots for you! And it looks like it's mutual."

"Shh!" Mack hissed. "You're crazy!" Or was she? "He's not what I'm looking for." Or was he? "I've had way too much to drink." Well, that much was true.

She felt something touch her fingers and looked up to see Dan's hand next to hers on the table. Their eyes met, and he smiled softly as he nodded to something Owen was saying about a baseball game on the television behind the bar. Mack felt an unfamiliar flutter in her abdomen. She was definitely feeling reckless tonight, but the past was whispering warnings even the alcohol couldn't silence.

Mason had been a charmer, too, in the beginning. Mason was handsome and so very civilized in his actions, but he seemed driven to make sure he was always the center of attention. Dan was far more comfortable in his own skin, but he was Gallant Lake's version of Superman. And she had a feeling the *ice queen* wasn't the Lois Lane the locals had in mind for their hero.

Dan walked to the bar. Shelly was calling to her over the loud music. "You're looking mighty dreamy-eyed, girlfriend!"

Mack rolled her eyes. "Wasn't it you who told me we're not in high school anymore? The next thing you know, you'll be asking me to carve our initials inside a heart or toss a coin in the old wishing well on Gilford's Ridge."

Shelly laughed. "Wow, I haven't thought about that old wishing well in ages... I wonder if it's still up there? I should take my kids hiking and see if we can find it. Look, you don't have to *marry* the guy, Mack. Just have some fun. Dan's a good guy, and Lord knows he deserves some fun, too. And after watching you two dance... Well, let's just say there was some hotness goin' on!"

Dan returned, thankfully ending the conversation. He handed her a glass, but it wasn't beer.

"I thought you might want some water to hydrate yourself from all your...uh...activity."

"In other words, you agree I've had enough beer tonight? You're right—this is not a typical Friday night for me." Remembering she was here to start a more fun-loving life, she lifted her chin. "At least it wasn't before tonight."

Owen leaned forward to make himself heard over the music. "Hey, Dan, you bike, right? A bunch of us are going to do the loop around the lake Sunday. Wanna join us?"

Mack's eyes went wide. "Dan, you still have your motorcycle? I used to love the way that thing rumbled..."

Kiara's eyebrows rose, and Mack realized she sounded gushy. But she hadn't thought of Dan pulling up behind the liquor store on that dark red Harley of his in a long time. He'd been every teenage girl's bad-boy dream—handsome, reckless and restless. She used to run to the back window when she heard him coming, just to watch him pull that helmet off and run his fingers through his hair, wearing those tight jeans.

Was it hot in here, or was it her memories that were heating her up right now? She gulped down the cold water, nearly emptying the glass in one pull. Dan was saying something. Oh, damn. Dan was talking and she wasn't even listening...

"...think Owen's referring to *bicycles*, not motorcycles." He nodded toward Owen. "I've got Chloe this weekend, so I'll have to pass." His mouth slanted into a half grin as he turned back to Mack. "But yes, I still have the old Harley. It's been in mothballs for a few years, but I can't seem to part with that last vestige of my misspent youth."

That bad boy might still be in there...

"You know, I've never been on a motorcycle. You should give me a ride sometime..."

Dan coughed and the others laughed. That wasn't the kind of *ride* she'd meant, of course. Or was it? Rather than apologize, she just met his gaze and shrugged.

There was a spark of something in his eyes. Interest? He closed them and shook his head, as if chasing away whatever thoughts she'd put there.

"Okay, Miss New Leaf, I think it's time to head home." He looked toward the entrance, where several men were standing. She recognized Nate Thomas and Asher Peyton among them. Asher was smirking in Dan's general direction. "Looks like my friends are ready to head out. I didn't drive, but Asher and I can drop you."

Owen spoke up. "I can drive her home."

Dan glanced at the cola Owen held. The two men had a brief stare down before Mack had enough of it.

"Before you two cavemen start pounding your chests, I'm *walking* home. Alone." She held up her hand when they both started to object. "I'm a big girl, it's not that far, and there are sidewalks and streetlights the whole way." She glanced Dan's way. "And I have it on good authority that this is a very safe town."

Owen sat back in his chair. "Suit yourself. You coming back next Friday? Third Fridays are…" His forehead furrowed in thought. "Oh, yeah. Classic rock. Always a good time."

"I don't know what my plans are for next week. I have to make living arrangements for Dad at some point." Shelly and Kiara both gave her a wave good-night, with promises to stop by the store. Dan didn't move until she headed for the door, then he fell in step with her.

"I'll walk you home and have Asher pick me up there. You shouldn't be walking alone."

Mack came to an abrupt stop. "Oh, please. Stop being such a knight in shining armor. I'm a grown woman." She pointed at Asher, whom she'd met just that week. Nora's husband, he owned the custom furniture shop a few doors down from the liquor store. "Go home with your pals and leave me alone."

He stared at her, then shrugged. "Fine. Go do your independent thing."

She hadn't expected him to give up his protector role so easily. When he didn't say more, she brushed past him.

She was almost by when he spoke softly, "Text me when you get there."

It wasn't an unreasonable request, so she nodded before heading out the door. It didn't take more than fifteen minutes to get back to the apartment, and the walk through a quiet Gallant Lake helped sober her up. Before she unlocked the door, she sent a quick text to Dan, simply saying, I'm home. As soon as the notice popped up that the message was delivered, she saw headlights come on in the parking lot behind the strip of stores and apartments. A Jeep slowly pulled away, and she recognized it as Asher's. Which meant Dan had made sure they followed her home anyway.

Maybe she should have been annoyed, but the way he'd done it was pretty chivalrous and sweet, and he *was* a cop, after all, and probably couldn't help himself. She waved as she went inside, just to let him know she was onto him. She locked the door behind her, and Rory trotted down the hall to wind between her legs, complaining loudly.

"Yeah, yeah. I hear you, cat. Your dish empty? Whose fault is that?"

She tossed a few pieces of kibble in, and they

were gone in a flash. If she fed this cat as much as
he thought she should, he'd weigh fifty pounds instead of twenty. She had another glass of water before going to her room and crawling into bed. She'd
just turned the lights out and Rory was settling on
the pillow next to her when her phone chirped with
a message. It was from Dan.

Drink some water or you'll have a headache.

Why did he have to be so freaking nice? And
why did she like it so much? She debated how to
respond, then grinned. Maybe she could get him to
blush again.

You know, I have a bicycle-type bike, too. If you ever
want to take a ride.

The bubbles appeared, then stopped. Then appeared again, but nothing came through. She chuckled, and Rory let out an annoyed mew next to her.
Was Dan lying in bed like her? Staring at his phone
in the dark, wondering what they were doing? The
bubbles started up again.

Chloe and I are taking a bicycle ride Sunday if you
want to join us. Pick you up around noon?

She had a sneaking suspicion one of those first
unsent responses was more interesting, but the invitation was a pleasant surprise. And a family bike ride

was something new and different, if not all that risky.
Bert was covering the liquor store this weekend.

Sounds good.

As she rolled over and closed her eyes, she knew
she'd be dreaming of a teenage Dan riding that Harley.

Chapter Seven

Dan took Mack's bike out of the back of his truck and looked it over as he held it for her to take. Just like her hiking boots, she'd gone for the top-of-the-line.

"You might want to remove the price tag."

She laughed and tugged at the tag attached to the handlebars. "That does look a little tacky, doesn't it? Don't want anyone to think I'm riding a stolen bike with the local sheriff."

He really wished people would stop saying stuff like that. "I'm not the sheriff today, okay?" He reached into his shorts pocket for his folding knife, reaching over to cut through the cord holding the tag in place. "There you go."

Mack's forehead furrowed. "You said something

like that Friday night, too. That you weren't the guy with the badge. Does it bother you being Sheriff Dan all the time?"

He watched his daughter pedaling her purple bike in circles behind the truck. "Chloe, ride on the bike path, where there aren't any cars, okay?" He turned to Mack, handing her helmet to her. "The whole *Sheriff Dan* thing started as a term of affection. Respect. I guess it still *is* that, but sometimes it makes me feel like a cartoon character. Like that's all I am—some 24-7 do-gooder crossing guard or something."

"Uh…you just moved your daughter to the nice safe bike path from the equally safe parking lot. And reminded me about my helmet. And you followed me home Friday night to make sure I got there safely. And you were clearly trying to determine everyone's alcohol consumption at the Chalet. And people like my dad give you the keys to their businesses…"

Dan set his own bike on the ground with more force than he intended. "The job is hard to turn off, Mack." She started to speak, but he talked over her. "But that doesn't mean I don't *want* to be treated like I'm just…Dan…once in a while." He jammed his ball cap onto his head. He wasn't even making sense to himself. Since when had he resented the *Sheriff Dan* thing? Maybe since drugs moved into his town and made him feel impotent. Maybe he didn't mind it when he felt like he might really be the hero. Maybe that made him a jerk. It was all too much to digest at the moment. "It just gets to be a lot sometimes, that's all." He turned away before she had a chance to say anything. "Come on, Chloe. Let's get this show on the road. You ride between Mack and me, especially on the main roads. Mack, you take the lead. We're taking the lake trail as far as we can, then up the hill to the resort, which means we'll be on the main road for a little way, but there's a wide shoulder. It's a busy road, so be sure to look both ways…"

Mack was straddling her bike, giving him a smirky grin.

"What?"

Her shoulder rose and fell. "For someone who doesn't want to be School-Crossing Dan, you really *do* tend to fret over things and boss people around."

She wasn't wrong. "The one job I *don't* want to change is being a dad. I'm just keeping her safe." He looked at Chloe, who was waiting impatiently for somebody to do something. Mack considered that, then tipped her head.

"Fair enough. But let's explore this conversation more at a later date." She waved at Chloe, and he noticed the purple bracelet sparkling on Mack's wrist. It matched the one on Chloe's arm. "I haven't ridden a bike in years that wasn't stationary and in a gym, so don't laugh at me."

He *did* laugh. All three of them did as Mack wobbled and zigzagged and had to plant her feet on the ground more than once to keep from falling over. But she eventually got the hang of it, and Dan wasn't laughing anymore. Riding behind her, watching her rounded butt go up and down, back and forth, over and over...it was enough to make *his* bike zigzag a few times. She was in capris and a knit top—just snug enough to show off all of her rounded lines. Mack used to be obsessively thin in high school. Always on some crazy diet some Hollywood star raved about in a magazine. Ryan used to tease that a good wind would blow her over.

That sure as hell wasn't the case anymore, and it was a vast improvement. She was far more interesting with those lush curves everywhere. She was far more interesting, period. He couldn't believe he'd texted her at almost midnight on Friday, telling her to drink more water. He rolled his eyes at himself. Could he get any nerdier? And then she'd responded by carrying on that embarrassing innuendo game that she'd started in the bar, about him giving her a ride. The Mackenzie Wallace he'd known as a girl would have *never* spoken that way, at least not intentionally. But Mack had been *very* intentional.

Just like when she pressed up against him on the dance floor. Intentional.

"Oh, hell!" His bike went off the path and he barely managed to get it through the grass and back onto the path without going head over heels. Mack and Chloe both stopped, looking back at him in surprise. Not his finest moment. He felt his face heat up.

"Sorry. Bad dad language. I owe you a buck, Chloe. Can I put it on credit for now?"

She nodded with a bright grin. "Sure, Dad. What happened back there?"

As if she knew she'd been responsible for his lapse

in attention, Mack joined in with a fairly wicked grin. "Yeah, Dan. What happened back there?"

"I got distracted, smart-a…" He cleared his throat. "Smarty-pants. We're almost to the road. Mack, you remember the way to Halcyon, right?"

"I haven't been gone *that* long, Dan. It's the biggest landmark in town, after the resort, of course." She started pedaling again. "Didn't you and Ryan used to go up there and sneak into the place looking for the ghost?"

He and Ryan used to sneak around the overgrown property surrounding the big stone castle, but they sure as hell weren't looking for some ghost. They used to break into the carriage house through a back window and smoke weed and drink with pals like Owen Graber. Once in a while, they'd take a couple adventurous girls with them and have fun trying to get past second base. He and Ryan really had been a couple of punk kids back then.

Chloe called back to him. "Dad! Did you really break into the castle? Did you *see* the ghost?"

"I did *not* break into the castle." Just the carriage house. "And there is no ghost, Chloe. It's just a story. Mr. and Mrs. Randall live there now with their kids. They wouldn't do that if the place was haunted." Of course, they'd named their daughter Madeleine, after the woman rumored to haunt the place, but they must have just liked the name or something. A large truck passed them but was courteous enough to swing out into the far lane. "Pay attention to the road, sweetheart."

The hill to the resort and Halcyon wasn't steep, but it was long, and Dan could see Mack was struggling a little. He called up to her, "You okay up there? Need a break?"

"Nope…" She sounded winded. "I'm fine. It's not much farther…is it?"

There was so much hope in those last two words that he had to laugh. She must have been exhausted, but she didn't quit.

They passed the entrance to the Gallant Lake Golf Club, and a low stone wall stretched ahead along the road all the way to the main entrance of the resort. The Gallant Lake Resort was nearly a hundred years old, built back in the days when people flocked from the city to the Catskills for weeks at a time during the summer. The movie *Dirty Dancing* wasn't *all* fiction. The resort had even had waterfront camp cottages at one time, and the main building had several hundred rooms.

Most of the cottages were gone now, and the resort had almost met the same fate. When Blake Randall bought the three-story fieldstone and timber hotel, his plan was to tear it all down and build a ten-story casino in its place. But then he met his now-wife, Amanda, and she changed everything. She remodeled the historic castle named Halcyon and captured Blake's heart in the process. They adopted Blake's orphaned nephew and had a daughter of their own, and Blake went from being despised in Gallant Lake to being a community leader and benefactor.

The stone wall rose to form two large pillars on

either side of the entrance to the resort. A limo pulled
out as they rode by. These days, the remodeled resort
was bringing in well-heeled guests from Manhattan
and all over. Beyond the resort entrance, the fence
changed from stone to wrought iron, signaling they
were almost to the Halcyon entrance. When they
were opposite it, Mack pulled her bike to the edge
of the shoulder and looked back to Dan. Her face
was red and shining with sweat, but she was smiling.

"What now? Are we going in?" She winked.
"Wanna see if there are any windows unlocked in
the carriage house?"

So she *knew* what her brother and Dan had been
up to all those years ago. He shook his head. "No,
thanks. The place is very much occupied these days,
not to mention it's monitored by the security team at
the resort. Cross over when it's safe, and we'll grab
an iced tea down at the resort."

"Yes!" Chloe gave a little fist pump. "Can we
walk down to the lakeshore? Can I go to the ballroom where the fashion show's gonna be? Can I go
up the big tree stairs?"

He gave his daughter a don't-push-your-luck look.
"Yes. Probably not. Maybe."

Her face scrunched up as she tried to apply the answers to the questions and determine if it was good
or bad. Traffic was clear, so they crossed the road
and went down to the resort, riding between the big
stone pillars and putting their bikes in the rack near
the front door.

Mack took off her helmet and shook her hair

loose, frowning at her brand-new bicycle. "I don't have a bike lock. Will it be safe here?"

Dan directed her attention up to a small camera on the building, aimed directly at the bike rack. He waved, and grinned when the green light below the camera blinked twice. Either Nick West was in the surveillance room, or his employee Brad was, and they'd seen him. Dan flashed a thumbs-up and took his daughter's hand, smiling over her head at Mack. "No one will touch the bikes. This place has tighter security than Fort Knox, and probably more cameras."

Mack was amazed by the transformation of the old Gallant Lake Resort. She remembered it being a nice, but really tired even then, place. It had always seemed trapped in a time warp of 1950s mountain lodge kitsch and even more questionable 1980s "upgrades," with gleaming brass everywhere. But there was no sign of that now. The lobby was open and inviting, with a very contemporary nod to camp motif. The main staircase used to be a wide, curving oak affair. It wasn't ugly, but it wasn't pretty, either.

It had been replaced with a massive round pillar in the center of the lobby, carved to look like a tree trunk. An open wooden staircase wrapped around the pillar with a metal banister that was designed with leaves and scrollwork. Large copper leaves were scattered across the ceiling three stories above, hanging down in some places. The effect as a whole made her wonder if there was a wondrous tree house hiding up there. No wonder Chloe had wanted to climb the big tree stairs. Mack did, too.

Dan noticed her gaping and gave her a nudge. "A little different than you remember?"

"Uh, yeah. I feel underdressed." She watched an older couple walk by, the woman in head-to-toe designer resort wear. The kind of stuff Mack used to wear every weekend at Glenfadden.

Dan nodded toward the back wall, where a row of french doors opened to a spacious veranda. "We might not get into the main restaurant for Sunday brunch looking like this, but we're fine for the out-door grill."

Chloe was already headed outside. They sat at a bistro table overlooking the outdoor pool and enjoyed iced tea while sharing a tray of nachos. Chloe told Mack about the fashion show she was going to be part of in June, and how much she hoped for a pur-ple outfit to wear. She even wanted purple hair. That announcement made Dan blanch a bit, but Mack as-sured him there were plenty of safe *temporary* hair colors Chloe could use.

When the nachos were gone, so was Chloe. She was determined to see the water, and one of the re-sort's employees, whom Dan introduced as Brad from Security, offered to take her down the expan-sive lawn to the lake. Dan watched closely as Chloe ran ahead of Brad, making Mack laugh.

"Do you not trust your friend? The guy from *security*?"

He finally dragged his eyes away from his daugh-

ter. "She's my child, Mack. With the job I have...
You don't know what it's like to have a child..."

She took a sharp intake of breath and he rushed
to backtrack.

"I mean... I just meant that a parent doesn't ever
stop being a parent..."

"Which I wouldn't know because I'm *not* one?"

His lips pressed together, and he looked everywhere but at her. His eyes flicked to the lakeshore,
where Chloe was running back and forth as Brad
watched closely.

"Was that on purpose?" he asked, still not meeting her gaze. "That you and your husband didn't
have children?"

From anyone else, the question would be way too
personal. Offensive, even. But this was Danny, and
she'd known him her whole life. He'd be fine if she
told him to mind his own business. But she didn't.

"It wasn't on purpose, but it turned out for the
best, I guess. We didn't have to worry about screwing up a child when we..." Her eyes closed. Now it
was her turn to be embarrassed.

"When you got divorced, like me and Chloe's
mom?" There was no accusation in his voice. If anything, he sounded amused. "One thing's for sure—
we're not in high school anymore, Mackie. Let's
establish a judgment-free zone between us, okay?"

She looked into his warm eyes and smiled. "Fair
enough." She watched him check on Chloe again.
"What happened with you and Susanne?"

His mouth twisted. "I don't know if any one thing

happened. It just ended, and we both knew it. Instead of hanging on so long that we'd end up hating each other, we worked out a split that kept things as easy for Chloe as possible." He looked at her. "What about you? Did something happen, or…?"

She huffed a small laugh. "You could say that. Remember how I was always the good girl?" He nodded. "Well, I never gave that up. Good student. Good college. Successful husband. And I spent every bit of my energy being the good wife." They both stood as Chloe ran up the lawn toward them. This conversation was going to end quickly. "Until the day I learned he was cheating on me with a cocktail waitress at our country club. I was so busy being Patty Perfect, but my husband only wanted Patty Perfect as his respectable arm candy. He wanted a naughty girl in bed."

Dan's eyes clouded, but Chloe was there before he could speak.

"Dad! There were great big fish right next to the shore! Brad said they were carp. What are carp, Dad?"

Dan looked straight at Mack.

"They're bottom-feeders, honey. Nothing but scummy, no-good bottom-feeders."

Mack tried and failed to hold back a smile. He wasn't talking about fish.

Chapter Eight

Dan walked around his old Harley and whistled. "Damn, Wyatt. It looks brand-new."

He'd gone to school with Wyatt Henderson, and they'd both gotten married the same year. But Wyatt's wife died of breast cancer before she reached thirty. Wyatt had poured his energy into building this classic car dealership and service shop just outside of town. It had always been his dream, and his wife made him promise to do it after she was gone.

Wyatt nodded with a smile. "It basically *is* brand-new. These babies shouldn't be left sitting in a garage without being run once in a while. She needed new tires, new brakes and a new carburetor. But she's all inspected and ready to roll." He handed Dan the keys. "What made you dust her off?"

He mumbled something about it being the right time, but the truth was he couldn't stop thinking about the gleam in the eyes of a sassy blonde who'd never ridden a motorcycle. The way Mack had talked about listening to the engine's rumble made Dan think it was more than the bike she'd liked back then. Which was a complete shock, because he'd never looked at her that way when they were kids. Not that she wasn't attractive to him, but she was his buddy's kid sister. It felt like she was *his* kid sister with all the time he'd spent at the Wallace home. His brain just never went there, and then she was gone.

Mack's desire to take a walk on the wild side made a lot more sense after their chat on Sunday. Her ass-hat husband had cheated on her. With a younger, *wilder* woman—at least in Mack's eyes. She wanted to see what she thought she'd been missing by being a good kid and a faithful wife.

Before Dan's shift started on Monday, he'd rolled the bike out of the garage and called Wyatt to pick it up and do whatever it took to get it roadworthy. When it was done, he had Asher drop him off at Wyatt's. His pal made a few comments about a midlife crisis before he drove off. But this wasn't about Dan. It was about Mack. It was about helping her find the kind of spirit that had her dancing in a mountain meadow a couple weeks ago.

He realized Wyatt was saying something and followed where he was pointing—to the plywood covering a shattered window. He was asking about the investigation into the break-ins. Dan coughed and nodded as if he'd been listening all along.

"Well…um… I don't think there are any new leads, but Sam's still working the case." Sam Edgewood was the state trooper who'd answered the alarm call. He and Dan were friends, and both were on the new antidrug task force in the county. "He won't let it go until he has something. He's one of the best."

Wyatt shook his head. "I'm sure it was some kids looking for easy money. A pro never would have left all these vehicles and parts here. They went to the cash box and that was it." They started walking up to the showroom so Dan could pay for the bike. "It's probably a good thing I did what you suggested and left forty bucks in there every night when I cashed out to make the bank deposit."

Dan nodded. "Always a good idea to leave a little cash available. Sometimes it's enough for them to snatch and run without trashing the place looking for more."

"My heart just about stopped when I got the call from the security service at three in the morning. I'm looking into installing a camera system along with the motion detectors."

Dan pulled out his wallet. "Talk to Blake Randall or his head of security, Nick West. They've got a primo system up there and might be able to recommend something that would work for you." He'd been looking down as he walked, searching for his credit card. He looked up when Wyatt brought up his least favorite subject.

"I've been hearing stories about drugs in town. It's hard to believe." He printed a receipt and handed it to Dan to sign. "I mean, they're everywhere, but why would they suddenly turn into such a big deal in our little town? Did some drug lord just move in or something?"

Dan shoved the receipt in his pocket. It was a question he heard daily, and he was sick of it. But he also understood the frustration. And Wyatt was a trusted friend. Susanne had been his wife's nurse during those awful final days.

"I don't know, man. We've got a whole freakin' task force on it, and we still can't figure it out. We think the town somehow got selected as a waypoint between the city and upstate, but they must have a local connection that's helping them stay out of sight." He looked Wyatt straight in the eye. "We'll find them, Wyatt. I won't let this happen to our town. I won't give up until we have them."

"I believe you, Dan, And you know I wasn't trying to pin it on you." Wyatt walked outside with him. The air held the promise of summer today, warm with a hint of sultry. Wyatt must have thought the same thing. He clapped Dan's shoulder. "I know you're determined, but you still need to make time for yourself to rest and regroup. It's a great day for a nice long bike ride to clear your head. You'll be better for it, I promise."

Dan was off duty, but the task force was never off the clock. He could check in with Sam and Terry and see if there were any new developments. The sunlight glinted off the mirrors on the Harley. Or he could go cruise around town and see if he could find an adventurous blonde looking for her first motorcycle ride.

He pulled out onto the highway with a wave, and it was even more fun than he'd anticipated to accelerate around the curve at the top of the hill and take in the countryside as he drove the bike back toward town. There was a little spot in his chest that woke up for the first time in years. The sense of freedom that the open road instilled was something he hadn't exactly been nurturing in himself.

He took a deep breath and smelled the damp, overturned earth of the farm he was passing. He smelled the freshness of new leaves on the trees. As he got closer to town, he could smell the clean, sharp scent of the lake itself. He might be doing this for Mack, but there was no arguing that he was enjoying this far more than he'd imagined he would.

"I'm sorry, Dad. I'm pretty sure my hearing is going. *What* did you just say?" Mack was surprised she was able to move her jaw enough to form words after the way it dropped at her father's announcement. He leveled a gaze at her that made it clear she could quickly be on thin ice with him, but she didn't care. "You're moving in with Cathy Meadows? Wha…when did this decision get made? When were you going to tell me? Are you two…?"

He sat on the edge of the bed, fully dressed, bags packed. If she hadn't stopped by this morning, would he have even bothered telling her he was leaving the rehab center?

"Lower your voice, Mackenzie." His tone was even but brooked no argument. Her father wasn't a big guy. He wasn't a loud guy. He was the kind of guy who just plugged along, doing his job, being nice and respectful to everyone he met unless they gave him a reason not to be. He was *not* the kind of guy to hang out with an aging hippie like Cathy. He gestured to the chair near the bed. "Sit down and hear me out before you go gettin' excited."

She never considered *not* obeying him. She'd never disobeyed her father, who'd been the one steady constant in her life. So she sat down and did her best to smooth the shock off her face, folding her hands in her lap. If her fingers were clutching at each other, that just couldn't be helped. He gave a brief nod.

"First, you know I'm ready to get out of this dang place. The food stinks and the bed's uncomfortable and the lights are on in the hallway all night long. I haven't had a good night's sleep since the accident, and I really need one. The only reason they haven't released me is that I can't get up the stairs to the apartment." His gaze darted away from hers. "Cathy has a very nice double-wide with a floor plan that'll be easy for me to maneuver that scooter thing around." He gestured toward the tri-wheeled scooter he had to rest his right leg on for the next six weeks. "Cathy and I have been friends for years.

She helped take care of your mother. She's a lovely person, Mackenzie."

Her mouth opened and closed a few times. She had a sneaking suspicion there was more to this than Cathy being a generous friend.

"So are you going to sleep in a guest room there, or…?"

Dad's cheeks went red, and his mouth thinned to a hard line.

"Where I sleep is none of your damned business, young lady."

Mack straightened. Dad never swore—not even "damn"—in mixed company. She'd heard rumors that his language was a lot saltier when he was playing cards with the guys, but *never* if a woman was present. The fact that he'd just dropped a "damn" on her meant she'd ticked him off big-time.

"Dad, you might be right, but…" He started to argue, but she held up her hand. "*But* I don't think it's an unreasonable question. I'm not judging…" She was, kind of, but she was really trying not to. "And if you have a…relationship…that makes you happy, then…good." Fine. Wonderful. Great. "I just want to know what's going on. I'm your daughter. I mean… I don't need details, but are you and Cathy… an item? Because I sure as hell…*heck*…haven't heard anything about it."

"He didn't know how to tell you." The voice came from the doorway behind Mack. "And he made *me* promise not to." Cathy walked over and sat on the bed next to her father. Mack's *father*. When Cathy took his hand, Dad gave the woman a soft, tender smile with a gleam in his eyes that Mack hadn't seen in twenty years. Her breath came out in a whoosh that left her feeling dizzy.

Her father was in *love*. How had she missed this? And how did she feel about it? He gave her a truly repentant look.

"It started about the time you and Mason were... having problems. You were upset, and I started talking to Cathy over coffee, and then we started talking over dinner, and then we started having nightcaps at my place, and..." He shrugged, knowing he didn't have to fill in the rest.

"So you're saying this..." She gestured between them. "Is *my* fault?"

Her father shook his head. "No."

At the same time, Cathy was nodding. "Yes. And thank you."

A startled laugh bubbled up. "I'm glad my divorce made *someone* happy."

There was a beat of silence as the three of them stared at each other, then they all started laughing. Her dad was laughing so hard he had to wipe his eyes with his free hand, because he wouldn't let go of Cathy's hand with the other. Mack sat back in her chair, shaking her head in amazement.

Cathy's laughter faded. "Honey, you know I loved your mama. She was one of my dearest friends, and..."

Mack waved her hand in the air, as much in surrender as anything else. "I'm sure Mom would approve. She's been gone eighteen years now, and she loved you both. I…" She straightened, then stood. "I don't *object*. I just need to wrap my head around it." Her eyes narrowed on her dad, who glanced quickly away. "It would have helped if I'd known more than fifteen *minutes* before you move in together."

"It's only temporary…" Dad started, then stopped when he saw Cathy's face fall. "I mean…we were going to *say* it was temporary. But the truth is…it's probably not…temporary. This way you can have the apartment to yourself. Do whatever you want to it. Cathy's got a great little place, and it's paid for, and if I start collecting Social Security…"

Whoa. Was he *retiring*?

"What about the liquor store?"

He chewed his lip, and Cathy jumped in. "We were thinking maybe *you'd* take the store. It's past time for Carl to retire. He could still come in and help, like I did after I sold the coffee shop to Nora. But the pressure would be off. He and I could… travel."

Since when did her father care about *traveling*? Mack put her hand over her eyes. This must be what it felt like when a person's head was getting ready to explode. A little dizzy, a little fuzzy, losing the ability to speak coherently. Yup. Her head was going to explode any minute now. She held her hand out to stop Cathy from saying any more.

"I need to go. I need…" She swallowed hard. "I need to go…think. Or something. Do you need any help getting to Cathy's place?"

Her father and his…his *girlfriend*…both shook their heads. "It's all set. There's only two steps up to the front door, and the railings are sturdy enough for him to be able to hop up there. Once he's inside, there's plenty of room. I took up the area rugs for now so he won't get hung up on them. You should come. Well…" Cathy cleared her throat, her cheeks going pink. "Of course you *need* to come. Maybe for dinner? Tonight? Tomorrow? This weekend?"

Her dad nodded. "Yes. And you could bring some of my clothes. I mean, I have some there now, but…"

So her dad already had a stay-over drawer at Cathy's. It would be cute if it wasn't so mind-boggling.

"Do you have enough clothes to get you through to the weekend? Tomorrow's our first official wine tasting at the store. It's just a test, with invited guests, but I still have a lot to do. And I should get started on all that work right now." She really needed to get out of here. "Uh…let me know if you need anything, and um…have fun, I guess."

She stopped at the store long enough to finish getting the tables and chairs in place and lined up the four wines and two craft whiskeys they'd be tasting. It would just be Nora and her cousins, plus Shelly and Kiara. Bert seemed to have everything else under control, which left Mack with little to do. So she changed into her sneakers and went for a walk, heading up the hill toward the resort, her head spinning.

Her dad. Cathy. Mack's failed marriage. Danger Dan. All those boxes she'd put people into. None of those boxes seemed to fit anymore. Was it good? Bad? Or just…life?

She was approaching the resort's golf course when a motorcycle came roaring over the crest of the hill ahead of her. She thought nothing of it until the bike slowed dramatically, then pulled into the entrance of the golf club and stopped directly in front of her. Awkward. And a little scary. She didn't know anyone with a motorcycle in town, and this guy was staring straight at her through his black helmet visor.

He pulled the helmet off, and she started to laugh in surprised relief. Danny Adams. On a motorcycle. Talk about people not filling their assigned boxes. Or into tight jeans. Or…she totally lost her train of thought. Dan's denim-clad legs were braced to hold the bike upright, and he was smiling at her. Wait. He was reaching a hand out to her. For *what*?

"Perfect timing, Mackie. Wanna take that first-ever motorcycle ride?"

The bike was idling with a rumble that vibrated in her chest. He looked like sex on a stick right now, with that leather jacket and his usually neat hair standing on end, clutching the gleaming black helmet in his hand. The thought of wrapping her arms around his waist and straddling that machine was extremely tempting.

"Isn't there a helmet law in New York?"

He reached behind him with a grin, pulling a dark purple helmet out of the saddlebag and handing it to her. What a strange, through-the-looking-glass sort of day this was turning into.

"And you carry a purple helmet with you at all times because…?"

"Because you never know when you might see someone who likes purple and really needs a ride."

Her lips trembled a little. He had no idea. "Was it that obvious?"

His smile slipped. "Is everything okay?"

She looked down at the noisy bike and her smile strengthened. "It is now. Let's blow this Popsicle stand, Luke Perry."

She stepped forward, but he stopped her, looking at her feet. "Whoa. Sneaker laces and motorcycle-wheel spokes are not a good combination."

"I can tuck the laces into my sneaks." She bent over and did that, then straightened and took the helmet from his hand. "Is that better, Mr. Safety First?"

"Much." He helped her adjust the strap under her chin. "Watch the muffler. It'll burn your leg if you're not careful." The seat was more slippery and rounded than she'd anticipated. It also sloped forward so that body contact was unavoidable. Dan pointed out a couple handholds next to the seat and behind it, but *he* was the handhold she preferred. He tensed for a second when she slid her arm around his waist. Then he relaxed and patted her hand. "Good girl. Your body follows my body, okay? If I lean, you lean. If I don't lean, you don't. Got it?"

"Yes, sir, Officer, sir!"

He rolled his eyes and turned forward. His foot jiggled something, his hand moved something on the handlebars and they were off. He went back up the hill toward wherever he'd come from.

It was loud. And different. She felt very exposed, especially when a big truck passed them from the opposite direction. She lowered her head at first, resting it on the back of his shoulder and hiding her face from the wind. But when he turned onto the side road, she raised her head and kept it up. Cars had plenty of windows all around, but the view was nothing like this panorama in every direction. It felt like she was a *part* of the scenery instead of just driving through it. Dan seemed confident and at ease with the bike, and her grip loosened as she relaxed and took it in.

The lake stretched out below them on the left. On the right, Gallant Mountain rose high above, with heavy forests broken only by the occasional home. They went beyond the mountain and Dan made another turn, taking a road between two high ridges and heading into the rural countryside. She pressed up against his back and raised her voice so he could hear. "Come on, you can go faster than this!"

Dan shook his head, but he accelerated. She was tempted to put her arms out to the side, *Titanic*-style, but she wasn't sure if it would bother Dan. So she tried it with one arm, pointing to a herd of dairy cows and leaving her arm out there. He didn't react, so she slowly moved her other arm away from his stomach. She felt him tighten, but he didn't say anything. And then she was doing it. She was flying, arms out, chest pressed tight against Dan's back for security. They rode like that for a minute, then he glanced back and shook his head. She understood the unspoken command and behaved herself again, holding on to him and the bike. But the sense of freedom remained, burning bright.

Chapter Nine

Dan couldn't believe his luck at finding Mackie walking just as he was headed into town to seek her out. And the look on her face when he pulled off his helmet in front of her. Priceless. And then she'd put her leg across the seat, pressing her body so tight up against him he wasn't sure he'd be able to concentrate enough to drive.

If he thought he'd felt free before, that was nothing compared to how he felt with Mack's arms wrapped around him as they leaned into the curves along the country roads. Then she'd put her arms out like a bird behind him, and, as crazy as it was, he'd let her do it. At least for a mile or two. Because he knew she was feeling it, too. Freedom. No judgment. No responsibility. No labels to live up to…or run away from. He wasn't Danger Dan. Well…maybe a little. She wasn't prim and proper Mackenzie. He wasn't a guy with a badge right now. They were just two people cruising down the road on a sunny May afternoon. Dan and Mack.

He headed up the next hill and remembered that Paul Cooper's place was out here and the farm stand might be open. Paul had one of the biggest sugar maple groves in the area and made the best maple syrup around. Dan slowed down as they approached and saw the green banner flying that indicated the stand was open for business. Mack straightened and looked around as Dan brought the bike to a stop.

Today was an honor day at the stand. There was a covered bucket nailed to the post to collect payment and a limited amount of product out. A small sign sat on the plywood counter.

There's the price →
← There's the pay bucket
We have faith in you to do the right thing.
And if you don't pay us, we have faith in karma evening the score.

Mack slid off the bike and laughed at the sign, unbuckling her helmet. "Does that really work?"

"Most of the time." Dan nodded, mesmerized at the sight of her thick hair tumbling free. "Paul doesn't leave enough product out to hurt too bad if someone gets carried away. Usually the worst of it is someone walking off with a can of syrup." He pointed up under the eaves of the rustic-looking stand. "And that digital camera will usually catch the license plate, and maybe even a nice portrait." He waved, not expecting a response. Paul's truck wasn't there, but he might have an alert on his phone for the camera.

"What is up with all the cameras around this town? Is there some vast criminal underground you people are dealing with?"

Dan sorted through the maple sugar candy display and pulled out two small white paper packages from the back, where the afternoon sun wouldn't have melted them. He tossed one bag to Mack.

"These days, half the doorbells in this country are minicameras. You probably had just as many cameras in Greenwich, but you didn't have me around to point them out."

"Fair enough." She bit into a piece of candy molded into the form of a maple leaf. "Oh wow, this is delicious. But the sweetness makes my teeth tingle."

"Yeah, it's pure maple sugar. When Paul cooks the syrup all the way down, it turns into this."

"Do I know this Paul?"

"No. He bought the old Kraddock place ten years ago. He's done well with it. Has kids here for field trips, and he and his husband have a big party when the sap starts running in March." Dan popped a piece of candy in his mouth and let it melt there. He'd always been a sucker for anything maple flavored, even as a kid. His phone vibrated with a text. He grinned and nodded up toward the camera. "It's from Paul. He must have gotten an alert on his phone."

The texts came in rapid succession.

Scott and I are staying in the city tonight to catch a show.

When did you dig out the BIKE?

Who's the hot chick?

Dan turned his phone so Mack could read the messages. She joined him in laughter when she read the last line.

"I haven't had anyone think of me as a *hot chick* in a long time." She gave a thumbs-up toward the camera, then walked over to the large tree between the stand and the road.

"I can promise you that's not true."

Her laughter came to an abrupt halt.

"What?"

Dan walked over to where she was leaning against the tree. He brushed her hair back from her face, leaving his fingers on the silky-soft skin behind her ear.

"Come on, Mack. Even if *I* wasn't thinking it, every other guy would be."

Was it possible she didn't know? But then, no other man had seen her dancing barefoot in a mountain meadow. Her eyes went wide and unblinking. Her breath stilled, and he realized his had, too. His hand slid to curl around the back of her neck. What was this woman doing to him? His nice, orderly life was suddenly sliding toward disaster as if a cat was walking along and smacking everything over the edge.

Ryan's kid sister. He'd accosted her in her dad's store. He'd had a drink with her. He'd watched her dancing on the mountain. He'd danced *with* her. And now he was taking her for a spin on the Harley he'd had in mothballs for years. And he was thinking about kissing her. *Really* thinking about it. From the heat in her eyes, she was on the same wavelength he was. They stood like that, staring at each other, for what seemed like a very long time.

Time enough for him to realize that the exact color of her eyes was that of honey and hot cocoa layered over each other, with just a little gold glitter added in. Her thick lashes were approximately three-eighths of an inch long and were the same dark gold as her hair. She had exactly seven freckles on her right cheek and eight on her left. And her lips... Her lips were full and softly tinted pink. And they were parted. Waiting for him.

This was nuts. *Nuts.*

He hardly touched her at first, just brushing his lips against hers so softly he could barely feel it himself. His head lowered a fraction, increasing the pressure. That's when she responded, pushing against him and thrusting her hands up and into his hair, pulling him down. The kiss heated up exponentially second by second, until he had her flattened against the tree trunk, his tongue deep in her mouth and his hands cupping her butt.

He was a man who was trained to be constantly aware of his surroundings. That didn't turn off just because he was off duty. It *never* turned off. But he didn't even hear the approaching car until it was racing past them, a bunch of teens hanging out the windows hooting and hollering. Mack flinched, but he tightened his grip on her. Those high school kids would never recognize his Harley. And they'd never guess dear old Sheriff Dan would be necking with some blonde at the maple syrup stand.

The absurdity of it set off a bubble of laughter deep in his chest. He tried to hold it in until he realized Mack was shaking with laughter, too. He lifted his head and immediately missed the warm comfort of her lips. Her eyes shimmered with humor and heat. She moved one hand to his cheek, smacking him playfully.

"People our age usually know better than to have a make-out session in broad daylight on the side of the road." She tipped her head toward the bike. "Is this a side effect of that?"

"Do motorcycles make women horny? Sometimes."

Her playful slap got a little bit sharper on the side of his face. "*Women?* Excuse me, Officer, but *you're* the one who seems to have a thing for throwing me up against walls and trees and stuff."

"Yeah, I do, don't I?" He kissed her again, sliding her around behind the tree as he did. She giggled against his mouth. The sensation was electric. Her laughter. Her body, all soft and warm. Her mouth moving against his, doing her own exploring. Kissing this woman was like handling dynamite.

Another car went by, but they were out of sight now, and neither of them had any intention of stopping. Which was nuts, right? They were in Paul's front yard, for crying out loud. On a Thursday afternoon. He gave a deep groan of frustration. Mack clutched at him, probably guessing he was going to pull away. This wasn't the time or the place. He lifted his head, and now it was Mack's turn to groan. She grabbed at his shirt, but he took a step back. Time for a reality check.

"Mack…it's four o'clock in the afternoon. And we haven't even talked about…anything." The corner of his mouth lifted. "I know you want to be adventurous, but going any further out here is a little *too* far, isn't it?"

She raised her fingers to her lips and nodded. "Right. Of course. Sure."

A commercial truck went by at a rate well above the speed limit. She flinched, then stepped away from the tree. He watched her eyes, which dimmed for a moment before brightening again. Her mouth curved into a sly smile. She patted his chest and walked by him toward the bike.

"I guess there's a little Danger Dan in there after all."

That was exactly what he was afraid of.

Mack's heart was racing. Not only had she ridden a motorcycle for the first time—with *Danny Adams*!—

but she'd also *kissed* the man. Under a tree on a quiet farm road in Gallant Lake. And he'd said she was *hot*. A hot chick. Tears burned her eyes.

She'd *never* been the hot chick in high school. That had been Shelly and Kiara's role, in their short skirts and cropped tops. Not Mack. She'd been the good student. The good sister. The good daughter. The good wife. The good chairperson of half a dozen charities through the years. She hadn't stopped trying to be *good* until she'd opened the storage room door at the country club and found her husband humping Charity Williams. *The irony.*

All that trying. In the process, she'd left friends like Shelly and Kiara in the dust. She'd left *herself* in the dust. So eager to escape Gallant Lake. So eager to be Miss Prim and Proper Housewife. So eager for approval from everyone else. With never a thought about what *she* wanted.

She pulled in a ragged breath but didn't feel any oxygen reaching her lungs. Of all the places to gain clarity on the falseness of her entire life, it had to happen at a maple syrup stand in Gallant Lake.

"Hey…" Dan put his hand on her shoulder. "What's wrong?"

She started to laugh, and then, to her horror, she began to cry. To ugly cry, with big ugly tears as well as big dramatic sobs for complete humiliation. She leaned over, hands on her thighs, wheezing in breaths between the cries racking her chest.

She was vaguely aware of Dan leading her farther away from the road. "Jesus… Mackie, what is it? Did I do something? I'm sorry…"

There was a picnic table behind the stand, out of sight and shaded. As soon as they sat, Dan folded her into his arms. She shook her head sharply before giving in to the crying jag that had clearly just been waiting for a chance to humiliate her properly.

"It's not…you. It's me…my life…"

The fear left Dan's voice, leaving only warmth and caring.

"Oh, Mackie. Go ahead. Get it out, baby."

She obliged, sobbing into his shirt while he held her, his hand running slowly up and down her back. He was speaking, but it was more a murmur of comforting sounds than actual words. Her tears didn't seem to intimidate him or make him want to run. That was new. Mason hated it when she cried. He told her it was childish. That was rich coming from a guy who cheated on her with a girl who was barely above the age of consent.

A laugh bubbled up, making Dan's hand freeze. Did he think she was having a breakdown? Who was she kidding—she *was* having a breakdown. And for some crazy reason, that made her laugh harder, with tears still covering her face. She lifted her head and gave him a watery smile.

"I'm sorry. This is horrible timing for an emotional collapse. Don't take it personally. I just…"

She wiped her cheek with the back of her hand, and Dan fished in his pocket for a handkerchief. What kind of man still carried a cotton handkerchief? Her dad. And Dan. She laughed again, then the tears returned. She was completely out of control. He pulled her back into his embrace, and she cried some more, but more softly now. The tidal wave had passed, and she was finding her center again. Slowly. Dan didn't rush her. He didn't talk. He didn't ask *her* to talk, either. He was just…there. Like a rock. Like a good guy.

She pulled in a long, slow breath and put Dan's handkerchief to use. She knew she wasn't a pretty crier. Her face had to be red and blotchy and puffy and wet and…

Dan's fingers raised her chin and his mouth brushed hers before he came in for a deep, hypnotic kiss. He lifted his head and grinned, saying exactly what she needed to hear.

"You're still a hot chick."

She huffed out a genuine laugh, no longer feeling on a razor's edge.

"I'm a hot *mess* is what I am."

He stared into her eyes, then shook his head. "Nah. You're human. A divorce is like a death, and it hits you at weird times. And then with your dad getting hurt…"

"My dad. Yeah." She looked up through the bright green leaves, filtering the sun and looking like a kaleidoscope. "Did you know Dad's been shacking up with Cathy Meadows? He moved into her double-wide today. Dad's gettin' luckier than I am. How is that fair?"

Dan's brows shot high up his forehead. "Carl and

Cathy? Wow, I…well…yeah, I guess I've seen them together a lot lately. But I figured they were friends. How old is your dad?"

"He's sixty-eight, Dan."

He winked at her. "Good for him, the old dog."

She straightened. "Ew. That's my *dad* you're talking about. No one wants to think of their father getting it on."

"My dad's had a girlfriend for ten years now. Her apartment is right next to his at the senior center in Florida. I'm sure they've had a few sleepovers."

Mack grimaced. "My brain isn't ready to embrace that yet. I just found out this morning."

"Ooh." Dan stretched his legs out in front of him, leaning back against the table. He stared at the ground for a moment. "What bothers you more—that your dad's seeing someone, or that he didn't tell you?"

She didn't answer right away. Did it matter? She pressed her lips together.

"Honestly, being blindsided pissed me off. A lot. Then they told me it all started when Dad started talking to Cathy about *my* problems. How weird is that? My failed relationship led to them being together." She sighed, staring out across the freshly plowed fields on the opposite side of the road. "Oh, and he's *retiring*. They want to 'travel' together." She formed the air quotes with her fingers. She knew she sounded resentful. "He wants me to take over the store for good."

Dan was quiet, then he started to chuckle softly.

"Man, you really *have* had quite a day, haven't you? Is that why you were out walking when I found you?"

When he found her. There was something about that word…*found*…that made her feel warm and fuzzy inside. Like he'd been looking for her. Like he cared. Like he'd pulled out that motorcycle just for her. Maybe she didn't need him to be Danger Dan after all. Because she was really starting to like Good Guy Dan.

"Mack…" There was gentle warning in his voice, and she realized she was leaning into him. She also hadn't answered the question he'd just repeated a second time. She pulled back.

"I was walking to settle my head, yes. And then you found me."

"And did I help or make it worse?"

She held up his handkerchief, saturated with her tears, and shrugged. "Both?"

He grinned. "Fair enough. You hungry?"

"I don't need any more maple sugar—my metabolism is buzzing enough already. And my face is way too messy for dining in public."

"I was thinking more along the line of burgers on the grill." He stood and held out his hand. "At my place."

She took his hand. Bad idea? Good idea? Who knew the difference anymore? The only thing she knew for sure was that she was sliding on the back of Dan Adams's bike and having dinner with him. At his place.

Chapter Ten

Dan put the perfectly charred burgers on the platter and set the buns on the grill to toast. Mack was just coming out of the house with a tray of condiments in one hand and two bottles of beer in the other. They'd stopped at the store on the way home and she'd juggled a container of macaroni salad and a box of cupcakes on the back of the bike, laughing all the way. He already had some baked beans in the cupboard. It wasn't fancy, but then again, it was Thursday night, which meant it didn't need to be fancy. This was just a midweek dinner between friends. Friends who'd kissed each other's lights out an hour ago.

Right before she'd burst into tears. But if there was one thing Dan was used to, it was dealing with people in emotional situations. He'd learned the worst thing you could do was try to tell someone to *stop* once a hysterical crying jag came on. Best to just support them without judgment while they worked through it.

Knowing what to do and *liking* it were two different things, though. It had broken his heart to see Mack, always so pulled together and in control, just… lose it like that. He wondered how long she'd been holding all that in. How painful that must have been.

"I didn't realize how hungry I was until I stepped out here." She smiled at him. "Those burgers smell amazing. I think I found everything we'll need." She held up the beer. "Even adult beverages."

She hadn't said much about the white Victorian he lived in, or all the signs of Chloe everywhere, from drawings on the fridge to trays of beads on the dining table. Mack knew he was a single dad, of course, but he wondered how she felt about being confronted by it. They sat at the glass patio table.

"You okay?" he asked. "You were quiet after we got here."

She took a sip of her beer. "Always the detective." He tensed, and she set her beer down with a frown. "Sorry. I forgot you don't like being reminded of your job."

"It's not that…it's just…" Dan wasn't sure *what* it was. He didn't want Mack to see him as his job. He wanted her to see him as a man. Maybe even as *her* man.

"I know. Cartoon character and all that. I get it."

She looked up at the house. "It's a bit surreal to be here at your house. It's so…domestic."

He chuckled. "That's me. Domestic Dan."

She laughed. "Who knew?" She took a bite of her burger. "Oh my God, you really *are* Domestic Dan. This is delicious."

They ate in comfortable silence, interspersed with an occasional comment about the food or the nice weather or something else with no meaning. They were opening the package of cupcakes when things took a more serious turn again. Mack gave him a level gaze over the top of her bright pink frosted cupcake.

"So you know why I got divorced. What's *your* real story?"

He didn't answer right away. Partly because his mouth was full and partly because he wasn't sure how to answer. He swallowed hard and shrugged as casually as possible.

"I usually say we grew apart, but that sounds like such a cliché. Our jobs didn't help. She's a nurse, and her shifts at the urgent care center tended to be the opposite of mine, until we were just passing each other in the hallway most days. We planned it that way at first, so one of us could be with Chloe. In hindsight, it wasn't the best idea for the marriage." He took a bite of his cappuccino cupcake. "Oh, man, this is good."

He told Mack how he and Susanne became more like roommates than husband and wife after a while. How neither of them seemed to mind that it happened. And how sad that realization made them both.

"She tried. She took a job at the clinic here in

town, with more regular hours. But after the local
police department dissolved and got absorbed by
the sheriff's department, I didn't have much control
over my hours. And being a cop is…" He blew out
a breath. "It's not a nine-to-five job. We're on call
all the time if something big goes down. And we're
spread thin, so I might be thirty miles away dealing
with an accident at the end of my shift, meaning I'd
be way late getting home. And often not in the best
of moods. Add in the fact that she was always worrying about me…"

Mack nodded. "It must be hard. What you do.
What you see."

She had no idea. No one did, except other first
responders.

"Susanne would try to get me to talk about it,
but that's not anything a cop wants to bring home
with them, you know? She'd freak out if I *did* tell
her anything, and it would just make her worry that
much more. It reached the point where she was texting me twenty times a shift to make sure I was
okay. So I stopped talking about it." He took a swig
of beer. Quite a combination—beer and cupcakes.
"Eventually she stopped asking, and that's when we
knew it was over. We decided to split while we were
still friends instead of hanging in there so long we
hated each other."

"Much better for Chloe that way."

"Exactly."

"Susanne's still here in town, then?"

"About a ten-minute walk."

Mack set what was left of her cupcake down.

"You live in the same neighborhood as your ex?"

"I live in the same neighborhood as my *daughter*. And technically, they're different neighborhoods, just close. This place is a hundred years old, while their house is in a more recent development." He looked up at the house. It had taken him a couple years of hard work to bring it back from the brink of disrepair, but it was turning into a home he was proud of. "Chloe can ride her bike back and forth easily, she can catch the same school bus from either house, and she's close to her friends no matter where she's staying."

"Wow." Mack finished her beer. "That's very… civilized." He started to roll his eyes at the sarcasm, but she quickly corrected him. "No, I mean it! Not many people would be willing to do that, even for their children's sake, but you and Susanne figured it out. Good for you."

Yeah, good for him. Their marriage had failed. Because of who he was. But at least they *had* managed to do the right thing by Chloe. He nodded, staring at the table for a minute before meeting her eyes.

"There was no single trauma that tore us apart. No affairs. No big fights. No games. Our marriage faded more than died. Not like yours, I'm assuming."

She huffed out a laugh. "My marriage blew sky-high, Dan. Nothing left but ashes. If I'd been paying attention, maybe I'd have seen it coming. All the signs were there. Staying in the city overnight. All those work trips. Late nights 'with the boys' at the club. The way our social group—I can't really think of them as friends—couldn't maintain eye contact with me after a while. They all knew, of course. Not one of them told me I was being made into a laughingstock."

She told him how Mason loved having her on his arm at business functions and formal parties. How well she'd played the part, charming his clients, chatting with their wives, golfing with the ladies at the club every Thursday, running fund-raisers for the trendiest of Greenwich charities, sitting in the same church pew every Sunday at her husband's side. It was all about appearances.

"It wasn't even a so-called friend who told me. It was Carly Fitzgibbons, the backstabbing president of the ladies' charity society at the club. She and I had tangled over which charities the society funded. I didn't think the ritzy private school in town needed help as much as the homeless shelter might, and she never forgave me for calling her out on it at a meeting."

Mack went quiet, and Dan had a feeling she was done talking. That was okay with him. He already knew her husband had cheated on her. He didn't need the sordid details. He started to stand, figuring they should move inside before the bugs came out. Springtime in the mountains meant blackflies, or what some called "no-see-ums." They were nasty, tiny bugs with bigger appetites than the summer mosquitoes, and that was saying something.

He was just starting to stack the plates when Mack spoke again.

"Carly sent me to the storage room in the middle of the annual fund-raiser for the society. She said they were short a centerpiece and asked me to go get one because the staff was busy serving appetizers. Made a big deal out of it and said the florist must have left one in there when they were setting up." Mack ran her finger around the top of her empty beer glass. "I thought it silly, but I was on the committee and she was chair, so away I went. I walked in on Mason and one of the cocktail waitresses." Her gaze met his. "She was up on a stack of boxes. His tuxedo pants were down around his ankles, and her legs were wrapped around his waist like a nutcracker. The three of us just looked at each other, then I walked out. I left the door wide-open behind me and told everyone I passed that there was free champagne being served in there. Quite a few guests got an eyeful before Mason could hobble over and lock the door."

"Good for you, Mackie."

"You'd think so, but people were more scandalized over *my* actions than his. I ruined their very classy event, you see. Mason's behavior was bad, but boys will be boys, right? Wives aren't supposed to be tacky about it."

"Screw that."

"Indeed."

They both laughed, and the tension that had been growing around her eyes disappeared. They moved everything inside and loaded the dishwasher. She asked if he wanted another beer, but he declined.

He wasn't on shift until tomorrow, but with the task force investigating the opioid crisis, he was always on call.

"A crisis? In Gallant Lake?"

"The theory is we've somehow become a substation for a supplier who's funneling the stuff into the city, but they're very happy to sell it locally, too. It's getting bad fast. We're losing too many good people. All incomes. Any neighborhood. The task force is working with the DEA and the state police to figure out who the local connection is and where they're stashing the stuff. Hopefully we'll get the head of the snake, but right now I'd be happy to just get this crap out of my town."

She hung the dish towel on the oven handle. "I'm sorry. That must be tough."

She didn't pry any more than that. Didn't ask for details. Didn't shrug it off. Didn't get dramatic. Just empathized. It resonated inside of Dan. Maybe it was his nonstop focus on finding who was responsible and dreading that it might be someone he knew, like Owen Graber. Or maybe it was the way Mack made him feel. Like she *got* it. Like she accepted that he'd said all he could and all he wanted to. It was nice. *She* was nice.

His kitchen wasn't that big, so it was easy to reach over and pull her close. Was that first kiss just a motorcycle and maple sugar sort of thing? Or had it really been as good as he'd thought? Judging from the way Mack melted against him, she was more than willing to explore that question with him. In fact, it was Mack who went up on tiptoe to press her lips to his. It was Mack who went exploring—first with her tongue, then with her hands, which wandered down his back and squeezed his butt the same way he'd done to hers out on the farm.

The kiss heated up as if doused with gasoline. Their hands were moving, their heads were turning and they both grabbed quick gasps of air before connecting again. Faster. Harder. And he knew where this was heading. Right up that center staircase and straight into his room. He started backing up in that direction, pulling her with him. She laughed against his mouth as she followed. They got to the staircase, and he stumbled, too focused on what she was doing to him to be bothered with what his feet were up to. Their momentum carried them down until he was sitting on the steps with her straddling him. *Yes, please.*

He slid his hands under her top, fumbling with her bra while she did the same with his belt buckle. Dan normally craved control, but right now he was very okay with shedding their clothes on the wooden stairs and making love right here, right now. Green light all the way. They were both chuckling under their hurried breaths as they worked with all the frustrating fasteners keeping their clothing in place. His fingers finally moved the bra in the right direction and the hooks came free. Oh yeah. This was happening. He was vibrating with need. Vibrating...

Damn it. That vibration wasn't from need. It was the phone in his pocket. The pulsing vibrating pattern meant the worst possible thing. The task force.

No no no no no!

He considered ignoring it, but that wasn't a serious option. He dropped his head back and it thunked against the step. Then he reached around and pulled the phone from his pocket with a groan.

"Mack…babe…gotta get this…work…"

She froze above him, raising her head and staring, wide-eyed. Her mouth opened, then snapped shut when she saw he was swiping to answer the call.

"Adams." He barked his name into the phone.

"Easy, Dan." It was Sam Edgewood from the state police. "It's not like I'm calling at three in the morning."

He didn't bother apologizing. He was too distracted by Mack lowering her head and running her lips…and her tongue…up the side of his neck. He bit back a moan, sliding his hand up to fondle her breast.

"What is it, Sam?"

Mack giggled against his neck, but thankfully Sam didn't seem to hear.

"A car was stopped on the Thruway for speeding this afternoon. The trunk was loaded with little baggies full of little white pills." Sam paused for dramatic effect, which was almost Dan's downfall as Mack continued to unbutton his shirt, tracing kisses across his shoulder. He bit the inside of his mouth to keep from groaning out loud. He was grateful when Sam continued, giving him something concrete to focus on. "The driver clammed up, but the car's GPS shows it came from Gallant Lake. A parking lot at some abandoned ski slope, then out to the Thruway.

Oh, and he had a sawed-off shotgun under the front seat, as well as a handgun stuck in his belt. These guys ain't playin'. The trooper saw the guy reaching and drew his weapon before he could do anything."

Dan sat up and Mack moved off him, sitting on the step below and watching in concern. Fun and games were over. "A ski slope? Gallant Lake Ski Resort? That place has been closed for ten years." Dan did the occasional drive-by to check for vandalism, but he'd had no idea anyone was using it for drug trade. "You wanna meet me up there?"

"I'm on my way now. We won't have a lot of daylight, but we should see if there's anything obvious before this guy has a chance to warn off his bosses. Who knows where his one phone call will go?"

With a look of apology to Mack, Dan stood, extending his hand to help her up. She'd already fastened her pants again and was reaching back to hook her bra. It was one of those mysteries of women that men would never figure out—he'd practically needed an engineering degree to unhook it, and she had it refastened behind her back in seconds. He told Sam he'd see him in ten and ended the call. Mack gave him a slanted smile.

"Duty calls?"

"Damn, Mack. You have no idea how sorry I am. Of all the lousy timing. I…"

"Hey, it's okay. You told me you were on call. Task force?"

Dan hesitated. This is where he always got in

trouble with Susanne. Holding back. Or telling so much that she worried.

Mack stared hard, then shook her head. "And if you told me, then you'd have to kill me, right?" She tugged the hem of her shirt, covering the last tempting stretch of flesh above her waist. "Can you drop me at home?"

"Uh…yes. To both." Her brows lowered in confusion. "Yes, I'd have to kill you. And yes, I can drop you."

The corner of her mouth tipped up. "Right."

She started toward the door, but Dan stopped her. "Mack…this interruption might be a good thing. That was a little…crazy and…"

"Frantic? Dangerous? Fun?"

He pulled her in for a quick kiss. "All of that. It's been one hell of a day."

"I don't have any regrets. Do you?"

He looked her straight in the eye.

"Only that my phone rang when it did."

She patted his arm.

"Yeah, that was a mood killer." She opened the door, looking back over her shoulder with a bright smile. "But there's no reason we can't try again some other time."

"Wait, this is sauvignon blanc?" Nora raised her glass. "I don't like sauv blanc. But I like this."

Mack's role was more hostess than expert tonight, on the trial run of ladies' night at Wallace Liquors. She turned to Marie DuCoq, the sales rep from one of the wine distribution companies Dad worked with. Marie held up the bottle she'd been pouring from.

"Oh, yes, this is a lovely wine. The citrus notes are pronounced, but not as harsh as some lesser sauv blancs can be." She looked at the puzzled expressions on the women's faces around the tables and cleared her throat. "It's dry without being bitter." Heads nodded at the simplified explanation.

Mack felt a small pulse of panic. There was no shame in her friends not being wine experts. But *she* was going to have to learn a whole lot more than she knew now if she was really going to take over the family business. Marie was pouring a "buttery chardonnay with a soft mouthfeel and a hint of melon and baking spices."

Shelly caught Mack's eye and mouthed, "What?"

She gave a thin smile in response. She'd asked Shelly and Kiara to join them for a layperson's opinion, since the Lowery cousins were business owners and looking at this as a new event to promote the town. Her two friends admitted they didn't know much about wine, which made them perfect guinea pigs. Mack tried to pay attention to Marie's descriptions, but she could tell Kiara was doing her best not to giggle at the over-the-top phrasing. This was supposed to be fun, not feel like a college lecture. She wanted people to *buy* wine, not be intimidated by it.

Amanda Randall leaned over from the next table, her voice low. "I'll introduce you to our sommelier at the resort. He's a laid-back California surfer dude who grew up on a vineyard. He has a degree,

of course, but Gavin can help make this a lot less…"
Amanda glanced toward Marie and lowered her
voice. "…stuffy."

Mack's shoulders relaxed. It wasn't just her, then.
She nodded in thanks as Marie moved on to the reds,
pouring a pinot noir. Mack jumped up to replace the
cheese platters on the tables with plates of fruit and
chocolate. Mel Brannigan was the only one not drinking. Even if she hadn't been pregnant, she'd explained
to Mack last week that she'd had a problem with sub-
stance abuse when she was a young fashion model and
had been in a twelve-step program for years. Mack told
her she didn't have to attend, but Mel said it wouldn't
be an issue. She was sipping a "very fine vintage" of
peach-pear sparkling water from a champagne glass.

It was nice to have these women here to support
her, laughing with her behind Marie's pompous back.
She thought she'd had friends in Greenwich, but they'd
dropped her like a hot rock after the night she exposed
her husband's bad behavior. The divorce made her the
odd one out at events. She was no longer part of a couple, *and* she'd been tainted by scandal, so invitations
dried up overnight. Mason's father and grandfather
had been members of the Glenfadden Country Club,
so the members naturally gravitated to him, at the expense of all contact with her. It hurt. A lot.

Who'd have guessed that she'd come back to Gallant Lake and…*like* it? That she'd go for a motorcycle
ride with Danger Dan Adams? That he'd *kiss* her?
That they'd come so very close to having sex on his
Victorian staircase?

Marie took the ladies through three more wines, finishing with a white port. Mack thanked her and rang up the purchases she'd told everyone they didn't need to make.

Nora was the last to leave. Asher's Jeep was parked out front, and he was leaning against it, scrolling through his phone as he waited. He was tall and rugged, with a dark beard that was just touched by gray. Amanda's husband, Blake, had picked her and Mel up a few minutes earlier. The men didn't want their women to drive after the wine tasting. It was something she'd have to consider once she opened these events to the public. Limiting the number of wines and the amounts being poured. Maybe offering a discount to designated drivers if they agreed to drink sparkling water the way Mel had.

"Tonight was great," Nora was saying. "Something like this could really help increase evening foot traffic downtown. Maybe some of the other businesses would be tempted to stay open if they knew the sidewalks wouldn't roll up at six o'clock." Nora tipped her head. "Are you really taking over the store? Cathy said…"

Mack tensed. She still hadn't worked out her feelings about Dad and Cathy yet. "Did you know they were together? Dad and Cathy? Why didn't anyone tell me?"

Nora's cheeks went pink. "I honestly didn't know it was a secret. I figured you knew until Cathy warned me that your dad never told you. For what it's worth, they seem good for each other. Your dad anchors Cathy's flightiness, and she's made him a little less…reserved."

Mack sighed. That made sense, actually. "It was a shock, that's all. Not that I have anything against Cathy—I've known her my whole life. But that Dad wouldn't tell me… I don't know, maybe I can't blame him. There was a time when I'd have been horrified at the thought of my father shacking up with a woman as out there as Cathy can be. I still remember when she was growing pot in her loft. She's lucky Dan never caught her."

Nora laughed. "There's not much that goes on in this town that Dan doesn't know about. He told Cathy back then that if she started selling the stuff, he'd arrest her in a heartbeat. If not, he'd pretend they were tomato plants as long as she didn't get carried away."

"Good Guy Sheriff Dan ignored a marijuana operation in the center of town?"

"Dan knew Cathy only started growing that stuff after a friend of hers got cancer. That was before medical marijuana became legal. I'm not saying she didn't enjoy a little recreationally, but from what I heard, most of it went to people who needed it and didn't have the money or the nerve to get it on their own. Dan's always been a compassionate guy. He could have arrested Asher years ago for being reckless, but he knew Asher was in a bad place. Dan drove him home and checked up on him every night for over a year. That's how they became friends."

As if he'd heard his name, Asher walked inside.

"You about ready, babe? Or are you two gonna have a sleepover and do girl talk all night?"

Nora smiled and stepped into his embrace. "I was just telling Mack about how you and Dan became friends. How he isn't *always* Dudley Do-Right."

Asher nodded. "I kinda miss those nights when he'd stop by my place and have a drink after his shift. We had some good talks." He kissed the top of Nora's head. "Not that I'd trade it for what I have now, but I think it was as good for Dan as it was for me. It was a pressure valve for him, where he could shed whatever he'd seen on shift before he went home." Asher gave Mack a pointed look. "I heard he put his bike back on the road this week. He hasn't ridden that thing in years. Wonder what brought that on?"

She didn't answer. Judging from the speculation in Asher's eyes, she didn't have to.

After Nora and Asher left, she finished cleaning up and locked the doors. She'd just gotten upstairs and was giving Rory a late-night snack when her phone chirped with a text from Dan.

How'd it go?

She knew he was still on shift, but it made her heart jump to know he was thinking of her.

The wine lady was a snob.

She hit Send, then followed it up.

I thought you might stop by.

The bubbles floated on her screen.

In uniform? That would put a damper on the party.

She thought about what Asher had said about Dan needing to decompress after his job.

Stop by for a drink after shift? Still got that Macallan open.

There was a long pause before she saw he was typing again.

I'm sitting surveillance after shift on that other thing. Tomorrow?

She smiled.

Sure. Be safe.

Always.

Chapter Eleven

Dan was only five minutes late to Five and Design Saturday afternoon. Considering he was on shift, that wasn't bad. He could have been on the other side of the county, but he'd lucked out. He parked the patrol car in front of the boutique and called in that he was grabbing lunch in Gallant Lake. Only a slight fabrication, since he'd picked up a sandwich to go at the Chalet before dashing over to watch Chloe try on party dresses for her big modeling gig at the upcoming charity event.

"Daddy! Look at all these dresses!" His daughter ran to give him a quick hug, then pointed to the rack full of purple glitter and lace. Dan looked at Susanne and tried not to sound too much like an old grump.

"Those are a little grown-up for an eight-year-old, don't you think?"

He must have failed at the not-an-old-grump thing, because his ex-wife narrowed her eyes at him as Chloe ran back to the dress rack.

"They're *party* dresses, Dan. Little girls like to dress up. Just because it has sequins doesn't mean it's risqué."

Mel Brannigan walked into the shop from a back room. "*Risqué?* Relax, Dad. You know I'd never do that." She smiled at Chloe and pulled two sparkly, princessy dresses off the rack. "Let's try these first, okay?"

Chloe clapped her hands. Maybe Dan *was* being a fuddy-duddy. After all, Chloe was happy, and the whole thing was for charity. He was able to stay long enough to see Chloe twirl around in three purple dresses before he had to get back to work. Susanne gave him another dose of stink eye, as if she didn't know what he did for a living or what his hours were. He'd told Mack his marriage ended because of crossed hours and growing apart, but really his job had killed it. And Susanne's fears over it.

He was tempted to stop by the liquor store to see if Mack was there, but he'd been out of his vehicle long enough. Time to get back to work. Besides, he'd said yes to sharing a Macallan with her later tonight, so he had that to look forward to.

But by the end of the shift, he wasn't sure that was such a great idea. It had been a miserable Saturday night. An overdose on a country road, which he'd luckily been able to reverse with Narcan. But the screams of the woman's three young children in the back seat, thinking their mommy had died, would haunt him for a long time. Then there was a break-in at the hair salon. No one was there by the time he arrived, but they'd clearly been looking for cash. When they didn't find any, they'd crowbarred the cash register right off the counter and took off with it. That's when someone spotted them running out the shattered front door and called it in.

Martie Williams had owned the salon for thirty years. She'd been adamant that she didn't need an alarm system. And she'd told Dan he was crazy if he thought she was going to leave any of her hard-earned money around "as bait." She'd refused to listen when he'd explained that if thieves found easy cash they were less likely to destroy property. Now the old-fashioned cash register her late husband had bought for the shop decades ago was gone. And Dan had gotten an earful from Martie about it—if he hadn't let these drugs into town it wouldn't have happened, blah, blah, blah. Sometimes this job made him tired.

That call had been followed up with a domestic disturbance in the upscale Walnut Point neighborhood along the lake. The complaint was for noise. Mr. and Mrs. Quenton had enjoyed a few too many martinis and started a screaming match that escalated to bottle throwing. In their living room. It was the first time he'd ever been called there, so Dan got them both calmed down and made them a pot of coffee. By the time he left, they were sheepishly picking up their mess and apologizing to him and each other.

He was glad it had ended well, but every domestic call took a toll. They were fraught with the unexpected and were among the most dangerous calls an officer could respond to. He'd seen more than his share that had ended in injuries, jail time, restraining orders and, twice in his eighteen-year career...death.

And the night *still* wasn't done with him. He ended the shift with a vehicular call that put him on the scene of a fatal accident in the next town over. He suspected drag racing was involved, judging from the twin burn marks on the remote country road. But there was only one vehicle when first responders arrived. And it was wrapped around a tree, with a dead teenager in the front seat. A family would be forever changed because of a moment's decision to race a one-ton vehicle with nearly bald tires. It looked so easy in the movies, right?

It was after midnight by the time Dan got back to Gallant Lake. He stopped home long enough to shower and change, then drove his truck to the parking lot behind the liquor store. And that's when his momentum slowed and the shift caught up with him. He was both exhausted and wired. Not a good combination for socializing. He texted Mack.

Rough night. Rain check?

Her response was swift.

Get out of the truck and come upstairs.

He looked up and there she was, standing on the metal fire escape behind the apartment. She was leaning on the railing, looking straight at his car, bathed in the light from the open door behind her. Her hair was loose around her shoulders, nearly white against the darkness of the night. She looked like...

Dan gave his head a shake, but that didn't change the illogical truth. She looked like exactly what he needed right now.

She waited for him, studying his face silently as he walked up to her. Then she opened her arms, and he didn't hesitate to walk into the embrace. Her arms were firm and tight around him, like she wanted to hold him up. And she almost was. He dropped his head on hers with a deep sigh, and they stood there for a beat. No words. No need for them. He could feel her trying to infuse him with comfort, and damn if it wasn't working. He felt better already. But the night's darkness wouldn't be chased off that easily.

"Come inside," she whispered.

He nodded against her. "Yes."

Mack could see the tension pulsing under Dan's skin. She didn't know why or what happened, but she had a hunch that "rough night" was probably an understatement. They sat at the kitchen table, where two glasses of scotch waited. Dan drained his before Mack could even start hers. Her eyebrows rose, but she didn't say a word as she refilled his glass.

Dan drank this one more slowly, holding the amber liquid in his mouth and closing his eyes before swallowing. He let out a long sigh, then opened his eyes and started to cough and sputter.

"What the hell is *that*?" He pointed to where Rory was stretched out on the back of the sofa, easily occupying three feet of space with his legs extended the way they were.

"That is Rory. He's a Maine coon cat. Remember I told you I won him in the divorce?"

The cat lifted his head and gave Dan a bored look before dropping back to the sofa.

"I was about to call animal control and tell them a mountain lion had invaded Gallant Lake."

Mack chuckled. "I named him Rory because he looks like a big old lion. He's harmless as long as you don't scratch his belly. Do that and you'll see more bloodshed than you can imagine…" She looked at Dan. "Well, probably not more than *you* can imagine. Sorry."

He went still. She reached out and covered his hand with hers.

"It really was a rough night, huh?"

"I don't want to talk about it. And trust me, you don't want to hear about it."

"You're not injured or anything?"

He gave a sharp shake of his head and took another sip of whiskey.

"Just a long night, Mack. Let it go."

That was hard to do, when it was lurking in the room like a heavy shadow. She had a dozen questions. But she stayed quiet.

Dan's tension eased a bit as the minutes ticked by

and the whiskey did its trick. Mack shifted in her chair, and the corner of Dan's mouth lifted.

"It's killin' you, isn't it? Waiting me out."

"A little bit, yeah." She nodded.

"I'm trained in interrogation." He turned his hand to twine his fingers with hers. "You won't be able to outwait me. I will never feel the urge to fill the silence with the answers to your unspoken questions. But honestly?" She looked at him in curiosity, and his smile deepened. "It's nice to sit here with you. I feel better already."

"I'm glad." She squeezed his hand. "Anything else I can do to help?"

"Yeah. You can kiss me."

She was more than happy to oblige. She leaned toward him, and he met her halfway, just as eager for it as she was. And no wonder. Their kisses were like wildfire fueled with kerosene and sprinkled with gunpowder. *Hot.* The chairs scraped loudly across the tile floor as they both stood, eager to be closer as the kiss grew deeper. *Hotter.* His hands were under her shirt, sliding across her skin. Her fingers were in his hair, pulling him closer, even though their teeth were already clicking together as the kiss went out of control and their heads turned for better access. *Even hotter.* He pulled his mouth away long enough to say one word.

"Bedroom?"

"Yes. Upstairs."

Hottest.

She wasn't sure how they got there. There was a

vague recollection of hands and kisses and clothing coming off, and then they were in her room and on her bed. Not quite naked, but not exactly dressed, either. And thoroughly out of breath. Dan was kneeling over her, and she saw a flash of concern in his eyes.

"Mack…are you sure…?"

She arched one brow. "Seriously? You think we need the consent conversation after the way we just came up those stairs?" He started to answer, but she put her fingers on his mouth. "Kidding. It's a good thing. And yes, I'm sure." A thread of doubt went through her. "Are *you* sure? After your day…"

He lowered his head and kissed her without a word. The kiss confirmed her suspicion—Dan was, at least to some extent, using sex to forget his terrible shift. After she'd asked how she could help. So they both knew what was what. She returned the kiss with enthusiasm. They both wanted this.

What difference did the motives make? She was providing an escape. He was providing…hope. A glimpse at a new beginning for her that included a night of passionate sex with her high school crush. What could possibly go wrong?

Dan's hands slid up to cup her breasts over her bra. He squeezed, and she let out a groan, arching against him. He murmured something that sounded like "so beautiful" before his hand slid lower, slipping his fingers under the elastic of her panties. He sat up and slid the lacy hipsters down her legs. He removed his boxers and started looking around.

"Son of a…where are my pants?"

She huffed a laugh. "Leaving so soon?"

He gave her a crooked grin. "Not likely. But the consent conversation goes hand in hand with the safe-sex conversation. My condom is in my wallet, which is in my pants. Which are somewhere between the dining table and your bed." He started to move off the mattress, but Mack stopped him. "Nightstand. Top drawer."

"So you were prepared for tonight, eh? Naughty girl." He crawled over her and pulled the drawer open.

"Let's be clear—if it's okay for you to walk around with a condom in your pocket, then it's okay for me to have some by my bed."

He pulled a strip of packets from the box. "Absolutely. Didn't mean to sound judgy." He winked at her. "We good?"

"Nope."

His eyes went wide. "What? Why? Mack…"

She started to giggle. "I just meant that you're too far away."

"That's easy to fix." In the blink of an eye, he was settling between her thighs as he tore open a foil wrap. She pulled down her bra straps and shifted to reach behind her back, but he stopped her. "I can fix that, too." His body pressed on hers, and his hands moved behind her back and made quick work of her bra, which was soon flying across the room to land by the dresser.

They were both still laughing, and she loved that. The laughter was an expression of joy more than humor. As if neither of them could hold it in. Dan kissed her, his fingers twisting in her hair. She let out a low moan as he sank into her and began to move. He traced kisses from her mouth to her shoulder, where she felt his teeth pressing on her skin. Nipping her lightly, then moving to her breast, all the while moving inside her. She traced her fingers across the dragon tattoo on his shoulder—she hadn't seen it since they were kids. It was…hot. Her moans were no longer low. She cried out and rose to meet his hips. Her fingers dug into his back.

"Mackie…oh, Mack…" His face was against her neck now, his words growing more tangled as the pace increased. She curled her hand around the back of his head, whispering…something. They were her words, but she had no idea what they were anymore. All she knew was emotion and sound and sensation. So much sensation. She burned with it, and when it reached the point where she couldn't take anymore, she begged him.

"*Please*, Dan…please…"

"Just go, Mackie. I'm right there with you, baby. I'm right there…"

There was a burst of light behind her eyes, and she was pretty sure she screamed, but it was drowned out by Dan's bellow as he joined her. There was a beat of silence, or at least silence other than their heavy breathing as they lay there. And then they were laughing again, softly, both shaking from it. Like a pair of shell-shocked teens who'd had no idea what was going to happen just then.

"Mack...holy..." Dan spoke against her skin, as if unable to raise his head. She knew the feeling. Her heart felt like it was trying to beat its way out of her chest.

"I know. That was...really something."

It had been *more*. More than sex. More than... anything.

Dan shifted his weight from her and grabbed a tissue for the condom. Then he settled back at her side and threw his arm over her, burying his face in her hair. "I won't spend the night. But God, I need to sleep. Just for a little while."

She didn't bother answering, because she could tell from his breathing that he was already asleep. She listened to the steady rhythm, feeling her own pulse slowing to match it.

There had been chemistry between them from that night when she'd swung a bat at his head in the store. As much as Dan had insisted he wasn't that bad boy anymore, she'd tapped in to the thrill seeker somehow. She suppressed a laugh. She'd just had crazy wild sex with the local hero. She wondered how that would fly with all the folks in Gallant Lake who adored their Sheriff Dan and put all those expectations on him. His arm tightened around her waist, and he muttered something in his sleep.

Too late to worry about that now.

For tonight, Sheriff Dan was all hers.

Chapter Twelve

Dan was warm. Too warm. He went to toss off his covers, but there was only a light sheet over him. And a soft, warm body next to him. His eyes snapped open. It was dark, and he lifted his head to check the clock. Almost four. He should go. Mack shifted and murmured something, then settled back against him.

There was just enough glow through the curtains from the lights in the parking lot to cast soft shadows on Mack's face. He studied her, wondering what it was that made her completely irresistible to him. She was pretty, but he knew plenty of good-looking women. She was fun, and that was different, but then again… Gallant Lake was full of fun-loving people. But no woman made him laugh as easily as Mackenzie Wallace did. And for sure, no woman made him lose his head the way she did when they kissed.

And the sex. The sex was incredible. The stuff of wet dreams, not reality. He frowned. He'd been in a bad spot when he got here last night. He probably shouldn't have come up. But she'd ordered him to. He ran his finger down her arm. She twitched but didn't wake. Big bad police officer taking orders from a woman he couldn't shake. Not from his dreams. Not from his life. Not yet, anyway.

He kissed the soft skin behind her ear, and she stirred again. She made a low sound, and her eyes swept open. She turned and smiled at him over her shoulder.

"Hey, you." Her voice was still thick with sleep.

"Hey, yourself."

Tonight was great, but it wasn't serious. He had to leave. He couldn't sleep over. So many smart things he should say. He rolled her onto her back.

"I want you."

Funny how the truth always came out when he was with her. Her eyes went dark, and her smile deepened.

"You had to wake me to tell me that?"

"Yup." He kissed her, grinning against her mouth as her arms wrapped around him.

"Good choice."

Mack whispered his name, and any scraps of doubt left his head completely.

Their first time had been intense. Hard. Fast. Pas-

sionate. Fun. But this time was slower. Smoother.
Softer. Quieter. And even better.

Afterward, they stayed locked in an embrace.
Mack quickly fell asleep, but Dan was wide-awake.
He stared up into the dark. He hadn't exactly been
celibate since his divorce, but it wasn't easy doing
the casual dating thing when you were the local law.
He had to be careful about whom he socialized with
in public. He didn't need people seeing him partying or having a one-night stand with some woman
or catching him sneaking out in a walk of shame
afterward. His reputation wasn't just important to
him personally—it reflected on his job, his daughter, his ex, his whole *Sheriff Dan* shtick. He drew in
a long breath. It was a lot to live up to.

Right now, wrapped up in Mackenzie Wallace,
all he could think was how much he wanted to *stay*.
How much he wanted to make love to her again tonight, and tomorrow night, and the night after that.
How much he didn't think he'd ever have enough of
her. How she made him laugh. How she made him
relax. How she'd taken the blackness of a bad shift
and erased it with her kisses, her smile, her body.

But in the real world…his truck was parked out
back, and everyone in town knew whose truck it
was. Nora's coffee shop opened at six for early birds.
It was almost five now. A groan of disappointment
escaped him, and Mack pulled her head back to
look at him.

"Are you in pain?"

He kissed her pillow-soft lips. "Yes. I'm in pain at the thought of leaving this bed. But I have to."

"Why? The sun isn't even up yet." She burrowed closer. "And you must be exhausted after all that sexing."

He huffed a soft laugh, lowering his head to press his face against her neck. "That was some pretty amazing sexing, that's for sure. But people will recognize my truck. The café opens at six. I don't want people thinking...you know."

"That two grown-ups spent the night together? Has Gallant Lake grown so provincial since I left that consenting adults can't have sex?"

He lifted his head, serious now. "Mack, it's a small town. Small towns talk. And I'm Sheriff Dan, remember? That name carries a ton of baggage and expectations. Not to mention I have a daughter and an ex-wife living here."

Now it was her turn to groan. She threw her arm over her face. "Okay, okay. I get it. I wouldn't want Chloe hearing about us from anyone but you. If there is an us." She sat up, not bothering to cover herself with the twisted sheet. "I couldn't care less what anyone else thinks or knows. I spent twelve years worrying about what people thought of me, and I'm over it." She stood, her body bathed in the soft gray light. "But you do you, Danny. I'll just remind you that it's Sunday, and Nora doesn't open until eight on Sundays, so you have time for a very early breakfast before you sneak out of here and make me feel like a scarlet woman." She yanked on a long robe and tied the belt snugly. "Omelets okay?"

Once again, he was stuck between what he *should* say—*no, thanks*—and what he was *going* to say. The internal debate wasn't even worth the time it would take.

"Sounds great."

They gathered up their discarded clothing on their way downstairs without saying a word. Dan made the coffee while Mack chopped up mushrooms and spinach and whipped the eggs. The sun was just turning the sky a peachy pink when they sat at the table where this had all started a few hours ago. When a kiss turned into a race up the stairs and into her bed. Mack must have been thinking about that, too. She reached over and put her hand on his arm.

"I know you didn't want to talk about it last night, but if you ever do want to get a bad shift off your chest, I'm here to listen. I know you used to unwind with Asher some nights, and…"

Dan couldn't stop his grin. "Asher and I never unwound like *that*, believe me."

She barked out a bright, sharp laugh. "I'm sure you didn't, but you know what I'm saying."

He frowned at his plate. "I appreciate it, Mack, but it's hard to talk to civilians. Susanne used to get mad that I didn't share stuff, and then she'd get upset if I *did* share. And frankly, her anger was easier to handle than her tears and the way she'd worry. So me not talking is really just me protecting you. No one needs the gory details." He took her hand. "But having you waiting up for me helped. Having someone to just sit with. To help me reenter the regular world again. And I gotta say, all that sex was the icing on the cake."

Mack smiled. "Glad to be of service, Sheriff Dan." He winced, and she rushed on. "I'm sorry. I know you don't like that, although I'm not sure I understand why. The more I talk to people here, the more I can see how much they love you. There's even talk about a push to start the police department up again, and your name is on everyone's lips as the future police chief."

Dan had spoken with Mayor Malone a few times about that possibility, but the plan was supposed to be hush-hush while the mayor lined up both support and funding. "At the moment, there *is* no Gallant Lake Police Department, so the talk is just talk." He leaned toward her. "And the only lips I want my name on are yours." He gave her a soft kiss, but the embers were right under the surface, ready to flare out of control all over again. It wasn't easy to pull away. "I gotta go. I need to grab some shut-eye before I'm back out with the task force and then my regular shift."

She followed him to the back door, still in her robe, which was falling open just enough to tease. She followed his gaze, then leaned back against the hallway wall in a movie-perfect pose, one arm over her head, the other hand tugging at her bottom lip. Marilyn had nothing on Mack. She gave him a sultry smile, half in jest, but there was a very real heat in her chocolate-colored eyes.

"Will I see you tonight, Officer?"

She squeaked in surprise when he moved against her, holding both hands over her head and pressing her against the wall with his body. Turned out two could play this movie-scene game, and she knew all the shades of what happened in that infamous elevator kiss. Her mouth fell open, and he took her chin in his hand, holding there as he kissed her. Hard. Deep. Hot. Then he stepped back, trying his damnedest to look cool and detached—and knowing he'd probably failed.

"My shift won't be over until after midnight."

She straightened with a sassy wink.

"I'll wait up."

He didn't bother answering before he walked out the door. They both knew he'd be there.

Nora couldn't take her eyes off Mack as they sat in the coffee shop later that morning. Finally, Mack couldn't take it anymore.

"Do I have spinach in my teeth or something? What are you staring at?" Naturally, her outburst brought the other women's attention to her, so now all three cousins were staring.

"I don't know," Nora said. "There's something…" She gestured in Mack's general direction. "…different this morning. Your hair's a little messy. Your eyes look sleepy, but your face is freakin' glowing for some reason. And your mouth…"

Mel raised a manicured eyebrow as she sipped her

herbal tea. "Oh, yeah…those lips look like you've either used a good volumizer or you've been kissing somebody. A lot. And recently."

Nora nodded in agreement with her cousin. "That's what I was thinking. She did not have this sexy, satisfied look Friday night when we left the wine tasting. Which makes me wonder what happened on *Saturday* night?"

"And with whom?" Mel asked.

Amanda snorted. "Please, we all know *that* answer. Paul Cooper told Blake that Dan got caught on camera making out with some blonde up at his maple stand this week. Paul was teasing that he might put it on Facebook, but Blake talked him out of it."

Nora reached for a croissant. "That must have been Thursday. My daughter Becky lives over by Dan's place, and her husband…" She glanced at Mack. "Who happens to be Asher's son…long story. Anyway, Michael saw Dan and a woman leave the house together Thursday night and get in Dan's truck."

Mack's cheeks were burning. First from embarrassment, but then anger took over. "Wow. Dan wasn't kidding about how bad the small-town gossip is around here."

All three women sat back a bit. Nora spoke first.

"Mack, just because we share with each other doesn't mean we share it with the world. I'm sorry…"

Mack waved her hand, freshly embarrassed. The whole gossip thing reminded her too much of Greenwich, but that wasn't fair. "No, it's okay. I know you all can be trusted. I just didn't believe Dan when he said how careful we'd have to be. How much people would care." He was well-known and much loved. There was nothing some people enjoyed more than bringing down a hero. And wouldn't they love it if the ice queen Mackenzie Wallace was the one to ruin their precious Sheriff Dan? She shuddered at the thought.

Amanda's blue eyes went round. "Excuse me, but did you just say you and Dan are a 'we'? It's not gossip if it comes straight from the source, so *spill*, girl."

She'd come home to Gallant Lake to find some peace and quiet. Help her dad for a while. Lick her wounds in solitude while figuring out her next move. And here she was, thinking about taking over the liquor store for *good*, falling for the local lawman and making friends who wanted to know all about it.

Mack was exhausted from very little sleep and very much activity last night. Her feelings were all over the place, and she was having a hard time putting them in any order that made sense. She glanced around the café, but it was quiet at the moment, in the lull between the before-church crowd and the after-church crowd. Cathy was behind the counter, keeping her distance from the younger women today. Probably because of Mack. And because Mack's father was now *living* with Cathy and they hadn't had a real discussion about it since he left the rehab center Thursday.

"Dan spent the night," she blurted out. "Or...most

of it, anyway. He stopped for a drink after work, and we were at the kitchen table and…"

"And one thing led to another until you were in bed together?" Mel smiled. Her smile was warm. Even a little dreamy. "I love when that happens. Shane and I started in the kitchen the first time."

Amanda nodded. "Our first time started in the living room before we headed upstairs." She winked at Mack. "But our first *kiss* was in the kitchen."

Nora chuckled. "We were in a half-built house on the side of the mountain when…" She winked. "One thing led to another." Her smile faded a bit. "Mack, Dan's one of the best guys I know. You couldn't find a better one, other than the three we've already taken." The others nodded in agreement.

Mack ran her finger around the top of her coffee cup. "I know he's a good guy. I just don't know if that's what I need right now. I'm a newly divorced woman who never took the chance to be footloose and fancy-free. I don't even know what we're doing. But when we're together, it's…wonderful. We laugh all the time, at the silliest stuff."

Nora's forehead furrowed in thought. She pulled apart the last bit of croissant and popped it into her mouth, staring off into space somewhere over Mack's shoulder. "You know, as well as I know Dan, I don't know if I've heard him laugh a lot." She tipped her head. "That's so weird. I mean, he's funny and kind and always smiling. But he's had dinner with us tons of times, and I'm sure he's laughed, or at least made *us* laugh, but…huh." She frowned. "I honestly don't think of Dan and immediately think of laughter."

Mack didn't know what to say. His easy laugh was one of her favorite things about Dan. They'd laughed all the way into bed last night, giddy and breathless with the joy and adventure of the moment. Was he different when he was with her? The thought made her pulse quicken. She looked up at Nora.

"He laughs with *me*. We took a motorcycle ride…" She gave Amanda a pointed look. "Where we stopped at the maple syrup stand." Where Dan said she was hot. "Then he grilled some burgers at his place and things got crazy and funny and pretty amazing. And then last night, he'd had a rough shift, and was looking for a way to unwind…"

Mel grinned. "Oh, is that what they're calling it these days?"

Mack joined the laughter. "Well, it seemed to work. For both of us. But now I don't know where we're going with it. He's got an ex-wife and a little girl and a job that seems all consuming. I've got an ex, too, but he's nowhere near here, and we don't have any kids tying us together for the rest of our lives." She drained her mug of coffee. "I'm looking to kick my heels up, but Dan's so serious about his responsibilities. I'm not sure there's a long-term there."

"You say Dan is serious, but you also say you two laugh and have fun together. So maybe you're just what he needs." Amanda stood, gesturing for Mel to join her. "I'll drop you off on the way back. Zach has a Spanish-class project due tomorrow that he just told me about last night at dinner. He wants to teach the class how to cook paella. Which means *he* has to learn to cook it. And have me video him doing it. After I teach him the recipe. God save me from teenage boys."

Mack helped Nora clear the table, carrying the empty mugs and dishes to the small kitchen behind the coffee counter where Cathy was working. The older woman's hair was usually in a braid, but today it was wound into a knot low on her neck. She used to be a lot more bohemian, with a wardrobe full of floor-length broomstick skirts and peasant-style tops. But Cathy seemed to be changing up her wardrobe. Today she was in slightly rumpled chinos and a dark green Gallant Brew polo shirt. She'd been avoiding Mack's eyes, and that wasn't what Mack wanted. She may not have fully embraced what her dad was up to, but she didn't blame Cathy for that. She waited until Cathy was done filling a customer order before she spoke.

"How's Dad settling in at your place?"

"Uh…fine." Cathy sorted out the customer's change, then broke a fresh roll of quarters open, dumping it in the drawer. "He says it's nice and quiet there—a lot easier to sleep there than the hospital." Cathy finally stopped moving and met Mack's gaze. "You should come over for dinner tonight. I'm making lasagna. Well, I'm reheating lasagna from the grocery store—you know I was never much of a cook—but there's plenty."

Mack nodded. Dan had said his shift wouldn't

end until after midnight. "I'd like that, Cathy. And...
thanks for being there for Dad. He put us both on the
spot by not wanting to tell me, but I'm okay with it.
Really. If he's happy, then I'm happy."

Cathy's smile brightened. "Thank you, Mack. I
told him keeping it secret was a bonehead move, but
your dad can be stubborn. What about the store? Are
you going to take over?"

"I don't have a choice at this point. It's the family
business, and Ryan doesn't seem interested. If Dad
really wants to retire, I'm the last one left."

She'd texted her brother after Dad's bombshell
announcement on Thursday but hadn't heard from
him yet. That wasn't all that uncommon. He was
working as a firefighter out west, and he'd texted a
week ago that his team was headed to a fire in Ari-
zona and might be off the grid for a while. Ryan
had his hands full just surviving, and she was sure
he'd be happy with whatever decision she made. Gallant Lake didn't hold warm, fuzzy memories for her
brother.

He'd called Dad right after the accident, and again
after the surgery. But he hadn't called his sister. Just
because he was sober these days didn't mean he
couldn't still be a jerk. He'd told Dad this was a bad
time of year for him to get away, when the wildfires
were just getting started out there. Dad told him not
to worry. He was proud of Ryan for pulling his life
back together.

Cathy's hand rested on Mack's arm. "That's going
to make your dad really happy, Mack. He was having

a hard time imagining that store leaving the family, but he really wants to retire."

Mack nodded absently. One more thing her father hadn't mentioned in their regular calls. What was he afraid she'd do? Cry? Get mad? Refuse to come home?

She walked back to her place, unable to avoid the truth. All of those things were possible. If Dad had asked her to come home while she and Mason were married, she'd have been horrified. It wasn't until she'd lost everything that she'd come back into Dad's world. He knew that as well as she did.

The sting was no less painful that night, when her dad confirmed it over dinner.

"I've been ready to cut back for a few years, Mackie." He scooped an enormous mound of lasagna onto her plate and handed it over. "I didn't want to pressure you or Ryan to take over the business," he said, "but I didn't want to *sell* it, either. It was great timing when you ended up getting…well…"

"Great timing for me to get *divorced*, Dad?" Mack smirked. "Yeah, I thought so, too." Dad's face went red. He didn't like talking about the failure of her marriage. He and her mother had had a forever kind of love, and it was tough for him to understand that not every marriage was like that. He cleared his throat awkwardly but didn't argue, so she pressed ahead. "I get it. If my marriage had lasted, I wouldn't be here helping you. Just like Ryan finding the firefighter team and finally figuring out who he was meant to be. Your kids are late bloomers, Dad. But we're figuring it out."

He mulled her words for a moment.

"So you're saying you'll take it on?"

She huffed out a laugh. She hadn't known what she was going to do until that moment.

"Sure, Dad. I've got nothing else to do."

He stared at his plate, frowning. "Not exactly the enthusiasm I was looking for."

"Give me a break, Dad. I'm here, aren't I? Isn't that what you want?"

Cathy cut in. "Your dad is very proud of both of you, Mack. You and Ryan. He says it all the time."

Mack's fork rattled against her plate. He *did*? Her father wasn't one to talk about feelings or affection, although she'd always felt he supported her and Ryan. And loved them in his quiet way. To hear that he talked about his feelings with *other* people—with his *girlfriend*—stirred some mixed emotions. On one hand, it was nice to think he was so proud of her that he'd say it out loud to someone. On the other hand, it hurt more than a little that he couldn't say it to *her*. She looked across the table at him and realized she needed to hear the words.

"*Are* you, Dad? Proud of us?"

The only other time she'd seen his face this red was when he told her he was moving in with Cathy. His jaw worked back and forth a few times, and he gave Cathy an annoyed look for starting this. Cathy cupped her chin in her hand and stared right back at him in mock innocence. The corner of her father's mouth lifted in a smile that had warmth and—uh-oh, was that *heat*?—in it. If she'd had any doubt about whether or not her father and Cathy were more than just friends, that silent exchange between them confirmed it. And Mack was surprisingly okay with it. Her dad shook his head and turned to Mack.

"Of course I'm proud of you. Both of you. You were always a good girl, of course. And Ryan? Well, Ryan worked hard to get himself right."

The words were the ones she'd wanted to hear. But then he'd ruined it.

"Was it just because I didn't cause problems that you were proud, Dad? Compared to Ryan?"

He gave Cathy a quick glance, looking for help. But Cathy sat back in silence, her face carefully blank. He was on his own with this one. He harrumphed a few times, but eventually he leaned forward and looked straight into Mack's eyes.

"Mackenzie Elizabeth Wallace, your mother and I were *always* proud of you. Not because you behaved. That's a pretty low bar, don't you think? We were proud because of *why* you were such a sweet girl. At twelve, you decided to do that for us because Ryan was getting in so much trouble. We tried to get you to ease up on yourself, but you just became such a driven kid. And when Mary got sick, you stepped up again. We worried, but there was no stopping you." He took a long drink of water, as if this much personal conversation was exhausting him. "When you and Mason got married, I was relieved. I figured you'd finally relax and live your own life." He gave her a sheepish look. "I guess I was wrong, huh?"

She started to answer, but he waved her off.

"And now you're back. And I have a feeling you're *finally* starting to live for yourself. So don't take on the store only to please me. I'll be proud of you no matter what, Mackie."

A thick silence fell on the table. Mack's throat was so full of emotion that she wouldn't have been able to speak if she wanted to. Dad looked like he'd just run a marathon and was ready to collapse of exhaustion. His glance darted around the room for a safe place to land. Cathy was biting her lip, her eyes shining with tears. She started to nod and kept nodding as she stood.

"I almost forgot dessert!" Cathy spoke rapidly. "I bought strawberries and angel food cake today. Let me just clear this…"

Mack got up to help, and as she passed behind her father, she patted his shoulder, still not trusting herself to say anything. He nodded, and she almost laughed. The three of them looked like a bunch of bobblehead dolls right now.

Wait until she told Dan about this later… His was the very first name that came to mind. Not her brother. Not her new friends. Dan Adams.

She checked her watch. Still a few more hours until he'd be at her place. Her heart jumped in anticipation. Good thing she'd grabbed a nap that afternoon.

Chapter Thirteen

Sundays tended to be quieter on-duty days. Not always, but usually. Dan's biggest challenge that day had been exhaustion and impatience to get back to Mackenzie. He'd texted her to let her know he was headed her way, just in case she'd fallen asleep. Or changed her mind. But her response came back almost instantly.

I'll pour the scotch.

When she opened the door and saw the box in his hand, she started to laugh. He'd missed that sound all day. He'd missed *her*.

"You brought a *pizza*?" She looked at her watch. "At twelve thirty in the morning?" She stepped aside to let him in. He gave her a quick kiss as he passed.

"Don't be too impressed. It's cold and half of it's been eaten. A pizzeria dropped half a dozen of them off at the station tonight. One of those thanks-for-your-service things. I haven't had dinner, and it smelled too good to leave it there." He took his jacket off and went to toss it on the chair, then stopped cold when an orange pillow started to move. "Damn, I forgot you had that mutant cat."

The cat was curled up on the chair seat, but a cat that large couldn't curl up enough to hide his gargantuan size. He studied Dan with tawny eyes the same color as his thick coat. Dan reached down, and those eyes narrowed dangerously. Then he stretched just enough to brush his head against Dan's fingers.

"Ooh, you should feel honored." Mack put a slice of pizza on a plate. "That's *almost* a sign of approval."

"What's his name again?"

"Rory."

"Right." He moved his fingers against the cat's head. Rory tolerated it for a minute, then reached up and put his teeth on Dan's finger. He didn't bite, just held him there. Dan waited until Rory released him, then slowly pulled his hand back. There was no malice in the cat's expression, and he finally lost interest and started cleaning his paws. Dan wasn't much of a cat guy, so he'd accept this truce as a win.

He took his glass of scotch and sat. "There's enough pizza for two in there if you want to join me."

"I had lasagna with Dad and Cathy." She sat next

to him and propped her chin in her hand. "You had an okay day?"

"Blissfully boring. How did your dinner go?"

"Um…not boring, but not bad." It was nice, sitting there discussing their day. She told him about her conversation with her dad while he ate. When she said she was ready to take over the liquor store, he set his pizza slice down and stared. Something weird fluttered inside him at the thought of spending more evenings unwinding with Mack.

"So you're really staying in Gallant Lake?"

Her mouth twitched. "Would that be a problem, Officer?"

"Not for me." He leaned over and kissed her lips, pulling back quickly to avoid being pulled into the kiss vortex that tended to spin the two of them out of control.

They chatted more as he devoured the rest of the pizza. As always, Mack was easy to be with. As he drained the last of his scotch, he said so. She tipped her head, and her honey-colored hair tumbled over her shoulders.

"You're pretty nice to be around, too."

They continued chatting as they cleaned up. She told him about her father's unexpected declaration that he was proud of her. To Dan, that seemed obvious. But when he saw how much the words meant to Mack, he wondered if maybe it was a guy thing to assume people knew your thoughts. It was a damned shame Mack had gone all these years not knowing for sure how much her father cared. The next time

Dan saw his daughter, he'd be sure to tell Chloe how proud of her he was.

Dan put the empty pizza box into her recycle bin. They were being so very domestic at one o'clock in the morning. After this weekend, he should be exhausted, but being with Mack energized him.

"So you're going to run the liquor store. I'd have never guessed *that* one twenty years ago. Is that part of Mackie's adventurous new leaf?" Another question rose up before he had time to think it through. "For that matter, am I?"

They stared at each other for a long moment. He wanted to kick himself for taking the conversation in such a serious direction. He had no right to press her for a declaration of her feelings about them when he hadn't examined his own yet.

She blew out a quick breath. "I guess it is. And you could be. We haven't really talked about what it is you and I…" She gestured between them. "…whatever this is we're doing…"

He took the towel from her hands and set it aside, tugging her close. "I didn't mean to be such a wet blanket. Sorry, babe."

She considered his words, frowning. "It wasn't a bad question, though. What *are* we doing? Is this a relationship now? Is it serious or just for fun?"

He had no idea how to answer.

"Can't we figure that out as we go? Take it a day at a time? No strings…"

"No strings?" She pulled back and looked up at

him, her brows furrowed. "You don't think we've already created strings?"

Yeah, they had. Strings slicing right through the center of his heart. He released her and scrubbed his hands down his face.

"I don't know, Mack. I haven't had a serious relationship since my divorce, and I'm guessing you haven't, either."

She laughed. "Turns out I didn't have a serious one *before* my divorce, either. This is new territory for both of us." She shrugged. "Maybe we should stick to that one-day-at-a-time plan for a while."

"If nothing else, I need to make sure Chloe's okay with it before anything gets serious." He gave her a wink and ran her fingers down her arm. He loved the way her skin trembled at his touch. "But we don't have to worry about any of that tonight."

Mack started walking backward, taking his fingers in her hand and pulling him along. "Agreed. And just because I didn't want any pizza doesn't mean I'm not hungry for something else."

That was all the invitation Dan needed. They were upstairs, undressed and in bed in less than a minute, but then he took his time exploring her. He hadn't seen her naked body in almost twenty-four hours, and he wanted to memorize every inch of it. He didn't just explore with his hands, either. He kissed her from her toes to her thighs and beyond. Just as dangerous to handle as ever, she came fast and loud when his mouth found her. And again when he sank into her.

They moved together in perfect time, whispering and pleading and saying very naughty words. But it was her name he cried out when he came, right after she'd shuddered in his arms with another orgasm. She had a hair trigger, and he'd never realized how exciting that could be. How exciting *she* could be. He pulled her in close, their hearts and their breathing falling into sync. She was asleep in seconds, but Dan lay there wide-awake, trying to make sense of it all.

He'd never wanted a woman the way he wanted Mack. With every fiber of his being. With a love so strong...

Wait. *What?*

She shifted in his arms, as if sensing his tension. He kissed her temple and whispered for her to go back to sleep. She did, but he couldn't. Was he falling in *love* with her? Was it possible for that to happen so quickly? Mack let out a little sigh in her sleep, and his heart swelled.

It felt very possible right now.

Mack barely woke when Dan whispered an apology and slipped out of bed, saying something about meeting someone named Sam. She brushed her hair up off her face and tried to remember what day it was. Wednesday? Thursday? He'd spent every night, or at least part of every night, at her place this week. They hadn't had a chance to discuss what they'd do when Chloe was staying with him. Well, they'd *had* the chance, but they'd decided to use those chances for *other* things, like making love all night. Every night.

She was so tired when Dan left that she'd just muttered something and rolled over. When her phone rang ten minutes later, she figured it was him, calling with something naughty to say. He did that a lot, but not usually this early.

Her voice was still husky from sleep when she answered. "Hey, lover boy, did you decide you'd rather come back and have *me* for breakfast?"

Her brother coughed on the other end of the call, choking on laughter. "Well, hot damn. I was going to ask how you were coping after the divorce, but it sounds like you're handling it just fine, sis. Way to get back in the saddle again!"

Mack groaned, sitting up and rubbing her eyes. "Jackass." She glanced at the time. "Aren't you three time zones away? Why are you calling so early?" She was suddenly fully alert. "Did something happen? Are you okay?"

"Relax, Mother Hubbard, I'm fine. We're working wacky shifts on this fire, and I don't get a lot of downtime for family calls." Ryan hesitated. "I talked to Dad yesterday, and he dumped a few surprises on me. Is he *really* shacking up with Cathy Meadows? And are you *really* taking over the store? Is that what you want?"

"Why?" She pulled on her robe, wondering if she'd misread her brother's plans. She worked her way past the hungry cat, who seemed more determined than usual to trip her up. "Do *you* want the store? You know I'd never do anything official without talking to you first. If you…"

"Seriously, Mackie?" Ryan sounded as tired as she felt. "Gallant Lake and me is not happening. Been there. Done that. Know I'm not welcome. At least not by some people. And I get it. Mrs. Michaels doesn't need to be bumping into me on the sidewalk."

Mack stopped so fast that Rory ended up two feet in front of her instead of between her feet. He looked back in annoyance, clearly frustrated that he couldn't trip her from that far away. Ryan rarely talked about the accident that took the life of his friend and nearly his own. When she didn't respond, Ryan filled in the silence.

"I talked to her a couple months ago, you know."

"Mrs. Michaels? *Why?*" Both boys had been drunk that night, but the police report determined it was Braden Michaels who was behind the wheel, just as Ryan had said. Braden's family refused to believe it at the time and took Ryan to court for wrongful death. Mom and Dad used up most of their savings defending him, but the case was eventually dismissed.

"There are twelve steps, Mack. And I'd reached the atonement step. I was too chicken to face her, but I did call and tell her how sorry I was."

She drew in a sharp breath. "Was that wise? *Apologizing?* Doesn't it make you sound responsible?" She pushed the button on the coffee maker and brushed her hair back again. She really needed to find a hairdresser.

"It's part of the program, sis. Had to do it. I wasn't driving, and I told her that. But Braden and I stole that booze from Dad. And I hopped in the car with him,

knowing how trashed he was. I was, too. Anyway..."
He sighed. "I called. She listened. She couldn't give
me more than an 'okay' when I was done, but that's
probably more than I deserved." There was a pause.
Mack had no idea what to say. Ryan sighed again.
"And that was a really long-winded way of saying
I have no intention of returning to Gallant Lake. It
wouldn't be fair to them. And as far as the store is
concerned, probably not the best idea for an alcoholic
to be selling booze. The store's all yours."

"Thanks, Ryan." She grabbed the box of day-old
doughnuts Dan had brought with him last night and
opened it. *Breakfast of champions.* "I'll be buying it
from Dad, so I'm sure you'll get a share, either now
or later." There was a rustling in the background
on his end, and it sounded like he was settling onto
a cot or sleeping bag. He'd been working on this
fire for weeks, and he had to be exhausted. "To
answer your *other* question—yes, Dad *is* shacking
up with Cathy. And no, I couldn't believe it, either.
But they're actually pretty cute together, which is
weird. He seems...happy."

"Well, good for them, I guess. Mom's been gone
a long time, and he deserves to be happy again. And
speaking of getting some...who the hell is 'lover
boy'?"

Mack hesitated, not sure if Ryan would want to
know she was sleeping with his onetime best friend. But
she'd been mad at her father for keeping secrets, and
she didn't want to turn around and do the same thing.

"It's just casual. And very new."

"Considering you just got free of the other jerk a month ago, I would *hope* this is new. Anyone I know?"

"Um…yeah, actually." She took a steadying breath. "Dan Adams."

The silence stretched on for what seemed like hours. And then her brother started to laugh.

"Are you kiddin' me? Dan Adams?" He laughed some more, and someone there must have said something about the noise, because Ryan wasn't speaking to her when he said, "Sorry, man, but my kid sister is screwing my best friend. Or former best friend. Like, she's got a whole town to choose from, and she chooses *that* guy." His voice got more clear as he started talking to her again. "So how *is* Danny? And I don't mean how is he in the sack, 'cause I don't need to know."

They talked for a few minutes about Dan, and Ryan seemed genuinely cool with it. He said he regretted the way their friendship had faded after the accident, but he understood it. After Braden's death, Dan had found the righteous path of law and order, while Ryan had continued drowning his sorrows in a bottle for a decade or more.

"I suppose I owe him some apologies, too. I gave him a lot of crap when he turned his life around. The truth was, I was jealous." Ryan paused. "He made it look so easy. Just woke up one day as one of the good guys. And I never figured out how to do that."

"Yes, you did. You're a good guy, Ryan. A hero firefighter."

"Don't call me a hero, sis." His voice hardened. "I never know what to say when people use that word. I've got a job and I do it. That's it."

Dan had said something similar more than once. He was uncomfortable with the whole Sheriff Dan, Hero of Gallant Lake legend. Ryan ended the call after explaining that he had to get some sleep before his next shift. The good news was the fire was 70 percent contained. The bad news was it was still 30 percent *un*contained. He promised to call again the next week.

Mack finished her doughnut and gulped down some coffee before starting a load of laundry. Once in motion, she stayed there, vacuuming and picking up around the apartment. Dad had told her it would be hers. Did she *want* to live here, where she'd grown up? Or would she be better off buying a house and renting this out? Her divorce settlement had been generous enough that she could probably afford it. The settlement was *too* generous, according to Mason, but he'd wanted the marriage to be over with as badly as she had. She'd taken a lump sum instead of alimony, but she didn't want to spend it all on buying the store. Her conversation with Ryan had made her realize she'd have to find a bank and get a loan.

Bert was manning the store until five, so she headed down a little before that to see how things were going. He was a funny guy—quiet and introverted, but knowledgeable about their inventory and happy to share his knowledge with customers. As Dad told her, Bert wouldn't come close to hard selling anyone, but he managed to do well just because people liked and trusted the former schoolteacher in his cardigan sweaters and comb-over hair. If he recommended something, they didn't hesitate to buy it. Dad called him an accidental salesperson. Bert didn't seem to sell anything on purpose.

She and Bert went over their stock orders for the next few weeks. There was a big charity event coming up at the resort that apparently brought a lot of high spenders to Gallant Lake, so they were planning for that with more upscale product than usual. After Bert headed home, Mack went through the wine section, dusting shelves and bottles while taking inventory. The bell over the door tinkled, and she turned to see one very familiar young face and an adult one she didn't recognize right away. But she had a hunch who it was.

"Mackie!" Chloe released the hand of the woman and ran over to Mack. "We were just looking at websites with Mel to pick out a dress for me. I'm gonna be a model, remember?"

Mack smiled and walked toward the front of the store with her. "I remember. Did you find something pretty?" Mack looked up. "You must be Chloe's mom. Susanne, right? I think I remember you from school. I'm Mackenzie Wallace."

Susanne Adams gave her an appraising look. It didn't feel adversarial. Yet. She was petite and trim, with shoulder-length brown hair and a very put-together look. An *expensive* look. Dan had mentioned his ex was dating a doctor now.

"Yes, I think I remember you, too. And of course, I know your dad. How is Carl?"

"He's recuperating well, but not quickly enough to suit him."

They were being oh so polite. This was brand-new territory for Mack, and probably for Susanne, too. Dan said he hadn't been in any relationships to speak of since the divorce. Dan had also said he hadn't told her yet, but Mack definitely got the vibe that she knew. Chloe was checking out the mini bottles on the counter, straightening them on the little display shelves.

"Be careful with those, honey," Susanne said. "Don't drop any."

Mack waved her hand. "Most of those are plastic these days. She's fine. Are you looking for anything in particular?"

Susanne didn't answer right away, studying Mack. Finally, she tilted her head toward the back of the store, where the wines were. Oh yeah—she knew. Mack followed. When they were far enough from Chloe, Susanne turned and got right to business.

"I hear you're dating my ex."

Great.

"Yes, I guess I am." Although this week they'd spent more time in her bedroom than out on any dates. But his ex probably didn't want to hear that detail any more than her brother did. She wondered who'd been talking.

"I wasn't sure how I felt about it, but we had a teacher's conference yesterday, and Dan was more…

relaxed…than usual. Happier. It was nice." She pursed her lips, lost in thought, before looking up with a soft smile. "It's a small town, Mack. People talk. And *everyone* knows Dan, so they're even quicker to talk. And everyone knows Carl, so *you're* on their radar, too. And not always in a good way— you were a bit of a brat in school."

Susanne shrugged as she continued. "I just wanted you to know the word's out there. Chloe told me Daddy had a new friend. She told me you three went bike riding together. And I'm totally fine with it. I mean, obviously." She held up her left hand and flashed an enormous diamond. "I'm remarrying, so there's no jealousy between Dan and me." She glanced toward Chloe. "But the simple truth is, he and I will be connected for the rest of our lives because of our daughter. And anyone coming into our lives needs to know that." She leveled her gaze at Mack. "I guess you could say we're a package deal."

Was this a warning or a welcome? Mack couldn't tell. Susanne was being nice enough but still guarded. Mack gave her a bright smile. "I totally get that. But just so you know, Dan and I are…new. Casual. That being said, I adore Chloe and I'd never want to upset her. If people are talking, Dan should probably…"

"Exactly. I'd rather Chloe heard it from her father than some kid at school joking about Sheriff Dan's new girlfriend." Mack cringed. She appreciated how cool Susanne was being about all of this, but that didn't make it any less awkward. Susanne picked up a bottle of Finger Lakes chardonnay. "Do you want to talk to Dan about it or should I? I'm assuming *you'll* see him before I will."

Without thinking, Mack glanced at her watch, and Susanne laughed.

"I'll take that as a yes." Chloe was just finishing up the last shelf of tiny bottles. Susanne pulled a folded piece of paper from her pocket. "Here's my contact information. Cell phone. Work phone. Chloe likes spending time with you, and you should probably know how to reach me if Dan has to leave and Chloe needs anything. He's basically on call all the time, you know."

Mack took the card, then shook her head with a grin. She remembered the call he got when they were making out on his stairs a week ago. "Yeah, I know. You're making this feel very…normal."

"Dan's a good guy and a great father. We were lucky enough to part as friends, which will make the rest of Chloe's life a lot easier." She smiled at her daughter, who'd just walked over to join them. "We're a team, and that includes the people we… well…" She rolled her eyes in Chloe's direction. "The team includes our new friends. That's why I thought we should meet."

"I'm glad we did." Mack slid the bottle of chardonnay into a paper bag. "Take this home with you. On the house."

Susanne's eyes brightened. "Really? I used to tell Dan he had good taste in women. I guess I was right. Thanks."

Mack watched Chloe and her mom head out the

door. She'd worried a little about the whole family dynamics issue of getting involved with a single dad, but it seemed that was one thing she didn't have to worry about. Now she just had to figure out what she and Dan were really doing, and how far it was going to go. The one thing she *did* know for sure was that she couldn't wait to see him again tonight.

Chapter Fourteen

"Just hold my hand and step in, Mack. It's a lot more stable than a kayak, I promise."

Dan tried not to laugh at the doubt and fear in Mack's eyes. She'd told him about her experience trying the kayak with Nate and how she'd freaked out when she couldn't get out of the thing. That wasn't going to be a problem in his aluminum fishing boat. Sixteen feet long, with three bench seats and a reliable outboard motor on back, it was his getaway from the real world. At least, it *had* been. For the past week or so, Mack was his getaway. When he was with her, some of the pressure always simmering under his skin seemed to ease. He could laugh with her. Or laugh *at* her, which he was about to do if she didn't get in the boat.

"Mackie, trust me."

At that, she reached out from the dock at the public boat launch and took his hand. She was shaking, but she managed to get into the boat and quickly plunk down on one of the bench seats. When she realized the sturdy old boat was barely swaying from her entry, she grinned up at him.

"That wasn't so bad."

"Told you so. Now hang on—I'll get us over to Muskrat Bay and drop anchor, and we'll see if we can find any fish."

Gallant Lake was a little choppy that afternoon, but the rainstorms had let up and the afternoon sun was warming things up in a hurry. Summer was definitely on its way, and there was already a touch of humidity in the air. The bay was protected from the breeze, so the water was quieter there. Dan got the anchor set and handed a fishing pole to Mack. She looked at the pole with the same amount of suspicion she'd had for the boat.

"I know I grew up here," she said, "but Dad was never big on fishing, and I certainly wouldn't be caught dead touching a worm back then. So I have no idea what to do here."

Dan opened the container of worms he'd picked up from the bait shop near the park and put one on Mack's hook. She didn't squeal in fear or anything when he handed the pole back to her, just inspected what he'd done in fascination, then watched as he put a jointed lure on his fishing rod.

"Why aren't you using a worm?"

"I probably will later, but as long as you're using worms, I'll use the lure and we'll see what works."

An hour later, they were both using worms. And they had a basket hanging off the side of the boat that was quickly filling with lake perch. It was fun when you found a school of perch like that, and Mack was having a blast. She'd start laughing the minute she got a nibble, and Dan couldn't help joining her. She was putting her own worms on the hook now, even if she made a lot of faces while doing it. But Dan took the fish off the hook for her. She had no interest in touching the fish while they were still wiggling, and he didn't want her stabbing herself.

Eventually, the perch moved on and things slowed down.

"This is perfect fishing," he told her with a smile. "We had our fun. The basket's full. And now we can just relax."

Mack frowned. "You don't want to move the boat to find more fish or something?"

"Sometimes the best thing about fishing is the peace and quiet. No one around. No demands. No complaints." He nodded toward the village in the distance. "It's nice to see the town from this perspective. Close enough to enjoy it, far enough away to not have to…react…to anything."

She nodded. "It's like that thirty-thousand-foot view they talk about—far enough removed to see the big picture, but not the details."

"Something like that."

She dropped her hook back in the water, letting

the line out a few more feet. She was up in the bow of the boat, and she leaned back and stared up at the sky, which was beginning to darken again.

"Do you take Chloe fishing?"

"I've tried, but containing all that energy to a boat this size is…challenging." Frankly, the girl freaked him out on the water. She had zero fear, and sitting still was next to impossible for her.

Mack laughed, sitting up again. "I can imagine. And with you being Mr. Safety and all, I bet you're a nervous wreck. That girl is always on the go." Her smile faded. "Have you talked to her about us seeing each other? Is she okay with it?"

Dan jiggled the fishing rod to move the bait around before setting it back down again. "She was excited about it. She likes you, Mack. We made sure she got counseling after the divorce, and she still goes once a month." Dan hadn't want to think his little girl needed professional help at such a young age, but Susanne had insisted. And she'd been right. Having someone to talk to had helped Chloe process all the changes in her life without taking things personally. "She's already seen her mom dating and getting ready for a wedding, so I think she gets it. Don't be surprised if she starts talking weddings, though. I think she figures that's how it works after Susanne and Samir got engaged. Boy meets girl. Boy dates girl. Boy and girl get married. Little girl gets a pretty dress and a part in the wedding." The tip of his fishing rod dipped and he reached for it, but it was just a nibble.

Mack's forehead furrowed. "I hope you told her not to expect any wedding bells with us."

He absorbed the sting of her words and tried to smile. "Is it such a revolting idea? Wedding bells?"

"Slow down, Danger Dan." Mack moved her fishing pole, mimicking his actions. "We've been together less than a month. I'm looking for fun, re-member? Not a shotgun wedding." She laughed. "I don't mean *that* kind of shotgun wedding, but you know what I'm saying. We haven't even said the *L* word yet, and I think the proper order of things is for that to come before wedding bells."

Dan swallowed hard. There were some big things in those few sentences. The first was the reference to a shotgun wedding. Meaning she'd be pregnant. He hadn't even considered more children, but the idea of Mack carrying his baby filled him with anticipa-tion. Pride. Desire. And then she'd mentioned love. Not directly—she'd used "the *L* word" as if saying it would be some sort of jinx. But he'd already been dealing with feelings for her that felt a hell of a lot like love. She was right, though. It was probably too soon for that.

"Do you want kids?" The words tumbled out be-fore he could stop them. Mack's eyes went wide.

"Where did that...? Oh, the shotgun-wedding thing." She looked off into space for a moment be-fore continuing. "It never happened for Mason and me, but the doctors said they couldn't see any rea-son why it shouldn't have. So I guess it's possible it could happen, even at this late date."

"Mack, you're thirty-six. That's not a late date." He hesitated, not sure if this conversation was a good idea. "If that's what you want. And that's all I was asking."

A smile played at the corners of her mouth. "I've *wanted* a lot of things, Dan. And I got a lot of them. And most turned into dust. I don't mean to sound melodramatic, but I kinda stopped wishing and wanting. If it happens, it happens. And if a baby happens someday, I'd be thrilled. I think." She gave her head a quick shake, nearly losing her brimmed hat in the process. "I have a hard time picturing that, but it would definitely qualify as an adventure, wouldn't it?"

Dan thought of his boisterous daughter and grinned. "I can tell you that every day is an adventure with the one I have."

"As long as we're on the subject, how do you think Chloe will feel if there's a new family member? Are Susanne and Samir planning a child together? Would Chloe welcome that?"

"*Would* she?" Dan laughed. "She's already asking for a brother or sister or both or several of each. Chloe's always been a the-more-the-merrier kind of kid. I know she's only eight, but she's never been selfish about people or things." He paused, emotion filling his throat. "She has the biggest heart of any kid I've ever met."

There was a gentle rumble in the distance, and Dan pulled out his phone to check the weather. "Looks like more rain might move in. Let's get back while we're still dry." They both started reeling in their lines. He hadn't had a chance to address the whole *L*-word thing. But Mack was staying in Gallant Lake, and they had plenty of time.

Even with a storm on the distant horizon, Mack was relaxed as Dan steered the boat toward the public docks at the park. Getting him away from town had done a world of good for all that tension he'd been carrying. No one was around to bug him about solving crime, and he'd gradually shed that hero cape that usually weighed him down. His joy when the fish started biting was infectious, and they'd both been laughing and teasing as they brought the fish into the boat. He said it was plenty for a meal and promised to fry them up that night. Mack had never eaten a meal she'd caught herself—unless you counted shopping at the fish market—so it was another adventure to add to her list.

Dan helped her out of the boat, then had her hold the lines while he backed his trailer down the ramp and into the water. A few minutes later, he drove the truck forward, with the boat safely on board and secure. She hopped into the passenger seat, and he started to drive, then stopped abruptly.

"Look at that!" Dan pointed past her, out the window toward the lake. Although it wasn't raining where they sat, it clearly *was* raining on the other side of the water. A soft gray curtain of rain blurred the rounded mountains in the distance. As the rain approached, the surface of the lake changed from smooth blue gray to rain-dappled pewter. They watched as the little downpour came all the way to the shore, then swept over the truck and over Gallant Lake. It pounded on the roof of the truck cab.

"Wasn't that cool?" he asked. His eyes were bright and…happy. Mack thought about what Susanne had said. That Dan seemed happier since meeting her. The thought filled her with warmth. She nodded in agreement.

"Very cool. At one point it was raining on the end of the dock but not over us. We got back just in time."

His smile dimmed. "We weren't in any danger, Mack. That thunder we heard was off to the north. I'd never—"

She rolled her eyes at him. "Oh my God, Dan. Do you become Captain Responsibility the minute your feet touch land? I never once thought we were in danger. I just meant we didn't get *wet*." She looked back out at the rain, still coming down straight and heavy. "But then again, what's the big deal about getting wet?"

When she grabbed the door handle, Dan reached for her, but it was too late. She was out and jogging backward away from the truck, gesturing for him to join her. "Come on, Danny boy. You won't melt!" She twirled, arms outstretched. The rain was cold, but it felt great. Refreshing. Daring. She turned away from the truck, away from Dan's shocked and disapproving face, and looked out over the now-silver lake. If only that carefree guy she'd seen in the boat could find a way to exist on shore.

The clouds looked so low she could almost touch them. The top of Gallant Mountain was completely hidden. She lifted her head, closed her eyes and let the rain hit her face. This felt better than the best facial she'd ever had. Her eyes snapped open when she felt two strong arms wrap around her waist. She was tugged back against a solid chest. A familiar voice spoke right next to her ear.

"You're crazy. You make *me* crazy, Mackenzie Wallace." His voice lowered so she barely heard the next. "And I think I'm falling in love with you."

"What?" She spun in his arms, laughing at the sight of his hair plastered on his forehead, raindrops rolling down his face. She could only imagine what she looked like, but…she honestly didn't care. "What did you say?"

He shook his head with that half grin she'd thought was his mask to hide his emotion. The one that said the world amused him, but that he wasn't part of the world. But the deep, dark flame in his gaze told her he was very present in this moment.

"I'm not going to repeat what I know you heard." He lifted a shoulder. "Probably shouldn't have said it so soon, but the sight of you out here, dancing in the rain… Thinking I'd join you…" He kissed her, hard and fast. The rain made the kiss taste fresh. "And here I am. You do something to me, Mackie. I don't know if it's good or bad, but I'm pretty sure that *L* word is behind it. And I'm falling. I'm free-falling. You pushed me—or maybe pulled me—right over the edge." He cupped her face in his hands and kissed her again. The rain was coming down so hard she could hardly keep her eyes open, but she couldn't not look into his emotion-filled gaze. "So tell me, baby. Are we falling together?"

She felt a quick shiver of fear, followed by another shiver…of desire. She wrapped her arms around his neck.

"The question isn't if we're falling, Danny. It's where are we going to land? And what's going to happen then?"

"Well, girl. You said you were looking for an adventure. Tumbling through the unknown is about as adventurous as it gets. Let's see where it takes us." He tugged her arm and took her hand, entwining his fingers with hers. "At least we'll have good company. But you didn't really answer my question. *Are* you falling, too?"

"I'm falling, Dan. Believe me, I'm falling."

The truth was, she'd fallen already. She was in love with Danny Adams. Before she could say so, he looked up at the still-pouring heavens and tugged her toward the truck.

"We'll both have pneumonia if we don't get out of this rain."

They went to Dan's house. Susanne had Chloe that day, and Dan didn't expect her to bike over for a surprise visit in the rain. They parked the boat next to his garage. Dan tossed the fish into the spare refrigerator in the garage. Then they ran inside to take a steaming hot shower—together. And then, well… then they made love, of course. In the shower. Then again in his bed. They probably would have continued the activity straight into the night, but Dan reminded her they had fish to clean.

"Uh-uh. *You* have fish to clean. I'm not going there." They'd tossed their clothes into the dryer, so she was fully dressed again, standing in the kitchen.

He shook his head. "Haven't you ever heard of the rule—you catch 'em, you clean 'em?"

She lifted one brow. "Haven't you ever heard of the rule—you could have thrown them back?" She pulled a head of lettuce from his fridge. "I'll put a salad together and mix up a box of brownies. While *you* take care of the fishies."

An hour later, they were sitting down to a delicious meal of pan-fried perch. The small fillets were mild but still flavorful. She thought of their conversation and realized that if they landed like this, sharing meals they caught in Gallant Lake and laughing about who did the most work, she'd be a very happy woman.

They were talking about her dad and Cathy while they were washing dishes later, and Dan asked how Ryan took the news.

"He's fine with it." Mack set her towel down and turned to face him. "What happened between you and Ryan, Dan? You were best friends, and now you have no contact at all. He said he understood, but I'm not sure *I* do."

Dan's smile was gone in an instant, and his face went gray. "You know what happened. The accident…"

"Uh, yeah. I remember. But you weren't even in

the car. Ryan was in the hospital for weeks, and you barely showed up. You stopped coming to our house. You avoided my parents…"

He put the last of the dishes in the strainer and stood staring at it as if he wished it could remove him from this room. But they'd handled some big topics that day, and she wasn't going to let this one slide. She really wanted to know. She put her hand on his shoulder, shocked at how tight and tense he was. He kept staring at the clean plates when he spoke, his voice devoid of emotion.

"I couldn't face your parents, Mack. I never knew when they'd show up in Ryan's room, and I couldn't face them. Or the Michaels family, for that matter. I didn't know what to do."

"Why couldn't you face them? I don't understand…"

He closed his eyes, his fingers curling into the towel he held. "I got them the booze that day, Mack. I wasn't in the car, but only because my dad had grounded me for mouthing back at him. He was drinking a lot back then—hell, so was I—and we had a stupid argument. One of those rite-of-passage arguments where teenage boys take their first swing at their dad. It was a mess. Anyway, he grounded me for the first time ever. I had to go straight home after baseball practice at school. But I didn't go to practice. I met Ryan and Braden up on Hill Road, and I gave them two bottles of gin I'd lifted from my grandparents' liquor cabinet." He shook his head, his eyes still tightly shut. "I got them drunk. It was *my* fault. My fault Ryan was in the hospital." He finally turned and looked at her. "My fault Braden was dead. I'm sorry—I didn't know how to tell you. If this changes anything…"

Mack started to laugh, low and soft. Dan recoiled from the unexpected reaction. She took his hands in hers and held tight.

"Dan, have you really been thinking that all these years? That night wasn't your fault." He started to object but she talked right over him. "Okay, fine, you contributed some booze. But that was in the afternoon, and they didn't hit that tree until three in the morning. I remember the night as if it was yesterday. Ryan and Braden took something like half a case of bourbon from Dad's store. And by took I mean stole. Mom and Dad were visiting my grandparents in Syracuse. The boys were supposed to be watching me, but they were playing video games and doing shots for *hours* that night." Her parents kept trying to give Ryan responsibility in hopes that he'd grow up, but it didn't work. "I put myself to bed. Ryan told me afterward that they got into an argument about whether Braden's car was fast enough to catch air on that little rise out on Marshfield Road. They got the bright idea to go try it." Dan was scowling at the counter, and she squeezed his hands again to make sure he was hearing her. God, had he been carrying this around all these years? "I don't know how they even made it to the car, much less drove it up there, but they did. Those two bottles of gin eight hours earlier didn't cause it. It wasn't your fault."

"Maybe I could have stopped it if I'd been there."

"I just let you off the hook for one guilt trip, and you're grasping at another one? Stop, Dan. You didn't do this. And honestly, I'm *glad* you weren't there. I'm glad you were safe at home that night. The thought that you could have been killed, too…my God." She leaned forward and kissed him softly on the mouth. He didn't respond at first, but then his hand came up to cup the back of her neck, tugging her closer.

The kiss deepened, and Mack felt something shift between them. As intense as their lovemaking had been before, she hadn't realized until this moment that there'd been something between them. Something he'd been holding in. But that something was gone now. His head tipped for better access, and he murmured her name against her lips. His arms went around her, sliding up under her top, hot against her skin. *Yes, please.*

"I need you, Mack. Spend the night." She hadn't done that yet—stayed at his place. He'd been worried about Chloe stopping by on the way to school or something.

"Dan…"

"It's okay. It'll be okay. We'll make it all work. Stay the night. Stay with me…" His hand slid beneath the waist of her jeans, his fingers curling around her backside and pulling her in tight. She let out a low moan. Who was she kidding? She was putty in his hands when he let down his guard like this.

"I'll stay, Dan. I'll stay."

Chapter Fifteen

"Wow, what a view!" Mack was staring out the windshield as Dan parked the truck in front of Asher and Nora's log house on Gallant Mountain.

Dan stared at her for a moment. Her hair was pulled back in a low ponytail. She was wearing crisp white jeans and a fluttery blue top that just brushed across her curves. It was low cut, and as she leaned forward, he couldn't help but smile and agree.

"Yeah. The view's *very* nice."

She looked over, then followed where his eyes were focused, promptly sitting up.

"What are you, sixteen?" She frowned at her outfit. "Is it too low? Too fancy? Not fancy enough?"

"Whoa, calm down, girl. You look perfect. Just do me a favor and don't bend over like that in front of Asher." Dan opened the truck door and winked over at her. "I'd hate to have to punch my best friend in the nose because he couldn't keep his eyes where they belong. And relax. It's just dinner with friends."

They walked up the steps hand in hand. Asher was an architect as well as a furniture maker, and he'd designed the big house to look like it had just grown there at the edge of the trees. The dark green metal roof blended with the pines, and a wide porch wrapped around three sides.

"I know I've said this already," Mack said, "but… wow." She stopped and looked at the lake far below. "When Nora said she lived in a log house, I pictured *Little House on the Prairie*, not *Architectural Digest*."

"It was actually featured in the magazine last year. Asher designed it and basically built it all himself, too. Wait until you see the…" The door flew open, and Nora stood there with a dish towel in one hand and a bottle of wine in the other.

"You're here! Come in! I just pulled my famous shrimp toast out of the oven, and Asher and the guys are out front at the grill." Nora waved them in. "Mack, why don't you join Mel, Amanda and me in the kitchen, and Dan, you can go watch the fire with the other cavemen."

"Actually," Dan started, not ready to lose Mack's company just yet, "I was going to give Mack the grand tour, if that's okay."

Nora froze, her eyebrows slowly raising. Mel and Amanda had stopped talking and were staring at

Dan. They all seemed to be biting back laughter. Nora regained her composure, but he couldn't help noticing her southern accent deepened.

"Why, sure, Dan! Y'all go on ahead and tour the place. With your girl." She leaned toward Mack and spoke in a stage whisper that could be heard on the second floor. "Dan's never brought a girl here before." Nora looked back to Dan, holding the dish towel over her heart. "And he doesn't want to leave your side. Which might just be the cutest thing ever."

Dan had taken his share of razzing from Nora since she came to town and bought the coffee shop next door to Asher's business. She and Asher fought like hellcats right up to the moment they'd fallen in love. Dan had been happy for the two of them. But right now he was wondering if he really needed Nora Peyton teasing about how cute he was.

Mack was looking at him funny. "You've never brought a date here to meet your friends?"

"What friends?" He glowered at Nora, but that just made her laugh harder.

"You don't scare me with that lawman glare, Dan Adams. And to answer your question, Mack, no—he hasn't ever brought a date here. I don't know if I've ever *seen* him with a date, now that I think about it. He's a bit of a hermit when he's not working." She stepped back and gestured toward the curving staircase. "Feel free to explore the place. Dan helped Asher build a lot of it. And despite the way he's pouting at the moment, he loves me."

He sighed. "Yeah, yeah. You're pretty irresistible."

He flipped the bottom of her hair as he walked by, making her squeal and smack at his hand. "Like an annoying big sister."

The men and women separated again after dinner, and this time Dan joined the guys on the screened porch. Mack had gone to the kitchen with the women. He'd heard another bottle of wine being uncorked in there. Good thing Mack didn't have to work the next morning.

Blake settled into a large wicker rocker and pulled a slender cigar from his pocket. He leaned forward and peeked into the house to make sure he couldn't be seen before lighting it. "I was at our Barbados resort last week, and a guy hooked me up with some hand-rolled cigars." He looked around. "Anyone want one?"

Shane took one, but Asher and Dan were satisfied with their brandy. Shane sat and looked over to Dan. "So things are getting serious with the woman you body slammed against the wall a month ago?"

Dan shook his head. He'd probably never live down that night. But *last* night, he'd had Mack against the wall in a whole new way, so that was his new favorite memory when it came to walls.

Shane chuckled. "From that grin on your face, I'm guessing the answer is 'why yes, Shane, things *are* going well.' Not that it matters, but I like her. She's got sass."

Dan tried to think if he'd seen Shane and Mack together. "Is this your first time meeting her?"

Shane took a puff of his cigar. "Other than a quick wave in passing, yes. I've been on the road nonstop, man. The basketball draft is in a few weeks and I've got two kids who might make the first round, and I've got a baseball player looking to make a big move this summer."

He glanced at Dan. "I hear there's been some drug drama in our little town. Mel said there's actually a task force now. Are you any closer to figuring it out?"

Dan didn't answer right away. He was tired of the question, but he understood why people asked. They were concerned. So was he. And these guys were friends with an interest in the safety and reputation of the town they did business in as well as called their home. But still, he couldn't divulge too much.

"We think it's a New York gang looking to expand north. We're not their target market, but they seem to be stashing the stuff in our area. Treating this like a warehouse between the city and upstate. The volume is more than we've ever had in our area, and they're tossing it around like freakin' candy. We just can't keep up with where they're hiding it. Every time we think we have a line, it dries up. We thought they were using an old grain mill on the north shore, but we searched the place and found nothing." Nothing other than a suspicious amount of tire tracks and fresh scrape marks across the old plank floors.

"I heard the old mill was in foreclosure," Blake said. "You might want to check with real-estate brokers."

The other guys nodded, and Dan drained his glass

in one gulp. They were trying to be helpful, but did they really think he hadn't thought of that already?

"Good thought. We're looking into all angles. We'll find them."

Asher patted his shoulder. "We know you will, Dan. I'm glad you've got Mackenzie as a distraction."

Dan went still. "Nothing distracts me from my job. You know that."

"Easy, big guy." Asher leaned against the railing. "I didn't mean she was taking you *away* from your work. Just that she gives you an escape from it when you're off duty. A chance to relax, like tonight. You know what they say about all work and no play." He hesitated. "She's good for you. She makes you laugh. She makes you more… I don't know…happy?"

Blake nodded in agreement. "Amanda said the same thing. You're different since Mack came to town. In a good way."

Dan wasn't sure he wanted to be different, but he knew they were right. Mack was changing him. Love was changing him.

"She wants me to go to the llama farm."

Asher choked on his drink. "There's a sentence I never thought I'd hear you say."

"You and me both." Dan shook his head. "I don't know what's happening."

The three men looked at Dan, then at each other, and started to laugh.

"Oh, I think you know exactly what's happening," Blake said. "Only love could get *me* to a llama farm. Don't bother fighting it. And whatever you do…" He snuffed out the cigar. "*Whatever* you do, don't screw it up. And if you *do* screw it up, which is likely..." The other guys nodded. "Make sure you fix it fast. Seriously. If you're in love with her, don't let her go."

Dan glanced into the house just as Mack threw her head back and laughed at something. She was sitting up on the counter, wineglass in hand, smiling at his friends. Her friends. In his world. Right where he wanted her to stay.

One of the weirdest things about moving back to your hometown was the way you kept running into familiar faces, but not *completely* familiar, because you've been gone twenty years. Mack looked around the bank and blinked, trying to put names with faces. Kiara was the easiest—she was a teller behind the counter and waved as soon as Mack walked in. Her braids were down and swinging around her face today. One of the other tellers looked familiar... Joy something? The big-haired lady who owned the hair salon... Martie Kennedy? Between the teased and sprayed-solid hair and the scowl on her face, Mack was pretty sure she'd be going outside Gallant Lake to find a decent haircut.

And now here was Wes Compton, former class president and all-around Mr. Popularity in school, walking up to her with a wide, toothy smile and his hand extended. His dark hair was trimmed short and neat.

"Mackenzie Wallace! Wow, it's great to see you!" He gripped her hand and shook it hard enough to make her neck snap a little. "Come on back to my office. Your dad called yesterday and said you might be stopping by. You're really taking over the store, huh?"

She didn't have much of a chance to answer, as Wes just kept talking. He'd always been a charmer in school, too, but now his charm almost felt aggressive. He was dressed in the new-slash-old *Wall Street* style, with his blue shirt with the white collar, pleated trousers and…suspenders. It was a trend Mack didn't think needed to return. Especially in Gallant Lake. But she returned his smile and shook his hand without grimacing. She needed this loan, and he was the loan manager at the only bank in town.

He barely looked at the store's tax records and profit reports she'd brought with her once they sat down. Wes was too busy talking. About himself. Thirty minutes later, Wes had filled her in on his success as a banker and investor. He had a big house on the lake with a wife and three kids. He'd married Mandi Sue Moore, who was probably the one girl in school disliked more than Mack had been. Mack had just been laser focused on grades and *accidentally* ignored everyone else. Mandi sincerely thought she *was* better than everyone else. Made sense that she'd go after Wes and his family's money. Mack looked at her watch.

Dan had agreed to go to the llama farm out beyond the maple syrup stand today. Mack had read about it online and saw that they had baby llamas now. Dan had been so tense and tired this past week, working long hours and getting frustrated with the drug case he was on. Doing something silly like watching baby llamas would be a great stress reliever. But the place closed in three hours. She tried to catch up with what Wes was saying.

"...let me tell you, the difference between a Mercedes and a Bentley is night and day. I mean, Mandi doesn't mind the Mercedes, but I'm just not impressed."

"Well, they both sound expensive, that's for sure." She wondered how much the little bank in Gallant Lake paid him. He must have read her expression, because he rushed to clarify.

"Oh...uh... I've had some recent property investments do very well."

"Really? Around here?"

"Yes. There's money to be made in foreclosed properties, if you know what I mean."

She didn't, but she really needed to speed this along.

"So about that loan..."

He waved his hand at her. "It's a no-brainer, Mackenzie. It's a local business with a local family. Your credit's stellar. Just the sort of thing the bank wants to promote. Fill out these forms and let me bump it up the ladder, but I'm sure there won't be any problem."

She blew out a sigh of relief. As she filled in the paperwork, Wes kept talking. He was an adviser for the business chamber in town. Chair of a committee exploring growth opportunities. President of the parent-teacher organization. He was even thinking of running for mayor. Mack was looking forward to the *quiet* of a llama farm almost as much as she was looking forward to seeing Dan. Her ears were practically ringing from the constant sound of Wes Compton's voice.

He was ushering her out of the bank when a man walked in whom Mack didn't know but Wes clearly did. He went completely still—and silent—at her side as the broad-shouldered man approached. The stranger was dressed in dark jeans and a black T-shirt two sizes too small. His hair was slicked back with so much hair product it was almost shining. Wes's smile abruptly changed to an angry straight line.

"What the fu—" He glanced around, then at Mack, and that smile returned like magic. "What a *fun* surprise, Carter. I didn't ever expect to see you here at the *bank*. Where I *work*. In *town*."

Carter shrugged, clearly unconcerned. "The boss needs us to move on something. Now."

Wes was a completely different man. His face fell, and instead of anger, Mack saw a hint of fear in his eyes. What the hell was going on? It was like the most puffed-up man in town had been deflated right in front of her. He hustled her down the sidewalk and toward the parking lot with a hurried goodbye and a promise that he'd take care of the loan.

An hour later, she was telling Dan about it at Larry's Llama Farm. He didn't seem concerned. But he'd had a bad overnight shift and was sleep deprived as well as frustrated over their lack of progress on the drug ring.

"Wes likes to be involved with everything in town. He's an overachiever."

"But who do you think that slimy guy was that showed up and freaked him out so much? He called him Carter."

"I don't know, Mack. Maybe a disgruntled customer. Wes can be annoying, but…"

She nodded and took his hand as they walked along the path toward the paddocks. He was probably right. "He told me he's making a bundle from foreclosed properties, which seems like a conflict of interest, but he's getting me a loan, so I guess it's none of my business. Oh, Dan! Look!"

The path curved to the right, and there in front of them was a large pasture with a dozen llamas wandering about grazing, or just lying in the grass, their jaws moving back and forth rhythmically as they watched Dan and her walk by. Some were solid colored—white, brown or gray. Others were spotted black and white.

"They're so big!"

Dan's shoulders began to ease, and he smiled. "They look like they were made from leftover parts, don't they? Chloe came here a few weeks ago on a field trip, and she said they can be three hundred pounds or more. I didn't know how *tall* they could be." A steel-gray llama walked toward the fence, his tail curled tight over his back and his eyes fixed on Mack. Dan took her hand and tugged her away from the fence. "Don't forget they can spit."

"Yeah, he wouldn't be so cute if he spit regurgitated food at me." Dan laughed at that, and she knew he was beginning to relax at last. His pace slowed, and he slid his arm around her shoulder.

"It's pretty up here." The lake was hidden by the mountain, but the farmland rolled over the smaller hills. Crops were showing bright green shoots in the plowed fields across the road, and the pastures looked lush and green.

She leaned into his embrace. "It is pretty. Summer's almost here—you can feel it in the air."

Dan kissed her temple. "All the better for dancing in the rain."

Oh yes. That *was* a good day. She grinned up at him.

They didn't see any babies until they walked a little farther. There was a smaller paddock near the barns, and a cinnamon-colored llama mama stood in the corner. A tiny baby of the same color was toddling around.

"Oh my God, look at that fluff of hair on his head! He looks like you, Dan!" He grimaced at her, which just made her laugh more. "He has gorgeous big eyes like you. And he's frisky!" The baby started jumping around, then ran a mad dash in circles around his mother.

They sat at a nearby picnic table to watch him. Dan checked his phone and frowned.

"Damn it. No signal out here. I was afraid of that. We should probably go…"

"Are you on shift today?"

"No, but…"

"Are you on call today?"

"Technically, but…"

She took the phone from his hand.

"Just put this away and let someone else save the world today."

"Mack…"

She darted in quickly to kiss him and stop him from thinking. Judging from the way he reacted, she was successful. His arm tightened around her, and she let him take over. He was hungry, demanding. And neither of them cared if the llamas watched.

But it was the middle of the afternoon, so they eventually cooled it and settled back against the table, watching the baby llama prance around. They didn't talk much, just sat there in the sun, pressed close together, and breathed. It was nice. It was perfect until Dan couldn't sit still any longer. The real world was out there, and he didn't like being cut off from it.

He checked his phone three times on the way back to the truck, muttering every time. As they crested the first hill on the way back toward town, he pulled the truck over.

"Seriously, Dan? You can't wait? This is supposed to be a break."

"It *was* a break, babe. And I appreciated it. But I can't hide from the job."

She was beginning to realize the absolute truth of that statement.

Chapter Sixteen

Dan's phone lit up with a string of missed calls and texts. All from Sam Edgewood. He muttered a curse and called Sam.

"Where were you, Dan? We've been calling for two hours."

"What happened?"

He'd known there was no reception on the far side of Gallant Mountain. He'd *told* Mack that. But she was so determined to go see that damn llama farm. To give him some much-needed fun. And Lord knew he couldn't say no to her.

"What *happened* was that we had the bastards, Dan." Sam's voice was angry and clipped. "We missed the actual exchange, but Terry's DEA guys told us a car matching this one was seen going in and out of the auto shop in Brooklyn where they think the ring is being run from. We know he's part of it. But we lost them just outside Gallant Lake. You know, that place where *you* live? That town where *you* want to be police chief?" Sam took in a long, heavy breath, then blew it out again. His voice lowered in resignation. "Sorry, man, that wasn't fair. It was a souped-up Dodge, bright blue. Stolen tags. I swear that thing had jet engines. We were too far behind him and never had a chance." He paused. "And we don't know the area as well as…you."

Mack watched in silence from the passenger's seat, reading his expression plainly enough and knowing to stay quiet. If he'd been near town and gotten the call, he could have intercepted the car. Maybe.

"I'm sorry, Sam. I was in a freakin' dead zone. No signal." Mack reached over and put her hand on his, but he jerked away. He wasn't sure why, and he regretted it as soon as it happened. Especially when he saw the hurt in her eyes. He cleared his throat and spoke into the phone. "Where did you lose him?"

"He came down by the Chalet…"

Dan stiffened. "You ran a high-speed chase through *my* town?"

"Of course not, you idiot. We were a couple cars back, tailing him. Everything was fine. Then he turned onto Hill Road on the other side of town. There's no traffic out there, so he made us right away and took off. Those roads have so many twists and turns and dirt roads that aren't on the damn GPS. He was just…gone."

Dan pinched his nose, closing his eyes tight. He thought of that poor woman who'd OD'd in her car with her kids in the back seat. In *Gallant Lake*. She wasn't a local, but that didn't matter. It had happened in his town. These drugs were coming into *his* town. He cleared his throat.

"Okay, Sam. We'll recap with Terry and his DEA team in the morning. This gives a lot more weight to his theory that Gallant Lake has become a waypoint between New York and their expansion into Albany."

He ended the call and stared out the windshield. He almost forgot Mack was there until she spoke.

"Something bad happened." She didn't state it as a question.

"Yes."

"Have there been casualties?"

He huffed out a humorless laugh. "Have there been *casualties*? Christ, Mack, do you have any idea how many OD calls I get these days? It feels more common than traffic stops. In Gallant Lake! And I just missed a chance to stop it." His teeth ground together as he turned the key and pulled back onto the road. "For llamas."

"Dan, you're off duty until tonight. It's a Wednesday afternoon. Even cops get to have lives once in a while."

"I was on *call*. I should have made sure I could actually receive a call, don't you think? I told you it was a dead zone, but no, you had to see the baby llama." He was being an ass. He knew it. But that mother and her kids…

Mack recoiled, but her voice stayed calm. Steely calm.

"I know you're upset. But this is not my fault. It's not *yours*, either. It's not feasible to be on call every hour of every day. You'll have another chance to get them…"

"Yeah? You're an expert on how often law enforcement gets a chance to shut down a drug highway, huh? That's great. What would you suggest we do next, *boss*?" He turned onto the main road, driving past Halcyon and the resort. He was baiting her, looking for a fight. And she wasn't going to give him the satisfaction, sitting there in silence.

He parked behind her place, his fingers tight on the wheel. She didn't leave the truck. He didn't say anything. Knowing he was acting like a jerk didn't make it any easier to stop. He scrubbed his hands down his face.

"I think I'd better just go home tonight, Mack. I clearly won't be good company."

"Dan…no. Come upstairs. Tell me what happened. Let's—"

"No. That's not what I need." He had a feeling it was *exactly* what he needed, but it wouldn't help him figure out how to break this drug case. And that had to be his focus now. He glanced at Mack. He couldn't afford to be sidetracked. The town was depending on him.

Mack shook her head, but she reached for the

door handle. "You're wrong. But you're too stubborn to listen, so…fine. When you're ready to talk, I'm here." The door opened, and she looked back over her shoulder. "For what it's worth, today was great until you got that call."

His chest went hollow. "Don't you get it, Mack? That's my life. There will *always* be a call that ruins a fun day. I am *always* going to have half my mind on my job at any given moment. And I won't be able to talk to you about most of it. I won't want you to know. I won't want to answer the questions. I won't want to bring the crap I see into your world. But that's what you get with me. The people of this town rely on me, and you have no idea what that…" His words caught in his throat. He was so damn tired. Her hand touched his, and he froze, closing his eyes. "Don't."

He wanted to follow her up to her bed and bury himself in her. Let go of everything weighing on him. But he couldn't do that. He had a responsibility, and today, he'd dropped the ball. That couldn't happen again.

Mack waited for a moment, then muttered something and pulled her hand away.

"You know, you complain about feeling like a cartoon character with the whole Sheriff Dan thing, but here you are, acting like you really *are* some kind of superhero. But you're not. And the sooner you realize that, the happier you'll be." And she was gone.

He couldn't fault what she'd said. But his priority in life wasn't being *happy*. It was…

His tires spun on the way out of the parking lot. Damned if he knew *what* it was anymore.

People hadn't been kidding when they told Mack the Travis Foundation charity weekend was a really big deal. Not only did it raise tons of money for the foundation to help veterans, but it was also a boon to Gallant Lake. Mack couldn't believe the swanky crowd strolling the sidewalks on Friday afternoon. Athletes—many of them clients of Mel Brannigan's agent husband, Shane. Hollywood faces recruited by the cousin who ran the event, Bree Caldwell— a former reality-TV star turned North Carolina farm wife. Dad had warned Mack to be stocked and ready for crowds, and she was glad she'd listened. He also told her to make sure she had lots of top-shelf stuff, and she'd been selling it.

She should be happy. Hell, she should be *ecstatic*. Her dad was wheeling his scooter around the store and smiling ear to ear as he made recommendations to customers. He loved being in the store, and she suspected he was loving it so much because he didn't *have* to be there. She hadn't realized how much pressure he'd been feeling the past few years trying to keep the store going while she and Ryan figured out what the heck they wanted to do with their lives. So now Dad was having a great time and the store was doing hot business. Why wasn't she happy?

Dan hadn't been back to her place since their argument on Wednesday. She wasn't sure if she could really call it an argument, since Dan seemed to be carrying on the whole thing on his own. He'd wanted to fight, but she wasn't going to be a part of him beating himself up. And she sure wasn't going to take the blame for whatever it was that went wrong while she and Dan had—horrors!—been having fun on his day off.

He'd said he liked coming to her to forget what he dealt with on his job. But what if he couldn't ever *really* forget? If he'd never be able to share more with her than his *need* to forget? What was there for *her* in a relationship that revolved around Dan basically using her as a release valve?

To be fair, it wasn't like he ghosted her completely. He'd texted, explaining he was on surveillance with the task force when he wasn't on shift. She knew he was trying to make up for what happened Wednesday by working nonstop. He couldn't keep going like this. But she didn't bother pointing that out. He'd rewired himself from Danger Dan to Sheriff Dan, and he seemed determined that there was no middle ground between the two.

Because she loved him, she was willing to give him a little more time to figure things out. She'd been through it herself after her divorce, finding the sweet spot between People-Pleaser Mackenzie and Free-Spirited Mackie. Dan had helped her with that. So she'd return the favor. If he'd let her.

"Mack! Oh, good, you're here!" Mel rushed into the store, waving at Dad. "Hi, Carl!" She turned back to Mack. "I have a double-malt scotch emergency."

"Well, *there's* something I never thought I'd hear from my pregnant, alcoholic friend."

Mel barked out a quick laugh. "One of the resort guests is being fitted by Luis for a gown for tomorrow's gala. Her husband is running out of patience, and she's afraid he'll tell her to just wear the dress she already has. She doesn't want that to happen, and considering the cost of the dress she's looking at, Luis and I don't want it to happen, either." She paused for a breath. "She says hubby *loves* top-shelf double malt. Got any that might impress him enough to soothe his grumbling?"

Mack turned for the counter, but her dad beat her to it, handing Mel a bottle.

"This'll keep him happy," he said.

"You're a lifesaver, Carl!" Mel clutched the bottle to her chest. "How much…?"

"A lot." Mack's dad winked. "But you can catch up with us later. That's what neighbors are for."

Mel turned to go but paused as she passed Mack. "Your dad's the best. You and Dan are coming to the gala tomorrow, right?"

"I… I'm not sure." She and Dan were supposed to be going together, but she wasn't sure where they stood after this week.

Mel came to a full stop. "What happened?"

Mack glanced back at her father, but he'd moved to the back of the store, out of earshot. "Dan's really busy this week…"

Mel waved her hand. "He'll be there—his daughter's a model. And even if he's on call, you should be there for Chloe. All she talks about is how you and she both love purple. In fact…" Mel looked Mack up and down. "Stop by the shop later. Luis has a dress that would be perfect for you with a little nip and tuck here and there."

"That's sweet, but I can't afford a Luis Alvarez gown, Mel." Luis Alvarez was Mel's best friend and business partner. He was also a well-known fashion designer. He maintained a fashion studio above her boutique that was usually appointment only, but he and his husband, Tim, were in town all week for the big event.

Mel reached for the door, distracted and on the fly again. "Don't be silly. It's a loaner. You can be one of our models. My cousins are all modeling dresses, too. They do it every year." She winked over her shoulder as she left. "And it's got purple in it. You'll be Chloe's hero!"

Mack was pretty sure she'd never worn a purple couture dress in Connecticut. She couldn't help smiling. If it was something the old Mack wouldn't have done, then it was something the new Mack should embrace. And what better way to knock Dan's socks off than showing up in an Alvarez Designs creation?

Chapter Seventeen

Mack paced nervously as she waited for Dan to pick her up Saturday night. She had no idea where they stood. The weight of the heavily sequined gown gave her some comfort. Between the shapewear she wore under it and the way the gown hugged her body, it was like wearing her very own ThunderShirt, like the snug ones dogs wore to comfort them during storms. The bold colors gave her a jolt of confidence, too—swirls of deep purple, turquoise and white. The off-the-shoulder design was simple and formfitting, with a thigh-high side slit and a plunging neckline.

Luis Alvarez had made a few adjustments to accommodate her ample cleavage, and Mel had shown her how to tape those babies up and secure and then how to tape the dress to her skin to avoid any nip slips. She felt strapped in and ready for battle.

She opened the door almost as soon as Dan knocked, and they stared at each other in silence. Dan was in a tux. A *tux*. And the man, who wore a uniform like it was his second skin, was doing the same with this tuxedo. He looked as cool and comfortable as he did in his cargo shorts and T-shirt out in the fishing boat. And just as delicious. But after the past week, she didn't feel she could jump into his arms and tell him so. So she waited, chin held high, tummy pulled in, hand on her hip as if she was just waiting for him to fall to his knees before her. It was all an act, of course, as she tried to suppress her fear that things were worse between them than she'd thought.

He let out a low whistle as his gaze traveled up her body. When his eyes met hers, there was a welcome and familiar heat there, and his mouth slid into a slanted grin. Danger Dan was back.

"Damn, Mack. You look…" He gestured at the dress. "…amazing. I mean, you're always amazing, but…hot damn. That dress looks like it was poured onto you. And this…" His gesture moved to her chest. "How are you keeping those things in there?"

The blurted-out question made her laugh, and just like that, the tension eased between them. "Don't worry, there's enough tape in here to keep everything in place."

He stepped inside, and he smelled as good as he looked, all spice and pine and mountain air. The minute his fingers brushed hers, she started wondering if they really *had* to go to the gala. Would they be missed? Could she convince him to follow her upstairs, where she'd relocated her things to the large master bedroom this week? The master bedroom with a king-size bed?

Clearly reading her mind, Dan shook his head slowly. "As much as I want to untape you piece by piece, Chloe's waiting for us." His smile faded. "I know we have a lot to talk about, Mackie, but for tonight..."

"For tonight," she finished for him, "I'm Cinderella and you're my Prince Charming. And you have another little princess who needs you, too. The clock won't strike midnight for hours yet, so let's enjoy it."

His arm slid around her waist, and he kissed her lightly. "I don't want to mess up your makeup." He winked. "At least not yet. But God, Mackie, it feels good to be with you right now. We both know I've been avoiding you, and I'm sorry. I'm just trying—"

"Hey, Prince Charming." She cupped her hand on his cheek. "No talking until later. It's been a hard week for both of us." His eyes glowed with warmth and regret, and she almost bolted the door behind him so they couldn't leave until they'd solved this problem. But Chloe was waiting. "I love you, so I'm giving you time to figure your nonsense out. For tonight, let's just go live the fairy tale, okay?"

He tugged her in close, kissing her again, a little more passionately this time. "I'm always living a fairy tale with you, Mackie. You make me feel...well, you make me feel *everything*. It's a blessing and a curse, to be honest. Maybe we can find a fairy godmother to lift the curse part, because my heart and my head are so damned tangled up right now." He looked down at her chest pressed tight against his, so close to overflowing the confines of her dress. "This dress isn't helping. I'm going to be watching all night to make sure that tape is really going to hold. And I'm damn sure looking forward to peeling it off later."

"Be careful, Caveman Dan. This is a borrowed dress, and if it's damaged, it might turn into a very expensive pumpkin."

He rubbed the back of his neck. "I'm wondering how I'm going to get you up into my truck. Maybe I should have hired a limo."

She managed to get into the truck just fine, thanks to that very long slit in the side of the dress and a little boost from Dan. She wasn't sure if he did it to help, or if he just wanted a chance to put his hands on her butt. Either way worked for her.

Hell, everything worked when they were together. Maybe this week was just a speed bump for them. A blip on the story of their love. Because she *did* love him.

When they walked into the ballroom, it took Mack a moment to realize this was the same Gallant Lake Resort ballroom she'd been in as a girl. When she was growing up, she'd been to a few weddings and parties in this room, but it never looked *anything* like this. The walls and chandeliers shimmered. Thousands of tiny fairy lights strung across the ceiling made it feel like she really *was* in a fairy tale. Multiple French doors opened onto the wide stone veranda overlooking the lake, which was smooth as glass as the sun sank low in the sky. The round tables had floral centerpieces that cascaded down from the tops of tall glass pillars, creating the sensation when you sat down that you were sitting under an arbor of roses and lilies.

The crowd was just as spectacular as the setting. Television celebrities. Broadway stars. Athletes. CEOs. The men were in tuxes, and the women were in the most beautiful dresses Mack had ever seen. She breathed a silent thanks to Mel for providing a dress that held its own in this room.

"Dad! Mackie! You're here!" Chloe came running at them, hugging Dan before turning to Mack. "Your dress has purple in it! We match, Mackie!"

Chloe twirled, the grape-colored organza skirt flaring out around her as she did. The skirt had glittery three-dimensional flowers scattered on it, and the top was a lighter shade of purple, with puffy sleeves of organza and lace. Mack laughed.

"We *do* match, but your dress is better for twirling than mine! And look at your shoes!" The flats were covered in purple crystals. "They look like something you could click together and get any wish you wanted!"

Chloe extended one leg, admiring her shoes. "Mel said I could *keep* the shoes. I'm going to wear them every day."

Dan frowned. "I don't know how practical—"

Mack cut him off. "You get to keep the magic wish shoes? That's awesome. Isn't it awesome, Dan?"

She gave him a pointed look. He didn't have to be such a Be Honest at All Times buzzkill. He apparently got the message, shaking his head with a smile.

"It *is* awesome. Make sure you thank Mel later. You look really pretty, sweetheart."

Chloe beamed. "Thanks, Dad!" She turned back to Mack. "Wouldn't it be cool if they really were magic shoes and granted wishes?"

"That *would* be cool." Mack started to lean forward, then thought better of it. No sense testing the strength of that tape. She grabbed Chloe's hand and bent her knees instead. "You know, when I was a little older than you, my friend and I found a magic wishing well just outside Gallant Lake. Have you ever heard of the wishing well up on Gilford's Ridge?" She had no idea if it was still a legend or not. For all she knew, the old Gilford homestead on the ridge had been bulldozed and built over years ago. But Chloe jumped on the story.

"Really? A wishing well in Gallant Lake? Dad, did you know about that? Is it still there? Can we go to it?"

Dan rolled his eyes at Mack, but a mischievous grin played at the corners of his mouth. "It's been a long time since I was up on Gilford's Ridge, honey. And I wasn't there for any wishing well."

Mack blushed. She'd forgotten the abandoned farm had been a popular lovers' lane for horny high school kids back then. Of course, *she'd* never been taken up there for that. She'd been a serious student. But she and Shelly *had* walked through the woods one summer afternoon in junior high and found the wishing well.

After a five-course dinner and a fashion show put on by *real* models as well as a quick walk about by volunteers like Chloe and Mack, the dancing commenced. Dan and Mack were seated with Nick West and Cassie Zetticci. The newly engaged coworkers were clearly head over heels for each other. No one could miss their affection. The furtive, heated glances. Hands held under the table. The occasional quick kiss. His hand brushing the back of her head, fingers twisting in her dark hair briefly before he sat up straighter and pretended it was accidental.

Mack leaned over to Dan when Nick and Cassie were out on the dance floor, cheek to cheek. "Are they the cutest couple or what?"

He gave her a bemused smile. "Yeah, I love to look at my friends and think how cute they are. Adorable, even."

"Stop being such a Joe Cool, Dan. You keep forgetting I know there's a heart in there." She tapped her fingers on his chest, right over the top of one of the round buttons on his shirt. Before she could pull back, he grabbed her fingers and held her hand there.

"I'm sorry things got weird with us this week. I'm tryin', Mack. It's just these drugs are coming into town out of nowhere, and I can't let myself be distracted. It's my town…"

Mack stood, still gripping his hand, thinking of their first dance at the Chalet. "Come dance with me, babe."

He stood but didn't move toward the dance floor. "That won't solve anything, Mack."

She gave him a soft smile.

"It'll make you forget, if only for five minutes." She patted his chest again, this time over where his phone was tucked inside the jacket. "And you're not in a dead zone here, so relax. You're still on call, locked and loaded." He hesitated, then nodded.

They'd barely taken a step when Sally Vincent from the post office stopped them. Mack always thought she was a sanctimonious old busybody. "Oh, Dan, you look so fancy in that tux! And Mack…" Her eyes took in the neckline on the gown. "You look…very daring tonight." Sally turned back to Dan, clearly her target in this conversation. "I heard about Kyle Alderwood overdosing last week. How awful! Where are these drugs coming from? Are you close to solving it? Why haven't you arrested anyone yet?"

Well, this wasn't helping at all. Mack tried to intervene.

"Thanks for admiring my dress, Sally. It's by Luis—"

Dan squeezed her fingers, talking over her. "Mrs. Vincent, we're chasing down every single lead, and believe me, we'll get the people responsible."

Mack nodded briskly, trying to move Dan toward

the dance floor. "Yes, he *is* working hard, but right now he's—"

Sally held up her hand. "Look, Mackenzie, we all know you're only here to help your dad. Lord knows your brother can't. Not after he killed that Michaels boy."

Mack couldn't answer. Not without air in her lungs. Sally rounded on Dan again.

"I hope you solve this problem soon, Dan. The Alderwoods are neighbors of mine. Kyle is a friend of my grandson. Thank goodness he survived, but everyone's very upset..."

"Yeah, well... I'm upset, too, Mrs. Vincent." Dan's voice sharpened, catching both Mack and Sally by surprise. "I'm really goddamned upset." He jammed his fingers through his hair. "I said I'll *catch* the bastards, okay? I won't quit until I do."

Sally looked at Mack, her lips pressed thin, then back at Dan.

"And you think the drug dealers are out on the dance floor?"

Dan released Mack's hand like it was on fire.

"You're right. I was here tonight for my daughter, but I need to get back to work."

Sally just sniffed and walked away. Dan headed for the exit, and Mack had to move fast in her stilettos to keep up with him.

"Dan, it's just one obnoxious old woman. Don't..."

He yanked his arm away from her when they got to the hallway. He kept his voice low, but his anger made it heavy and thick. "Just one? Mack, that's

the *third* person to ask me about the drugs *tonight*.
And who can blame them? People are dying and I'm
here in this penguin suit sipping champagne. They're
right. I *shouldn't* be here. I shouldn't be with you.
I'm dropping the ball and it's..."

"And it's *my* fault?" Mack glared at him. Enough
was enough. She wasn't going to be his scapegoat.

"No." The edge dropped from his voice. "No, it's
not. Look, my job destroyed my first marriage, and
it'll do the same with us." He dropped his forehead
to hers. "I was right to back off this week. It's hard
for me to think straight around you, and now more
than ever, I *need* to think straight."

"You're saying you can't do your job and love me
at the same time?"

He stepped back. "I don't think I *can*, babe. I want
to, but I really don't think I can." His devastated
expression told her those words hurt him as much
as they did her. He gestured toward the ballroom.
"Those people are relying on me. They all remember what a screwup I was, and now they'll think I'm
one all over again. I have to—"

"Those people are *killing* you, Dan, and you're
letting them do it. Your *job* is law enforcement, but
you're a man who deserves to have love in your life.
And you *can* do both. You made mistakes when you
were a kid. So did Ryan. You have to stop taking
responsibility for every bad thing that happens in
Gallant Lake." She put her hands on both sides of
his face. She could feel him slipping away from her.
"You're a good man. A good cop. You'll solve this.

But you can't carry the whole town on your shoulders. You need a safe place to rest."

The hallway was silent and empty, with only the muted sound of music in the background. He stood there, eyes closed, as if absorbing her words and trying to hold on to them. She willed him to be successful. She needed him to believe.

"Dan, I love you. And you love me. That's a good thing. The *best* thing. Let me be where you come to rest and laugh and love. To let go of the expectations and all the darkness with me. Let me be your safe place, Dan. Go do your job and know that I'll be waiting with open arms and a glass of scotch. You deserve that. We both do." She took a deep breath. "And if I'm not the one you can talk to, find someone you *can* talk to. A professional."

She held her breath until his eyes slowly opened. There he was. The man she'd fallen in love with. The tender glow in those green-gold eyes of his. She saw a flicker of hope there. He was trying so hard to believe. She stared at him, silently pleading for him to accept her help. To accept her love.

"Mackie…" His voice broke. "I don't know…"

"Yes, you do. You *know*. Let me in, Dan."

He moved closer, his hand gripping her waist. Before he could speak, there was a commotion at the end of the hall. Nick West came rushing at them. Dan stepped back from Mack, leaving her feeling suddenly cold and lost. Blake Randall was right behind Nick. Both men looked grim.

"What is it?" Dan's voice was all business now.

"We've got trouble." Nick was talking fast. "Some guests got their hands on the tainted Oxy."

Blake's face was like thunder. "There are ambulances and state police out front, Dan. It was an overdose. At *my* hotel!"

Mack bristled. "That's not Dan's fault!"

Blake looked at her in shock. "I *know* that. Christ, I wasn't *blaming* him, Mack. But this is a big damn problem, and he's..." Blake looked at Dan. "You know this isn't your fault, right?"

Nick, a former cop himself, shook his head. "We don't have time to hold hands and sing 'Kumbaya' right now. We need to contain this. We don't need the gala interrupted by flashing lights in the parking lot."

Dan moved farther away from Mack. "Fatalities?"

Nick shook his head. "The guy was touch and go, but they should both pull through."

Dan started walking away with Nick. Mack called his name. He stopped and turned back as if he'd forgotten she was there. Nick and Blake walked on.

"Mack, I gotta go."

"I know you're going. Just tell me you're not *leaving*."

Dan stared at Mackenzie, his heart heavy. She was everything. Everything he didn't deserve and couldn't hang on to.

"These drugs may not be my fault, Mack, but they *are* my responsibility. My community—my friends—are relying on me. If you can't get that..."

She shook her head, refusing to listen. "I understand your responsibilities. But you're letting everyone else define your success or lack of it. No one's working harder on this problem than you." She took his hand and squeezed, like a mother would to a child. "Trust me, I know from experience that you can't make everyone happy. It's impossible. You'll lose yourself—"

He stopped her with a kiss. It was a dangerous move, because their kisses so often spun out of control. But this one was necessary. And sweet. And... final. He lifted his head and looked her straight in the eyes to leave no doubt to his words. He steeled himself against the tears he saw shimmering there.

"This job saved me, Mack. It's who I am, so how can I be losing myself?"

Truth be told, he felt like he was losing himself right now. Losing himself in her eyes, which were quickly filling with tears. Why couldn't she understand? His shoulders fell. How could he expect *anyone* to understand what he couldn't fully understand himself?

He brushed a loose strand of hair behind her ear. "Maybe I am stretched too thin. I don't think I can be what *you* need and what everyone else needs. I need my focus, and you're bad for it." Nick barked Dan's name from the end of the hall, and Mack flinched.

"Are you saying *I'm* what needs to be out of your life?"

Dan looked at her with regret pressing him down like an anvil resting on his shoulders. There was a voice in his head whispering this was the wrong choice, but he dismissed it. He had to be able to control one effing thing in his life, and he could control *this*.

"I'm no good for you, Mack. Look at us. You told me once that it felt like I was using you. You were right. I am. And I love you too much to do that to you. You deserve better."

"Dan…" His name came out on a breath. Her tears were ready to spill over, and he wasn't strong enough to watch that happen.

"I'm no good for you, Mackie. I'll ruin us one way or the other. If not now, then eventually."

Her eyes went hard behind the tears, and she jerked away from him.

"You've been hiding behind your Good Guy Dan disguise for so long that you actually think it's *true*." She poked him in the chest with a brightly polished fingernail. "You're a coward, Dan Adams. You're afraid that wild, reckless kid you used to be is going to bust out, take over and destroy you. But you don't have to worry about it." She poked him again. "You're doing a great job of destroying yourself, twisting yourself in knots, determined you deserve the worst. Which is a damn shame." She backed away, putting her hand on her own chest as if it ached. He knew the feeling. But she wasn't done with him yet. "That wild, happy kid is who you really are. But you're killing him, and you're killing us." She pulled her shoulders back. "I can't be the only one fighting here, Dan. That's not the kind of adventure I came home for. If you're too scared to believe in a future for us, then what's the point?"

Her mile-high shoes clicked like gunshots on the marble tiles as she walked away and left him standing there alone.

Chapter Eighteen

Mack thought she'd braced herself sufficiently before knocking at Dan's front door the following Saturday, but...no. She wasn't at all prepared for the sweet stab of loss when he opened it. He stared at her in steely silence. He was in uniform, physically and mentally. One hundred percent pure cop. Annoyed cop.

"Mack, I don't know what you want, but I don't have time." Even his tone was on duty—authoritarian and cold. He'd clearly made his decision on who he wanted to be. "I'm on duty in just..."

"Mackie!" Chloe came pounding down the stairs behind her father. "You remembered!"

Mack ignored Dan's confusion and smiled at Chloe. "Of course I did. A deal's a deal, right?"

"Right!" Chloe plunked down on the bottom stair and pulled on her sneakers. "Girl code." She gave her father a disdainful look. "You wouldn't get it, Dad. But when girlfriends make promises, we keep them. We're going to find the old wishing well today, and then we'll each make a wish and it'll have to come true! Did you bring an old penny?"

Mack reached into her shorts pocket and pulled out the 1936 coin. "That was a great idea you had. It took some digging, but I found a treasure trove of them. Do you need one?" After searching the apartment for old pennies, she'd called her father. Turned out Cathy still had her old penny jar from when she owned the coffee shop, and it was loaded. So loaded that when Mack left, Dad was sorting them all out on Cathy's dining table to see if maybe they were rich.

Chloe shook her head. "Nope. Mom's boyfriend, Samir, had some. But now you can make more than one wish!"

Mack shook her head. "You can't get greedy with wishes. The wishing well might get mad and not give us *any*."

Chloe's mouth dropped open in horror, but Dan spoke before she could say anything.

"What the he…heck are you two going on about?"

Chloe finished tying her sneakers and ran to Mack's side, grabbing her hand. Mack gave Dan a cheery smile, hoping it wasn't trembling as much as her heart was.

"You remember the story, Dan. About the old well up on the ridge, where the Gilford farm used to be?

Stories say their well has the power to grant wishes. I was up there once as a little girl with Shelly, and we tossed in quarters and made wishes, but it turns out we were doing it all wrong." She gave him a quick wink to let him know her speech was for Chloe's sake. "Your daughter figured it out. She thinks maybe the well only grants wishes for *pennies*, and the pennies have to be from the years when the Gilford place was an active farm. The house burned down in 1945, so…" She held up her old penny. "We had to find pennies that were older than that, because that's when the well was magical."

Dan's gaze went from the penny to Mack and quickly back again. He seemed distracted by her presence, and she had a feeling he hadn't listened to a word she'd just said. This friend zone was new territory for both of them, and he was wearing it as uncomfortably as she was.

"Bye, Dad!" Chloe waved, tugging on Mack's hand. "Let's go!"

Dan shook himself out of whatever thoughts he'd been lost in and gestured to his daughter. "Hey— you're not going anywhere without a kiss, kiddo. Come here." Chloe obliged, but only long enough for her father to barely brush his lips on her hair before she was out the door. He straightened with a resigned half laugh. "Pretty soon I won't get her to hold still for even that little bit." He looked into Mack's eyes. She wanted to ask for a goodbye kiss too, but she could see he was slipping into his protective cop-mode armor again. "It's…nice of you to do this with Chloe…" He swallowed hard. "After… you know…you and I…"

For some strange reason, she felt compelled to come to his rescue. "There's no reason you and I can't be civil to each other, right? Or why Chloe and I can't be friends."

Dan's shoulders dropped a bit, and there was a quick flash of sorrow in his expression before it hardened once again. "Right. Friends. Uh…" He straightened, reaching for his gun belt and avoiding her eyes. "Do you mind dropping her at Susanne's when you're done? She's staying there this week."

"Sure. No problem. I'll text Susanne when we're on our way. Should only be a few hours. I'd like to find the old well, but I have no desire to spend the entire day traipsing around the hills looking for it." Dan nodded, busy buckling his gun to his hip. Mack couldn't resist a little jab. "Look at us, all grown-up and mature, carrying on a casual conversation as if we…"

He met her eyes then, his angry gaze slamming into her as he barked a one-word command.

"Don't."

And there it was, all the emotion she'd been trying to convince herself she didn't have anymore. "Don't *what*, Dan? Don't stop pretending that we're suddenly just *pals*? Don't act like I still love you? Don't push you to admit you still love me too? What is it you *don't* want me to do, exactly?" Her words were low and sharp, just between them. "'Cause I've got a news flash for you—whether I'm your

so-called *friend* or your lover, I *still* don't take orders from you."

He scrubbed his hands down his face, eyes
squeezed tightly shut, lips pressed tight.

"God*damn* it, Mack. I don't have time for this
right now. I… I can't do this, okay?" His eyes
opened, his golden gaze level and cool. "It won't
change anything. We made our decision." He looked
out toward the street. "Chloe's waiting. I gotta go."

He ushered her out to the porch, then locked
the door behind him. She wanted to argue. To rant
and rave right there on the porch. But he was right
about one thing—this wasn't the time. So she followed him down the sidewalk to where her car was
parked. Where his daughter was waiting. He rubbed
his knuckles in Chloe's hair, chuckling when she hol-
lered in protest. Then he walked away.

"Do you think the wishing well will grant us
anything we want?" Chloe jumped out of the car as
soon as Mack pulled off the side of Marshall Creek
Road, behind Gilford's Ridge. Shelly had agreed
with Mack's memory that they'd found the well ages
ago by coming up the hill from this direction, rather
than from Ridge Road. There were some worn and
faded no-trespassing signs on random fence posts
and trees, but this was Gallant Lake. She knew pretty
much everybody, or had at one time. It wasn't like
she and Chloe were looking to do any cattle rustling.
They were just hiking. After covering each other in
bug spray, they headed into the woods.

Mack finally answered Chloe's question. "I don't

think the wishing well can grant *anything* we ask for like a genie in a bottle, honey. But sometimes the act of wishing and hoping for something specific can create the right energy in our lives to make it happen. Does that make sense?"

Chloe dashed toward the trees. "Not really, but kinda. I know what I'm gonna ask for. Do you?"

Mack didn't reply, instead directing the girl to the left, where she thought the old homestead might be. What *would* she ask for? Dan back in her life? In her bed? What point was there in that if he didn't stop being so tough on himself? If he didn't see himself as a man outside Sheriff Dan? That's what Mack had to wish for. Dan's job might have shaped him, but it didn't have to be who he *was* at heart. She'd wish for him to see that. But she wasn't very hopeful as she hurried after Chloe. He was a stubborn one.

Two hours later, they'd zigzagged their way to the top of the ridge. The view of Gallant Lake stretching out in the distance was beautiful. But Chloe was unimpressed. The eight-year-old wasn't here for sightseeing.

"Are you sure this is the right hill? I haven't seen anything that looked like an old house *or* barn *or* well." Chloe's brows bunched together as she gave Mack a skeptical look. "You are getting old, you know. Maybe you forgot which hill you climbed."

"Thanks a lot, kid." Mack handed her a water bottle from the small pack she'd carried. "Enjoy the view for a minute while I try to get my bearings." Mack looked around the ridge. It would have been easier if she could use the map app on her phone, but the area was yet another dead zone, with no signal at all. They seemed to be hugging the western end of the ridge. The homestead must be to the east. "This is the right hill, just the wrong end of it. We need to go east. Do you know how to tell which way is east?"

Chloe rolled her eyes. "Duh. The sun rises in the east, so it's that way." She gestured widely, basically covering every direction but due west. "How much farther is it?"

"Do you want to quit? Are you tired?" She wouldn't have objected if Chloe was ready to pack it in. It was getting warm, and they only had two bottles of water left.

But kids were resilient, and Chloe shook her head emphatically. "No way! I want to make my wish!"

They walked east for half an hour, and the trees started to thin. Mack could see an overgrown field, and the roof of an old barn straight ahead. The old Jessup farm was on this end of the ridge, but as far as Mack knew, no one had lived there in a long while. That's why she was surprised to see the glint of windshields and chrome from several vehicles parked there. She and Chloe stopped at the edge of the woods. Those were all late-model cars, and there were four of them by the old barn—two sports cars, a luxury car of some sort, and a pickup truck. One of the sports cars was low, sleek and electric blue.

Something sent a trickle of warning up the back of her neck. She remembered the call Dan had gotten from his task force friend about the guy they'd missed. The guy driving a souped-up bright blue Charger. Just like the one she was looking at right now. She took Chloe's hand and stopped her.

"We've gone too far, honey. This isn't the place we're looking for. Let's go back toward the car. We'll have to come back another time to look for the wishing well."

"But maybe those people know where it is!" Chloe pointed as four men came out of the barn. Three were wearing ball caps pulled low on their foreheads, with loose-fitting dark clothing, carrying large duffel bags. But one was in chinos and a bright white business shirt and tie. And suspenders. His gait was familiar. So was his dark hair, short and neatly styled. He carried a leather satchel. All four of the men's heads were on swivels, looking around as if they sensed they were being watched. Just about the time Mack realized who the businessman was, he looked up the hill and straight at her and Chloe. Wes Compton from the bank. She *knew* he was up to something fishy that day in the parking lot.

Chloe started to wave, but Mack squeezed her hand in a signal to freeze. The girl seemed to pick up on her sense of danger, staying quiet and alert at her side. Dan seemed to dismiss her suspicions about Wes, but she was more certain than ever that she'd been right. Wes said something and the other men separated, two heading toward the vehicles and one—the largest—jogging to the south side of the ridge. The guy loading the back of the blue car was

Carter, the man she'd seen at the bank. Wes waved at Mack and Chloe.

Mack tugged Chloe under the shadow of the trees. Something was very wrong here. She and Chloe should not have seen this. Her heart started racing. Maybe he hadn't recognized them. But where had that other guy gone? Wes shouted something up at them. She couldn't make out all the words, but she clearly heard her name. She waved, giving him a wide smile.

"Hey, Wes! We got turned around hiking up here, but I know where we are now." Somewhere they shouldn't be. "Gotta go! Bye!"

She backed up, ignoring whatever he shouted in response, and started jogging into the woods with Chloe running at her side.

"What's wrong, Mackie? Why are we running from Mr. Compton?"

"I think Mr. Compton is doing something... secret...on that farm, honey. And he might be mad that you and I saw him. Let's get back to the car." They headed down the hill, but she could hear footsteps keeping up with them. *Damn it*. Wes's voice called out again, closer this time.

"Mackenzie! Stop! I just need to talk. You're not going to outrun us."

Us.

The other man was chasing them, too. That couldn't be good. She and Chloe ran past a huge downed tree, roots sticking up in the air at the base. She tugged Chloe behind the roots and up against the thick trunk, holding her finger to her lips to silence her. It wasn't a perfect plan, but she needed to do *something* to protect Chloe.

"Don't question me," Mack said in a rushed whisper. "I need you to hide here. I'll cover you up. Don't make a *sound* until your dad or I come for you, okay?" Chloe's eyes were wide as silver dollars, but she immediately knelt near the trunk of the tree. Thank goodness she was wearing dark clothing. It would be hard to see her through the leafy branches Mack was tossing over her. "I'm going to pretend you ran down the hill, so don't say anything if you hear me calling for you. Don't make a sound, okay?"

"Okay, Mackie. But...what about you?"

"I'll be fine. I'm gonna text your dad to come." Hopefully a text would get out, even if a call wouldn't. They heard heavy footsteps getting closer. "You'll be safe here. Wait for your dad or me—no one else." Their eyes met through the leafy shelter. Mack's chest went tight. "I love you, Chloe. I won't let anything happen to you."

Mack turned and started running straight west, as far away from the tree as she could get. When the footsteps got close enough that Wes didn't have to shout when he told her to stop, she kept her back to him, putting her hands up to cup her mouth. She started shouting off to the west at the top of her lungs as if Chloe had run in that direction.

"Run, Chloe! Run to the car and call your dad! Run!"

She pulled out her phone, but Wes grabbed her

arm and knocked the phone to the ground. He spun her around, glaring at her as he tried to catch his breath.

"Damn it, Mackenzie! Why did you have to run like that?"

The second guy, looking angry and rough, ran up behind Wes, who nodded off in the direction Mack had been shouting. "Go find the kid. She's trying to get to the car, which must be over on Marshall Creek. Don't hurt her—just get her back here."

As the man took off, Mack pretended to be upset, but she was secretly relieved. The ruse had worked. They were moving away from Chloe's hiding place. Wes released her, shaking his head as if he was deeply disappointed.

"Mackenzie Wallace, what are you doing? I just wanted to talk to you both so there weren't any mis-understandings about what you saw. There was no need to panic."

"Really? Then why did you just send that guy run-ning to catch a *child*? You could have cleared up any misunderstanding with a phone call. You didn't have to chase us through the woods. In fact, you know what?" She stepped back, testing him. "I think you *should* call me later and explain it all. Or not. What-ever. I need to go…"

He took her arm, less gently than before. "I don't have time for this, Mack. Your boyfriend and his posse have been getting on my last nerve these past few weeks, so I need to get this barn cleared out today." He started walking, pushing her ahead of him. "It's too bad. We had a good thing going in Gallant Lake."

"Look, I don't know what you're doing up here, and I don't *want* to know. Seriously, I don't want to be involved. I don't care. And Dan isn't my boyfriend anymore, so don't worry about that."

His eyes narrowed. "You expect me to believe you and Dan broke up, and you just happen to be out here with his *kid*? That's quite a coincidence, don't you think? I'm not an idiot, Mackenzie."

Before she could answer, the big guy came thumping through the trees and back to them. He shook his head at Wes.

"No sign of the kid. The car's still there. No one else around, so she hasn't raised any alarms yet. Maybe she got lost. Maybe she's hunkered down in the woods somewhere, hiding."

Wes gave Mack a long, calculating look, then gave her another shove as he answered Big Guy. "Forget the kid. Let's get the rest of the stuff loaded and get the hell out of here." He looked at Mack. "You're staying with us, at least for now."

Resisting made no sense. Running would be futile. And if she cooperated, they might forget about Chloe all together. She yanked her arm away from him but started walking back to the farm.

"Fine."

The radio in Dan's car crackled before Terrance Lewis's voice came over it, low and steady. "Everyone's in place. Hold tight for now. Let's see if any bigger fish show up." Terry was with the DEA and the leader of the task force operations.

"Roger that. They're loading the vehicles now. Canvas duffels. Looks like Carter, Martinez, Compton and some big guy I haven't seen before," Sam Edgewood replied. Damned if Mack hadn't been right about good old Wes Compton being up to no good. Mr. Clean Cut was the local freaking drug lord, right under Dan's nose. He shifted in the seat of the unmarked sedan, parked under the shade of a maple tree just fifty yards from the dirt driveway leading up to the "abandoned" farm currently in foreclosure. That's why they could never catch up with the product. Wes kept moving it from one vacant, foreclosed property to another.

They'd caught a break when the woman who'd almost died at the resort last weekend told investigators that "some guy at the bank" had sent her and her brother to meet the man who sold them the drugs. Dan remembered what Mack told him about Wes, and they'd started checking all the foreclosed properties. There was a suspicious amount of activity at this place, with the buildings up a long curving driveway, out of sight from the road. They'd had someone sitting on it for days now.

"Hold on. Something's happening." Sam's voice was quiet on the radio. He was hiding behind the barn. "Compton and the big guy just went up to the woods in a hurry. Maybe there's another stash up there?"

Dan didn't want this bust going sideways after

all this work. "Have they made us? We have anyone up there?"

"Negative," Terry responded. "Too many of these gangs use wildlife cameras with motion detectors, and we didn't want to risk triggering one. We've got one agent at an upstairs window in the old house." The agent acknowledged with a click on the mic. "One of your fellow deputies down by the road. One with Sam." Two more mic clicks. "Two cars of federal agents waiting on side roads for once it all goes down. Hopefully without a fight." There was a pause. "If it goes sideways, just remember Yosemite Sam up there is the best shot of us all. Those guys won't sit for a week."

Sam would never be able to live down the day he'd shot a carjacker in his left butt cheek. Dan chuckled, then pressed the button again. "Jesus, don't say that out loud. His ego's bad enough."

One of the SUVs full of DEA agents clicked their mic so the raucous laughter could be heard. Sam was also laughing softly. "I keep telling you guys I hit him right where I was aiming." There was a quick pause. "Hold on." Sam's tone was suddenly all business. Something was wrong, and everyone went silent.

"Jesus. Okay, be advised Compton and his buddy have emerged from the woods and are returning to the farmyard. They have a woman with them. I repeat, they have a civilian woman with them, and I don't think she's there voluntarily."

"A hostage?" Terry asked. "That's not their style."

More static, then Sam's whisper. "Style or not, her body language screams 'unhappy.' Disgruntled customer?"

"We've been camped out at this farm for two days," Terry replied. "They haven't had any clients here. Description?"

"Long blond hair. Average height. Jeans. Blue sweater. Small backpack."

Dan's vision blurred, making him blink almost as rapidly as his heart was pounding. It took all his concentration to draw in a breath and hold it, trying to slow his adrenaline to a more functional level. Mack had been wearing jeans and a blue sweater this morning. He remembered noting the bright pink stripe around each cuff and the hem. It matched the thick socks she'd been wearing. The socks *he'd* bought her after she got those blisters weeks ago.

He squeezed the mic button so hard it was a wonder it didn't snap. "What color are her socks?"

Silence. Then Terry spoke. "Did you just ask about her *socks*?"

Before he could reply, Sam answered with the one word Dan had been dreading.

"Pink."

"Is she alone? Is there a little girl there? An eight-year-old?" Dan was almost shouting, which he knew was a no-no when guys were using earbuds.

"Dan…" Sam started, still in a near whisper. "Are you asking about Chloe? Do you think your daughter might be out here? I haven't seen anyone but the woman… Oh, crap. Are you saying this woman is Mackenzie Wallace? Your girlfriend?"

A new low voice came on the radio. "Smith here, from the upstairs window. I can confirm it's Mackenzie Wallace. My sister went to school with her."

"She's arguing with Compton." Sam's voice was level, as if he didn't know Dan's entire world was falling away from his feet. "He's pointing to the barn. She's pointing to the ridge."

"Gilford's Ridge." Dan didn't bother stating it as a question. That stupid wishing well was on the burned-out Gilford farm. Mack had taken Chloe to Gilford's Ridge. Which, by some ridiculous chance of fate, was where Wes Compton's current storage place was. Dan had been too distracted that morning to make the connection, but then again, this operation hadn't been on his radar when Mack picked up Chloe. Sam had been on surveillance today and noticed the jump in activity. Suspecting Wes and his men were clearing out, Terry made the call to grab them.

"What are we doing, guys?" It was one of the federal agents from the waiting cars. "These roads are remote, but they're not abandoned. We've had two local cars pass us already. All it takes is someone getting nosy, or sending a text to one of Compton's guys, and we're blown."

Terry said something about waiting for *bigger fish* again. Smith was talking about the men loading more duffels into their trucks. The feds were offering to grab the trucks as they left the farm. But the only thing Dan cared about was where his daughter was.

The radio buzzed with static, and another unfamiliar voice came on. "Okay, we're on Marshall Creek Road behind the ridge, and there's a blue Ford compact here. Parked and locked tight. No one around."

"That's Mack's car." Dan's mouth was dry as cotton. "My daughter was with her. She's *eight*." He swallowed hard. "If Compton's done anything… I'm going up there now."

"Negative! Sit tight, damn it." Terry's command was quiet but firm.

Sam joined in. "Agreed. Don't make things worse, Dan. Chloe's not here, and the woman isn't sobbing or distraught. She's just pissed." There was a pause. It couldn't be easy for Sam to be operating so close to Wes and his well-armed men. He was hiding in the old pump house, but the thing wasn't soundproof. Or bulletproof. Terry's mic clicked again.

"Dennis, take your team up the hill from the car. Use stealth, but find that kid."

"Roger. On our way."

It was the logical course of action. Dan would have made the same call in Terry's position. But Terry wasn't in *his* position, with his daughter and the woman he loved in danger. The *L* word settled his pulse more than any breathing exercise ever could. He *loved* Mackenzie, and his job didn't have a damn thing to do with that. His job sure as hell wasn't more *important* than that. Than Mack. Than Chloe. They were his *family*. He opened his car door slowly and slid out, moving along the tree line near the road as he inserted the earbud and tapped the mic.

"Be advised, I'm out of my vehicle, moving closer to the driveway."

Sam let out a string of hissed obscenities in his ear.

Terry's voice came on again, sounding more resigned than angry.

"Roger that. Do *not* come up the drive until we know what's happening. A shoot-out doesn't help anyone."

"Affirmative." Charging in, guns blazing, only worked in the movies and would put Mack and Chloe in more danger.

The next few minutes of silence felt like an eternity as Dan hunched under a large eucalyptus bush. He was so tense that his whole body twitched when the earbud finally clicked.

"Be advised," Sam said. "Two of the vehicles are preparing to leave. Carter's in the blue one. Martinez is in the other." A pause. "The woman is sitting on the back of a farm wagon in the yard. She keeps glancing up the hill when Todd's not looking. Dan, I have to think your girl is still up there."

He closed his eyes, praying to whoever might be listening that Chloe was okay. Going forward without that little girl in his life just wasn't an option.

Another click. "Dan, we found her. She had a good hiding spot." Dennis's words were the sweetest Dan had heard. "She said she was ordered not to move until she heard from the woman or you. Say something so she knows we're the good guys."

Dan's eyes burned, and his throat was thick with emotion. "Baby girl, it's Daddy." The word broke as it came out. His whole body shook with relief. "Dennis is a friend of mine. I need you to go with him, okay?"

Silence. Then Dennis responded. "Got her. She's fine, just scared about the woman. On our way to the vehicle now."

Sam said the words Dan couldn't form. "Thank God. Now let's get this son of a bitch."

"Team Two will grab the vehicles heading out now," Terry whispered. "Everyone else stay outta sight."

"Roger that."

Dan flattened under the shrubs as the two vehicles raced down the drive, throwing up dust and stones. They both headed east, toward the interstate, but he knew they'd never get that far. Using the dust cloud as cover, Dan moved farther up the drive. He could see the remaining two vehicles, but they were blocking his view of Mack and the two men.

Sam came on the radio. "Be advised. Compton said something that pissed off Dan's girlfriend. She's up and arguing, dropping f-bombs all over the place."

Dan grinned through his worry. *Thatta girl, Mackie. Give him hell.*

"Compton wants her inside the barn, and she is not having it." A pause. "Be advised, the big guy is heading down the drive in his truck, which is loaded with product. Don't let him get far."

Terry chuckled. "I'll take care of him. Go get your girl, Dan."

Dan moved up the hill, only stopping long enough to duck when Elliot went by. His eyes narrowed when he saw Wes grab at Mack's arm.

"Roger the hell outta that. Everyone else stand down. Compton's *mine*."

Chapter Nineteen

Everyone knew that you never let a bad guy take you into a vehicle or an abandoned barn. Mack had read it a dozen times. *Don't let them take you anywhere alone.* Wes grabbed her arm again, fingers digging in hard enough to make her cry out. But not so hard that she couldn't call him every name she could think of while digging her heels into the dirt driveway. His face reddened with anger.

"Damn it, Mack, I'm not going to violate you or anything. I'll just tie you up in there and let my bosses decide what to do with you after I'm long gone." He yanked sharply. "You're not that hot that I'd risk my escape taking the time to do you."

She tried to pull away, but he wasn't letting go

this time. Fear and fury were fueling her in equal measure now.

"A—I'm *totally* hot enough, you ignorant ass hat. And B—I am *not* letting you tie me up in some barn in the middle of nowhere. I'll die out here!" And who'd save Chloe?

His grip tightened again, and he pulled hard enough to send her stumbling forward. "Okay, okay. I'll tell you what—forget what I said about my bosses. We don't need to get them involved." His voice was so smooth and smarmy that she knew he was lying. "I'll call your boyfriend and tell Dan where you are once I'm at the airport and ready to book outta here. You'll be fine. Now be a good girl and get moving. I wasn't kidding when I said I don't have time for this."

He pushed again, and she didn't even try to stay on her feet. Let him drag her if he wanted. She hit the dirt and glared up at him, slapping at his hands when he reached down to grab her.

"I am so sick and tired of men saying they don't have time for me, Wes. And I am damn sure *not* anyone's good girl. Oh, and I'm not going in that barn either, so you can just—"

A glint of rage in his eyes silenced her. Maybe lying on the ground under him wasn't the best idea she'd ever had. His hand curled into a fist, and he pulled his arm back.

"No wonder Adams dumped your obnoxious ass," he snarled. "You never know when to shut the hell up."

Before he could take the swing, there was a roar

from her right and a blur of dark motion. Wes vanished under whoever had just tackled him. Mack rolled away from the scuffle, only to have someone's hand wrap around her arm as she stood. *Oh, hell no.* She came around swinging, connecting with the stranger's face right about the time she noticed he was wearing a bulletproof vest and a cap with the letters "DEA" printed on it.

The tall black man shook his head and grimaced, but he was laughing. "That's a hell of a right hook, Mackenzie. I'm one of the good guys. It's over." He let go of her arm and stepped back. Law enforcement officers were coming at them from all over, with the same dark hats and black vests. On the ground, one was wrestling with Wes. She saw a familiar shock of sandy hair. *Dan.* He was on top now, throwing a flurry of punches at Wes and cursing him in a voice filled with rage. She heard him say something about his daughter.

Chloe...

She must have spoken out loud, and the agent she'd just punched tipped his head at her. "Chloe's safe. She's with my team." He looked over at one of the men watching Dan beating on Wes and raised one brow in question. "Sam, you think you might want to get your friend?"

Sam jumped forward and grabbed Dan's arm before he could land another punch.

"Enough, man. I think you made your point."

Dan struggled against his grip for a moment, then stopped, glaring at Wes. "It'll never be enough for me, but yeah. I'm done. Facedown, asshole." He spun Wes over in a flash, cuffing his hands behind his back, then standing. His eyes went right to her. And...wow.

Her knees nearly buckled from the emotion swirling in his gaze. Rage. Desperation. Relief. Love. He swept his gaze up and down her body, checking for damage, then pulled her into his arms. He nearly crushed her, but she didn't object. She knew he needed it as much as she did. She soaked it up, then started trying to explain.

"I'm so sorry. I had no idea. I never would have put Chloe in this—"

His hand cupped the back of her head, holding her against his shoulder. "I know. I'm just glad you're both okay." A shudder went through him as he drew in a deep breath. "You're all that matters to me. You and Chloe. That's it."

"Did I mess up your bust or sting or whatever this is? I punched your boss. Will you be in trouble? I'm sorry..."

"Baby, hush." Another shudder. No, wait. That was a shake. He was shaking. He was...laughing. And so were the agents around them. Mack pushed away, but Dan kept her in the circle of his arms. One of the two female agents spoke up.

"It's true. She clocked Terry right in the nose. It was pretty sweet." The woman winked at Mack. "Couldn't have happened to a nicer guy."

The man she'd hit—Terry, apparently—rolled his eyes. "Ha ha, very funny." He smiled at Mack. "No harm done, I promise. And I was in charge today, but I'm not Dan's boss. In fact, I'm thinking he won't have *any* boss before long. After today, I think he's a shoo-in for that chief of police opening I hear is coming."

Dan started introducing her around as two agents roughly lifted Wes to his feet and walked him to the waiting black SUV with dark-tinted windows. Just like in the movies. A matching SUV pulled up behind it. As soon as the door closed on Wes, the back door on the second vehicle flew open.

"Daddy! Mackie!" Chloe bolted out of the car and ran to them. Moving as one, Dan and Mack bent and opened their arms to pull her into their embrace. She ended up sitting on Dan's hip but had a death grip on Mack's hand. She realized with a wave of sadness that she didn't belong in this family embrace. But when she went to move away, Dan's hold tightened around her waist. He shook his head at her, even as he talked to Chloe.

"Baby girl, I am *so* happy to see you. And I am so proud of you for listening to Mack and doing what she told you." He kissed her cheek, then let her slide to the ground. "Why don't you let me thank Mack for a minute, then we'll go home, okay?"

"But Dad, I have to tell Mack—"

"Just give me a minute, okay, baby?"

Chloe opened her mouth to argue, then shrugged and walked over to climb on the old farm wagon. Mack smiled. Dan had been right about her—perpetual motion.

"Dan, I really am sorry…" He wasn't listening, intent on examining her arm where Wes had grabbed her. Rings of bruises were already visible.

"Do you need to have this looked at?" His hands slid up to her shoulders, resting at the base of her neck. "Are you hurt anywhere else?"

"What? No. I'm fine. I'll just catch a ride back to my car with someone and be out of your hair. I should never have brought Chloe up here. I wasn't thinking…"

"Mack, you had no idea this was going to happen. Hell, *I* had no idea this was happening until a few hours ago. And I never connected in my mind that this place was on the edge of Gilford's Ridge or that that's where you were going to be. It's not your fault. And the way you protected Chloe, at your own expense… Mack, I don't know how I'll ever thank you enough for that." He put his thumbs under her chin and raised it until she was looking right at him. "But I'll spend the rest of my life trying."

Her heart jumped. He didn't mean it the way she hoped, of course. He only meant they'd be living in the same town, as *friends*, and he'd be grateful. How nice. But there was something shining in his eyes that made her go very still. Something warm and deep and true.

"Mack, I was an idiot. You were right about me hiding in the job, using it as an excuse, being a coward. All of it. You were right. I love you so much, and when I thought I might lose you…" He swallowed hard. "Everything just fell into place in my head. Like tumblers in a lock. Boom. It was clear as a bell. This job might be my calling. But it's not my life. *You're* my life. You and Chloe." He cupped her face in his hands. "I *love* you. And if it's not too late, I'd really like you to love me back. It still won't be easy. I might end up being the local police chief, which is a big job. I don't know how we'll make it all work, but Mackie... I need a safe place. I want that safe place to be you."

He kissed her, and she kissed him back with everything she had. Neither of them cared about the catcalls coming from the agents milling around the farmyard. It was Chloe's voice that finally pulled them apart.

"Yes!" She shouted from the farm wagon. "It worked!" She gave a little fist pump, and everyone laughed.

"What worked, sweetie?" Dan asked.

"The wishing well! We found it, Mackie, on the way back to the car. Mr. Dennis didn't want to stop, but I told him it was *very* important. He carried me over and let me throw my penny in real fast. I made my wish, and it worked!"

Mack had a feeling she knew the answer before she even asked. "What did you wish for, Chloe?"

The girl gave them a wide, gap-toothed grin. "I wished that you two would get married!"

There were more catcalls while Dan coughed and Mack's face went burgundy.

"Well, I don't know if I'd say it really worked then..."

But Dan stopped her, sliding his arm around her waist and reaching up to the wagon to hold Chloe, too.

"Actually, baby, I think your wish did come true. Or at least, it's *going* to." He looked into Mack's eyes with a heated gaze that made her toes curl. "What do you say, Mack? Do you think Chloe's wish will be granted?"

She settled in the crook of his arm, trying to hold her smile back, but failing badly.

"I do."

Those two words made Dan straighten with a smile. "Perfect answer."

* * * * *

MILLS & BOON

Coming next month

THE PRINCE AND THE WEDDING PLANNER
Jennifer Faye

Bianca shook her head. With him gazing into her eyes, her heart had leapt into her throat. Was that desire reflected in his eyes? The prince desired her? Her heart tumbled in her chest.

She didn't know how long they stood there staring into each other's eyes. It was like Leo had a gravitational force around him and she was being drawn in. Though she knew letting anything happen between them would be a mistake—compounding all of the other uncertainties in her life—she remained rooted to the spot in front of him.

Her heart raced as she found herself getting lost in his dark gaze. Her fingers tingled with the urge to reach out to him—

Someone cleared their throat. Loudly. Annoyingly.

And in that second, the connection dissipated. Bianca blinked and glanced away. Heat rushed to her face. She was grateful she didn't have to speak because she didn't trust her tongue to work correctly.

Leo cleared his throat. "Yes, Michael. What is it?"

"You are needed, sir. The call from Canada."

Leo sighed. "I'll be right there." Once the man moved on, Leo turned his full attention to her. "I'm sorry. I've been expecting this call all day."

"I understand. You have important business to attend to."

Reality had come crashing in on them. And none too soon. He was a royal prince. She was a wedding planner with an uncertain heritage. They did not belong together.

"About this…" As his voice trailed off, he looked at her with confusion reflected in his eyes.

He wasn't the only one to be confused. Her heart had betrayed her mind in wanting what it could not have. And now that her feet were once again planted firmly on the ground, she couldn't forget that she was here to do a job. That needed to be her focus. Not getting swept up in some fairytale.

"It's okay," she said. "You have important work to do."

"You're not upset about ending the evening so soon?"

She shook her head. "Not at all. I understand that business must come first."

As he escorted her back to the palace, he didn't offer her his arm. And she made sure to keep a reasonable distance between them. Because as much as nothing had happened between them, something most definitely had almost happened.

Continue reading
THE PRINCE AND THE WEDDING PLANNER
Jennifer Faye

Available next month
www.millsandboon.co.uk

COMING SOON!

MILLS & BOON
MEDICAL
Pulse-Racing Passion

Set your pulse racing with dedicated, delectable doctors in the high-pressure world of medicine, where emotions run high and passion, comfort and love are the best medicine.

MILLS & BOON

THE HEART OF ROMANCE

A ROMANCE FOR EVERY KIND OF READER

MODERN

Prepare to be swept off your feet by sophisticated, sexy and seductive heroes, in some of the world's most glamourous and romantic locations, where power and passion collide.
8 stories per month.

HISTORICAL

Escape with historical heroes from time gone by. Whether your passion is for wicked Regency Rakes, muscled Vikings or rugged Highlanders, awaken the romance of the past.
6 stories per month.

MEDICAL

Set your pulse racing with dedicated, delectable doctors in the high-pressure world of medicine, where emotions run high and passion, comfort and love are the best medicine.
6 stories per month.

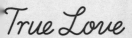

Celebrate true love with tender stories of heartfelt romance, from the rush of falling in love to the joy a new baby can bring, and a focus on the emotional heart of a relationship.
8 stories per month.

Indulge in secrets and scandal, intense drama and plenty of sizzling hot action with powerful and passionate heroes who have it all: wealth, status, good looks...everything but the right woman.
6 stories per month.

HEROES

Experience all the excitement of a gripping thriller, with an intense romance at its heart. Resourceful, true-to-life women and strong, fearless men face danger and desire - a killer combination!
8 stories per month.

DARE

Sensual love stories featuring smart, sassy heroines you'd want as a best friend, and compelling intense heroes who are worthy of them.
4 stories per month.

To see which titles are coming soon, please visit

millsandboon.co.uk/nextmonth